The Mothers

Keith Botsford

THE MOTHERS

The Toby Press

First Edition 2002

The Toby Press LLC
www.tobypress.com

Copyright © Keith Botsford, 2002

ISBN 1 902881 57 5, *hardcover*
ISBN 1 902881 58 3, *paperback*

A CIP catalogue record for this title is available from the British Library

Designed by Breton Jones, London

Photography by Adolfo Crespo

Typeset in Garamond by Jerusalem Typesetting

Printed and bound in the United States by
Thomson-Shore Inc., Michigan

To NFG

Si monumentum requiris, circumspice.

Contents

Part one

Felicità

The four perturbations,
gladness and desire, fear and sadness
(Augustine)

O ld father and young son climbed the bare hill directly
behind the convent buildings and there they finally found a tall
plain cross in the middle of a plot with hedges on three sides. Jim
said to his son: "I think this is it. Somewhere here. And if it isn't,
your i will forgive you."

The Kid—fair and slight himself, still sporting his summer
freckles and making sure his hair was parted in two neat waves—
stood there figuring out what his *nonna* might want to hear about.
For instance, Mrs. Vojtyla's cat, Mrs. Vojtyla being his piano teacher
and a neighbor to both Jim and me.

"Her cat's deaf," he said to his invisible but present grandmother, Feli... "You can drop a plate or something and he doesn't
even move."

This struck him as a wonderful attribute: to be ever calm and
more inscrutable than cats were. It was also logical to talk to the
dead. He talked to his dead sister Rory, why not to his *nonna*? As
one talked to oneself.

Wishing to be both calm and inscrutable, he said nothing about what he felt. He was being Mrs. Vojtyla's deaf cat. It was better that way. Grown-ups, even dead ones, had a way of asking dumb questions.

Maybe he felt nothing at all. After all, they were looking down at a patch of snow like any other patch of snow. There was no real grave. No stone, no name. If she lay down there under the ground it was no longer as a real body but as ash.

Jake said his prayer as his mother, Francine, had taught him. Then when he'd done with that, his hand in Jim's was deeply restful and confident.

I often wished Jake were my child, and Jim my man, which would have made him our Jake. Not in this life, Aissa, I said to myself. My Dakota Grandma I can still see as she stood before me, sternly making a sharp gesture with her hand before her mouth. That meant say no more. She didn't want to hear what I was about to do. And I must never tell Jim. Fifty odd years have gone by and I still haven't said a word.

It was All Hallows Eve, when the dead shake hands with or embrace the living. Not hobgoblins from scare-flicks but the people who'd gone before us and were glad to renew acquaintance on their annual day off.

Wherever you come from, you know Hallowe'en can often be a beautiful day. The last day of the year to Celts, who feared it. A fall day. On which leaves crisp and can be stripped from the trees by wind and rain, but the air might still be smokey, cool and clean. Less so where I've always lived, right here in Chicago. A little ways out, now.

All Jim's oldest friends—myself, Frank, Milo, Igor, Otto and Heda—knew Hallowe'en was a tough time for him, and I knew better than most, since I'd been tracking his, our, disasters since we played fatal boy-and-girl games on the South Side.

Hallowe'en was when he and his latest wife Francine swayed,

mentally, like highwaymen on a gibbet. Every candle-lit pumpkin on a sill reminded Jim and Francine that All Hallow's Eve was the right time to talk to their daughter, as August 14 was the right day for her to die, if she has to—so that the next day she would be assumed up to heaven.

Carrying Rory up the hill had been painful. How could something so terribly small and angry weigh so heavily? He wept and Francine was all in white.

True, Jim liked to weep anyway, that was the Italian in him, and his good heart, which had so hard a time showing itself.

As far as I could make out from a distance, Francine, who was all French in the head, didn't and couldn't cry. She just withdrew. Which was understandable. What had happened in Pisa on that night was bad stuff. You shouldn't die two, angry pretty and smart.

The idea of All Souls Day, October 31, was that the dead and the living could get back together, and families after all were the only dependable community the dead had: who else but their descendants would remember what they had been? As Milo had started saying, shaking his head, what was the point of spending a whole lifetime storing up memory and knowledge if death then rips all that careful accumulation off and kids like Jake, Jim's last son, all have to start off from scratch again?

Jim and I, we started off Catholics. On the last day in October we learn what it's like for the dead, who no longer have any need of a calendar or any fear of death.

And deep in her little box of ashes, by a stir in her spirit, Jim's mother Feli knew this was the day she had been looking forward to. She was expecting her twelve-year-old grandson Jake, the Kid. And with him, her son Jim. The dead have only an even-steven chance of getting what they want, but if she'd had a choice, Feli would have wanted to see her Jim, too, as a child, when he had been still loveable and nice. Luckily, anyone could come along and put flowers on her grave, far away from her progeny as it was.

Her other son, Tony, was with her in the realm of the dead,

which was comforting—as long as he didn't put in an appearance and start arguing with his younger brother. And maybe her husband Jacob would turn up, whom she hadn't been able to find in the after-life because he had killed himself and suicides had a different status, they died apart and remained apart.

When I saw Jake in those days (and I'm talking about a couple of years ago when he still looked like a changeling), it was obvious he was tuned in to what was threatening his house. He bounced balls in his room, he talked to himself or his sister (the dead one), he had imaginary stomach ailments, but he avoided questions that involved him with his parents, such as what he felt about what was going on. "I don't want to discuss that," he said.

Milo Frankel might be wrinkled like an apple in a cellar, his hair might be in wisps, but with his one good eye he was a great noticer. He reported catching the Kid sitting on the top step of the back stairs eavesdropping his parents' moods and said, "I feel sorry for Jake. Jim and Francine are like lousy actors in a bad play. They piss him off with their personal problems. And he's right. He wants to know how come grown-ups can't see life is fun as long as they don't muck it up."

The truth is, Jake is a thinking kid. He spends a lot of time working out Mothers himself, what makes them different from girls in general, like me or any of his playmates at school, or from fathers who, when they weren't busy "working" were at least playmates and knew how to throw a ball or how you worked up a curve. Mothers were mysterious, turbulent creatures with a strict sense of order and right and wrong.

Jake said to his Papa, whom he called "Popeye"—because he smoked all the time and spinach was his favorite vegetable—"I don't really remember your *Maman*. All I remember is she was very old and had just one tooth."

"He's my last child," Jim said to Milo. "If you're my age, it's scary the way Jake may remember me. The way I have to talk louder to be heard, how I leak and hack, how I'm on my last teeth and how

I can choke on a leaf of lettuce. Is that how Jake is going to think of me?"

The once-beautiful Feli, his mother, with her shy elegance, her oval face, light olive, and its framework of delicate hair, was long lost and gone. Some other nature took over when she busted her hip in her seventies; she added fat and anger first and then reverted to Agrigento—a sort of dark place in the past under a very bright sun that she squinted at with her weak eyes—and stomped and hobbled about her tiny apartment in New York where the boys, Jim and Tony (Tonio) had grown up. Who else remembered her as she once was—almost a girl, still young and pretty and desirable?

Jake must have been around six and she well into her nineties when Jim took him to see Feli in her "home." On the sixth floor of Cardinal Spellman (you got moved down floor by floor for convenient access to the basement and disposal) she sat all day in an armchair in front of the TV which was mindlessly and loudly on for the nurses and cleaners. Neither the TV nor much else had any real interest for her. TV or people were just moving shadows and noise; so were father and son, son and grandchild. But Jake's hand was small and warm and she took it and swung it backwards and forwards as if skipping rope or in memory of a swing. Another kid had come to play; it had given her a simple joy.

On Hallowe'en, then, while Francine nursed her grief and grievances, Jim took the Kid a hundred miles out into the country to see his grandmother's grave. By the time they got going, the day was resolving itself into mildness and thaw, the kind of day that dirtied the snow of the first, early fall. They had trouble finding the convent where she'd been buried. With the clocks turned back, an early dusk threatened, the landscape blurred. It was as if Feli were deliberately eluding them.

Finally the Kid spotted the nuns' discreet sign on how to reach the "Queen of Heaven" and they went a long way (much longer than Jim remembered its being) on a dirt road with deep tracks and a high middle, churning up mud and snow. Then they tramped around the convent grounds a good half-hour looking for the cemetery.

Mamma was here. No, she was there. Jim said, "I remember the graveyard being on a hill."

"We are on a hill," the Kid replied.

"You were here with us at the burial, Kid: if you're so smart, you find her."

Jim couldn't remember where his mother was buried? Feli's tactic had always been reproach. "Jim, you haven't been here since they buried me, not once! Don't you love me any more?" This she now said (gently at first) into his ear. But since her gravestone was flat and buried under old snow, under brush and bramble, it was anybody's guess where her ashes actually were. All they saw was some hungry crows pecking and a few black-and-white nuns in the distance hurrying from building to building.

Why hadn't Francine come, who always knew where everything was? Why was she stranding them?

They were stumbling about stupidly, so Feli raised the stakes, and her voice: "At least Tonio loved me. If he were still alive he'd be here. He'd know where to find me. You were off on one of your trips when I died." And more of the same as they continued to tramp aimlessly: "Your brother was accepting," she added. "You devour, Jim. That's why I'm here."

Jim, who told me this, who—today as from the very beginning, whenever there was a hole in his life, told me everything (including all sorts of things I didn't want to know)—said: "Don't kid yourself, Aissa. It was perfectly real." Her ash-box (not from Ashes-R-Us, Funeral Directors, as Milo joked, but mailed to him in Chicago) had presumably rotted in the ground, releasing her bleached remains into the air, where they now reassembled themselves before his eyes: the way you see snow or clouds take on shapes. The late afternoon light was fading fast, the air was thick with smells, like apples, smoke or soil, and the palpable ash, stinging, shifting, started speaking: "Over here. Give me a kiss."

In their new form, the cinders—the "cremains" they now call them—were no more than a pitiable wisp of her, but they reproduced: first a skull to which stray bits of singed white hair clung; then swaying in mid-air, a mouth with a single yellow tooth, eyes a faded watercolor grey; and finally, seeking to come close to him for a cuddle, a body curled on itself in its original fœtal position. "Give me a kiss...Why won't you give me a kiss? Is that too much to ask?"

Her hands reached out like bare branches and sought to pull him down to her, to her own world of the dead; she wanted to talk and lure, and hold. "I could tell you now why I had to marry your father, I could tell you..."

Should you kiss the dead? "Get away from me!" he wanted to shout.

"...what I suffered as a child." Her voice came on the chilly wind of dusk, carried this way and that like the ash of paper rising up a flue. "I could tell you..."

"I know, I know," he heard himself say. "You don't need to tell me. There are also things I could tell you about me, and about you. Things that you don't know or never understood. Like how hard it was to love you, and how urgent the need. It's too late, isn't it?"

What the Mothers—Jim's various Mothers, Feli and the sunny (but for Francine) young girls he made Mothers—had to say could go on forever. However much they were part of Jim's life, every one of them still had unsettled claims; they wanted to know where they had gone wrong and what might still be done to right their lives: which Jim had enriched, leavened, wrecked: which was their fault, his fault, nobody's fault, a fate, a sign of the times.

Reproach and retribution, love, loss and other perturbations were Mother subjects. If he hadn't come, his mother would claim he had a cold heart and a forgetful disposition; and now that he had come, that he refused her a kiss.

Why? she wanted to know.

And what if I'd become one? A Mother? Fifty years ago there might have been a Jake, and Jim and I might now be an old couple. Our Jake would be fifty. My imaginary child would have been as like Jake as possible, whom I hardly ever saw, unless he was taken along to a party at Milo's, but from the window in my bedroom that gave on to Hemperle Road. When Jake went by. On his way to somewhere else…

Well, I had been one, hadn't I? However briefly.

I, too, felt sorry for Jake. The way I see it, only the Kid was game and up to this visitation and all it entailed. The Kid was in much better shape than Jim was. His mother was less extreme, more balanced, more rational than Jim's had been, but also dangerously sharp. And Jake's aged father, confused though he might be and sixty years up on the Kid, was at least still there (for how long?) holding his hand, which Jim's father, Jacob, hadn't been. Jake liked to hold hands. He was learning life from scratch.

Which was smart of him, acquiring a Mother while she was still young and pretty. Jake could lust after her and adore her too much to actually study her in the shower. To him she was still a girl. But also not a girl. More like a prototype: the first of its kind you know. Time was going by, but still kindly.

Jim said it was different for him. "There was no one else whose hand I could hold. It was always her telling me what to do. I murdered her daily in my heart."

After all, he wasn't like her. He wasn't a girl and there wasn't a pattern laid out for his life, the way there had been for Feli. He was not going to make dinner, wear a bra, do his hair and put himself out for his father. Who wasn't around anyway.

Francine was just past her fatal forty, an age at which all Mothers reconsider their lives. That was the borderline of an okay age. Feli still had her looks but she was neither any longer a girl, nor was she a generic girl, she was a Mother, which was a very different story.

By fifteen, which Jake would get to soon enough, Jim no longer even thought about killing his mamma. He was too distracted. Girls, wonderful and terrifying, complete with boobs and innards he knew nothing about—all connected with that awesome capacity to turn into a Mother—had sopped up his rage like so many paper towels. The girls Jim knew, me included, wanted to keep their metaphorical kitchens (that is, the kinds of men they'd allow to walk about admiringly inside them) clean. Where we'd once, when Jim and I were thirteen or fourteen, held hands, gone for walks, bathed in the lake, danced awkwardly, kissed in Father Pzyrnik's car, the mid-teen-age Jim had become a beseeching mass of nerves: Give me what I want, please, forget the mess!

What he couldn't foresee was that in no time at all, unkindly, the girl would say yes. Which I did. By the time that happened, he had become accustomed to his mother looking old and it had become hard to think of her as young once, doing what he was so busy doing; or know what had made his father, however briefly, love her.

No, Jake had been lucky. He knew his father adored his mother. Jim loved Francine. It was as natural as **Jim ♥ Aissa** scrawled in chalk (mirror-image) on Father Pzyrnik's parish steps. And Jim's brother Tony had also been lucky. He could remember Feli at thirty-something. Which was why Tony could adore her to his dying day. Because she was, indeed, a beautiful woman. But was she lovable? After her sons there wasn't much room for anything else. In wartime Chicago she was sniffy with me. Class. Later she said, "You were a pretty little girl." And towards the end, before she vanished definitively into Cardinal Spellman, she would complain to me about Jim and his wives and children. "At least," she said, "You didn't grow up and marry him."

The last stage was bound to be painful. When his mother got very old and Jim himself started to look like her (like "Feli the Bearded Lady"), which may not have been what he wanted to look like. People thought he would be pleased when they said, looking at her many portraits on his walls, "You look more and more like your mother," and told him what parts of Feli he had. He wasn't pleased. "It's worse than looking like her," he said. "It's becoming her."

When he said that, Jim was showing me his doting grandpa photographs. He said he got a kick out of his kids staring at their babies and fighting over who Freddy or Tilly looked like. "The fact is babies don't look like anything; and you don't look like anything at all until you've got the better part of your life behind you. Then your true character comes out and shows. Alas!"

Maybe he didn't like looking like his character either: his nose and mouth expanding; his ears elongating like queer, big mushrooms on the bark of his hair; his eyes burning more fiercely; his beard savage, his teeth busy disintegrating. Other parts of him were also distrusted by the Mothers. They nattered about buying him new clothes; he ruined them or seemed to have slept in them.

"Go ahead," Francine said after sixteen years. "Ask the others what it's like living with you." She knew the answers, she'd polled them at weddings and funerals and on his birthdays. The man who was absent even when he was present. No one of them ever said he was idle or stupid, but what were the Mothers and their kids compared to his work? How much time did they get?

It was worse than ever when he said that he was writing about them. He did turn out a lot of pages on his computer up in his attic. But they were all for himself. Or for me. The Mothers were afraid of this *Nachlass* of his life with them: Feli in her box, and the others—Lou and Maria and Natasha and Francine. It would be compulsive stuff; private things; even intimate things; like that picture of Mother Number Two, Maria, naked on his wall.

"He has problems with his Mother," Francine told them. "That's where it all starts and that's where it all breaks down."

Jim was bright and charming, very, they agreed; but he was also a Prime Shit. He had far too much history, too much rage, too many kids and not enough grip on daily life. Where did that rage come from, that both he and his brother had, that I faced when I was young myself?

"You're trouble and strife," Francine rose to say to him in her closing argument. "Ask them. You have no idea how very utterly and thoroughly you use people up. We (girls, women, Mothers) are not bottomless pits."

Right now she could tell how angry he was at her leaving, maybe.

"God knows I've tried," she said.

The difference was that now, now that she'd given up trying, it turned out easy enough to get out. He couldn't stop her. She could see the persistence of his anger as his mood fluctuated: on low mornings she was sure he harbored thoughts of killing her, or he'd give up the Kid and head to the South Seas. Nothing new about that, people who read Milo's books knew; the world was full of people killing what they loved.

Most of the time he was simply torn in two. It happened before my eyes.

He'd have done almost anything to keep her. And keep the Kid. So he said.

Why? Because he loved her and loved the Kid.

"O...kay," she said. "When it suits you."

"I don't ask to have the thoughts I have," he told me. "There's nothing much I can do about the past. They're both dead, aren't they? Mamma and Tony. And how could I miss what was left of her at the end? She's better out of it. But Francine is right. I neglected my Mother. That is, I didn't see the point in, or couldn't bear, seeing someone who wanted to be dead but wasn't, who didn't know where she was or who I am. Anyway, her umbilical attachment was to Tony, not me."

Tony and Mom were both gone; then again they weren't. Not really. They had statements to make; they could be pretty insistent, like the Mothers; they liked to button-hole him at odd hours, from nowhere. In a way, writing them was giving them fresh life. Even if the hand was mine, the intent was his.

"Now it's Tony's kids who pepper me with e-mails," he said. "They want to know what did their Dad live on? Did Tony really hold up convenience stores? And in the obits I sent them, where it says her maiden name, they ask me how come it's not Bergonzi? They ask me what was my father like? Was he anything like Tony, or was he more me? How the hell would I know?"

I can attest to that. The one time I saw her, his niece Mandy said, "Hey, Uncle Jim, you make it like there are secrets out there."

She loved that, this niece of Jim's, firm-fleshed and mind-blown. She wished she had some secrets of her own. But her art was presentational. For several hours she told me—two girls on the porch while Jim had his nap on my bed—who and what she was, her astrological sign (Cancer), her designs on her boss ("Jewish, I'm part-Jewish you know, and going bald"), why she hated family get-togethers ("because they're family get-togethers and nobody likes anyone else"), and her faith in the Moon Goddess.

But there were. Secrets. Things about his Mother and Jacob that Jim dug at with his nails. How Feli had "suffered as a child." Who Jacob really was, who was sometimes known by different names. Which was why, as Jim put it, his mother went on talking to him: "Posthumously she still wants to be loved. Or understood. And she wants us, me, to have the straight dope. I promised her I'd do my best."

Which was to entrust the whole thing, boxes of it and endless conversation, to me. Who really didn't want it. Really. And could never say no to Jim, who for most of my life has been the most lost and most present.

2

You couldn't tell if Hemperle Road, once a country lane, and the area round where I'd lived for forty-some years and where Jim moved to when he came back from a trip in the mid-eighties with his French bride, Francine—pronounced the way they said "France" in France—was going up or down; whether it had been up and was going down or been up and was declining. He bought the house that had been the original farm house, I lived a few houses down and across the way. We were a typical mid-western neighborhood—all kinds of people, fewer children than we'd have liked, the cars mostly sensible, the gardens well-kept.

Just about opposite me was Mrs. Vojtyla and her deaf cat, whom I've already mentioned. She'd been a piano-teacher until her hands had cramped up on her, early. When the Mounts moved in and asked if Jake could have piano lessons she had demonstrated and said no: the rest of her might be beautiful and youthful (and also sorrowing) but her hands were like talons, and with those talons she described to Jim and Francine how, during one morning earlier that winter, a flash of lightning had sent the row of plastic bunnies on her front lawn scampering across the snow. With dignity, then, her hands crossed on her black silk dress, she said she had once played Chopin as he ought to be played, intimately. But there were no recordings.

She relented about the lessons because Jake melted her heart. Hers was another world for the Kid, who loved and feared her: and would never practice enough. It was Mrs. Vojtyla who told me about the new couple moving in.

My old cottage had probably housed field-hands in the old days. It is blocked from the street by hedges, and by a gnarled apple whose roots have reared up and sloped the porch back toward the house. From the porch, the spring of their arrival, I watched out for them, saw Jake first, then Francine driving to market, and finally Jim. There was no reason for me, back then, to intrude on them; or for them to intrude on me. I am Jim's in-between-Mothers, off-season moth. He takes up with butterflies and then they flutter away, and when they do, I re-emerge. Frankly, I'm dug into his very fabric and was a butterfly once myself, one who went into a long hibernation. If I'd ever asked him why he came out here, whether it had been for me or out of sheer co-incidence, I would have been laying a claim on him, something I have never done.

"Changed my life, changed houses," he would say. It was a pattern.

I was his first girl: when he was in tenth grade and his mother had moved from New York. We were all so young, it being war-time, and high school running right through our sticky summers.

Every Sunday he'd served mass for Father Pzyrnik and in return got fifty cents, a bag of orange slices and the keys to Father's car which he had been supposed to wash: and did, between our fumblings in the back seat. Why did he pick me, of all people? My exotic name? Jim says it was my daydreaming and my eyes which are very deep-set and dark like my Grandma's.

He says that no sooner had he and Francine moved in, he rang my bell to see if it could possibly be the same Knoblauch.

What time of day would that have been? If it was evening, probably I'd passed out. Drinking and thinking my thoughts. If it was bright and early, I would have been asleep. Anyway, I didn't answer. Knowing you, Jim said, that doesn't mean you weren't there. Maybe you were scared.

I've got plenty of reasons to be scared and I always have been scared with Jim: the first time, and afterwards. And because of him, of everyone. Mrs. Vojtyla had her concert programs and I had all the scraps I'd kept about Jim all those years I more or less made up my life as I went along, teaching until I got sick, then writing books about my Grandma and her people which didn't sell much until I got even sicker and had to quit. Oh, there'd be an unsuccessful flutter between Mothers, but what you can't bring off when you're young and in love you're not going to bring off when you know, as I knew, why it would never work. I wasn't a help, was I: not answering a single one of the letters he sent through other school friends and Father Pzyrnik? Because I was scared of him. However, fear and coincidence or not, I did live there and Jim, a night-time walker, soon began dropping by to see both Mrs. Vojtyla and me.

I knew their house from when the last Hemperle had still lived there. And a few times Francine would call and ask why didn't I come over for dinner, or lunch, or because there were a lot of left-overs she thought I could use, they'd be wasted otherwise. I rarely said yes. Jim was happy. What business did I have there?

The big house was old, needed work, and was crammed with Jim's past and his magpie nature. It had his African masks, batteries de cuisine, books on sagging home-made shelving, his Italian grandmother's trousseau lingerie slowly disintegrating in trunks, two pianos battered by generations of moving men, and the equally bashed-about leftovers of his former wives and dispersed army of children who—at his request, and despite the fact that they have always been central to his life—I have left out of this story.

"They're only just starting to ask questions about me," he said. "Why whet their appetites?"

It was Otto Pribisch, another schoolmate of ours from the old days, who told Jim about the house in the first place, and I did see Otto. So the coincidence may not be one. And when Jim and Francine moved in, I told Otto all that old stuff between Jim and me was dead and gone, which it was. Anyway, Otto, another Holy Child alum who's worked all his life for the Archdiocesan charities, is far too discreet to have mentioned my name to Jim. All I said to Otto was, it was nice having Jim nearby. I just loved him and missed him, as I'd done all my life.

When they arrived, the bridal pair, he presumably on his last and best and she presumably on her first and only, the word was that they seemed happy there. Francine was cool, I was told. And easily his match. A match in a different sense, Otto said, a woman who'll finally bring some order into his life. Jim's housewarming parties, in his grandest manner—the one that scares me—convinced all his friends that he'd finally settled down. It was Milo who said that the other Mothers had proved, (post-Jim) by how they wound up relieved and calm and happy—no matter how relatively ordinary their later men—how different Francine was! She knew all about those Mothers and had no intention of succumbing as they had. "More than his match," Milo said, whom I'd also known for almost as long as I'd known Jim.

What did Jim tell Francine when he started visiting me? What did she think of me?

He was in the tenth grade and I was in the ninth. In 1942,

when the government transferred Jim's mother from New York to Chicago, she was busy reading Italian newspapers for army intelligence. His brother Tony, six years older than Jim, was in the army and he was Jim's hero, his adored big brother. By 1945, when Tony was invalided out of the army, they moved back to New York. So I had two years with Jim, and a lifetime.

Of course he is most vivid to me as the slight, wayward Jim his Mother saw when he was Jake's age—unfilled-out, smooth, delicate, not yet much touched by real life. But I can't say that in that lifetime his face, which I love for its passion and mobility, its swift shifts of mood, has changed that much. It only became more his. His eyes, a deep blue running to black, brilliant as headlights and ready with tears as with fierce anger, still dominate his face. They have barely altered with age and retain their capacity to engulf and repel me. His nose, fleshy and Italian, grew wider and heavier; the olive of his skin darkened and folded into deep long fissures; his broken, wide-spaced, tobacco-stained teeth, which later he tried to hide with a beard and Milo had likened to the menhirs of Brittany, upturned stones, continued to deliver a broken smile, still touching and trusting as a child's.

When we were both kids, I used to envy the Mount apartment and all those bits of it that reflected their earlier, better days: its silver bowls for calling-cards, its gilt clocks that pinged, its delicate tulip-wood chairs no one was allowed to sit on, its walls hung with lachrymose views of Palermo and Rome. The very smells (Otto confirms this) were alien: of unobtainable cream and lardy hams, and overwhelmingly of Parisian perfumes I was questioned about when I went home.

I knew I came from a different world. Otto Pribisch and Aissa Knoblauch both came from a different world from Master James Mount.

Maybe our homes, Otto's and mine, were as exotic to Jim.

The Pribisch apartment smelled of sewing-machine oil, sour cream, dill, and violin cases. Mine smelled of my Grandma, who was a full-blooded Dakota.

"I used to envy you, too," Otto said. "And Jim. The two of you were so innocent and so excited. I'd moon about you, but Jim would hug you as if he knew what happened next."

"Nothing happened," I lied. "He scared the daylights out of me. He still does."

It was Milo who pointed out that all the women in Jim's life, starting with his mother, had alien blood in their veins. Lou's mother, the one with the stiff curls, was, I think, half English; Maria had a grandfather from the Azores; there was Natasha's Russia; and now Francine with her French name and manner. "He may live in America," Milo said, "but you notice he never married the girl next door."

My grandparents were a Czech soldier and a Dakota.

On those walks of his, the ones he took in all weathers when he came to live on Hemperle Road, he said he'd seen mostly women—apparently stranded here (by death or divorce or failure) by their men. I suppose that's true about our half-mile of the original road. We have women who've been here a long time. The men seem to come and go.

"They're probably not lost at all," Francine said. "They just seem that way to you. Maybe they can't afford to be anywhere else. They might have attachments."

Her sense of the real and the true was far greater than Jim's, and this he both admired in her; and hated. Everyone else loved Francine for that clarity, as I did, who've seen three Mothers come and go, and the fourth leaving. Less so now, maybe, when she has to think for herself and not just play off Jim.

Their arrival did alter things in the immediate neighborhood. As Mrs. Vojtyla said, we all felt just a bit more dowdy and alone. Francine gave the big old house on Hemperle Road a new tone: one of freshly-polished hardwood floors and long windows, of decorated plaster ceilings, and people (a lot of them legal clients of Jim's or friends famous enough to be in the papers.) I told Otto I was happy for Jim. I thought he and Francine would last in that house. And with Jake, that it would be a happy house.

So how is it that with all they had going for them—enough money coming in, a son they worshiped, being settled—that Jim kept asking if their house was as solid as he thought? Was this belated family of his, that little trio, safe? Could it be that Francine saw Jim as coming up to the end, and—alone enough with Jim absorbed in his work—she foresaw herself as alone for the rest of her life?

Francine was coming up to the fortyish age at which his parents had split; or, the way it would have been put back then, when Jacob Mount had walked out on his wife. Cast now as his mother, the one being abandoned, Jim would watch Francine—still young, still lovely—as she emerged from her shower. She would stand there, a Mother herself, with a mirror propped on a shelf blow-drying her hair, with which she was never satisfied: buck naked for all five-foot-eleven of her excepting for a towel round her trim waist. Pert, lovely and fresh. Nothing abundant about her, but everything perfect. And every time he thought, good, she was still there.

Then it was the turn of the Kid, still half-asleep, who came into the kitchen hopping on his left sneaker and hoping to get into it without untying the laces. Jim gave the Kid a good long look and told him to sit down and put his shoes on properly. As usual, he wished Jake looked a little less smart and a lot more strong. This precariousness bothered Francine and it bothered Jim. But it wasn't something Jim could do anything about, and once Francine lost Rory she never felt safe with the one she still had. Which is probably why she bent down and undid the balled-up knots on his laces. Just in case.

It all seemed normal. Life as usual. Something he could count on, this being the seventy-plus-year-old father of a kid he adored, a wife to hold his hand at the end. What mattered would still be here when he was gone.

However, turning on the espresso machine, what did Jim see? Too much of everything. The accumulated mess of his life. "Do you really need all this stuff?" Francine asked. How often (how well) did he play his Bechstein back-to-back grands? Was he really attached to those genre paintings of bakers baking bread and muleteers struggling with mules? Who was that boy peering out of a cupboard in a wedding dress with daisies in his hair? And what did it mean? (It was himself playing Tatiana at school.)

He explained her sniping away at his past as just Francine's way with things. She had always been into cleaning up and throwing out; she regularly purged her wardrobe at Goodwill; she was as ruthless with the Kid's toys.

"You know what I wonder sometimes? That maybe I'm next in line? Next to be tossed?"

So, "No," he told his friends and his particular pal Milo Frankel, "you wouldn't be wrong to think I'm undergoing a radical critique of my life—just when and where I least expected it."

He looked up at Milo—who was himself two wives up on Jim, the latest being the very pregnant Prudence—and added: "Francine's come up with a total of twenty-two splits in the family. I've been counting ever since: my parents, six by my father's sister, the beautiful red-head, mine, Tony's, I mean, who makes lists of such things?"

"Well, wives do," Milo answered, his good ear tilted Jim's way, his throat slack, his voice weary. "There's a purpose to it. They want to show us we're bad bets."

"She's always coped so well," Jim said. "Now, suddenly, she finds this all too much? I said to her, 'What are you getting at? That we're in an unsettled period? What comes next? You want to be divorcee Number Twenty-three, assuming you've counted right?'"

"What did she say?"

"She said she'd counted right. And just yet she didn't see any more point in divorcing than in staying married."

Why was so much made of women marrying? Francine wanted to know. Surely it was men who felt this compulsion to marry, men who feared being alone; who couldn't navigate in the real world. Look at you, she said. Someone had to look after the children men unthinkingly made, and at the end women were a comfort, weren't they? Who wanted to die alone in a hotel room?

Who indeed? Jim was haunted by the very things this smart—

and often cold—young woman said; and by the obvious fact that
on any given day, which could be sooner or later, she could chuck
him out: as a book- and-history-laden irrelevance to the pursuit of
her own life.

"Love indeed!" she said to Dr. Klima on a visit (not a profes-
sional consultation): "I don't think it is me Jim loves, but rather the
state of being married. His affections are transferable to whoever
holds the office, *si je peux dire*, and anyone would serve as well as
I. Ask any of my predecessors. You've been around for most of his
wives."

An elegant, short, Buddha with soft fingers wrapped around
an extra-long cigarette, Igor would have harrumphed, for questions
belong to him, and those who answered were patients, patently sick,
not the wives of his particular friends.

Talking to Jim's friends, I realized how artful Francine was.
She said devastating things like that with such complete bonho-
mie—and reasonableness, as though that settled the matter, it was
just common sense—that they were all persuaded of her good intentions. And they all said she was right: Jim could be impossible.

From upstairs, Francine called down: "You make sure he eats."
If the Kid wouldn't eat, how was he going to survive?

As Jim repeatedly told me, daily life was sound enough—getting the Kid to school where his grades were minimal (he lived by
charm), doing the shopping for dinner on his way home—but he
felt an undercurrent. The neighborhood was an eddy in which the
three of them seemed to go round and round, getting nowhere.

Sometimes, walking the neighborhood, followed a ways by
Smax their haughty cat, Jim remembered other rows of houses, of
lawns and garages. He saw himself as a kid in New York running
errands for the Kaufman Pharmacy; or still a virgin, he found
himself in San Antonio on his first twenty-four hour pass before
being shipped overseas, proud of his neatly-pressed chinos, clutching his first pay and a box of GI-issue rubbers in his pocket. He had
tramped about for so long he got lost and all the girls he saw in back-
yards and porches looked beautiful. O so beautiful! Their Mothers

on the other hand looked tired and were in back somewhere. He only heard them when they called out to their daughters: to stop dawdling out on the porch and come back in and help out: "I mean right now. This minute."

It wasn't just his neighborhood that was so cozily filled with women but his entire life. At the time, still stepping anxiously on the brink, when Jim brought me his stories, his fragments of Francine-talk, he'd say: "You're the one who wants to be a writer. Not me."

He was fretful and I was reluctant.

"How could you not write about this?" he asked. "It's a great subject. The Mothers, all of whom were once girls. And my hard heart, the one I ought to have but don't. It will seem to be about the women in my life, but really it's about women in general, and how delicate our relations are with this different species."

When I pointed out I was a woman, he said beguilingly: "Indeed you are. But you're not a Mother."

That was a terrible thing to say, but an obvious one, for it was by my own will that I wasn't. But how could he know that? I could never quite get used to Jim as a lawyer, though remarks like that—caught in my own trap on the stand!—made me see why he might be a good one. When I was his girl, way back, I thought he'd be a musician. He'd come over to our house and make up dreamy sounds on our piano: and then suddenly go haywire with rhythm he said he'd just heard in Stravinsky. It was only years later he sent me an LP of Petrushka and I had to go out and buy a player to hear it.

His ear walked out on him, he says, and when he went to college it was with words in his head; then later, arguments. As a career, it made sense. I knew perfectly well he couldn't write his own story. He had no self-knowledge. Lawyers don't need any.

I suppose Mount & McIlvenny, Attorneys-at-Law, was a weird sort of firm for a big city. Jim and his older partner, Frank, were more like the family lawyers of an previous generation. Wives, husbands, cops, crooks, wills and going broke. They knew they'd never handle anything big. They didn't specialize. They did what

Frank called salvage—"flotsam, jetsam and lagan, who gets to fish what out of the sea once the ship of life had gone down."

I used to follow Jim from a distance, when his cases got into the papers. Jim got the guys who swore they hadn't bludgeoned little old ladies to death and Frank did divorce and property. Which was another joke, because good Catholic Frank didn't believe in divorce and Jim had no sympathy for thugs.

They were alike on law and different in every other way. Frank's once-black hair had gone white; his body had spread; his hands were clumsy and big and his hair remained wired, but in a bushy, projectile sort of way. Frank and Miriam had been together fifty years without making a child; Francine held the marriage record with Jim, sixteen years, which is not very long as such things go; and children he had plenty of.

The first troubles with Francine were begun about two years ago—at least that was when most of us first heard about them. Jim says it was at about the same time that he first heard from Sunny ("S-u-n-n-y, not Sonny") Farber, an attorney in Long Beach, California.

It appeared Sunny wanted to sell him something: "Your brother's dead, right? It's not something we can discuss over the phone, but you're sort of the heir." It had to do with his Dad.

"Heir to what?" Jim asked. "My father didn't leave a goddam thing."

That wasn't what Sunny Farber was selling. He had information. He knew his father's old telephone number in Los Angeles (Van Dyke 6545) and who his partner had been. He knew the joke between Jim and Francine, that Francine styled herself Jim's "current wife."

Jim's antennae bristled. He didn't like Sunny. He saw him as having long bright yellow hair and shades. What did this California shark want? What was in this for him?

Francine let it be known (since Sunny called more than once, and was insistent) that Jim was paranoid about Sunny Farber. And about his father.

"Who knows what's true about Jacob and what isn't?" she said to Milo. "We never talk about his father. With good reason. It always ends up this way. As usual he's turning everything into words. Words are real for Jim, a lot more real than we are. He doesn't know the effect he has on people, just how overwhelming he can be. If his father had been around... ?"

But his father hadn't been around. So what was the point of speculating? Was his father a mystery because he had something to hide or because what Jim hid about him was a terrible emptiness?

3

The most I can do is put down the few things Jim told me over the years about his father. Jacob Mount was also Harry Carey—a bad pun, but Jacob's own idea—and sometimes Walter, Mount or Carey. It was in California—as with Jim's brother, the West was where they wound up—that he turned into Harry and the others, depending on who he was writing or talking to. Jim said he had also come across people, long ago, who had known him as Walter: mostly money people with whom he dealt.

Dealt what? I remember asking.

Jim didn't even know what Jacob did for a living—he invested? He invented?—Or even what he had been doing out there in L.A. All he knew was his father went out to the coast in the spring of '39, the year when war broke out in Europe, while he and his mother and brother were in a hot hotel by the Sicilian sea. It was a summer of hot sand and black shirts. Late in that summer of '39 a typed letter came from his father. Feli read the boys just a bit from the end: about how he missed them all. From her face the boys read that summer was over.

When the war broke out (early September), they just managed to find a cabin on the *Rex* and sailed from Naples. "Tony and I were glad to be back in America. Mamma wasn't," Jim said laconically. Not taking into account she might have had premonitions, that war might mean more than just a change of locations.

They went West on the Empire State Express (Jim's first sight of Chicago) and the Santa Fe's Super Chief. As his mother said with apprehension in the dining car rolling through Arkansas, bound for a new life: "You'll see, you'll like the sun. It will be a better life for you."

Tony, who yearned for Italian girls (so like his mother), said: "Seeing is believing." When in fact he was a whole lot better at believing than seeing.

There was a huge papier-maché orange at the end of the line and girls in short (for the time) skirts handing out juice; there was Jacob's green Studebaker waiting for them at Union Station. It had the first push-button radio the boys had seen. Feli was wrong and Tony was right. There were good things, Californian exotica like the Brown Derby drive-in; but in fact nothing that good happened out there.

Jim remembers his Dad trying to sell Feli on California. It didn't work. Jacob's Hawaiian flowered shirt was criticized and, as in Philadelphia, he was only there in name and as a bunch of soft jackets that hung in the closet. Soon enough he vanished.

An agnostic even about his own name, his few letters before or after the split came typed and unsigned. His office door in downtown Los Angeles, of frosted glass, bore a number, 1015, but no name. The sixty-year-old shoe-shine boy in the dusty lobby where Jim's father sat high called him "Mr. Carey," and Jim recalled looking up sharply to see who that was. Not that Jacob answered. He could have said, "This is my son," but he didn't. God could not have been more unknowable.

Yet I was surprised at how sharp the memory of his father was in Jim's mind. There Jacob, enshrined in a half-dozen photographs, never changed. He stayed dark, quick and angular as he'd been in

26

Jim's childhood, flexible as a plaited leather whip, as if he were a hard-struck shot, hit for the corner and baseline. Untouchable, Jim said. He'd whizzed by you before you got a good look.

Some five years ago, after Tony died on a hilltop in Nevada—with that big smile on his face, with his shades on—Jim flew on to Los Angeles, and when he came back he stayed the weekend with me for the first time before going back to his own home.

He was all shaken up by Tony's death and, as he said, by not finding his father's grave. For all the wild tales he's told me about Tony—all true enough, tossing Roosevelt dimes in Central Park Lake (how modest political protest was in the 1940s!), the girls, Ginger and Rose, the way he died, the funny hats he wore when, for the sheer fun of it, he held up convenience stores—I know Jim loved and missed the man terribly. Among other reasons because now there was no one left to remember with him.

Jim brought back the flag Tony had been laid out under, neatly folded in a triangle, as per regulations, and told me how cold he had been to kiss. He'd been drinking on the plane, and drink never helped his anger. I tried to talk him down, but he said, handing me the flag, "The effing Army did its best to kill him, didn't it! You know about punishment brigades, Aissa? In first, first killed. Sicily, Salerno. That's what happened to him."

When he heard Tony was dead, snow had been falling in Chicago. In Nevada the wind blew flat; but the brown hills of the City of Angels were balmy. He told me how he'd tried to find out where Jacob was buried: to settle that at least. For as Jacob's mother and sister had both written at the time, the cemetery was supposed to be in Beverly Hills. Where Jacob died, or killed himself—depending on what you wanted to believe—was not so clear. Both those Christian Scientists, to the extent they accepted death at all, said Jim's father had "passed on" in Nevada: like Tony. Whereas his mother, never strong on American geography or America, period, said Arizona.

There was no death certificate registered in the Los Angeles County Hall.

Jim drove all over Beverly Hills, Santa Monica, Westwood and the like in a big, air-conditioned rental car. One cemetery, the largest, had been swallowed up in a vast Veterans' Administration complex; few others showed up on the map or in the Yellow Pages. Still, he visited every one there was.

"In 1947, you say?" That far back it would be hard to find. Was there perpetual care? (Yes, he cared.) "What did you say his name was?"

Mount.

"No Mount here."

I did my best to comfort him. He said, "There's nothing surprising about not finding him. When he walked out on us I did everything I could to get through to the man. I never even got close."

But then did it matter exactly where Jacob died and was buried? By the time Jim's grandchildren grew up, would there still be families—in the accepted sense? He doubted it. But it did mean something to him that both his brother Tony and his father had died somewhere out West, up in those cold and empty moon-mountains which they both fancied. Both died without for a moment having understood women, maybe no more than he did. They had no feel for them as people. It mattered because, for his father, Jim's filial piety ran deep and strong.

According to Jim, in the 1940s Jacob still had some hopes: "At least that's what he wrote from time to time." Certain "investments" could still pan out, and then in the background of a couple of snapshots with deckled edges there was the second wife, Hetty Short. (He was Harry to her, as though "Jacob" no longer fitted his new California life.)

She was a brassy blonde of the sort the seventeen-year-old Tony liked to be seen with going into night clubs, and ran a consignment shop just off Wilshire Boulevard: 'Fit for the Stars.' The one time Jim had seen her (during the boys' monthly visitations) she'd looked at the two of them without maternal ambition. "Hi, good-looking," she said to Tony, while Jim was allowed to feel a white fur she said had belonged to Ginger Rogers. Jim said he'd never noticed painted nails before, nor after, of such a hard, metallic red.

Hetty remarried within weeks of his father's death. But she had long since left Los Angeles, and her Harry, for New York. "Another busted flush," Jim said. "I tried hard to see Hetty. I had every reason to. I lurked by the marquee of her apartment block and made friends with her doorman, but never caught sight of her. Tony of course called her up one night Mamma was out. He pretended to be someone else, but she knew who he was and said she never wanted to see any Mount for any reason whatever, and Tony said, 'Silly bitch, she's got Papa's money; she thinks that's what we want.'"

What money? Feli struggled with two hundred bucks a month for child support, but she remained loyal. "I'm sure your father's doing what he can," she said regularly, still carrying her torch. While Jim's big brother Tony would sometimes get a greedy glint in his eyes and say: "You remember those oil wells he showed us in Long Beach?"

Jim did: their monotonous rocking motion. But he also remembered, which was not the way Tony imagined his life, that Jacob had failed to say, "Son, one day all this will be yours."

"Why else would he show us those wells?" Tony asked.

Jim said: "Because they were there. Because you could see them from the road. Because that may have been what he wanted you to think."

Tony wouldn't be shaken. When he wasn't dreaming girls, his extreme fantasy was being flush, his treasure out there beyond the Sierra Madre, rocking, pumping, making him as rich as he deserved.

"How about you, Jim?" he asked. "You have no taste for money?"

Not so much no taste as no idea of what it was, Francine would say.

Anyway, Long Beach was a dreadful place now, Jim said, seedy and desolate, with the Queen Mary bunkered among freeways and water-bed motels with dirty movies. He went there too before coming back to Chicago.

"I'm happy to report the wells—maybe even those—are still pumping: retirees can look at them from the picture windows of their heaped-up ranch houses. I'm always visiting these particles of the past."

That could be why, when Sunny Farber called from Long Beach, Jim saw him as a lure. No thanks, Counselor Farber, he said to Frank after the call. "I have to take it that's the way he wanted it: to be a Dad and husband that no one should get close to."

In a brief life, Jim explained, that was always possible; the longer we live the more explicable we become. He had seen his father just once after his parents' divorce, when, once again Jacob, he came through New York on his way somewhere and bought Jim his first blue suit. "He said he hoped he'd be proud of me. He went too soon to pronounce judgment, which is probably just as well."

When he'd more or less settled down after the dead, the gone West, our weekend together—a lot was drunk—he went back to the big old house and asked Francine if she thought dead folks remembered. "Do they loll about in paradise and still criticize us? Do they see what we're up to? Can they make us feel ashamed?"

She replied: "If we think about them, they do. They become part of our conscience."

Sure, but if there were no after-life and this life was all we've got, then there would seem to be no reason to be nice to the living. Once they were gone, they were gone. Worms didn't pass judgment; the living became laconic. When Jacob died, all he got was a telegram from his Aunt Ros, his father's sister: REGRET YOUR FATHER PASSED ON STOP ROS.

And his brother Tony had died too quickly for Jim to get there for the big leap. He felt it necessary to tell Francine, too, how cold his brother's cheek had been when he kissed it. It was coming up to that time of year when her daughter Rory had died, and she said, "At least you got to do that much." For with Rory there had been no such *au revoir*—she was there, hanging on, and then she wasn't. For she hadn't kissed Rory's cheek that one last time. At the critical moment she'd been asleep.

"My lucky Mamma," he said. "Having shed eighty years of sorrow, she spent the last ten years of her life wrapped up in her childhood. I'd gladly do so myself, if I knew what my childhood was really like."

When he and Tony once totted up on a yellow legal pad all they knew about their father, the result hadn't added up to much: maybe a dozen fragments. In about half the items listed their memories didn't tally: as to place, time, or even the bare facts—like the color of a car. Had it really been a green Studebaker he met them in at Union Station?

"That was all we had, period," Jim said. "Just a few fragments."

The early, independent memory, he thought, that part of it which belongs to no one else—the sound of fire-engine bells such as they had seventy years ago, the light-and-shade of big trees in the park, a hypodermic needle fat as a drug-store straw—contains the Big Secret. "Only we don't know what it is. That's why we spend so much of our lives lying about and to ourselves."

He supposed that his father had spent much of his last years in lawyers' offices not unlike his own. But it was as a Displaced Person, or as someone who wanted to be displaced. "Divorce will do that for you," he said to Frank. "Young Jake is just the age I was."

All the Mounts of his father's generation were gone. Fifty years down the line no one was left who knew him, at least no one Jim knew of. Jacob fell among the Missing, among the incomplete or abandoned lives, an eerie lot: old people in their retirement communities where no kids are allowed; young men who died in war before they could be explained.

Then there was the last thing he said to me on that visit, how Tony's nutty daughter Tessa (whom he saw at Tony's funeral for the first time in years) could hear unborn children. She heard them shriek in the middle of the night: "Few people can be silent enough to hear them," she told her uncle. In all seriousness. She was the sort who went on pro-Life marches.

"She listened."

Who to?

To all who could be remembered, but had lacked enough life to be held on to.

Jim said, "The composer Chabrier grew up with four of his miscarried brothers and sisters in glass bottles on the mantelpiece. He never said if they were communicative."

4

My Grandma was a real listener. In a Dakota camp, when she was still a girl—This is some time before her people's West was all lost— she could tell which dog barked or which child whined. She could hear rain when it was still miles away. The only thing she didn't hear coming was Sergeant Knoblauch, a Moravian who criss-crossed the Plains in his wagon repairing pianos and harmoniums and every kind of musical instrument. He stuck her in his wagon, carried her off to Chicago, and made an honest woman of her. That was her story, anyway.

I'm a listener, too. As Jim's a talker.

It started long ago, but it's never really stopped: the things he doesn't like about me, and his way of letting me know. These days he doesn't like it that I haven't got my busted hip fixed. He says my Knoblauch hair is dirty blond because it's dirty, and wants to know why I butcher it myself instead of going to the sa-LON. He thinks I'm getting fat because most of the time I sit in my rocking chair. There's nothing I don't know about my defects, believe me.

But at the same time he'll give me a hug and say, "I do love you, Aissa." By which he means I'm familiar, my smile's the same as it always was and it hasn't grown up. By which he means I'm a constant. He goes tramping back to the john in my little house and he sees on the hook behind the door the silly nightgowns that are just about the ones I wore when I first knew him: Sears Roebuck Mother Hubbards in winter, cotton in summer. He doesn't like it that my handwriting is crabbed, and he pretends not to like it that I take notes about what he says, just as I did when he was fifteen and sixteen and I found him so extraordinary, or save every letter and postcard he ever wrote me. They're part of the book about me I've never managed to get written.

Let me explain why we can't love each other like normal people. I'm not as ignorant about sex as he thinks. I'm not scared of that. I'm scared of him. I got married once, I had other men friends. I let them have their way, *je leur ai laissé faire*, it just didn't mean much. But his Thing is a threat. If I let that into me, I knew what would happen. So now I drink. Is that a crime?

The nights out here all you see, because the ground is sandy, is light spreading on the lawns and frost settling on the brown grass. And when he walks home down Hemperle Road the nights are brown overhead where the glare of the city spreads up from the south. My kitchen faces north: I see nights that are pitch dark, cold and scattered with stars.

The worst thing in his life right now, he says, is the illusion of solidity given off by the big old house, by the Kid, by their meals together, he and Francine and the Kid. "It always look so durable," he says. "And suddenly it isn't."

At present, his voice trembles; and sometimes his hands shake, too; or he's about to burst into tears. In those states, it isn't just his teeth that are broken and irregular, his whole face gets lop-sided, his eyes swim: as if the world's snatched a toy from his hand.

"You think Francine really wants a divorce?" I ask.

"That's what she's getting to."

"What are you going to do?"

"Fight. What do you expect me to do? I love her. She says she's lost the will, the desire, the motivation, whatever. She's exhausted her capacity for loving. I've talked to Milo, I've talked to everyone."

"And what did Milo say?"

"He said she was a virtuous woman, she'd done her duty for sixteen years and now she wants to kick over the traces. Francine says no one's going to be surprised if we split up. She thinks everyone knows she's had a hard time of it. Well, I don't know if I'm in her 'everyone knows', but I'm surprised! I did what I could."

"Yes, but did she love you? Ever?"

That was the big question, and the answer is that Francine—as do all of us—loved her man according to her capacities. For some love rose like yeast, unstoppable; others knew what would happen and never made dough. Francine struck me as the prudent sort.

I watched him start on the couple of hundred yards to the big house, where I could just make out the big fir by his driveway. Various gardens where the recent snow, before Hallowe'en, had melted now looked freshly ploughed. His hands behind his broad back, he never looked up or back. I knew what was going on. He was plunging among the talkative dead who were peering up at him, waiting for a word: mother, father, brother, daughter—Jake's sister to whom the Kid, with other things dying round him, had stopped talking.

He walked past Mrs. Vojtyla's house in which a light burned upstairs. Why had Francine scoffed at the piano-teacher's bunnies fleeing in the storm? The wind had taken them. Things fled all the time. The stars weren't animate but they rushed through the sky while Mrs. Vojtyla's music remained locked in her head: the way her Chopin had been, whom the Kid's fingers now harmed. How did she feel about that?

My question—had Francine ever loved him?—had thrown him. He might as well have been staring down at his Mamma's ashes and saying, "I didn't love you, I should have."

When families were looked at in time, over generations, what was certain?

34

You have to understand: he didn't just share all this with me, he imposed it on me. All I was supposed to do was find the words. There. He unlocked the front door and tiptoed back into the house which was silent and asleep. In his bedroom the Kid lay sprawled on his bed, the covers pulled off. Real enough. Through her door, Francine's sleep was deep and uncommunicative. Nothing changed there. Apparently.

Still, sleep remained as elusive as ever, the room cold, the bed narrow and solitary: but for Grandma Tilly Mount, his father's mother, who sat at its foot. Oversized and inconvenient, she had brought California with her: in the shape of the Pacific at Santa Monica, a row of formal palms, a crumbling red bluff, then the sea and its slow swells. This, in accord with the Science, was the material universe she shared with her red-haired daughter Ros. Tilly was the Keeper of the Key to the Scriptures in L.A.'s Second Church; Ros had written for the Monitor. Science would make them successful as well as healthy.

He waited for the uncomfortable chrome chairs of his grandmother's dinette set to form. And the expression on her face—silent and disapproving. For her to bite slowly on a biscuit the way a glacier might grind rock. How dared the two boys badmouth their Dad? They were spoiled, spoiled rotten, because that was what You-rup was, spoiled rotten. Here in the California she brought to his bed she was on her own turf. She was glad to have got rid of Feli while their lot played on the beach in Italy. Now her son—Jake, Harry, Walter?—was back where he belonged: with an American woman: even if that was only Hetty. An American was better for him, healthier, than an Italian.

Tony's charm didn't move her at all; she didn't suggest the boys could stay out there with their Dad as Jim had half-hoped.

"I guess we're not liked," Tony said when Jacob had picked them up. The way Jim put it, was that they were too "different" and that was the fault of You-rup.

When he turned on his bedside lamp Grandma Tilly had

gone, whom Science had not helped, since in the next decade her son was dead, Ros was to watch her sixth husband die at breakfast in Acapulco on their honeymoon, a spoonful of grapefruit halfway to his mouth, and Tilly herself went blind a few years after that.

There was no question of deserving or not deserving what happened to her children or herself ("Serves you right!"): blindness and "passing over" (death) were material events. So were divorce and having or not having money. She didn't and Jacob didn't. Sounds to me, when Jim talks about her, everything she said came out like one of those copy-book maxims she must have written out when she was a girl a hundred and twenty years ago. You are My Only Grandchildren. You Should Know Where You Belong in the Scheme of Things. You're going to have to Make Your Own Way. The Way Your Father Did. The American Way.

When in '39 they'd arrived back from their abruptly-ended holiday and landed in New York—for some reason there was no question of their going back to Philadelphia—Tilly and Ros had been there to Show them the Sights. American Kids Don't Eat Foreign Food. They had chicken pot pie at a Horn & Hardart's Automat. American Kids don't have Uncles who Brag; they don't have slinky, dark-eyed Girl Cousins who Flirt. There'll be no Popish Mummery Here. If they were Real Americans like Their Father they'd relish the material legs and zest of the Rockettes at the Radio City Music Hall, where Ros's fourth husband was in charge of the vast electric organ: its maintenance, not performance, Tilly said, proud of science. She'd had enough of the artiste with her husband Charlie: that was why they had no money.

When they got out West and Jacob said that was that to his marriage and Feli didn't understand, the three of them lived not far from Long Beach in one of those thousands of wooden beach-shacks that crowded the coast then and crowd it now, its walls so thin there was no escape from Feli's tears. They poured from her all day; her room was strewn with damp handkerchiefs and with sufferings that were Italian, Catholic, operatic, terrible, and as consuming as cancer—especially on a stage set of flimsy beach-houses and against a backdrop, where Jacob was, of orange groves and brown, burned hills.

Who ever heard of crying for two whole years? "Not in America," said Auntie Ros cheerfully, her hair a fiery sunset red. "Here we get on with things. You lose one husband you get another. Get her down off the cross."

When it wasn't grey and drizzling out at the end of the pier where Jim went fishing (get out of the house, get out of there), the sky was a super-perfect postcard blue. Whether in the bright yellow school-bus, or slinking pierwards or to the movies—Zorro and newsreels before the feature—the one thing he knew was that their summer beach house wasn't home. There was nothing of theirs in it. It had other peoples' furniture. It was a trap. His mother did all the feeling for him; he was supposed to rent his feelings from her like the furniture. On holidays and weekends there wasn't even the relief of school and the world outside.

When he could escape the nightly tomato soup—Feli was too distraught to cook—that outside world contained all the fauna he recognized as his America and he was proud of it. Out there were sailors and pert teen-age girls handing over popcorn, little old men with canvas hats and cancerous skin idly casting for mackerel or better, hucksters and probably perverts if he'd known what they were. But, above all, there was freedom from manners, from hours, from woe.

His real place was the Ocean, which I didn't see, or really believe in, until I was in my thirties. One weekend a month the boys were with Jacob. From the main Bus Station downtown they got on the trolley that ran right up Santa Monica Boulevard. It ended at the ocean and the bath-house with its wet rope carpets, its muscle-builders, and the brief beach beyond with its endless lazy breakers.

"I was happy there," he told me one night. "You want to know why Francine thinks I don't understand Jake? She says it's because I didn't have a childhood myself. Imagine a Sunday afternoon long ago, Aissa, and you'll see a kid Jake's age who didn't want to go home and face his mother's weeps. I didn't want to be around a sniveler. I could make comparisons between them, my Mother and my Father. Mom prayed reproachfully to God to send her back a man who was merely being misled by 'that woman'; my father got on with living. Who was right? What's Jake going to do?"

Those by-the-Pacific weekends were among the items in the brief list of what they remembered that he and Tony made.

Elegant in the long whites that concealed his thin legs, Jacob played tennis on the public courts where Bill Tilden played sometimes; he cruised the city in his, if it was green, green Studebaker, the radio turned wavy by Hawaiian ukeleles to match his flowered shirts. These hung outside his slacks—to Feli a terrible sign of degeneracy. How could he? And while Jim didn't much like Hetty, especially her hair and her nails, she at least belonged out there where Feli had assured the two boys they would be happy.

He begged his father, who swam well out beyond the swell, to stay as late as possible and they did: until the sun plummeted, hazy and orange, right down into the sea. "The Ocean was great, my dear. It faced nowhere I knew."

I told him I'd never really seen the sea, or stayed by it, watched it, and he said, "I could take you one day."

I wasn't taken in. Trips like that were for other people, and not with Jim. I saw the Pacific through his eyes: that was more than good enough. Wasn't Grandma Tilly right—about the Mounts, about Jim's Mother? At least for that old America, the one that no longer existed? And what counted more for Jim: the presence of his mother or the absence of his father?

In '41 Jacob gave Tony a second-hand Pontiac convertible for his seventeenth birthday: "Get you out from under your mother," he said.

The car was the first of Tony's many infidelities. He took his Mamma out. She had a scarf knotted under her chin, a brief smile on her lips, her delicately crooked front teeth showing. "A lot of the movies I used to see happy-ended the same way," Jim said. "The girl's hair blowing in the wind. I remember Tony's driving gloves waving goodbye as he revved away; they were a bright yellowish brown."

Once they went North as far as Santa Barbara for a whole weekend. They locked the door behind them and left Jim out front to be picked up by an Italian family who had a boy "just his age." That was the last thing he wanted. The moment the convertible reached the end of the road, he took a few bucks out of the household money that was in a pot in the kitchen and walked to the bus station.

Only when he got to L.A., did he realize it was a Friday, so his Dad wouldn't be in his office. He walked all the way from the bus station to the only place he knew the address of in the city—because it was in the phone-book: the store in Beverly Hills where Hetty sold her glad rags.

"She was a profoundly neutral bitch," Jim said sixty years after. "Didn't care if I was there or I wasn't. None of her business."

Hetty was calling up his Dad when in fact his car pulled outside the shop and he jumped out in a fury. "He was a strong man and it hurt when he whacked me. But it was better than being in Balboa and afterwards we had steaks out by the pier there used to be in Santa Monica. He said at least my getting all the way to Beverly Hills showed Gumption."

Jim said, "That was my first taste of violence first-hand: 'live' as we'd say today. Really my only taste. I don't count when Tony was drunk. I think underneath it all my father was proud."

In California that year, coming up to Pearl Harbor, all the storms that accompany an unwanted divorce—pleading for her life, her love, her marriage—violent, electric, garish storms of rage and humiliation, were magnified by the cramped quarters in which they took place: inside the house; in his father's parked car; at the clinic Feli went to, when under the drugs they pumped into her she decided she didn't care to remember who she was; at Mr. Steinmann's legal offices signing papers when he asked coldly just how much she thought her husband was worth.

One storm after another. People are pitiably naked in distress.

The weekend Feli went by bus to look after Tony when he had

a crash in Big Sur—there was a girl with him, her face disfigured by glass splinters. Feli sent Jim to stay with Jacob. "In fact, she couldn't bear to talk to Hetty or even mention her by name," Jim said.

"I could hear them arguing about me on the telephone, the kind that stood up and you had one part to your ear. Finally he agreed to drive me back Sunday night."

The trouble was, Jacob knew Hetty didn't like Jim. She called him "Mr. Smartass."

On Sunday morning—she liked to sleep late—Hetty was sore that Jacob had gone off to play tennis. When she got up, all she'd put on was a silk bathrobe. Her hair was up in rollers, the way it stayed all night. She plunked Jim's Shredded Wheat on the kitchen table and said, "Your Dad will be home soon, and don't stare at a lady when she's not fully dressed. Doesn't your Mom teach you anything?"

"I'd never seen rollers," Jim said. "Just very rarely something Mamma called *bigoudini*, little soft things you rolled round your hair to make it curl. She was very private, very convent. She could take off a bathing suit on the beach wrapped in towels."

Jacob came back a bit before noon and was in the shower singing *O Sole Mio* when Feli arrived. Whom no one expected. From the kitchenette Jim and Hetty heard the taxi door slam and looked out the window.

"For Chrissakes!" Hetty said. "Hasn't that woman got any common sense? Jacob!" She turned to Jim and said, "You go out there and tell your Mom she doesn't belong here. Jacob! Jake!"

Jim clung to the refrigerator door trying to be invisible, shaking his head but unable to get even "no" out of his mouth.

As Feli walked the stepping stones on the lawn to the front door (the grass thick and soaked by sprinklers) he could see the care his mother had taken with how she looked: her hair swept up and wearing the big boxy shoulders just become fashionable, her lips brightly 'sticked, her nails near as bright as Hetty's.

"Jake!" The doorbell rang. It rang again and again. His bike was against the side of the house, Dad's Studebaker was out there, and so was Hetty's station wagon with its gleaming wood frame. Everything was obvious, clear as California sky. Feli should have known and turned back.

Fixed by the counter, Hetty kept calling out "Jacob!" and "Jake!" from the kitchen: until finally Jacob appeared in a towel-cloth bathrobe, his dark hair plastered down. "What's up? What are you yelling about?"

Hetty just pointed.

By then Feli was sobbing hysterically at the door.

Jacob took her by the elbow and put her in his car: like something he didn't want to be seen with.

"You get away from that window young Jim," Hetty said.

But not quickly enough. He'd already seen his father grip the steering wheel while Feli tried to get her arms about him.

I said, "Can't you spare anyone anything, Jim? Don't write those things. Young Jake shouldn't know about them, they're humiliating. I think it's time you went home."

He stuck his head out the door and let the wind push at his face. The wind was wet and warm, and though it wasn't raining the moisture in the air made him feel like a plane pushing through a cloud. Reluctant to go, he turned around in the doorway and said: "The Kid reminds me of me, that's what's bad. He senses that he's stuck between Francine and me. He plays it cool of course. That's the virtue of the day. But I know what it's like for him. Been there, done that as they say nowadays."

"The only one you're hurting is yourself Jim. And me a little, I guess."

"I wouldn't hurt you for anything in the world," he said, stepping back in the door.

"Yes you would. Only you just wouldn't know you did."

5

By 1942 Feli had stopped crying—life being over, there was no longer anything to weep about. Still she dressed with care, as though back on the market, but a Mother, which overrules everything. She was forty-five, olive-skinned, lithe, and women still wore hats: in which she looked good. Often pillboxes, sometimes with erotically-charged veils which bore regular dots.

After school, Jim would wait for her on the corner of 59th and Lex and walk her home from work—Tony being much of the time away, with girls. Sailors on shore-leave wandered in wistful gangs, three or four abreast, hands thrust in pea-jackets, dark blue bell-bottoms jaunty, white caps askew, ogling. In the late summer, the sailors were in whites. Though it was Tony she'd rather lean on, she'd say, "It's nice to have you with me Jim. I don't like the way they stare at me."

Home in New York, that summer of '41, was two rooms with heat dripping through the asphalt roof and off their energetic bodies. Feli's eyes shone. Her boys were becoming men. Rice and peas on their plates at the little round table, Tony picking at a slice of bread, avoiding the crust, she watched them both. The Dad who ought to be at the table was a continent away on the other coast, which no longer seemed real. Had she really lived two years there? She denied it. Now only the boys were served, and had become the sole objects of Feli's unfocused hungers. She hardly ate. Instead it seemed her body softened, her lips smiled and she became desirable and expectant. Part of her said: "Sit up straight!" Another said, "Love, please!" Which was easy for Tony, hard for Jim, and dangerous for both.

They were merely uneasy, not unhappy: as though their legs had grown too big to fit under the table. She noticed also the extra heat they gave off: as though there weren't enough coming off the air-conditioning exhausts that rattled and whirred outside their open windows. This super power-supply was something they shared. They were both dying to get up and go out, to get away from the fussy furniture Philadelphia friends had sent them when their own burned in a warehouse fire. However, there was this to be considered: the insurance would pay for Tony when he went to college in September. He said bravely that he would be eighteen when classes started in the fall and he was ready to do his bit.

Feli, who had only Sundays off in war-time, tried to hold them back; she wanted to smile them into staying and keeping the home fire burning. They understood and did their best.

Before and after dinner—which she served as she always had, as though Jacob would be back soon, and this just happened to be the cook's night off—Tony sat on the sofa. His manner was entirely grown-up. He had a tall glass in one hand (iced-tea color) and his Dad's cigarette, with far more assured smoke spiraling up from it, in the other. Was the way he toyed tenderly with a lock of his mother's hair on her nape a conscious imitation of Jacob? Or his hand, which would stray to lie on hers or brush the silk of her sleeve?

He bantered ("Now, my girl…"). She giggled and flirted. His affectionate gestures were those of the man of the house. But no, they had none of Jacob's nervousness, his perpetual high tension. They seemed to come from the movies the boys went to several times a week (they had part-time jobs, this being the American way) and she with them only on weekend nights. Jim said Tony was like a film festival. There was Franchot Tone in Tony's affection, Charles Boyer in the way he tamped his cigarettes on a silver case. They were the signs of married love, its tiny rituals.

Jim was like Jacob in his anger and sensitivity, his demands. Feli thought to capture him in another way, as Jacob had been: by the touch and feel and smell of women, by the camphor of her winter coats coming and going morning and evening, the delicate scent of ironing and lavender sachets when she opened her drawers. Jim experienced her cupboards and her chests-of-drawers as being redolent of a secret life. Indeed, in one of his novels Milo has Jim, or someone very like him, say there had never been an alien closet he'd not ransacked for its traces.

Tony—*il bel' Antonio*, as Feli called him—said women were

simply bloody marvels; Jim wanted to know what they were like, what made them tick. While his brother ironed to be helpful, Tony fondled the pile of smooth, still-warm garments and thought of undressing the marvels. "And they weren't imaginary," Jim said. "They were many, real, and occupied all his time."

"Look at this stuff!" Tony said with wonder, raising a complex brassiere from his mother's early days. "Image unhooking that!"

I remember Milo saying that if you wanted to nurture a ferocious passion for the opposite sex, grow up only with your own.

The heat the two boys radiated in New York was expectation, and the only woman around was their mother, who teased them both, though it was Tony she coaxed.

After the long winters of Philadelphia the sunshine of California had freed up bone and flesh in Jim, as it removed layers of complexion and clothing from girls' lives, opening up the glory of their skins, shadow and glow. The differences between the two species became obvious, but neither reassuring nor comprehensible. What had they done wrong that boys couldn't be as frank, as open, as approachable as girls were? Men could be good-looking, Tony was, but the girls were beautiful. That was a big difference: That boys didn't dare to be beautiful, that their good looks didn't make them (Tony even less than most) feel guilty of a come-hither. So what sort of knowledge of their powers did girls have that they hadn't?

In California, everything had been out in the open and Jim could observe his brother's "moves." In New York, girls were wrapped up and lived in little boxes, while the parochial schools Jim went to were full of boys growing up on bread and margarine. Out West one could watch as the girls sprouted suburbs, lengthened and softened, acquired a freedom he marveled at. Occasionally scented, their necks were hung with delicate little chains; they sat or lolled about in recess, visibly tired of what their bodies were doing to them, their downy skins sleek against one another like slick, soft kittens, in a way no boy could have allowed himself. Or they crossed their legs like lazy scissors and caressed their calves, conscious of the beauty they had to offer, which could be theirs—his, if he understood the messages in their smiles and eyes. Had he been less awkward.

Growing-up had befallen the girls, a difficult chemical and emotional transformation which he understood not at all. Not that these ur-women really knew what had hit them: their insides had acted up and suddenly they'd passed from girl to woman.

Then they'd be Mothers.

I see these frustrations still at work in Jim when he brings Jake around, which he sometimes does now: as though by chance, on his way to Mrs. Vojtyla's or the market. None of this chemical complexity weighs on Jake yet. It's only his dead sister he dreams about (less now, he says candidly). "But it's not far off, sex, the whole bit!" says Jim.

Being attuned to dreams by Grandma, I asked Jake what he dreamed about her—when he did dream about her a lot.

Jake explained in detail. Rory was falling from the Leaning Tower of Pisa and every night he almost saved her so that he could play with her.

"It would be nice if she were here. I would never be alone."

Often enough Jake still talked to her. Their intimacy has given Jake the ease with which he admires, plays with and dreams of his Mother and all girls. Like Adam he knows no better.

Jim envies him, I think: who had no such ease with Feli. He had his face cleaned with her spit on a hankie; he knew the night-smell of her, of satin night-gowns, sleep and sheets, her often unwelcome and always demanding arms cuddling him while Jacob, collarless, stood in the bathroom next door stropping his razor.

These indulgent daydreams of Jim's irked Francine. "It's always your mother's perfume you talk about. Didn't you smell him? Your father? Or was it only your mother who got to you? All your kids loved her and went to see her. They found her kind and funny. You might think on that. It was one of the first things about you that shocked me. Here was this charming, frail, harmless old woman and you treated her like some mess the cat had dragged in."

"Charming yes, frail I guess, frail by the end; but harmless no."

Perhaps that was the way things were with boys: that Mothers drew an excess of love or fear and loathing. So when the Kid, slippers flapping, came in, pushed Smax the cat off his chair and sat down, Francine asked him: "Are you going to hate me when you grow up?"

Jake didn't answer. He was fine-tuning his selective deafness.

But the answer was obvious. Jake would never hate her. *Jamais.* He was besotted, though he didn't know it. He was a Tony.

That last August before Tony enlisted (Jim said it was on a bet he lost, but a letter from Princeton stuck in a book Jim lent me all those years ago, said the college was pleased the draft board had given Tony a deferment, "in view of your financial difficulties") Feli and the two boys spent two weeks in a cheap and crowded resort hotel in Maine with a frail wooden porch that ran round three sides. The young people seemed to be only girls. Where the forest grew like an obsession just beyond the huge lawn there was a tennis court on which Feli and Tony played with old deflated balls, all they could get. The girls were bold and joined in ("Gee, I think your Mom's great for her age!") and they played mixed doubles: Tony, two lanky girls and his Mamma, highly pleased with herself.

When the cold nights set in Jim was sent up to bed early (for his health, while Tony's flourished.) Though they shared a two-bedded room in which Jim read for hours into the long-lasting summer light, Tony's bed was nearly always empty when the book had fallen from his hands and he awoke in the early morning. About these absences Tony was nonchalant: obviously a mere kid couldn't understand.

Feli was often flustered that summer. She blushed easily, unable to relax her vigilance. As a family of three, weren't they always threatened? Surely they had suffered enough: "Your father still loves us," she said.

Only Tony always seemed to have a clear path, no burdens on his conscience. There was enough generic heat left over from

Mom-loving for him to pursue unsuitable girls after the hotel's spare, rationed dinners: always immaculate in a sleeveless golfing sweater with a checkered pattern and grey flannels that ended in shoes of white buckskin. Yet none of those girls—he constantly assured her—could match Mom. She was his best chum.

There are emotional incests, as there are physical. Back in New York, waiting to report for induction and Camp Dix, Feli became especially tremulous whenever Tony, freshly shaved and scented, spruced up with double silver brushes, went out on his dates. Yet Tony had been at girls or women since he was seven or eight: how could she not have known? There were friends of hers on the list of his "dates", and the daughters of friends, and cute, bobbed kids from the ground-floor cosmetics counters of Bloomingdale's where she sold frocks on commission. And no one said a word? Night after night she stayed up for him, waiting for his key to turn in the lock. Paz and Debby, Lorraine, Gigi and Felicia. Feli was unable to hide her disappointment: "I thought you were going to take me out to the movies."

"If they were nice girls," Jim said, "he'd bring them home to dinner."

While Tony was at Princeton, Jim hung around in the asphalt yard of Saint Joe's where Roger Horan boasted he could shoot his jism twelve feet or better. Jim made book and Horan was marched to Central Park where, under a tree, he hit a winter-bare branch. At least twelve feet up. And the temperature was twenty-two.

By the summer of '42, the year Tony was finally to go into the army—Tony a counselor, both of them in an Adirondack camp—there was talk, with second wife Hetty gone from California, of a meeting (on neutral ground) in New Mexico, or Arizona or Nevada. Just Feli and Jacob. Feli invested a lot of hope in this reconciliation, but not until she'd raised a stack of objections—how difficult it was to get time off from work or to find a berth on a wartime train—to test Jacob's good intentions. Tony said he was happy to be drafted so he wouldn't be around if it ever happened, which he doubted.

When she got back she wouldn't discuss the trip or Jacob. In the eyes of God she was still married to him.

Jim did inherit his Dad's diaries. "Feli," it says. With a week X'd out. And is otherwise blank.

Women floated dreamily through Jim's childhood sky: like parachutists or puffballs. From newspapers and magazines he clipped women: not strapping swimsuit girls, no big boobs. They were all women alone. Usually reflective, absorbed in some task. A large number were from paintings and each averted her gaze, making herself mysterious and unapproachable. Most of them were northern women. Several were Dutch or Scandinavian, though there were reclusive Italians among them, seated at a piano, dressed to the nines and staring out a window.

6

I think I actually got a glimpse of this Sunny Farber: a very clean forty-something fat man with porcelain skin, sparse thin hair tied in an inch-long rat's tail, piggy eyes and an elephant-hair bracelet on his right wrist. He was letting Jim out of a stretch limo up the street. Jim said the limo was filled with flowers, as though covering up death—"The way he waves at you, you know he'll be back, as if he owns you."

"I thought I'd bring Jake up here to clear the air. His blessed Maman is off with her one-armed friend Myra from the Art Institute."

I parked Jake in my tiny parlor and told him not to touch the box in the corner that held my Grandma's regalia. I said it was something you didn't touch, part of her spirit. He wanted to know, did I mean it belonged to God? I said it was all one thing, God and spirit: "You know that, it's like your sister."

He looked at the box. "And like my *Nonna*?" I nodded. He seemed to consider this. "Can I make a box for Rory?" he asked.

His father was elsewhere—in need—and I whispered hurriedly to Jake that I'd help him.

Jim said it still wasn't clear what Sunny wanted. Sunny was just an intruder, a go-between, somebody to remind you your life isn't as private as you thought: The state cop leaning in your car window ("Well now, Jim, I'm sure you know this is a forty mile zone.") Quacks hurting you; lawyers cross-examining.

And no, he hadn't got much further over lunch. An indigent patient had walked out of a California institution. "My father's partner, in fact."

"And?"

"That's it, so far."

"You remember him?"

"Vaguely. Very cool, crisp-pleated grey flannels, a cream-colored car of some kind. The truth is, I don't want to discover a different father. The one I have is hard enough to live without."

But I could tell he was rattled. He yelled at the Kid and said he hadn't done his homework. How could he? Jake asked. It was back at the big house. Jim said that wasn't why he hadn't done it, and next time some bloody pimp like Sunny Farber rings the doorbell, don't answer it.

"Okay, okay," Jake said. "No need to get mad about it. Jeez, where's your sense of humor?"

"Gone."

"You kidding?"

No. Not one iota of the current woman fix was funny. He had no generalized benevolence to see him through it. Wasn't that what they preached to the shipwrecked at Mount & McIlvenny? "Try not to hurt each other too much, pain costs."?

It got to be that I could hear them as clearly as Jim could: the Mothers, all five of them if you count Feli, singing away like Sirens; or more like ravens in winter, "Remember me, remember me!" They paid close heed to Francine as her bark sailed by—which of them hadn't gone through the same thing? But it was to him they sang, "I told you so, I told you so!" They were draining him, leaving him with even less sleep than usual. But I happen to know they were perfectly real. As real as Feli in her cigar-box, as real as Grandma Tilly at the foot of his bed. That's why Jim turned away Sunny: he didn't want any more spooks. That's what I'm for, maybe: to write them out of his head.

The nights were really bad, especially the hours before dawn, when he was at his most helpless. By the time he got downstairs into the frantic half-six to half-seven of dragging Jake into the new day, Jim might have left his mind upstairs communing with the Mothers. Other times, he might wait for his wife impatiently in the kitchen: a question the ladies posed upstairs might seem wildly urgent. For instance, what did she think love was? Just an illusion? A need?

The early-morning Francine, only half-awake, in a terry-cloth robe, her hair lank and wet but her body perfect, said,

"Wait at least 'til I've had my coffee." And that meant two English muffins twice toasted, butter, French jam, juice that couldn't be concentrate. Then she might say, "What was it you asked? Love. Right? To have somebody love you, and especially that love expressed in marriage, *quelle horreur!*—weighs on me like a stone. I'd much rather you didn't. Let's face it," she added sternly, "ours wasn't exactly a romance!"

Perhaps not. But Jim loved her, and that weighed on him like a stone. He understood what she said perfectly. To have an obligation to love, if one didn't! She's utterly consistent, he told Otto or Milo or somebody about this time. But he wasn't. Not a settled person. Not in the sense of having just one persona, a recognizable background, attitudes, habits. Being always the same: rational. Though he'd read about such people. And lived with one. Please tell me how they manage it.

Here Feli too, to hear Jim tell, stuck to her illusions, which turned out to be also irrational. From her buried cigar-box and to the Mothers upstairs she put on the sweetest and most seductive of her crooked-toothed smiles, lost somewhere in the '30s, beguiling and Madonna-like, her hair lit with fair strands and boyishly bobbed. A tall woman for the day, she had on a dress that fell below the knee; her minimal, vague hips wandered up and down as she walked, and she had long, sleek, silken legs like Francine's. As the weather warmed she liberated herself further: simple shirts in delicate colors, or in bed, cotton night-dresses embroidered in blue.

She sang for Jacob, the only man she was ever to know. She held her tea-cup just ladylike so, which Jacob appreciated. She said that of course Jacob had always loved her. Parish priests were always welcome and she was much on her knees, hoping that God would understand how great was her love: for Jacob, for her own mother, her boys, Him. Her pride in Jacob was genuine. He worked so hard, she said to her son, you have no idea! And sometimes he was just so worried! At what, darling? She thought it was investments, but Jacob never talked about work. To the other Mothers, shyly, she said: really he never left his suits, or his suits never left him. She was an innocent. Jacob appreciated that.

She too had been young, pretty and adored, Jim told Francine—who felt awkward listening, as if she were eavesdropping some secret part of the man she was married to and that she wanted nothing to do with. "And then a Mother," Jim said. "Only when I married in '48 and Tony, too, when Jacob had died, or killed himself, when she fell down and broke her hip and let herself go, seventy-odd then, only then did she become reproachful."

Feli had glared at him and slammed her walker on Jim's bedroom floor: "They devour you, don't they? Men. Boys, Husbands. Children. It's never the same again."

Quite a show she put on up there, for all the Mothers who'd had the misfortune of marrying a Mount. She fingered her long nose, the nose which Jacob teased her about, she patted her cheeks which blushed so easily at the loose talk from the other Mothers, especially Lou, who had a way of being deliberately vulgar. "He wanted me to be always beautifully dressed," she said. "Look at me now!"

The boys had been such a comfort, she was proud to wheel

them up the street and back, though the nearest park in Philadelphia was a long way away. Best of all, she confided, was to have them in her bed in the morning. They squirmed. Especially Jim, when she said, "I'm going to eat you!" He thought that was probably true, though he also recognized it was a game. For there were days, many days, when his father was fully-dressed and off somewhere. Then Feli wanted to be loved for longer, to stretch out time. She could fill him with her perfume, stroke his hair so it fell over his eyes, fold him into her night-dress, cosset him on her pillow. Make him into herself.

If Jacob was about, however, he would grumble that Jim was a big boy now and she ought to stop coddling him. Since nothing was so sweet to her as his command, nor so central as her desire to please, the hungry Italian in her was promptly quelled. Off and out Jim went. Later Feli would say that she'd thought her job was to keep her husband happy: years had gone into dreaming of being married and having children who would be all her own.

Mother love was this enormous, erotic power. When he marched with the tribes of Israel (Jim read his Bible young) through her Red Sea, the sea closed in after, every drop in that massive bulk of water being God's love, her love, where you could drown. Her embrace and arms were as insidious as water itself, which seeped and dripped, ever finding its own level, able to gouge out mountains.

And that Mother love was still there, though she was some years dead and lay under snow. Only now it reproached. So many things had gone wrong. Jacob had taken another woman. Then he had died out west, which she passed off as a heart attack, that being the only explanation that fitted the man she worshiped.

Had there been suitors? I asked.

Of course. Mostly Italians. And why not? She was still a beautiful woman, deserted by her husband and then widowed: a sympathetic figure. One at a time the suitors sat about on Feli's plum-colored sofa. They wore dark suits; their hair was thin and combed-back. Then Feli talked about her husband or her two boys, and her own self went missing. Or rather it lay behind her, and vanished in the fall of '39 when their train pulled into Union Station in Los Angeles.

Sometimes the two boys, converted into young men, coincided in her New York apartment, the one that she would never change. There were those secrets—the ones Tony's children e-mailed him with questions about—to be examined.

The old house creaked in the wind. The importuning Mothers fled, as they sometimes did, not wanting to press their luck. Only Francine lurked downstairs. The sound of the hair-dryer was heard in the land and the Kid had misplaced his homework. Again.

There's a parallel here, a complicity between mother and son. Both had been or were being rejected. Or so Feli whispered in her son's ear. Jim says his mother had a pre-skeptical sort of faith. Her big picture was Our Lady of Sorrows and The Sacred Heart of Jesus. She believed in salvation. She was sure that in the end God would console her for her ill-fortune. But Father, she confessed, "I feel this terrible shame."

If she'd been able to reason, she'd have known that mortal sin you can repent, but from shame you can only hide.

Who felt shame now, shame as Feli had felt it? Igor Klima asked. Igor had a swimmer's trunk, a refugee's bandy, thrifty legs. Across his large, black and empty desk and over his manicured fingers, Igor faced his patients' guilt every day: what they hadn't meant to do. They were guilty of this or that weakness, of their fantasies, their ire and murderous desires; but not ashamed. This was stuff they couldn't deal with: why else would they be in his office? Igor could cope. He was endlessly receptive.

In the same way Francine said, knowing what Jim was up to, talking to the Mothers (she was one): "So what if it's the truth? About your mother or anyone else. If they are ashamed and conceal the truth, it should not be revealed. Not to themselves and not to others. It's their property, not yours. There's nothing worse than betraying someone's confidence. Surely there's something between marriage and hatred."

Not for Feli, Jim told Francine. "The bonds of marriage held her in their tightest web; she kept weaving another fifty years."

It wasn't that way with Francine. She said she felt nothing from the neck down. Why should anyone feel ashamed if life didn't give what you expected, deserved, hoped for, etc.?

How come she was so intelligent? Jim asked. How could she see his every imperfection with such clarity, and be so cool about it?

She replied: "Because I have no heart."

Part two

Lou

"Miss Louise Inskip will play Donna Elvira
in the Spanish Department production of Don Juan."

Unwillingly I had allowed Jim to drag me to Igor Klima's house. Going out was the price I paid for re-entering Jim's life. The son of émigré Czech Jews, Igor is still full of Central European doubts, lavish manners and sweet understanding. But he remains foreign to me, though I fear I don't to him. In this I'm like Mother Number Three (though the children she mothered weren't Jim's), Natasha Gilpin. She refused to have any truck with Igor, saying he could see right through her and that made her uncomfortable.

Mind you, I think he's a dear, a sort of male Mother with gentle, soft fingers. But the little Self I have is all my own and it's all I have, so I don't like being probed.

The occasion was Milo reading from his new book and a large number of admirers had been invited: so many that the closest I could get was the doorway to Igor's immaculate kitchen, where I was in the way of the caterers. Jim, who'd arrived early, had an easy chair and Prudence, Milo's newest wife, just about at term and in a long dress of mauve velvet, was curled up at his feet right up under Milo's lectern. Just the sort of occasion I shrink from. I don't really know these people; they have only the vaguest idea who I am—possibly one of Jim's spooks, the women who are drawn to him? Or perhaps just insignificant, a fragment from his childhood, a mouse in Jim's paw.

I argued my point before he drove off to Igor's lakeside penthouse with Francine (Jake was on a sleep-over with his school buddy). "I don't go out, Jim, I don't. I love you, but in my kitchen only. I'm not a Mother, I'm not one of the Mothers." (Who would know how much it hurt me to say that? The last to know would be Jim.)

I could as well have said: I don't have anything to wear, my one pair of shoes is shot, I've lost the habit of people, they alarm me. I ought to have known better than to argue with Jim. He can be guileless and blue-eyed and take me over: So Francine and the Kid are off to New York for the weekend after the party, and Jim says everyone (well, just about everyone) who's there knows about me. Otto would be there and his wife Heda and I surely know them. "And you've met Milo. And I'll be there." As though that were enough.

That was years ago, having met Milo, and what did that have to do with anything? I responded by becoming a little girl whose Daddy is saying "Don't be afraid" about her first dance. "They know about me?" I asked. "What is it they know about me?"

He talked around that one. My going he presented as a sort of last chance—after all, Milo was eighty-something, he wouldn't be around forever. The message was clear: When am I going to grow up?

Please God, never. That's not quite true either. I've tried and tried. But I'm haunted by a long-ago morning when I went where Jim would never have sent me, thinking I was doing it for his good. I haven't grown up because I can't tell him what I did. Because he would pass judgment on me and I'd lose him forever. It's not something about which Jim can be rational.

Francine will be there.

I told him I didn't go out: "Once a year I look after the Professor's cats and that's it. The city is travel: I don't travel well. You've said that. I don't 'know' them all. You do. Milo was your best man. You bring me what they say and I put them on paper. I know about them, my dear, I don't know them. Frank and Mrs. Frank, Igor. All those people have public dimensions, they're in the papers, they're talked about. Not one of them, except Otto and Heda of course, and maybe Mrs. Vojtyla, has ever touched my hand, breathed in my face, passed me a plate or asked how I am. Why do I have to go? What was there to "know" about me? I went on. I live in my rocking chair. I am defined by tatty clothes, a bad hip, and my private self.

Milo was in college when Jim and I were kids. Same neighborhood, different spheres. Jews and us. We read his first story together. I have that old *Partisan Review* somewhere. And when Jim got married to Lou and left his old Chicago friends behind, I read about them in Milo's first novel. Jim was good material and Milo was a noticer.

Milo was teaching in Springfield, Jim was swotting up his first-year exams. I have a snap of the two of them on a tennis court. Milo wore a baseball cap, Jim's legs were terrific and muscular. Jim had style, Milo was never, in his own words, *sportif*. I have another photograph of Milo. He's pedaling a kid's bike, legs sticking out like jug ears. And maybe I saw Milo once or twice with Jim. Before he met Lou and before we took our disastrous trip together.

For all that, I'm glad I went to the reading. I was able to look at all of them as if they were in a portrait, most of them dark and heavily varnished. There was Igor with his huge, sad eyes; and Otto and Heda, always remarkably interested and eager, little busy people of the sort who get things done without complicating them; the Kid, who was eagerly talking to Otto about hockey; Jim, restlessly spotting who'd come and who hadn't; his hands whirl-winds of suppressed energy, even his legs never still; his partner Frank and Mrs. Frank, holding hands.

Then, when he was ready we all fell silent and Milo became an old guy standing dry-throated in front of a lectern. He was nervous. He dropped some pages, he picked them up. His hands shook and he made a self-deprecatory joke. Only when he started reading did the words give him fresh life. The words were so right I couldn't help smiling. They were words anyone could be saying, yet he used them in a way which was like being caught by surprise. What a seduction is art!

The book was about a friend of Milo's, recently dead. Milo hated his being dead. He hated any diminishment in his life. In one passage, he was near death himself. He said, in an aside to no one in particular, that curiosity had got the better of him. He'd wanted to know what death was like. But had been plucked back—this with a smile towards Prudence, who'd done the plucking.

After the reading I stayed for Igor's reception. I was standing talking to Otto and Heda about our old days in Chicago, the houses we'd known, the changes, when two women Jim later said he hadn't seen in years, came up in turn to him. They had memories. Of Jim's wives. The one remembered Maria (the naked wife on Jim's wall) and her ultra-short skirts: "A lovely girl"; "Wasn't she just!"). The other remembered Lou. Both Mothers were recalled as they had been in their early, heady days with Jim. Beautiful women, they said; in their memories they glowed; and they had always wondered how they'd fared. After. Would he remember them to both? Of course he would. But he didn't answer as to what they had become.

In Jim's memory, as in Milo's, nothing ever went away, least of all lives he'd held in his hands and fumbled. Even then, with Francine drifting away, it seemed to surprise him that these women could exist in any world but his own. The most he said was: to one, "She's fine," and to the other, "She's just fine." As though that in itself was surprising.

I know him well. The Mothers, viewed from the latest devastation, actually turned him on. He loved them all! But especially Francine, of whom this was my first, prolonged view. Close up, or as close as I allowed—though later we were to become friends. Most noticeable about her was her control. Control over her pain, physical (I knew from Jim that she suffered from some mysterious malady that occasionally laid her low) and mental (she was, she thought, as much to blame for the failure of her marriage as Jim.) She looked, as Jim often said she did, like a woman under threat: from something she couldn't talk about but was always with her.

Not that different from me.

2

It was Milo who suggested he take the show in, the Don Juan. Milo said the Donna Elvira wasn't his, Milo's, type, but hot stuff. "Smoldering" was the word he used. To show you how far back this is, and how safe America still seemed, how polite in language at least, consider the "Miss" before Lou's name on the program. Milo and Jim were fresh friends and Milo thought he was being generous by putting Jim onto a good thing. Far more dashing, a dandy with streaks of prematurely white hair and Paisley-lined waistcoats, he sometimes passed a young girl up. And by the nature of things, I would guess, could only marry a Jewish girl. Which Lou was not.

We are, literally, in the late 1940s. Jim was twenty with his first year Bar exam coming up in Springfield. Milo was an instructor after a number of years in Mexico, and even as Jim was about to take on Lou, he was about to shed Mercedes and their child, who in the pictures I'd seen was about four and had quizzical, high eyebrows. Tony had come back from the war, his skin yellow; Feli had stopped war work and was back selling on commission at Bloomingdale's; Jim had been to Poland and the camps as an interrogator; and Jacob had stopped his heart on purpose.

One morning back then, as April fled in capricious rain, he found Lou sitting at his kitchen table, a formica-topped job at 822½ Pearl Street in Springfield. The half represented the Upstairs. It looked out on a parking lot. A small, shaggy dog panted at her stockinged feet, and before her was a frying pan from which she took pieces of fried bread. She chewed on them carefully and after each piece she picked her teeth. A vision of greed and cleanliness. Of all things, and throughout the years they were married, teeth mattered. They were widely separated and large and she worked at them constantly. Jim said—whose own teeth were painful, missing and scattered—it seemed a strange choice of worries.

It took him several minutes to realize he was married to a girl who picked her teeth and owned a dog.

Miss Inskip was all he had really seen of the performance. She was outfitted in a black riding costume and significantly carried a crop in her hand which she swished during her speeches. A top hat sat on her vigorous mass of auburn curls. Tall and high-colored—her skin very pale, her lips a violent scarlet, her eyebrows dark, strong and straight—she was perfect for the part, that of an outraged woman powerfully betrayed and bent on vengeance. She looked extreme. She strode the stage in high boots, she stamped, fire flashed from her eyes, her long skirt swirled. She was wildly over the top.

Jim picked her up, she picked him up? They met back-stage, both holding paper cups of wretched wine. He was in awe, she was so smouldering and beautiful. As an artiste she despised the rest of the cast, and as a big girl she was hungry.

He picked her up, she picked him up? They met back-stage, both holding paper cups of wretched wine. He spent a quarter of that month's GI Bill check on a prime rib feast at an out-of-town roadhouse. Then, late that night in her room over a back-alley garage, half overgrown kitten, half unplayful tigress, she made love the same way: as though still Elvira-furious. He woke up with her sturdy legs locked about his waist. Neither of them had much experience. She was twenty-one, and—her stage presence apart—a one night stand with an apprentice brain surgeon was all she knew about sex. The rest was instinct.

"It was a long time ago," Jim said. "One thing I don't have is regrets. I fight hard, and if I lose, I lose. That's that. Lou is the only

Mother it didn't work out with quite that way. I mean, in the end she fought hard and she lost. Unfortunately, she has rancor. Or at least a kind of ironic detachment. As in, who is that man? Was I really married to him?"

Fifty years have passed. Does time heal all wounds? Kind of. Both of them have earned public transport and movie discounts. Lou's thighs have swollen, Jim's bones are brittle. Both have new partners. As Jim's Francine, his fourth, was departing, Lou's third, an ex-Rhodesian coffee-planter who leaned with his ear to one side or the other as though still listening to the BBC on shortwave, an utterly harmless man, was settling in. His mouth worked like a cod's, endlessly garrulous. Nothing worse. Lou now wore bulky wools, painted postcard-sized watercolors and tended to turnip and radish in her garden. Her kids (they were Jim's too, she occasionally admitted) said she was happy at last.

So you see, there is accommodation, Shakespeare's "smooth-faced villain." All Jim's Mothers (but not Feli) discovered accommodation as they bailed out. Natasha (Number Three), returning to her husband after a decade, said leaving Jim (or Jim leaving her, for Francine soon followed) was like filling a tub with hot water and lying back in it, luxuriating. With Jim it had been as though the plug was forever being pulled out and "everything you were went out with the water." I suppose the men they chose, like the one I chose (briefly), were relief expeditions, men advancing on the Mothers and saying, "You poor thing!"

The question is, when you reach summing-up time (Do I wish I'd borne Jim's child? Or for that matter anyone's, when that was no longer possible?), the what ifs multiply. What if the Mothers had stood their ground during marriages instead of retreating in disorder? I asked Jim.

"Then they wouldn't be happy," Jim answered.

"You always have to pay for your fun, Jim," said Milo. "Mind you, I'd as soon pay for it and have the fun."

"I just want to know why they married me, why Lou did, for one."

"You were a cute kid, that's why. I found you cute. Good-look-ing, bags of boyish charm and good intentions. Your women sniff out the artiste in you. It's a powerful aphrodisiac for some. Even if it doesn't last. And you rescued them from their awful parents: one after the other."

Despite Milo's advice to the contrary—and everyone else's—they married just after Christmas. Appropriately after Saint Stephen was lapidated. On the feast of the Holy Innocents. Jim and Lou did marriage the way we all did (those of us who married, anyway) back then at the end of the forties: with starry eyes and movies in mind. Milo was best man and made good use of the scene in an early story called "Babes in the Wood". The portrait was memorable and I read it with relish, not knowing it was about Jim. He got the event just right: two kids with perilous relatives signing on too young, the Justice of the Peace, the weak coffee and soggy breakfast before, the cold and expressionless Midwestern sky, their attacks of nerves, the standard v.d. certificates.

Was I jealous? No, I didn't hear about it for several years, until Jim came back to Chicago. And in between times I'd finished school myself, taught for a while in the backwoods, and married, briefly, the only well-read man in my neck of the woods. Theodore Apeyitou was a burly, forty-year-old Greek who taught philosophy at the nearby community college and he sweet-talked me with Plato and Schopenhauer and Nietzsche in the college library and during lavish meals in his tiny apartment. Theodore was a bright man, but self-destroying, more Nietzsche than Plato. Accommodation? There wasn't any. The "marriage"—my parents didn't even know about it—dribbled on for a year until he went off the road, drunk, in mid-winter. Is it that we women are all relieved to get our own space back? I know I was glad that no one else had been involved. Because it's harder when families are involved.

Jim's unhappy mother Feli only met Lou at the family get-together breakfast on the day of the wedding. She didn't like it that Lou whistled, she didn't like her boyishness or that she didn't wear makeup back then when she wasn't on stage. Europe and its prejudices sat on her boxy shoulders and right away, having only just shaken Milo's hand, she was tut-tutting with the long-divorced Inskips, Lou's folks, about how "one doesn't really know Jews socially." Meaning Milo. She didn't mention that her other son, Tony, was about to marry one, the one later known as "Mad Di."

Tony of course wasn't there. That wasn't unusual—as Jim acknowledged, few people came to Jim's weddings, when weddings there were, to Lou or to her successors. As though they knew something he didn't. As for the *bel Antonio*, Tony, Jim tells me he was in the Niger having one of his few, early and brief flirtations with the idea of working for a living. Which was why Feli asked Mrs. Inskip if Africa wasn't unhealthy. Mrs. Inskip's answer was that Africa was hot and that was all she knew or cared about it. Feli then turned to Milo and said she was sure "this Di was a nice girl but like should stay with like, don't you think so?"

Milo said mildly that he thought the bride was called Louise.

After the breakfast with its funereal eggs and slabs of ham, Milo said to his pal, "You'd have thought your brother had taken up with a homebreaker and was going to divorce your mother."

The only other thing Feli confided to several people was that she wished Jim still had his father.

In the background, Lou was with her parents. The one thing the female Inskips had in common, Milo noted in his story, was that they both had the jaws, and the appetites, of alligators. They, too, were talking about Africa with mouths full of biscuits.

A bright red spot shone on Lou's cheek. "Oh…We get letters and snapshots from Tony," Lou said bravely, playing the young wife, but laughing a little too loudly. "As far as I can see, he seems to spend a lot of his time playing polo and making sure the natives—'Wogs,' he calls them—don't steal him blind. And then there are French women who are bored and whose husbands all seem to be away a lot: 'up country' or 'in the bush.'"

"Quite the playboy is he?" her father said. "I hope your young man's not like that."

No, no, Jim was serious, she said; he was in Law School. "He's just slightly apprehensive."

"If I were marrying at twenty I'd be scared out of my wits."

Lied Feli with her sweetest smile: "Oh, I'm sure they're deeply in love."

From the Justice of the Peace at eleven, they drove in an old Pontiac the two blocks to a red brick hotel in downtown Springfield where the Rotary had its Wednesday lunches.

Milo wrote that he was sorry for those poor kids: "They deserved better of their folks. Her parents behaved as if they were giving him a Christmas present three days late. Her mother had wrapped the poor girl up in a bright red dress with a lot of sequins and ribbons looped through the hem and wrists. It's a wonder they didn't stay in their respective homes and have her delivered by UPS."

I've noticed that kids whose parents split are often pretty harsh about them, as if they were the ones being left out in the cold. I think that's because what parents actually feel is impenetrable to their children. Milo was only having fun with the Inskips, but Lou herself took an almost indecent pleasure in lampooning them, which they probably didn't deserve. Jim too, who had no idea of how harsh his tongue could be.

The Inskips had been so long split themselves, that they considered it the natural condition of men and women. That is, they had sussed each other out with the loathing that sometimes comes from familiarity. They'd barely met the groom when Hazel informed him Eustace drank too much and took up with "floozies," and Eustace said, "I hope my daughter doesn't take after her mother. Hazel's one of the free-spenders. Usually they're fun to be with, but Hazel isn't."

"Oh shut up, Eustace!"

"But it's true, my dear. For your sake, Jim, I hope Louise doesn't serve you dinner and then retire to take off her make-up and prepare her hair for the night. It's a frightful sight." Then, taking Jim to one side, he whispered loudly: "Worse, she was against divorce 'on principle.' Never heard that one before. But then her lawyer explained the financial advantages and she cottoned on."

Together only at funerals and this singular wedding, of an only child Hazel was glad to be rid of and a curious young man with a suicided father and an Eyetalian mother, only hard liquor made brief cohabitation possible: though neither thought it suitable for the other. Thus, by the time the cake was to be cut they had already decided the future Mr. and Mrs. wouldn't last much longer than they had. Sooner rather than later would suit them, so they could escape to the nearest bar. When the cake was cut Mr. Inskip distractedly pushed a wadge of cash into the pocket of Jim's tux. Did he even know who Jim was? Mr. Inskip, who was short and green in the face, had obviously drunk his way up from Baltimore in the Parlor Car of a Chesapeake and Ohio train and had no intention of changing diet. Mrs., who ran to a certain blowsy embonpoint, wore a violent green silk dress of which there seemed to be a lot. She was a cold, hard woman with two bright red patches on the fuzzy pink of her cheeks and her blond hair done up in statuary hair-do of tight, regimented rolls. Every time the young couple was addressed by one of them, Lou broke out into a rash.

Thereafter the three older people sat in a corner and complained about young people in general. They only rallied when the wedding party was about to leave. Mrs. Inskip, a tear poised on her powdered cheek, said they hoped the bride would be happier than they'd been. She threw her rice at her daughter: as hard as she could.

Milo went with them as far as the station. Lou said, not looking back even once, "Sorry about that. She's an odious woman. All through the war she stole our rations."

"A spirited girl," Milo said to Jim as he despatched them on a honeymoon to Chicago and Niagara with the advance on his novel. "She may be more than a match for you."

Fifty years later, as they discussed the departing Francine, Milo said: "I liked your Lou. Women are an area where you've always shown good taste."

"Fat lot of good that's done me," Jim answered. "Their Mothers all sniffed me out straight off. I was taking their daughters off into dubious territory." Still, as he remembered it, Mr. and Mrs. Inskip were only too glad to get their awkward, big, ever-hungry only child off their hands. Whereas at the Pasquiers, on his first visit after marrying Francine, he'd been told by Madame to put shoes on, because bare feet made the carpets smell.

"They had me figured out all right," he told Milo. "Hadn't they all had miserable lives themselves?"

3

That was how Jim found a strange woman sharing his "home" at 822-and-a-half Pearl Street. The apartment faced a tree-lined avenue along which black ice formed and the asphalt heaved, and it became a mighty fortress against their parents and their pasts. A Christmas later, when Jim was coming up for his first-year exams, Mrs. Inskip wrote asking what they needed. Mr. Inskip merely sent a check saying they shouldn't take it for granted. With the Inskip check, drawn on some mysterious trust fund which Eustace, her father, was speedily drinking away, Lou bought a dog she named Pushkin.

Jim didn't like animals—even today he barely tolerates Jake's cat Smax. Dogs least of all, their mournful slobbering attentions ("like bad students"), their public defecations, their dirty lives. Pushkin smelled of rotting, humid carpet. He had wiry, sandy hair and a long, always-wet beard under his chin. He lived in a cloud of murderous farts on the foot of the marital bed and growled whenever Jim came in.

She said, "If I'm not having a baby (and she wasn't) I can at least have a dog, can't I?"

He let Pushkin know how he felt about him by giving him

quick passing kicks whenever he could. Pushkin ran—on his short, disorganized legs, he resembled a slithering bathmat—to complain to Lou, and she wanted to know what kind of a man kicked dogs.

Answer: a bad man, one with a vicious streak.

Then she went to work. Not at painting which was what she said she had always wanted to do. She gave up her studio classes, got up every morning at five and inventoried and tagged body-parts outside the hospital's operating rooms: this is Mr. Schmidt's pancreas, that is Mrs. Belloni's miscarriage. By one P.M. she was home, sometimes with a smirk—a filling meal? an encounter, a guy, a girl, pals from her studio days?

There had been one guy before him, she said, fondling a drooling Pushkin on her lap: he studied the human brain.

"How about you?"

Was she, like Francine's younger sister, attracted to hospitals and doctor types?

"We need the money, don't we?" she asked. "It's a job, not a trysting place."

We have reached 1950, not our own times. As Eustace and Hazel Inskip—and indeed Feli—arrived in Springfield by train, expresses to sex were rare. Going "all the way" made you pregnant, so, like Jim (I know from my own experience) most boys alighted a stop or two before their destinations. If Jim remained silent about himself, chances are that, except for our one foray, he was all but a virgin.

He was convinced there had been guys after the brain-man. But only later, when there were guys after they married. She brought them home, never more than one at a time. These "callers" were more underfed than the young couple, and Lou extracted creased singles and a five from the blue tin cash-box, with budgetary slots, to buy them (and herself) roast beef and a bottle of cheap red. When they were filled up and done ogling her was when—dissatisfied, excited, a big girl with rock-like bones and solid thighs—she climbed on top of him. The mutt Pushkin fled under the bed when this happened. Lou pressed herself on him as Feli once had when he was a kid: he felt like a hand digging a tunnel in the sand and the sand suddenly collapsing, all dead weight. As with his mother, he felt possessed, and he knew there was nothing, nothing acceptable, that he could give in return.

What he never knew was what Lou's dissatisfactions were or whether he was responsible for them. She never talked about them. She was seeing him through his exams, wasn't that enough? She said: "Do you ever stop to think what I do for you?"

In the empty hours of those midwestern winter mornings, nursing tea in a mug to keep his hands warm, fat law books propped before him, the question was, where did she find her men (if she did find them) and when did she fit them in? Did she have assignations at dawn? Did the whine of the near-dead battery of their car correspond to some inner urge of her own? He could always tell when she'd been at it, though; she devoured whatever was put on the table for lunch and always wanted more. It seemed that for her, the two appetites went together.

"It's the war," she said by way of explanation for one appetite. "I was starved as a child."

Though sure there were others—He'd run across them near the hospital being dragged to the diner across the street on Lou's arm—he could only swear by one guy before the actor Richard Dever. This was Sam Bushkoff, a doe-eyed poet who regularly came to dinner and couldn't take his eyes off Lou; like most of her "callers" he looked as if every meal would be his last. Lou had a half-head on Jim, but over Bushkoff she towered.

"I want to make babies," she said. "Stop telling me to paint. I don't want to paint. I'd like to be normal, to have a normal suburban life. Why can't you give me that at least?"

"You call the wispy Bushkoff normal. How come you take such a shine to the weedy and needy?"

"Oh, you mean Sam…" She giggled. "You can't be serious, Jim. I'm just his infatuation. Come on up to bed."

4

After six years of Springfield she still had no babies, and it was big, strong women who now seemed to attract her, earth Mothers, coffee-colored or darker, with capable, healing hands. They showed up, when she began painting again, among tropical plants. In Lou's canvases they held babies in their arms; they were confident; they were content; they had large breasts which grew on them like breadfruit and melons. Her vegetable and floral world was openly sexual, made up of pistils and seeds of great complexity, red, green, brown; bloody, excremental.

Thinking back to those years—The Law was biting into him, but it was also a refuge—he detected in his tiny room a prevailing smell of linseed oil, like the ghost of Lou. He thought they were good pictures she painted; she exhibited at the university gallery and sold half a dozen.

But he shouldn't have said in bed that they were good paintings; certainly not that he cared for them. With that encouragement, the next morning she packed up her paintboxes and dismantled her easel. A week later, fetching the unsold paintings from the gallery and stacking them against the wall in what had been intended as a future nursery ("You like them so much, you keep them") she gave up her job at the hospital and started commuting to Chicago where she found a job painting sets with an experimental theater company. Her work kept her out very late; he couldn't call in the mornings either, because she slept in. He thought it very likely there was some guy up there she was seeing.

While she was away, her dog Pushkin was run over crossing the road. She blamed Jim. Then she said it could also be a sign that she was going to get pregnant. "How's that?" he asked.

"Because the dog's gone," she answered, as though that were self-evident.

Given the mother Lou had, why did Lou aspire to follow the stony-curled Mrs. Inskip down the bad bloodstock line? But aspire she did, and she started going to "fertility specialists" in Chicago while he discharged into a beaker in an antiseptic washroom, thinking of young Horan's seventh-grade jism and of the lower limb of an icy tree that he'd reached on a bet. Today you can hatch and incubate like a cuckoo and flush like a toilet with—as the I Ching (Lou's favorite reading) had it, "No blame" attaching, but not in the '50s when the pursuit of fertility was hard work, and undoing it, dangerous. As I well knew.

The desperate remedies proposed by the day's medicine were humiliating to both body and psyche. Lou's hips were broad, her periods regular and copious, her hormones intense, her disposition maternal (viz Pushkin). The quacks were baffled.

"What's the matter with me?" she would wail.

The vaginal douches were useless. Rhythm charts were useless. Bottling the stuff up in a syringe and squirting it at the very neck of the womb was useless; useless too, afterwards, was lying on her back, legs-in-air packed with towels to keep the vital high-motility fluid in.

Another year passed in ever more bizarre experiments and in a flurry of advice, dietary (Guinness or dates), oriental, hypnotic, and Feli saying Lou should pray. Then it was summer again and they abandoned the whole project. Copulation included.

Lou had a summer job as assistant stage designer at the Shakespeare theater in Niagara-on-the-Lake, and she may have wanted to punish Jim for the malfunctioning of her ovaries, for failing to make her into the (Bohemian) suburban Mum she craved to be; or maybe she was right, his sperm and her eggs just didn't get along. Whatever the reason, Richard Dever was an instrument to hand, yet another meager Hamlet playing in her repertory: this one married, gaunt, and in analysis. By letter she proclaimed herself blindly happy in his arms and begged Jim not to trek up there and destroy her idyll: it might not last, he should just keep busy at the office. They'd see at the end of the summer.

The letter was pain-giving, something like an unwanted invitation—stopping just short of "wish you were here" but making sure he would be—and slightly mad in its many details, like Dever's vital statistics. He realized her need to tell him the physical details; she knew they would sharpen his appetite. However, he restrained himself and didn't answer, though she thoughtfully gave him both address and phone number.

Twice he went up, a long drive in that same old Pontiac, the second time seriously drunk, the first time just to lurk, precise information being vital. On his first trip, he attended Dever's Hamlet matinee and evening. Dever was as described: in black tights his legs were thin, make-up exaggerated the black of his eye-sockets, spittle flew from his rouged lips, and his eyes were red—he wasn't getting much sleep? No sighting there of Lou.

After the evening show Jim went out with the after-theatre crew, the cast in a corner demolishing steaks. Which one was Dever's wife, the one he said caused him eleven years on the couch? But no Dever there and still no Lou. His table wasn't far from the cast's. He could ask after her; he was her husband. But who would he ask? Would he be laughed at? He tried to listen to their stories and drank greedily until they suddenly broke up all at once and the restaurant closed. He missed going out with them because he was paying his check, and he got out into the dry, chilly night only to see the tail-lights of their cars speeding away. Who with whom?

It took him a half-hour to find Lou's cottage. He stopped a few houses away and turned his engine and lights off, hearing the water lap on the pebbly shore. A light or two were on in her house, but the curtains were drawn on the side towards the road, and he crept around the side of the house, cracking dried end-of-summer twigs, smelling cigarette smoke and wanting one himself.

He was greedy: he wanted to see them at it. Then he might burst in or he might weep. Either one.

The lights went off first, then the front door slammed and he was just in time to see Dever striding along the winding road ahead of him: "Come back here," he wanted to yell. "Do you know what you're doing to me?"

The second time he went up he had worked himself into

a rage and stayed in a bar until after the performance. When he reached her house by a bright moon he slammed the car door, ran up the steps and bashed at the front door in swat-squad style: meaning to break it down, only to find it wasn't locked. There were wet towels in puddles on the floor and a trail of trousers and work-shirts. He pushed the door at the end of the trail and found Lou alone in bed, startled by the noise and clutching a sheet around her naked body. She fumbled for the bedside light but he grabbed her hand and forced her back down on the bed. She said, "Is that you, Jim?"

Then he wept and she pulled him into bed, stroking his head: "Poor Jim, poor, poor Jim…" He allowed it and then stumbled out of bed when she'd done with him and went into the kitchen and finished off an open bottle of wine, vomited by the shore, and hit a guard-rail just past the border at the Falls: either because he wanted to or because he couldn't see properly, though his tears, no fewer, had now turned to tears of rage. It wasn't until he reached Chicago the next day and could drive no further that he found out he'd fractured his ankle.

His partner Frank came up to Chicago, sold the car for scrap and took him back to Springfield. And it was probably Frank who wrote Lou at the end of the summer, when Dever had thrown her out of the cottage (his cottage) because his wife was coming up for the final performances, and told her Jim was in bad shape and she should come back.

Jim met her at the last train through Springfield in the used wooden-sided station wagon he had bought to replace the Pontiac. He had taken great care with his appearance. He wore clothes taken from her closet and drawers: her winter coat and hat, her gloves, her shoes. In the station parking lot he smoked one lipstick-tipped cigarette after another: being her, being the wife she wasn't. She walked right by him and into a taxi, carrying a suitcase as light as in the movies, one that contained nothing.

It was last summer that Jim told me all this. I'd just come back from my usual two weeks away looking after the Professor's cats. The Kid was away at camp, Francine was dong fast-forward on the

Art Institute social scene ("You'd be surprised how many interesting people there are out there"), and looking for an apartment in the city. He didn't want to be alone in the big, old house, so he took over my place, which was where he filled the usual yellow legal pads with all these scraps about Lou.

There was a deep disturbance in his life, matched by the dog-day thunder that rumbled somewhere South of the city, out on the lake. The heat was grave; no relief was in sight. He thought he might have fallen asleep in my chair. He only remembers coming to with a start and finding that the light had gone out in my kitchen. He padded three-quarters naked around the house—there's not that much to it—and then looked out the windows in front. All the lights had gone out on Hemperle Road, too. He thought about how the Kid was doing at his camp by the lake, whom thunder and lightning scared. He opened the front door, which is hardly ever used and sniffed outside. No storm. The ground was dry, the air still heavy. He described the moon as grotesque, full and a garish yellow.

Then on his way back to the kitchen he caught sight of what he called "that silly, frilly nightie of yours, you know, the one that's always on the hook on your bathroom door."

There was no air stirring, but nonetheless it swayed. "I thought you'd hanged yourself, but in a serene, benevolent way, the way you would. There was nothing frightening about the scene. If anything it was inviting. I lifted you down, put you on, and fell asleep in another body."

I simply let him relax a little, and gradually he unwound. As though I were talking to myself, or just reminiscing, I started talking about my grandmother. I said it was thought a special gift to be part-man and part-woman, to be now the one and now the other, not sexually but in spirit: for which reason they were early on given names which reflected this double state of theirs, and it was thought, my grandmother said, that such people, though apart, had a clearer understanding of the spirit world, in which men and women were not distinguished from one another. They were like prophets of another state that followed death and as such, half warrior, half squaw, they were valuable in council. Also, I added, much envied by the spirit doctors, being already the spirits which they, the doctors, could only invoke.

Later, Jim told me how the rest of the fall had gone. Lou had spent it picking up the pieces, from her busted affair with Dever, and the no-longer-so-young couple, time fleeing before them, started working with the rats. These were special rats. They got injected with Lou's urine and in return offered ovulatory marching orders, such as: they should go at it between 9.15 and 9.45 A.M. on the Thursday following. The rats were peremptory, they were sacrificing their own reproduction for Jim and Lou, but they did not make for loving sex, but rather something tawdry and dutiful.

Lou missed a number of those appointments; by the spring she dropped them entirely; in summer she agreed to one last attempt and bought a dog which, by agreement, she kept in Chicago.

5

Jim's never asked if I felt jealous. Of Lou or any of the others who took my place in his life. I would have told him no, I wasn't. I never expected it could work between us; I always hoped it would; and ultimately (after my Greek rolled off the road at high speed, unlamented) I decided defeat was not only acceptable but represented the inner truth about myself. If my Grandma had been alive, I'd have asked her whether someone had put a curse on Jim and me, and if there were something in her medicine pouch for us? But she died the week I went into the ninth grade in my new school: walking me there was just about the last thing she did. Who could keep up with her, even when she was in her eighties? She died the week I met Jim in the yard and we were walking the same way. So she wasn't around at the critical time—for that, Indian-fashion, she'd have had her remedy.

I say a "curse" because it's always the same way when he comes into my life: the opposite of what you might think. I'm a pokey little train speeding up on a downgrade—like that long downgrade runs that down the whole of Grandma's prairie—and Jim's the tunnel I run into. The walls close in on me. Suddenly I can't see a thing, I can't stop, I don't know what's at the far end, I put on the brakes. And nothing happens except the long screech of my voice, like metal heating up. I talk because I can't think, and when I can think I can't talk because I don't know what to say to him. The curse would be that: that I can only listen. It's not the cat's got my tongue, it's that Jim's my space and whenever he appears there's no place for me, only his embracing arms. My space thickens, his atoms expand.

That time in the late '50s when Lou was away with her new dog, Jim called up (his favorite way, out of nowhere) and asked me if I'd like to go to Mexico with him. I had no idea how he even found me; and in Evanston of all places, where I was practice-teaching second-graders. His offer flattered and surprised me, and right away I said no, I was sick, I couldn't possibly, I didn't want to go, I knew what he'd do to me. I hung up on him. Fear of what I desired, desire for what I feared, ran up and down my body like a tiny, tired mouse. As always. He was married; he was mad; when we talked, he took up too much room in me; I knew I wouldn't please. I became a footman whose job was to keep him intact, and one of my duties was to pick up pieces of myself that had fallen along the trail, or re-gather war feathers lost in a mighty love battle—he would need them again. I argued with myself all night.

In my head I kept saying to him, "I should have trusted you after that first time, out by the lake (but did he remember?). But I didn't. I vanished as soon as I knew it was true. I went far away so you wouldn't know. You were right: if I loved you, I should have trusted. I was going to. Next time."

But there hadn't been a next time. Jim went off to college and that was that.

I could have invented an illness, not just said I was sick. I don't know why I ever said yes when he called back. I didn't want to repeat my history? One's first loves, if there have been none since, count for something, don't they? I was too scared to say no?

No, what I wanted most was that he should be happy. Even if ten years had gone by.

I wasn't at my best when he arrived in the tiny apartment I shared (the bedroom too) with another teacher, even if Lois was away. My little single bed was piled high with mounds of old resort-type clothes left over from my "honeymoon" with the Greek. He had ridiculed them and I knew Jim would too. But with no idea of what would happen, I felt I should be prepared for every eventuality.

His kiss at the door was on my cheek, and chaste. But a look in the mirror, the hundredth since I got up after a sleepless night, showed me other defects. My hair had grown long and thick. It was dirty-blond in color. Or possibly it was just dirty. As usual, I found nothing to say. I said to myself it wasn't just that I didn't fit into his life: I didn't fit into anybody's. I couldn't even keep a job. Any bets what Lois would say in my school when I didn't show up Monday morning?

If I was edgy when we started out—he reminded me to lock the front door— I hadn't even shut it—it only grew worse. We did six hundred miles that day, virtually without talking. Lou couldn't be mentioned; certainly not by me. What I wanted, even if I knew, couldn't be said. I knew that at the first motel we stopped at, I'd panic. I panicked in every motel we stayed in, terrified of the night ahead.

Outside Arkadelphia I hung around the station wagon while he checked in. The thought of him writing "Mr. & Mrs." on the registration card felt acutely sinful, as a knife does violating skin. The next night, in the heart of Corpus Christi, with the air warming, I took a long shower and read on my side of the bed, half watching late-night movies until he fell asleep. He discovered me in the morning wrapped in a blanket on a hard chair. I said, "I thought I'd wake you up if I came to bed."

At every stop Jim would help me lug my two cases in, and then I'd hang my clothes up in cupboards which could barely accommodate them. Then just as we were getting ready for dinner in San Miguel Allende, I suddenly couldn't make up my mind what to wear. What I could wear that he wouldn't despise. I said, "Being desirable without any real desire's a bitch." I thought I was brave to speak at all.

"Just relax." he said.

The blouse I picked up showed my breasts. I felt like a tart. The word I picked up from Jim. I felt like a whore, cheap goods.

In Toluca I asked him. "Do you think some girls are born to be virgins?"

"Maybe. But they don't have to stay that way."

"I'm not a virgin."

"I know you're not. Why would you be?"

"Well, I'm one in my head. I was married for nearly a year."

"I heard."

"I felt I had nothing to do with what he was doing."

I guess what I knew—besides the fact I always had and always would love Jim, I clung to that—I got mostly from books.

In Toluca I was reading about a woman who was weak and passive, small and timid. Yet she'd fallen for a burly, thoughtless man (the Greek?) who smelled of a crude cologne, to the point that her whole body belonged to him. When he touched her breasts she knew they belonged not to her but to him.

When he was just about asleep that night I took Jim's hand and placed it on my breast. The effect wasn't as I'd expected. He stirred, but nothing more. His hand seemed remote and mysterious, as foreign as Mexico. I couldn't tell why, but it was as though he found my body useless, and me too. Nothing went in, nothing came out. And yet I'd always loved Jim: from the very first day. I still do, even bring this trip back from where I buried it forty years ago. It's taken that much time to figure out that he found my goucheness and my frightened self offensive, unadaptable to his needs or even his unstated desires.

On the way to Oaxaca I told him I'd felt uneasy the moment we crossed the border. At first, I said, it was not understanding the language and the strange food; on the road it was the heat, which was compact and smelly like pressed meat; then, wherever we arrived, it was being treated like dumb dirt, like white folk treated Indians in my Grandma's day. I guess I couldn't acknowledge that what had happened all those years ago had raised barriers in me that all the cute dresses in the world, as well as the love for him they represented, could not topple.

In Oaxaca, when we arrived, it was a bout of dysentery that lasted three days.

Then, on the steep climb up to San Bartolomé, the dead man on the road across the white line in the middle of the mountain road, his skull freshly split with a machete, the blood kept liquid in the mean midday, and not a soul about.

I didn't understand that Jim wouldn't stop when I shouted. I wrested the steering wheel from him so he had to stop suddenly—we nearly went over the edge—and the engine stalled. Jim was furious. We got out of the car and I was sick. We'd been traveling for hours in that wagon: gasoline fumes, and heat, rose through the floor. He got back into the car and tried to start it again. It wouldn't go. "Now you've done it," he said. "What if we get stuck here? All we've got to drink is half a can of hot Coke. How would you like to lug those suitcases in this heat?"

Way down, in the jungly Chiapas below, the road behind us wound like a garden hose left to rot in the sun. A single pick-up was heading our way; it kicked up a dust too heavy to rise high. Didn't I understand we had at most a quarter-hour, twenty minutes? That is if no one came the other way, down from the Guatemalan border. And if we could get the car started again, up that high and on a gradient. "That was a dumb thing to do," he said. "You know where we are? This is Mexico, not Evanston."

He had to shout the last bit after me because I'd gone off to be sick again by the side of the road, not daring to look back because of the dead man in the road and because Jim was so wrathful. Did he think I didn't know this was Mexico? I hated the place.

I heard him try the engine again. The carburetor was flooded from the climb, it was vapor-lock: whatever, the engine wouldn't catch. And we'd stopped beyond the body, therefore Mexican cause-and-effect was at play—we had struck the man. Not a mark on the car? "Señor, you cannot deceive us, you had plenty of time to wipe away all traces of your crime."

I could tell he was looking at me in the rear-view mirror as he pressed the accelerator, but to no effect. I knew what he was seeing and thinking. He saw a dumb broad down on her haunches looking at a dead Indian—as I supposed my Grandma to have done. Sad, but aware of fate. Luckily for me, this distant cousin, a brother in time, had been felled from behind and lay head-down, glistening black hair streaked with blood and bone. The back of a head has no expression: or here it had as much as that of a coconut split on a beach. But still, not a glossy black-and-white photo as Jim might have waved at a jury, but real. And wet.

I heard Jim walking toward me. His thoughts came before him like a bubble out his mouth: she dresses like one of her second-graders—that dirndl with broad, puffy sleeves and a skirt, sandals. Like a little girl being taken to a horror movie in a safely air-conditioned movie theater. She refuses to grow up. I thought, how savvy his wife must be in comparison!

We stared at each other. Nothing on the road, neither the dead man, the car or themselves, cast a shadow. His eyes were like that, too. He said: "We can't stay here. You hear anything coming the other way?"

"I don't hear anyone."

"We can't stay here."

The dead man shouldn't have been there. He was unspeakable. Someone had cleft his skull in two and left him there. I stood up, and I remember circling him, clutching the hem of my skirt, as in a trance. "Jim, who did it? Why?"

He grasped me by the arm and started to pull me away. The tip of my sandal touched the dead man's blood. Perhaps it reached a toe. I couldn't move. He thought I wouldn't. "I'm telling you, we can't stay here with him. If we're here when someone comes along, we'll be responsible for it. Nobody else has stopped."

"You can't just leave him here in the middle of the road."

"We have to leave him. We have no choice. Don't you understand? Mexicans love death. They love real blood and pain. And you've got blood on your foot. Come on, we have to get out of here. Stop being scared. It's got nothing to do with you. I'm going to give the car one more try, and if it doesn't work, you can forget the car and our things. We'll just have to get out of here."

This time the car started. "Get in!" he said. "It's someone else's problem, Aissa. He's not going to come back to life."

In San Bartolomé I was limp; I could neither move nor talk. Yet Jim walked briskly around the market place buying trinkets for everyone back home and cloths for his table, while I sat among the Indians on the steps of the church, staring inertly at my sandals, sweating heavily though at seven thousand feet it was cool and the Indians all wore heavy woolen serapes. He hovered about me, anxiously taking pictures—of them, of me.

Many years later he showed me his pictures. He said: "I thought you would like being among Indians."

"Dead ones?"

The body was still there when we drove back to Oaxaca, where I took to my bed without eating and stayed there three days. When night came on I saw him from our hotel balcony, walking about the plaza something-or-other. It was strung with bulbs and the dark figures of the young, male and female, performed their *paseo*, walking round and round looking at one another, kids selling peeled oranges thick-coated with pepper or waiting with a shoe-box for someone's shoes to shine. The girls and boys would marry; and the girls become Mothers, the boys Fathers.

On the fourth day he put me on the plane home because I said that was what I wanted. He carried my suitcases.

"Mexico was strange," is what he says now, when he refers to our trip. "But things have changed."

Maybe he has. I haven't. The Indians, dead on the road, prostrated on the church steps, were horrible. Life and death meant nothing to them. My Grandma talked the same way about cruelty and death, which is why I've never gone near where her people still live, though I think that's where I'd like to be—at the end. My father said to me before he died I had only two Indian things in me from his mother, my nose and drinking. Perhaps he meant to be nice. But I began drinking when I got home from that trip. Drinking like an Indian. To forget.

Jim wrote me when he went back to Lou. He said he understood that some women didn't travel well, or couldn't. If where they went to was unfamiliar, they were in someone else's hands. They weren't the persons they were at home any more.

I don't think he had expected to find Lou at home when he got back. And certainly not for her to say, "I've started puking. I suppose that must mean something."

It eventually meant carrying home this little creature in a French market basket Lou had bought the summer before they met.

Jim found it a sort of distant miracle and loved Lou for what she'd managed to do, and that first boy, Henry, was baptized with ash from Jim's pipe, which he seldom took out of his mouth.

Following which the sisterhood of all Mothers soon took over, to whom this was no unique event, no more than apples plopping from trees. Lou took all their congratulations with a distant expression, as though the other Mothers bending over the crib and making strange smacking noises were going through a weird, primitive ritual.

Jim thought she was in distress and appealed to his mother for help and Feli shipped to Chicago a red-armed widow friend to "do" for Lou. For a while, Lou was docile and tired and allowed Mrs.

Fostermann, to do whatever she wanted. Then she said—back then it was no more than a shadow fleeing along the ground—that she couldn't go through that again. Either there had to be another pair of hands around or she couldn't cope.

Nonetheless, cope she had to, being immediately pregnant again and the red-armed Mrs. Fostermann gone. During the long gestation the child-to-be was firmly imagined from Day One and for this second child Jim was present at the birth. Lou swayed in the delivery room in her chrome stirrups and her insides opened up while he watched: effluvia and the magical head appeared and, completed by a slender furless rabbit of a body, was borne away. Even as the doctor snipped with scissors and sewed with needle and thread, he had wept uncontrollably, grateful without knowing to whom. Or, as Lou—with whom he'd undergone the pregnancy—simply grateful it was over.

By all accounts this displacement of his was all up front, open, visible. He too became expanded and milky, was transformed into a Mother. It was as if Jim inhabited all the parts of Lou. He noted where fat might settle in later life, what sagged. He liked the smells, carbolic; the steam in their kitchen, like the vats of a giant laundry; the overwhelming health, like that of a champion pumpkin. Nothing was hidden from his imagination: the swollen breasts that weighed, the structures that supported them, the cotton pads that accumulated rich and sour milk; the slow draining of blood and the hardening of nipple and aureole that spread like inverted mushrooms; and even the hysterical fear in the middle of the night that something, many things, could go wrong.

Later, Francine would say to Milo: "Imagining himself lactating and how much his insides weighed, isn't that just like him?"

"I've imagined stranger things than that," Milo replied.

"Yes, but you haven't lost track of yourself."

Francine thought Jim had.

6

Neither Jim nor Lou had ever been far enough south for nature to be so fecund or constant as it was in Puerto Rico. And wasn't it typical, Lou complained, that she should have to pull up stakes at a moment's notice: just because he had a fancy to do some pro bono lawyer work in the Commonwealth's Public Defender's office?

"How about my needs?" she asked.

A fancy? Jim asked. By then there wasn't any money coming in from Lou's theater work, the firm with Frank wasn't bringing in much, and Mr. Inskip, who'd sent a check for the first-born, didn't for the second or third or any after that. In fact he said he hoped theirs wasn't going to be one of those awful Catholic families. "Why else would I take that job in Puerto Rico? It wasn't much, but it was steady money."

When Lou got into that long depression he was in the middle of a nasty case. For a while, it kept him balanced, as standing up in court usually did. He was defending six defiant prisoners who'd been caught up in a riot and attacked their guards, one of whom was killed, while two other prisoners had been shot dead. His clients were accused of riot and affray and, collectively, of the murder of the dead guard.

The case had began with a letter his clients had smuggled out to *El Mundo*, a letter which detailed the extortions of the prison staff, what they did to women and men, the food they stole, the beatings they administered. Ultimately these six short, out-of-whack little men with their thin moustaches and defeated eyes did the only thing they could do, since no one would listen to them: they turned on their guards. It had been the desperate act of men at the end of their tether.

At the same time Lou learned that she was pregnant again.

One early morning—Lou had apparently got up before him—he couldn't find the keys to the Volkswagen they'd bought on arrival.

"'I thought she was fine," Jim said. "She'd begun painting again. New stuff, more violent. Bigger canvases, simplified shapes. Her reactions to *la Isla*, I thought. But the subjects were almost all women. Women infolded in leaves, in the huge fans of banana fronds. Women who identified with Vegetable and Fruit. There were always bananas. Bright yellow or green. They were threats, like a penis. It was all there, perfectly visible. And yet I couldn't see it. Obviously she hated me for making her pregnant again. She wasn't fine, she was sick."

She wasn't in the little back room she used as a studio, she wasn't with the children, who were stirring, or in the kitchen with Raquel, who was making the coffee. Finally he spotted her—by the battered straw hat she wore, beneath which her piled up curls of strong hair fell well down below her shoulders, the hat standing out from the surrounding green—where she stood, her back to Jim, legs wide apart, alone in the depths of their garden in the island's gentle hills. A hundred yards away at least. Away from her life. From life altogether. Though there were five children in the house (two of his brother Tony's parked with them while their mother, the mad Di, had her breakdown; two of their own; and Raquel who looked after them, who was thirteen and still a child herself) not one could be heard at that moment.

He thought good thoughts, he said. Lou had melded with their tiny finca, and there, on the small country property with a little land around it, she was of a piece with the irregular globular universe about her, with the heavy bread-fruit that split and rotted on the ground, with the gourd-shaped avocados hanging among fatty leaves, with grapefruit and orange and lime and acerola. That's the way Nature was, big and round, fecund and rotting, superfluous, over-abundant—more than you could possibly need.

He said, "I had to leave soon, and I only walked down towards her to ask her if she knew where the car key was. I was maybe three quarters of the way down when I stopped. Because she didn't move, there was no sign she heard me pushing aside vines or walking through the tall grass."

He says his thoughts remained friendly. He took in the bulk at hips and thighs that had changed the shape of her body, the freckled copper color of her bare shoulders, the shapeless garment she wore under her cardigan—buttons down the front made for easy access to her creamy breasts—in which the irregular white blobs of the fabric she'd bought by the yard appeared on a background of faded pink. He thought the dress was not flattering, yet it made him feel fond, for he remembered how she'd run it up on her machine, put it on when they got to the island, and seldom taken it, or its like, off since. She apparently didn't care.

When he reached her, she hardly turned around. She said, "What if we were going somewhere by ship and it started sinking and I had to jump over the side. I have only two arms."

At the same time, and in the same tone of voice, she told him where the car key was: where he had left it, on top of the TV.

He took her hand without really noticing and said, "Why don't you come back to the house? It's still chilly down here, the kids will wonder where you are."

"I'll stay here, thank you. I have to think this thing through."

Then he saw that her hand, which he still held, had splashes of paint—red, ochre, a virulent dark brown on its back and, on her nails, black. "You've been painting in the dark again," he said.

"I have trouble sleeping. I'm serious. I want to get rid of this bloody baby. I've asked around."

Then Lou walked solidly away from him, as ever in espadrilles, and he turned back to the house and left for San Juan. The shadow had returned to him. What she'd said about aborting was like a zeppelin passing overhead, slowly casting its long, laborious shadow, heavy with pain and details.

When Jim had described this scene to Francine once, she had shown a brief silvery smile, fragile as mirrors. She said, "If she really wanted an abortion, she would have gone and done it and you'd have been no wiser. That's what I would have done. Though of course I wouldn't have. Why did she ask your permission? Was it because she knew you would refuse?"

The early years with Lou had been hard years, he told me, going back to quacks, rats and Lou's first and startling pregnancy, and however lucid Francine could be, this wasn't something she'd gone through. She'd borne their two children as if their presence in her womb had been an accident to someone else about which she hadn't wished to be informed. She felt well, neither of them impeded her in any way—in fact they were hardly visible during her pregnancies. They'd both been born before term, tiny and frail, and Jake had survived and his sister, eventually, hadn't.

"And what was the pain you say you felt?" Francine had asked.

"That I could have done more for her."

"And now?" I asked.

"That I didn't see it at the time—I mean, that she was sick and needed help."

All that day in court, while when lunch was brought in tin pails, in the afternoon session after recess, he thought of Lou wanting to be rid of her child. "And Sergeant Vasquez, did you think that in boxing both ears of the defendant you were simply administering a corrective? He is now deaf, you know…"

Even as he spoke to the jury in his very correct Spanish, so different from the way words were lost in local mouths, he thought of the child-to-be: not up in the hills yet, those lovely hills where everything grew so fiercely and in such bright colors, but rather in a landscapeless womb, stolidly multiplying cells and learning useful tasks, nurturing ever more complicated desires. *Quedate*, he thought. Stay with us.

Then, while Sergeant Vasquez was explaining the need for discipline with troublemakers, with people who'd already defied the law, *que es una cosa muy seria*, a serious business, he thought of what the child would see when its eyes opened, sunlight, color; what it would feel, warmth, its mother's skin; and no, not for the world would he deprive it of that, or her.

"And when later, Sergeant Vasquez, you felt it necessary, because the law is a very serious thing, to tie the second defendant to a post in the courtyard, in August, when everyone knows it is not cool in San Juan and especially not in a concrete yard that reflects the heat, and deny him water for three days, this too was merely discipline?"

The prosecution objected, for this was a question of murder; what was on trial was not conditions in the penitentiary which, however severe, could not be considered as mitigation of a capital crime. Here Sergeant Vasquez, who was heavy-set and sleepy after his midday rice and beans, said, "Who says he had no water?"

Jim reminded him there were witnesses, several hundred of them. And meanwhile thought of water, that simplest of substances. Of the water denied the prisoner that was later used to hose down the dead men's blood on the concrete pavement of the yard. About now Raquel would be spraying the children with a hose, and they would be slithering down their plastic slide.

He couldn't understand. Lou had undergone seven years of pain and humiliation, then the rats (and God) had removed her barrenness and made her fruitful. They were two wonderful kids she had, how could she want to be rid of the next?

When he got home he asked Lou, "Which of them would you have killed? Which one would you like not to exist?"

Lou said it was different, they were already there. This one wasn't.

But they wouldn't have been there if she'd done with them as she proposed to do with this one. So why did she want to do it now? What was the difference? Because it wasn't yet born? Think of the efforts it's making to be born!

It was a hot, thundery night. The children were in bed. Raquel was watching a comedy on TV, whose jokes and flickering light reached them on the porch that looked down onto the lights of the village in the valley. Above them the moon was veiled, the stars invisible, and in the distance, towards the sea, lightning flashed like a fish breaking water. Lou's voice was low and muffled. "Do you think it's an easy decision for me?" she asked. Her cigarette glowed, the smoke hung there in the ultra-still air.

"But it's not just your decision, is it? You're talking about something, someone, who's half you and half me."

"That's why I told you."

"And if I don't agree?"

"Then I won't do it. But it's what I want. What I don't want. I don't think I can cope with another one. I don't have that much to give."

"I'm not an Old Testament man," Jim told me. "All I know is I can't bear thinking of it even today. I feel as deeply sick about abortion as I felt then about the deliberate cruelty to which my defendants had been exposed or the Jews in their ovens. It's simply murder. I said, 'what should I tell the ones we allowed to be born? That it was just something you felt you had to do?' "

"What did Francine say?" I asked him.

"Oh, I said to her, 'You know how you and I feel when Jake is ten minutes late, or he's ill, or anything happens to him. We lost a daughter. It's not like just removing a wart from your hand."

Francine said, "I'll never really understand you, Jim. Most of the time you don't care; then all of a sudden you care too much. Because the child was part of you?"

At some point in their crisis, Jim's and Francine's, he asked her what she would do if she were faced, as many had been faced, with such a terrible choice that nothing she chose could possibly be altogether right. Say she had been in one of those villages in Poland where he had been after the war and there was a round-up. You know most of the people won't come back. Somehow you manage to sneak away with Jake. You know there's a rowboat tied up on the river bank, hidden in the rushes. You make it there and are just about to push your way off the bank when you see an officer looking down at you. He's cold and mechanical. He's smoking a cigarette. His belt-buckle gleams in the moonlight and he's smiling at the power he has over you. "You can go but you can't take the child with you," he says. "Or he can go and I shoot you." In other words it was down to Jake or her. The officer's in no hurry. It's all the same to him. He'll wait until he's finished his cigarette.

"Well naturally all the Mothers I've asked say, 'Kill me but spare the child.' I suppose because the child is young and is not guilty of whatever it is the round-up is about."

"What did she say?"

"She said, 'Kill him and then kill me too. I wouldn't want him to grow up alone. He has a right to die in my arms.'"

7

Then Lou's old man, Mr. Inskip, died. It was a routine matter, like getting from A to B. His liver gave out, which he'd known all along it would, and he checked into a Baltimore private clinic, which believed in allowing the alcoholic to go out happy. He was bored and had never found it easy to get up. Now he didn't have to. Eustace was content, Lou less so, for the clinic had cost a lot and Lou's expectations *of many readies* were seriously dented. As were those of Mrs. Eye, as Jim called Hazel Inskip, who had attended Eustace's funeral with high hopes: "Just bits and bobs left, darling!" she said on the phone from Baltimore. This was within days of Lou's fourth child when, on the first evening she got out of bed and friends came to the house, she hemorrhaged inch-deep on the bathroom floor.

To Lou's surprise, a few brief weeks later her mother contracted marriage with an Old World "yachtsman" and became—though she never used the name, nor ever pronounced it properly—the Señora Gustavo Ibarguengoïtia Sotomayor. I've read batches of these letters (which Jim kept, as he keeps absolutely everything) and clearly this new husband was a card. He also turned out to have concealed a number of debts, which she found herself paying off, plus the upkeep of himself and his vessel, so the "bits and bobs" could not have been all that inconsequential.

The letters were cheerful complaints. Who would have thought the wantonness of nature toward man and boat could cost so much? she asked. She detailed rapacious dentists and hormone injections—"The maintenance a man requires, you wouldn't believe it!"—and without skipping a beat, about how kelp fouled propellers and barnacles were a form of "nautical acne." What if we had to do this annually to ourselves, haul ourselves out of water and get scraped and repainted? she asked rhetorically. "I'm down to the last of what your father grudgingly left behind and Gustave is forever explaining the Swiss tax and banking laws to me that do not permit remittances to be sent. If I say we should go to Switzerland the old goat says this ship is his home and Switzerland is landlocked. That much I knew."

Mrs. Eye had never shown insight of any kind and Lou, saved from bleeding to death by ergot, was startled to find herself so intimately re-connected to her mother.

"She's human!" Jim said. She's got a sex-life again!"

This was evident in the jaunty cap she wore in the second-wedding photograph taken on the Keys—on which Hazel had scrawled, "BOARDED AT LAST."

Then, within a year, Mrs. Eye lost both her breasts. Lou was angry, as though first her father and now her mother were playing games with her. One had died and the other was greatly reduced. Lou took it hard. It was gospel in the early '60s that parents were to blame for the ills of their children, and accordingly Lou not only refused to visit her Mum in hospital, she concluded that these more or less concurrent and fateful events were the usual parental slights. Neither Hazel nor Eustace had ever shown the slightest concern for her, and now this, this just-about-dying, costing a fortune in hospital bills, was the living end. How could her parents be so recklessly stupid?

Thus, at the lower end of the scale, she disposed of her mother's premature *Nachlass*, mainly nautical effects, piously shipped north by Gustave, who said her mother probably wouldn't need this stuff any more—if she survived, he didn't think she'd want to see water again—without a glance. But upstairs, in her own being, Lou made her risky decision: that if life were going to treat her like shit, she could play that game too.

To everyone's surprise, the old girl survived. No metastasized cancers, de-toxed for life, she said. And she and Gustave went to sea again. When Jim asked her, on her farewell call, where they were going, Mrs. Eye answered, "We're outward bound."

In this period of their lives together there were times (frequent enough) in which Lou looked at her husband as though he were someone else, someone she hadn't seen for some time and wasn't sure she wanted to see. The same thing befell her children, now five, then six. They would come up to her and cling to her knee; she would examine them closely as if looking for an answer, then send for the two Hondurans who now looked after them. In his old age, the Rev. Sabine-Gould, sitting in an armchair like Lou, had accosted a child playing at his feet, saying, "Little boy, whose child are you?"

Lou didn't smile. You couldn't be sure she understood the little boy had been his own child.

After several increasingly spartan apartments and temporary houses in Springfield, where Jim lobbied at the legislature, they moved to Chicago, where Jim went back into partnership with Frank, and I began, rarely, to see them again. Sometimes passed off by Jim as an "old friend" who needed babysitting money.

Their new home was an enormous old apartment out by the University. Its halls, which wound their way among its red-brick turrets and bays—like a Norman castle—couldn't be defended against the changing times. Even the new baby's room smelled of pot. It took Lou some time to realize what their guests were smoking. The sofas and sometimes the kids' beds (from which they could easily be lifted in the middle of their nights) stank of copulation and urgent slurpings. There was no point in saying that what these people got up to was against the law—there were even young cops among them and law school instructors who were dealers.

At least once a week Jim would bring me stuff from his files. Once, this produced a name he'd practically forgotten. Niven. Suddenly summoning up his close-cut hair, his dull, eager features, the way his body looked like two boxes put on top of each other (two short legs and a big torso), Jim said Lou had "often been attracted to minds." She alighted on such men as though minds were a separate part of men that she could take for a walk. Nevin taught English Lit. at the university. Early English Lit.

How is it possible to carry on an affair between a woman's fifth and sixth child? Surely the body was attached to something else—to her children, to what had gone on or would continue to go on. You couldn't expect a woman in her late thirties, surrounded by diaper-buckets and a row of snow-boots and parkas by the front door—though of course she had the help of two Hondurans—to think about sex? Even if contraception was coming in, his and hers, they apparently didn't work. Or someone was lying. And if, despite feeling weary and being vague, Lou thought she had a lousy marriage, Jim didn't think she would be saying, "What's wrong with my marriage?" but "What's wrong with me?"

Now, of course, should any of their children ask her what was going on back then, she would deny anything happened.

As with other bits and pieces of Jim's past that kept popping up, Francine had her own reading of this unmemorable affair: that maybe it wasn't Lou who was that unhappy, but this poor little English instructor, what's his name, Niven. Unhappy with just his mind. Maybe he wanted something more. Plenty of women she was meeting now, she said, bonked guys just to make them feel better about themselves. Women were charitable. "Divorce is an act of charity." she said. "Men feel much worse if they stay married to such women."

Jim said that every now and then he read a book-review by Niven. Just as sometimes he came across people who'd known Lou in those days. That is, before she cracked up. To such people, mainly other women, not to her children, she had apparently admitted that there had been infidelities. "She'd claim they were her way of ducking my high-powered sperm. The other guys were the only way she could get out, out being what any sane woman would want, right?"

Otherwise Jim couldn't remember a blessed thing about Niven: except that he sometimes saw him in the Seminary Book Store, mostly in the Norse section. "Anyway," Jim said, "his stay was mercifully brief. And then we agreed we'd have no more children." This was less a matter of Christian withdrawal then of No Entry. As it was, she didn't have much to do with the sixth and youngest, who marked their last (willing) congress. The Hondurans looked after this one-baby-too-many who looked so exiguous the other kids checked first thing each morning to see if she was still there. They'd called her Fleur in fact because Lou said she looked so tired already and so wilted from being born she didn't think the baby would last long.

8

With her last pregnancy behind her and a black police lieutenant from Saint Louis (one with literary aspirations) taking her in tow, Lou started on her New Life. She cropped her hair, wore slacks and Jim's shirts, and exercised with weights. The Hondurans took over cooking as well as cleaning and walking the school-age kids to their daily business. Lou ate as plentifully as ever, but with more distraction, as though food were not so good for her teeth and her new self.

Under the new regime, the apartment enjoyed a different and tougher class of tramps: the said lieutenant who was on the Vice

Squad, Orientals polished like old-fashioned spittoons who did nails, another black who was a public school principal, four roofers of different South American nationalities, a ward-heeler, a man Lou had nearly run over who'd apologized to her for thinking about the market instead of watching where he was going, and a great number of shaggy students of a variety of sexes.

In that batch Liam Brady, a part-time poet, had to be the fatal exception.

He walked in one night—significantly just before dinner—with an introduction from Nevin who had recently left Norse, and Illinois, to run Spiritual Healing workshops out on the coast. Whatever Lou's reactions, the Hondurans would have added another plate and the kids would have made room without being told. They were used to living in the Hotel Lou.

Brady was from Belfast: "Don't worry, I can sleep anywhere," he said. Which he needn't have said, since it was obvious. With him he had a knapsack and nothing else. It contained a shirt, a pair of pants, a book and maybe a toothbrush. He washed and changed once a week (book, shirt and pants) and he'd been everywhere with it from Katmandu to the Tierra del Fuego.

"And of course he had to come to Chicago," Jim said. "Lou claimed he was 'marvelous' with kids."

Lou was coming up to forty by then (the Mother equivalent of the seven-year-itch) and fell wildly and conclusively (for her part) in love with the man. That is, she threw herself into his shallow waters and knocked herself out for him: publicly, privately, every which way. Where there was a nest a cuckoo always hung around, said Jim. "I guess our nest was attractive. More or less cheerful, wide open, hospitable. We took in priests, artists, revolutionaries, ne'er-do-wells. All that fertility attracted the ascetics."

As ever, Jim had lots of theories about Lou's guys, the latest being that she sensed they wouldn't board her unless she manoeuvered alongside them. Another was that her body, put through such work-outs every eighteen months between conceptions, bored her. A third was that she had aspirations to be as thin, sexless, and meditative as they (at first) seemed to be.

In retrospect, it seems to me we re-lived Lou that summer. One of Jim's sons, reaching forty himself, came through and began questioning Jim about his own Mum. He said, "She seems never to have liked you that much. Possibly she didn't like men."

"You kids discuss this sort of thing?" asked Jim, who had his proper side. "I thought Mothers were sacrosanct."

"You never inquired about your Mother? Or wasn't there time between rounds in the ring with her?"

"Where does your generation get this glorious freedom to sass your parents?"

"I always thought her really deep affections went to women. Emotionally, I mean."

"Why does there have to be an explanation for everything?"

"You're always offering one."

"Anyway, why just emotionally? Your mother was a potent woman. What was missing in her makeup was a mere appendage, a trifling physical detail. Which Freud explained."

Jim would dig into his briefcase and spread the enormity of their correspondence before me: acres of Lou's powerful, delicate, semi-italic hand, and the battered yellow-paper carbons which reflected the fury with which he had beaten up on the Remington of the day, answering her. He also showed me diary entries, because some entries shocked him now: "The rich curls of her bush, the depths of her gash, the muscles of her powerful arms, that broad, proud basin, all that now belongs to an Irish pederast!" That sort of thing.

Other entries were simple jottings-down of the obvious, that Liam Brady, like all his predecessors, was just an excuse. "May I ask what you see in him?" he wrote Lou. "He's such a brief man. Both physically and spiritually. Not there much, and not much of him when he is there. Just a repressed childhood and an overdose of John Calvin. Has he told you that when he and his sister snuck off to the movies she put a paper bag over his head during the kissing scenes? Or does he wear one for you too?"

When he looked back to those days it seemed Brady had been around forever. "Seemed" was right. His diary told him it was only some four months from start to finish. Long enough for a "house guest," for whom Scotch suddenly appeared on the sideboard before dinner. Encircled by his imprecise memories of his break-up with Lou, Jim consulted his pals, all of whom remembered Brady only vaguely.

Milo said Brady got "something like fifty bucks for making up crosswords; he saved all the big words for the blanks, the rest of the time he was all monosyllables, and sparing of even them." His partner Frank said Liam's skin, very white, came and went: it was so dry he scraped it non-stop. "The only time he took on a little color."

Igor Klima, his friendly therapist, ventured that Liam was frugal and had "a certain destructive charm." But then Igor was, by profession, against gossip.

As for Jim's kids on the subject, he thought that in their later life they suffered from selective amnesia. The daughters, Mothers themselves, had determined that he had wronged Lou; the sons thought the whole thing (breakdown, divorce, enmity) sucked so much it was better forgotten. So Jim stuck by the last of his many diagnoses: basically Liam was Lou's ultimate waif.

Was he? As everyone saw at the time—except Jim of course— no emotion was less dignified than jealousy. Jealousy was King of Detail. All sorts of little things hurt: at the time, and long afterwards. The interloper arrives, armed with his knapsack, and things change. Once Liam had more or less moved in—before moving on, he said—their bizarre apartment on very much the wrong side of the University (normally a place of rampaging or sage children, of long corridors obstructed with bikes and balls of every dimension, of vast plants whose tentacles and fronds desperately sought sunlight and prised open gaping sashes) became as full of Liam as an archaeo-logical site. Brady shards (bits of skin, xxx'd-out clues) turned up randomly everywhere: by the antique porcelain john alongside Drano, in the tea-caddy where coffee was kept, and of course in the marital bed. Sometimes at very awkward hours. Brady's conversation hung about long after midnight and made Lou rapt. It got quoted everywhere: the kids said, "Liam said…" and Lou said, "According to Liam…"

On weekends Brady played ghost-soccer with an imaginary ball (cheaper); the kids were entranced with his kind of make-believe. He could be heard explaining in short words that there was no cheating in heaven: they might not see the ball but it was still there, and if they mis-kicked they mis-kicked. "No goal."

For Lou it all seemed, this cohabitation, this *convivencia* (Brady had a smattering of languages and preferred the foreign ones), a wonderful *vie de Bohème* without the labor of making art. When Jim asked patiently when Brady might be moving on, she said Jim should stop being so stuffy: "You'd rather I moved out?"

The correspondence showed the distasteful side of this new form of existence. Jim objected to finding the Brady underpants drying on the shower curtain-rail: "Why can't the man keep his smalls to himself?"

There was a kind of gluttony about Lou's new life now: she consumed exotica such as guacamole (back then little foreign cuisine found its way past the stockyards) and basic stuff like Brady's furtive kitchen-kisses which made her pale skin redden: "Where are the paper bags of former years?" Jim asked querulously in one letter.

Then there was the matter of Brady's "friends" dropping in: at first for meals, then as they grew more confident (in their Latin way) for prolonged stays, draped in febrile postures (proof of their terrible dreams) on the sofas or floor of the living room, with the TV left on. Pablito, Carlitos, Kike, Brady's *amigos*, were all beardless and young. "Have you ever noticed," Jim asked with guileful innocence, "your Liam seems to have no women friends?"

"And what do you think I am?"

Well, Jim wouldn't stipulate.

Worst of all, however, was, thinking to be safe, to come back from the office on nights when Lou had retired exhausted (from what?), and find Brady reading Neruda or Voznesensky at the kitchen table and ready to discuss at length what was wrong with Jim, why his marriage wasn't working, his selfishness, his ingratitude, or Lou's plenitude of life, her fecundity, her high spirit. Anyone would admire these qualities, he said; Jim shat on them.

Bit by bit Brady, who would have started on the opposite side of the table and intently watched the brandy bottle by Jim's elbow diminish, found a pretext to get up ("I'll make you a coffee. If you keep this up you're going to have a terrible hangover tomorrow") and do something behind him ("A sandwich? You shouldn't drink without eating.") And each time he sat down, his chair moved around the table, so that eventually Jim found himself lending not just an ear, but also a shoulder, an arm, sometimes a hand ("I'm really fond of you, Jim. You're such a bastard. But I could help you if you let me").

It was all in the dossiers, including an unambiguous poem of Brady's in which he described himself as finding himself in Plato's cave being both parts of the soul, male and female, filled with love.

How could Jim have been surprised when, after a trying case and a bunch of hideously criminal clients that kept him out of town for eleven tedious and eventually unsuccessful days in Joliet—it was at this point that Jim told me the prisoners he'd defended in Puerto Rico had been convicted of second degree murder and were now in Hunstville, Texas—he came home and found the house empty and a note on the kitchen table announcing that, having considered all her options (what options?), she'd taken the kids to a better life in the sun? "Perhaps in the Dominican Republic, but Liam hasn't decided"?

The loss of Lou was one thing, the loss of his children another. In modern America he wasn't likely to get one back without the other. Again Lou had puzzled him. That was when he first sat down, feeling rocky, to think about the Mothers. What made Lou tick? Was her flight due to that new nostrum, that all anyone needed was love? Had the fiery Miss Inskip of Springfield, Illinois in 1950 transformed herself in the late 'Sixties into a flower child and hung herself with bells? He doubted that. He saw these grown-up adolescents in court. Lou had healthy appetites and very healthy teeth; she wasn't one of those unwholesome kids, prepping for Skid Row with tracks on their arms, too stoned to eat. So what were her yearnings now, that had formerly been so securely bourgeois and Inskip-like under the veneer of art and rebellion? And how would they happen to fall on so frail a reed as Liam Brady?

He consulted his partner. "Of course you denigrate the New Partner," Frank said. "But who knows what Brady does for her that you didn't do? If he's as you describe, she'll be the first to know."

"Some encouragement," he told me. "When every night you go home alone to a vast empty apartment."

As if he'd never before noticed the concomitant slow decline of his married life and its neighborhood, he now saw that large, ungracious apartment building, once occupied by prosperous, optimistic Jews—it had been sold to an obscure, anonymous, real estate company—was presently surrounded by a disintegrating landscape being bulldozed building by building and replaced by nothing more than migrating, drifting blacks with sincere emotional problems. They poked about in garbage cans and rubble looking for a life and, as though in mimesis, its interior imploded. "I hadn't noticed that, either," he told me. "I began to feel it was done for, and I was done for." No children used the countless toys any more; if he swept them into one room they turned out to conceal papers he needed and were shifted to another. Jars of pulses settled and festered on the kitchen shelves; Lou's bright canvases brought a mocking heat into rooms with knocking radiators. The intelligentsia of college instructors and second-hand bookstore owners, together with the remaining dentist who practiced on the ground floor, imitated the diaspora of their more respectable ancestors and fled the pogroms to come.

Would she come back? Did he want her back? As though mocking him, into the few remaining mail-boxes downstairs, mostly twisted out of shape, came pathetically joyous letters from his kids that sounded just like Brady at his worst, full of Celtic flim-flam.

These fat envelopes, filled with crayon drawings and plastered with crossed kisses, had traveled with their stamps and their utter absence of a return address from various staging posts—La Jolla, Guadalajara (the Mexican one), Eau Gallie (Florida), Baltimore—where Lou had friends, all women, from her theatrical days on whom she could impose her brood for a week or ten days at a time. But Brady wasn't mentioned. Lou's instructions? How could he be sure?

From Lou, however, there eventually came messages of peace and fulfillment, encomia to the virtues of calm. A postcard from former Hispaniola confirmed that Brady had finally decided, or so Lou said, to unpack his knapsack. "We are thinking of ginger farming. Or perhaps avocados," Lou wrote, adding that she expected at least six hundred dollars a month for upkeep. Out in the country servants were cheap, but she thought the kids would have to go to private schools.

"Ha!" Jim wrote Brady care of the *finca* at k.29.4 on Route 104, "You want to make that lot your responsibility? You're going to pay the bills? The maids?"

On Frank's advice—"Mothers need reassurance"—he sent the money down, though the partnership wasn't flush. The new generation of offenders didn't pay their bills.

The Chicago summer settled in; patches appeared on linen under-arms; the Loop trains pushed like worms against the air. On one of the dankest nights, Brady called him.

No, he wasn't in Santo Domingo, he was round the corner, could he come up? He sounded jumpy.

Well, the maid service isn't what it used to be, Jim answered grumpily.

Brady said he didn't want dinner. What he wanted was to talk about Lou.

"All right," Jim said. "But you can't move in."

Then there he was at the door with his knapsack, which looked about as emptied out as Brady did, who wasted no time asking for a beer and saying, "Jim, you've got to get your wife out of my hair. I can't breathe. I had to escape. I took this offer to teach in a poetry program to get away."

"And here I thought you were living an idyll among the palm trees. The peons are restless?"

"She's your wife, they're your kids, you look after them."

"And what were you in all this, an innocent bystander?"

"How could I help myself? You know what Lou's like."

He understood Brady's plight: Lou's sturdy legs were wrapped around poor Liam's waist. "Has she acquired a dog?"

"What was that?"

"I take it she's not pregnant at least. A dog is a good substitute."

I think Jim figured that Lou's character wouldn't change that much: it would simply off-load itself in a different way onto her environment, onto houses, food, people, children.

"Of course she's not pregnant," Brady said. He looked shocked.

"Well, you never know. It's a brief but enormous life that women undertake when they become Mothers."

"You're reading this all wrong."

"Am I?"

Jim felt damp and heavy. What was the wretched man trying to say? That there was no congress between them? Unlikely. "My mind was wandering," he told me. "Somewhere I'd recently read about a splendid machine, the Embellishing Machine. A piece of the brain that burnishes faded images—the way they can bring back old recordings or restore old snapshots. The Machine will bring back Yesterday: as though it were today!

He looked at Brady and saw the Machine at work. It helped him slip past the seducer's one, bald fact, that he can want and get, but then what?

"I'm talking to this wretched Ulsterman," he said. "He's fucked up my life and my family. I look down at Brady's appropriately-faded jeans and what do I see? I see a guy who's tramped all that way in this sticky heat just for what? To get away from bad student poems? Because he was lonely? Or did he want to confess his essential worthlessness as a human being? To tell me he'd wafted my family away simply by inadvertence?"

Then the Machine started working for him, too. Freed in his memory from an embalming fluid that smelled like linseed oil and damp, fresh canvas, Lou flooded back into his mind, vivid, high-colored. She appeared before him first in her full voracity, all curls and powerful eyebrows as well as engulfing thighs and bright teeth; but then, as miraculously, in her domesticity, tranquilly feeding babies, bent over that same frying pan as in her picture (picking teeth) but now sniffing up steam and odors, the two babes huddled together on cold Springfield nights against the dark rages of the Midwest.

It had to be, he explained, a movement of love and a life shared for good or ill. The sort of groundswell, he said, on which one's bark rises, falls, rises, falls. "Especially because of her pathetic lies. She can't have thought or even imagined that her illusory lover, Liam, was heading to Chicago to hand her back, to lean on me."

There she was in a finca from which one could barely see the perilous Mona Strait. She'd cast off, like her Mother. Cast off into currents that were carrying her away, against which it might be hard to swim back. "I love Liam and Liam loves me," she wrote. "The children are happy. Just leave us alone."

Easy enough to say. But there was Liam in his apartment. Not just that one time, but throughout the summer, once a week and sometimes more.

"Go back to the Dominican Republic," Jim finally said. "You owe her at least the truth. You realize what you're doing to me? It's all a fantasy. She gives details of conversations and encounters, mutual friends you see, that can't possibly be—you not being there."

"Why don't you tell her?"

"She's got them all doing it. Number One Son describes to me things 'Uncle Liam' is doing. In case you didn't know, you've just made them kites."

"I made them kites."

"Maybe. Long ago. You're not making them a goddam thing now: except a lot of trouble."

But when his poetry workshop ended Brady called him up to say his mother was sick and he had to go to Belfast. It didn't make Jim feel any better.

9

Lou was far away, so we all missed the early signs of the deterioration that occurs when someone like Lou widens the gap between herself and the real world. One of Igor's patients at the time—Jim had recently become one himself—thought he was the big clock in the station concourse and that everyone kept looking at him and readjusting wrist-watches.

"How do you tell a man he's not a clock without his mainspring busting?" Igor asked. And Jim was forced to ask himself how you could describe in detail the liberating embraces of a lover and yet be alone on a *finca* with nothing more than two Honduran maids, a lot of sugar cane, and six small kids (admirable as they were, with the last, Fleur, coming up to her first birthday) raising Cain.

Seen from Chicago, this chasm between what was and what should have been, showed up in the progressive augmentation of Lou's letters; they doubled or tripled in number and length in proportion to Liam's distance, who was heard of only once, in Australia. Apparently the sick mother in Belfast was fully recovered. Jim dutifully sent his wife the postcard he'd got from Liam, but she accused him of malicious lies and altering post-marks: "I wouldn't put anything past a sick mind like yours."

Back then both Jim and Igor were bright thirty-somethings: of a size, mental and physical, but not of the same shape. Hard cheese and butter, or tough steak and a kidney. They were both what Natasha—Number Three Mother well down the line—called "brain-boxes", but Igor, with his languid eyes, his soft, manicured hands, and his polished, delicate intrusiveness, had the self-irony and the perceptiveness Jim, all energy and unruly passion, lacked.

A sure way to make Jim laugh was to have him tell you of his first meeting in the Good Doctor's office, long before they became intimate friends (about which Milo quipped that Igor really thought Jim was the last person on earth who understood him, and Jim knew Igor was!) At the slightest tension, Jim's right knee, like his brother's, would jump up and down, his hands fly every which way: a sort of automaton whose twitches he mimed perfectly for his friends. Tension there clearly was: the tension of so patently lying about what afflicted him, much of which was perfectly unspeakable.

"Are you always like this?" Igor had asked of the fleshy, impatient, outsmarting patient sitting opposite him.

"Like what?" Jim asked, who was shaking with rage at the cards life and Lou were dealing him, his right knee literally banging against Igor's black-leather-covered desk. Then came the revelation, one of those rare moments when he saw himself as someone else might see him, and he said: "Oh, I see."

It was Igor who saw that Jim's sense of abandonment was nothing new. He and Lou had married out of mutual need. They could just as well have chosen other mates or, had they been smart enough, waited until they knew what each really wanted and why.

"Marriages are like a house of cards," Igor said. "Each card rests on another. Take one out and who knows what will happen? It's called Dependency, and dependency is always mutual."

And leads to sickness, he might have added.

10

When Jim got a letter from the Dominican Republic in a hand that wasn't Lou's and opened it to find that Mrs. Inskip had headed it "Santo Domingo," he figured that the *Merry Widow*'s charts were out of date. But also that the letter probably meant trouble. Otherwise, why would she write him and not her daughter?

It turned out Mrs. Eye was indeed troubled.

"Gustavo—yes, he's reverted to being Hispanic—kindly drove me to this desperate farm of Louise's. God knows what she lives on. She wouldn't even see me. Gustavo, bless the man, gave each of the kids a ten-dollar bill. I saw her snatch the money from them. The older maid, what's her name? Nelida. She told Gustavo that the *Señora* was *enferma*. Sick. I believe her. After all it stands to reason, doesn't it?"

Hazel wrote in a torrent of words, as if released suddenly into loquacity after twenty years spent staring through the bottom of a Martini glass at Mr. Inskip and another twenty fearing he would walk back in through the door.

"She should never have had all those babies one after another. You should have done something. She was different before. Not better. Different. I told Louise that I never let her father touch me after she was born. Once was bad enough."

Sensible, Jim said to Igor, who was the first to read the letter after Jim. But what Jim wanted to know was, had she seen Lover Boy? As her Mother, Hazel should have known that Lou hated to be conventional in any way—if only because that was what her Mum had wanted her to be. It was very simple, really, he told Igor. Her Louise was in her Bohemian-pastoral mode. Except for her teeth, demonstration-white, Lou had long been absent from bourgeois routines. Who needed money when Nature was so bountiful?

He turned the page. "I didn't see much. Drove up, got out, and was greeted like a cold supper." Pause. "Should I worry that

Louise doesn't like me? Gustavo says no and he's usually right. Being a Mother's bad enough, but without a father it's hell, let me tell you. But I bet she winds up cozy like me some day, well out of the fray. All I got for my pains and Gustavo for his fifty bucks—Hell, Fleur's neither healthy nor old enough to spend the money, otherwise he'd have laid out sixty—was a quick look at a French woman who seems to be living there with Louise: a sort of anorexic type, not at all like Her Majesty. In what capacity, I have no idea, having been shuffled off to a wooden bench under a tree and told my visit wasn't 'convenient' just then.

"I barely saw the children, who were engaged in trying to overturn a rowboat in a pond with a cloud of mosquitoes hanging over it. Those two Indian women Louise carts around were sitting in the boat with their skirts tucked up. I tell you, that woman's certainly not there to give French lessons. Too rich for that. She has a white Mercedes parked behind the house. They (Jim read this as Lou and the unknown French woman) seem happy by the way. The children I mean. (Oh). An incredibly filthy group of ragamuffins, led by the girls. (Pause) Louise was just like that of course."

Right. He seemed to remember Lou in one of her letters talking about a French woman. Her name was Odile and she'd married money. Jim had imagined her as taut, very upright, with long hair tied in a tiny bun and her long neck falling away below.

Well, that fitted. He'd once told Mrs. Eye he thought Lou would be happier with girls. She hadn't understood. She said, "Why? Whatever for?"

Not for the sex of it, he'd wanted to say to Mrs. Inskip.

No, Lou wasn't that sort, Jim told Igor—though that too befell her—but she was thoroughly receptive, and if Mrs. Eye had been capable of grasping his meaning, girls did had a certain advantage over guys. For instance they could lap around down there and (a) lazy as she was, Lou didn't have to do anything, except be generous, and (b) what girls did with each other had no consequences at all, at most it offered a vaguely pleasing sensation.

Igor, who already had some years of listening to men con-
structing their women out of their own fantasies, presumably
remained silent. Or Jim just ran on. What he meant, Jim said, was
that Mrs. Eye's daughter wasn't into come-ons. On the other hand,
she didn't say "no" much, either. "Be my guest" could be her motto.
As though "down there" was some sort of National Park or a Grand
Hotel.

Maybe Igor said, "Is that so?" Certainly, as their later friend-
ship shows, he was never taken in by Jim's addresses to Igor *qua*
Judge and Jury.

Some weeks later, he heard from Mrs. Eye again on the ship's
phone. This time from Havana, where Gustavo, she said, had some
"funny business" with shifting cigars under false labels via Miami
("No one knows like Gustavo how to use a Swiss passport"). She'd
called to say she'd managed to see Lou once more before leaving the
Dominican Republic.

"She came to see us with her French 'friend', Odile." The
implied quotes were in Mrs. Inskip's voice, as though considering
what Jim had said about Lou and women. Louise just ate and ate—
You know she has this terrific appetite, but this was kind of mind-
less eating. Reminded me of her father when he brought tins from
his PX during the war: chomp, chomp, chomp. That was before I
became a so-called 'war bride' and he adopted a liquid diet…"

"Mrs. Eye, have you been drinking?"

"Of course I'm drinking. How the hell would I get through
life without drink? Anyway, We're not talking about me, we're talking about your wife and your children. As I was saying, the old
goat was applying his charm to Louise, how much he admired her
bountiful nature, not having had the good fortune to have children
himself, no one to leave anything to—though what he might leave
is another question.

"While he was going through his paces aft, I managed to have
a few minutes in the galley with Odile. She said Louise often seemed
to forget the children even existed, and when she, Odile, reminded

her of something, like she'd promised to take them to the beach, Louise would say, 'Oh yes, I did say that.' Only she never did take them. To the beach.

"Frankly I'm worried. Odile says Louse will wander off to the nearest village and just stay away, the Indians are threatening to quit and Odile's had to bribe them to stay. School's starting and the children should be going, not the little one of course. But nothing happens."

"She'll come back."

"That's what Odile says. She says it's rather a burden having Louise on her hands."

"That's why Brady left. He's not the only one to have felt weighted down."

II

By then the pack of cards in Jim's life had been jostled, for Maria, fresh out of school and eighteen, had walked into the office of McIlvenny & Mount and the Embellishing Machine just gave up. It was no longer needed. Maria's arrival, outfitted in a miniskirt of a shortness Chicago hadn't yet seen, her dark hair bobbed, her shoes patent and bright and red, was Christmas beforetime.

An upheaval was taking place all round him in which we both shared. To be in one's forties in the 'sixties was no easy task. Forty-year-old males were old-model cars caked with mud and habit. The temptation to trade oneself in for a new model was overwhelming, America's salesmen overpowering. According to the new pundits Jim wasn't happy or conscious enough in his jalopy self. Reinvent yourself, man! Didn't he know the *Saturday Evening Post* was dead and Jack Kennedy had let everyone down by getting himself killed? The same thing befell the sweet domesticity of women like me, fuddy-duddys with unpierced noses and little blue notebooks in which we wrote up grades and steered children to what we'd been ourselves. We too had to emancipate ourselves, as mattresses had been emancipated from beds and sex from privacy.

I got second-hand news about changes in Jim. Apparently bracelets had sprouted on Jim's wrists, nearly bells on his ankles; bright Mr. Fish shirts from London gleamed on his broad chest. Other changes, Otto told me of, such as (despite the coltish remains of her adolescence) the prodigious generosity of her body, its yielding, its wholesomeness, her discretion—as though they had a life together that was no one else's business—were taking him to places he hadn't imagined existed.

All very nice, Lou being elsewhere. I kept my distance, but I heard a lot. It seemed that Jim's kids—after a hard-fought battle with Lou's lawyers (Jim reckoned Odile was footing their bill)—were coming up for three summer weeks: "not an hour more." Dear Otto Pribisch, custodian of our youths, of what Jim and I had once been, was as delicate as he could be. I can only remember two things he said at the time: one, that the holiday was costing Jim a lot of money he didn't have, and two, that the kids doted on Maria.

Apparently the two girls furtively studied her; handled the patterned tights in her crammed drawers; stomped about in those heavy heels of her shoes with their blunt toes. The boys noted (with anxiety and pride) the way men on the El studied the lie of her thigh-high skirts and, while adopting her wrong-side-of-the-tracks Pawtucket Rhode Island accent, compared her to their mother Lou. There, thighs were hidden under felt and quilt, legs bare and shoes soled with rope. The older boys' pre-sexual aspirations wandered and they pretended to be looking at the ads over the straps. The youngers, as eager to please, invented dreadful pun-jokes at which Maria laughed so frankly, covering up various stages of color on her lips, cheeks and eyes, that the whole car turned round to look.

"How does the girl take to it?" I asked Otto. "What is she? Eighteen? She's going to take on six kids?"

III

The word "cool" had just come into use. What was nice about Maria, Otto said, was that she didn't even notice she was a beauty; she was in love.

The family danced on the beaches that mid-sixties summer with a battery-powered LP-player, to the sounds of "No Milk Today." All learned to cavort from Maria. It was a state of mind.

When the kids were gone back to the Dominican Republic, Jim and I had a few telephone conversations. (I note that back in the early days Jim only talked to me when he was safe in some new love.) The impression I got was that he felt the world was shifting. The whole country was like a big river flowing between steep banks, Utopia and Discontent. He was going to jump in. He felt as if made for this new world, which was Maria's. He swam in a vague current of liberation, of naked feely freedom. No need to conceal anything any more. As I recall, the motto of the day was to let it all hang out: so everyone was a flasher. Jim too.

And Lou? I asked him.

During the winter Lou did come back, briefly. Jim sent the tickets and the whole family flew via Miami into O'Hare on a crisp fall day, all nine of them, count them! Lou, six children and two Hondurans under a temporary visa which Jim had fixed up. Among paleface Chicagoans they looked next to black, all of them unsuitably dressed in tee-shirts and shorts (the kids) or thin shifts (Lou and the maids) with flip-flops on their feet. Lou didn't seem to notice where they were. Nor that it was winter. In Chicago.

While Jim collected their baggage (raffia cases, cardboard boxes, Brady-like knapsacks), Lou wandered off and was found finally in the Departures, staring out the plate glass windows as though waiting to go somewhere. From Reason to Mad on a charter flight.

After a visit to one of the first suburban malls to buy them all sweaters and warm gear, they had dinner at a spanking new McDonald's. When they weren't carrying on fights and bickerings that went back to the beginning of time the kids seemed all right. They talked Spanish to the outside world and English to each other. The two "babies" held their at-homes on Honduran laps. Henry, the oldest, who was twelve, read all the way through the meal and told everyone else to shut up. Lou went up to the counter and asked for toothpicks, then came back and picked up what was left of their fries and went out into the parking lot where Jim saw her through the windows, picking her teeth and trying to feed cats who weren't there.

Maria had tactfully taken her vacation back East. That didn't mean Lou hadn't had an earful about their new, jolly, young step-mother-or-what-have-you from the kids, I mean, if you had an Uncle Liam, why wouldn't you have an Aunty Maria?—only that not much was registering with Lou. She hung up her voluminous dresses alongside Maria's skimpy skirts and said to Jim, "I'm not staying, if that's what you think."

The only time she left the house was to go to her lawyer.

Lou never made a go of it back in Chicago, and it wasn't because she had a rival. What ultimately tripped her wire was the news that at the end of the jetty in a Florida yacht basin her mother had fallen into the drink off the stern of the *Merry Widow*. When Gustavo called, distracted and confused, the immediate presumption among Jim's friends—no one told Lou right away—was that the old girl, having outlived her usefulness, had been pushed, and Gustavo would soon set sail for the next widow. That was to jump to a gross conclusion. In fact, Gustavo was genuinely distraught, and the local police confirmed that he'd been in the galley with a real estate dealer when the "unfortunate accident" occurred.

Mrs. Inskip had been drinking since lunch-time—despite the lessons from the past, nothing unusual about that—and she'd told her guest she needed air. She'd gone up the companionway and there, apparently confused, had walked off the stern still bearing the cocktail-shaker, by then three-quarters empty of its straight gin. No one had heard or seen a thing. The proximate cause of death was that she'd knocked herself out on a plastic buoy and slithered down from there: hence the lack of an audible splash or protest. Her absence hadn't been noted until Gustavo went up on deck to tell her dinner was ready.

The cocktail-shaker, bright and shiny in the sunset, was retrieved immediately from the tie-dyed oily gold of the basin; Mrs. Inskip, only after many puzzled telephone calls from Gustavo wondering where she'd gone and asking boat-by-boat if anyone had seen her—somewhat later. By floodlight.

The effect on Lou, when Jim finally told her, was immediate. It wasn't grief, but fury. Once again life was treating her like shit. Gustavo sent a check (on their joint account) for nine air-fares back. Lou told him flatly she wouldn't go. And no, the kids couldn't go either.

"What did Mum ever do for them?" she asked in a rage. She hadn't buried her father when he drank himself into a slow and painless death, in the process drinking up all the money she might have had, and she wouldn't go now. "What would be the point?" she asked. "It would be sheer hypocrisy!"

Gustavo sent up mementos to remember her mother by: chunky, jangling bracelets and impossible linens, outsized dresses and scandalous negligees, suspender belts and yachting caps, the boxes themselves as well as their contents still imprinted with the smell of Mrs. Eye's motherly flesh. These things of the here-and-now Lou disposed of in the trash. But upstairs in her mind, in her fragile head under its immense and taut curls of auburn hair—and out loud too, tripping on a tricycle, sending one of the babies into a howling fit, bringing the Hondurans racing back from the kitchen—she dwelled exclusively on her resentments.

They poured out of her as though she were once again on stage in Springfield in top hat and riding skirt, the crop in her hand swishing on her parents' flanks and withers.

"This woman," not Mum, not Hazel, had dressed her up like a mutton chop to marry her off and get her out of the house, she'd insulted and humiliated her throughout her adolescence—how awkward she was at dancing, how she ate too much: now she should go and weep tears by her grave or urn or whatever?

These more or less sequential and fateful events, the deaths of her father and mother, were yet another parental slight to add to the many. Maybe she hadn't cared for them much or at all, yet now they were depriving her of what she'd never had! You could tell her in a hundred ways that it probably wasn't that way at all, that this maternal neglect was only her perception of the problem, that quite possibly Mrs. Inskip just didn't know how to express affection, this being so totally inexpressible with her father, or that, indeed, Mrs. Eye had called up several times from the southern latitudes to express her concern: this didn't matter to Lou.

Here were two people who'd never shown the slightest concern for her, both of them dying stripped of all their assets. It was the living end. How could they? What earthly reason was there for children to forgive their parents? What special indulgence attached to the fact of having been born of those loins and not another set that one might have preferred?

No, she'd been dealt shit and what she wanted was to be shed of everything she'd ever been or done. A New Life for God's sake!

Accordingly, when Odile showed up one October afternoon after school—Jim at the office, the Hondurans in charge—Lou took off with her and wasn't heard of for the better part of a year, during which she fell into a deep silence. As she'd been saying for weeks: So the children had lost their paradise and felt all cooped up in a Chicago apartment, why should that weigh on her? The whole Mother business was a ghastly mistake. Like marriage. Yes, she was deeply attached to the children, but less and less so: dwindlingly, as the peas in a pod grow smaller. It was a terrible thing to say, she agreed, but then she was a terrible woman, she'd learned from her mother. Let Jim cope. He could be the maternal breast.

And wasn't that what he'd wanted all along? Fulfilling his reproductive urge at her expense? He wanted to know what it was like being her; now he could be her. No, no, no, she had to go, or she would go mad. Which she did, completely, but in Switzerland.

There had been no tearful scenes, the Hondurans testified. Lou had been there when the *Señor* left in the morning, she wasn't there when he came back. *Es evidente*, they said, showing him around an apartment complete with her absence. *La Señora francesa* had come with wonderful cakes from Paris and steered *la señora* Luisa out the door, as they said, steered her out by the shoulders: after they'd all had this very expensive and *estupendo* meal of cakes *y mucho màs*. They wanted him to know they had the greatest respect for his wife, but as a mother *le faltaba algo*. There was something missing.

And what was that? He asked sternly.

They looked abashed, as though they'd offended the Master. They said, *sentimiento*.

Sentiment or affection? They felt it necessary to explain that they weren't merely respectful; they sympathized; he could count on them, they wanted him to know that. *Pobre Señor. Primero ha sufrido mucho por hechar de menos a sus hijos, y ahora esta sin su Señora esposa.* First no kids then no wife.

Yet all their furtive, tropical gestures said that the Hondurans, too, were children; they'd grown up in a world which had bosses and peons, in which murder flourished as much as poverty, and it was miles away from modern America, which had outgrown physical, economical and political disaster. The States was a place where the whole had fragmented into its many-millioned parts and just ignored anything that didn't relate to an individual ego, a legal entity, a plausible plaintiff. That fatal fragment, the Pursuit of Happiness, was the paradise of lawyers, as Jim well knew. You couldn't imagine the two sisters, fervently short, brown and long-haired, suing because they were servants, indentured, far from home and no doubt often unhappy. They couldn't relate to acts and their consequences or to a possible justice that would solve their condition. Lou was gone, therefore Lou became *pobrecita*, poor Lou, just another victim of circumstance.

So that when the next day movers came and removed Lou's effects, they were startled. You might as well cart off the roof of their *bohíos* or send burly men to move the palm trees along the strand. Things should stay in place. Women too, who above all things were, in their simpler world, loyal.

The apartment gained little space (Lou didn't own much) and

into that space Maria, back from holiday, came some evenings, some nights, some weekends. To her ready-made family. As Natasha and Francine were to do. All three fell for his family, and some of the time—never enough—for Jim.

"Bloody little realists," Jim said of the kids. "Even when they die they think of death as just another fact."

Only Igor Klima recorded Jim's ambivalence. Every time he asked his new patient if he wanted Lou back Jim simply looked blank: not as though he didn't know the answer, but as though he wished the question hadn't been put.

That year, we learned later, Lou spent in the brightly-colored (like a first-grade playroom) but sterile confines of Dr. Sainmont's Clinic, "Les Pins," suffering alternately from depression and manic episodes. A lot more of the first, Odile finally wrote, announcing Lou's forthcoming rehab and return: all those children had been too much for her, she was going to need care and consideration for some time, and not to have "all those children on her back all the time. Do you still have the Hondurans?"

He didn't.

Feli, now in her late sixties, temporarily freed of Jim's brother Tony—on expenses exploring the fisheries of South East Asia—volunteered to come out. She said "If you want me to" in a way that made it *extremely* difficult for Jim to say no. Feli made it plain what her priorities were: Lou was the children's Mother and it was his responsibility to see that she could come back to her family and a "proper home." By which Feli meant the one she'd not had herself since that now-distant day in California.

Jim held out against giving her a room in the apartment, but even in the small apartment he found for her a few blocks away, she was a constant presence. No, more than that, she was in charge.

Always demure, ever innocent ("They have far too many toys, anyway, most of them broken. I gave them to the Cardinal's charities"), deeply and tactlessly inquisitive ("I don't quite understand this Maria of yours? She comes to help you? She is paid?"), she saw Jim's home life as deplorably fallen off from the standards in which she had brought up her two boys: young girls didn't wear trousers, boys needed to learn table manners, one does not chew with one's mouth open, napkins sat on laps and were put in rings at the end of each meal.

Of the Hondurans she made short work. They were dirty and went round the house in bare feet; they hardly spoke English and by now nor did his children that much, and she didn't want her grandchildren speaking "that kind of Spanish."

She hired a limo and took the Hondurans and their squalid purchases of durable goods to the airport. They were in floods of tears.

On her return, Feli took the children triumphantly to church, then went back to New York, mission accomplished.

It was not a period Jim and she could sort out on a visit to the cemetery at the convent of the Queen of Heaven. In effect, it brought Lou lurching back toward Chicago. Month by month, week by week, she came inexorably closer: from Villars to France, where she convalesced in the miniature castle Odile's husband had bought her; from the Loire valley to New York through which she wandered still pretty much in a daze; from New York by slow stages to theatrical friends in California (where she saw her erstwhile lover Richard Dever, now married, now fifty pounds heavier, now no Hamlet); and from California to Springfield—as though she were starting life all over again.

"To gather my thoughts," she said. "Shall we discuss what's to happen? I don't feel quite up to Chicago or the children, can you meet me in Springfield?"

From within shouting distance, because Jim couldn't bring himself to answer, she wrote letter after letter. Maria was not mentioned. Did she not know about her? Of course she did. Divorce papers were filed. Igor said: "They're her children too, and you know the courts, she'll get them. Are you hoping she'll just go away? It's not enough to go round saying your wife abandoned you. Not when you're infatuated yourself. She apparently doesn't want you as any part of her package; you don't want Lou back, say so. You owe her that much, and you owe Maria a lot more than that."

Easier said than done.

Lou was the more determined of the two and when she'd recovered—The Up can be as powerful a swing as the Down—it's possible that in her eyes she had a chance to regain some terrain, even the upper hand. Her lawyers kept her informed, or did friends from the old days, or Odile? Did she come up to the city from downstate on spy missions? Did she hang about Jim's known haunts? She talked to Milo? Milo was no consolation—he was under financial siege from Luna, his own Number Three. Some people said Jim missed her; others said Maria was just a kid, she hadn't moved in, and Frank and Mrs. Frank were disapproving. And Igor, whom she undoubtedly saw, preached the reality principle, not the Embellishing Machine. But Jim had high principles and at least he would negotiate: it was in his interest. Yes, she had a chance.

But what's weird is that Jim, who is the sort who in a wreck grabs the first lifeboat, solo, did exactly as his Mother had done with Jacob, and to the same effect. "What's to happen" in Louise's letter was read as reconciliation, and so he went down to Springfield.

Essentially, the trouble was, his soul was treading water. Often it didn't seem to him his ship was going down.

12

A lot of empty air wafted along the straight Springfield streets. The hotel seemed familiar, though Jim couldn't place it at first.

"I was unfamiliar to myself," he was telling me recently. "Then I remembered—It was where we had held our wedding reception.

Trust Lou." But then the hotel was unfamiliar to itself. The kind of red-brick hotel where the Lions Club had met weekly on Wednesdays for lunch had fallen, nearly two decades later, into the excavation that the capitals' downtown had become. Within were some welfare families, a restaurant long shut, plexiglass at the reception, no elevator boys: eight floors of red brick with the wrecker's ball poised.

Such was the place, full of memories ("Meet me there Friday at 7.30," she wrote on a postcard without a return address showing the state capitol), Lou chose for reconciliation or rift: the scene of her early humiliation and the rice nastily flung at her by the departed Mrs. Eye, of Pearl Street, of the hospital where she'd registered human detritus, of her one-and-only theatrical performance.

I can only guess what was on Lou's still-troubled mind. In stress she had regressed? She really wanted her dog back and her cash-box with its compartments? Or she had taken resolutions? The divorce was merely a threat? She truly wanted Jim back? If so, why? Two years had gone by—only a few letters and presents had arrived—without her children. Anyone in her shoes, if what she wanted was her old life back, would have been afraid and expectant. She had relinquished, squandered; now she had to recapture. As Mrs. Eye had confidently predicted, she wanted to wind up cozy?

She began on the wrong foot by not turning on Friday night at 7.30 as she'd said she would. Jim sat in what remained of the lobby, watching the door; he walked around the block. When by ten she hadn't showed up, he got in his car and went out in search of somewhere to eat.

Driving down to the lake he found an Italian bar. The kitchen had closed but they made him a bologna sandwich. What they had for wine was Gallo generic red. At the bar his neighbors were two barbers called Sal (both of them, he specified) and an undertaker called Dom who exuded good cheer. Jim told them his story, they told him theirs. Just ordinary men with ordinary fates: "What can you do?" Dom said. "You roll with it. I don't know no-one hasn't got some story."

Then Jim told them about the Inskips and the two Sals said, "I don't believe it. You can't tell about people."

Past midnight, Jim told them about getting married right there, right there in Springfield: "I was just a kid," he said. "I'm staying where we had the reception. Sick, no?" He didn't say anything about Maria, though as I remember it would have been impossible not to smell how much in love he was. It came off even his letters like burnt meat. Maybe mixed with exotic fruit.

The two Sals agreed. Jim's wife sounded like she was a beautiful broad ("But, you know, that foreign blood..."—meaning not from here) and started talking about how kids were today, doing pot in the school washrooms, ducking the draft, busy "getting laid by all those chicks with long hair." But not their kids, though Dom said nothing about his boy. Their kids would get killed for doing things like that. Dom's boy, Dom Jr.? He might have been in Canada dodging the draft or taking deep drags for the silence about him.

What they didn't like, when they found out, was Jim being a lawyer, and they summoned an old one-eyed man from a booth up front to tell Jim just what he thought about lawyers. Jim had drunk too much to work it out that the one-eyed man was a lawyer until Dom, fun-loving Dom, called him "Judge." Then they all laughed and offered to walk Jim back to his car if he "didn't feel so good."

He didn't and nearly backed his car into a dumpster and just as nearly off a temporary bus shelter before flinging himself fully-dressed on his hotel three-quarter-size bed. Chenille bedspread, he said. Street-lights and street-glow from three floors down. A TV he didn't remember having turned on was the only light.

He thought he'd fallen asleep when instead, trying to kick his shoes off, he saw Lou standing there right by the bed, close enough to touch, in a dress of bright green silk.

At least he thought it was Lou, though those strong arched eyebrows of hers had been plucked into thin lines and her cheeks bore red spots as bright as her dress but neither as bright or as shiny as her lips. Then as he raised his head to take a better look he thought something was wrong with her hair, too, as though it had been ironed first, then crimped into voluminous rolls down either side of her head. Big earrings hung from below the fat rolls of hair and a choker, beadwork of some kind, glittering, clutched her neck. Her body also appeared much larger than it ever had, though that could have been the effect of the dress that had no waistline. Certainly her legs, which showed through, looked even more solid, strong as they'd always been.

It seemed to him that she didn't say anything for a long time, as though waiting for him to work out who she was, where she'd come from (the door to an adjoining room seemed to be ajar) and what would happen next, which was entirely in her power. Or that was what the slight smile that now formed on her face said which, when he reached out to turn on his bedside lamp, she forbade: still without saying anything, just reaching out and holding back his hand. And continuing to smile.

"Lou? Jesus! What time is it? You scared me. How long have you been here?"

"Ssh. I'm not wearing anything underneath." She moved around the end of the bed to stand against the flickering lights of the TV. From where he was lying it now looked as though she just stepped out of the screen which itself, in black-and-white, was showing a garden and a porch and, down in one corner behind her, a boy bicycling and tossing newspapers. There was no sound from behind the screen, except that Jim could see Lou's lips move. She was saying, but not loudly enough to be heard, "Shall I take my dress off?"

Even as Jim remembered the dress—it was surely the one Mrs. Inskip had worn at their wedding, and that hair, too, was her mother's—she put her arms behind her head to unhook the dress. It was not a graceful gesture, though it was perhaps meant to be.

She continued to struggle with the dress and finally, with a whimper, started to lift it up over her head. At that moment he hated himself for the wave of pity that flowed in him. "Help me," she said. "Can't you help me?"

He lay there rooted to his bed. He could have helped her, but he didn't want to. He didn't want to look either: it was like prying into some dirty secret. Her head now concealed in green silk, metallic and with too much sheen, her body emerged below: the forty-year-old breasts that were losing their shape, in whose ducts and glands danger lurked; the lines and circles of her sunning, white-and-brown (Where? In California? In Switzerland?); her belly with its corrugations.

"Get undressed," she said, and tried to force her own dress up over her head, catching it on her chin.

He tried to get up to help her, but his head spun. He staggered to the basin in the corner of the room and put his head under the tap. "Don't go away!" she said. Was she crying? He threw up into the basin, then brushed his teeth hoping to get rid of numberless foul tastes: vomit, Gallo, onions, peanuts, lies, Lou's kisses that hadn't started yet.

It did no good (Like this you make me sick, he thought) and he went to stand by the open window to get fresh air. She said: "Are you there, Jim? Just rip it off me." And when he didn't, she lowered the dress back down and tore it down the front herself, kicking off her red shoes and stepping out the dress.

As he stared out the window she put her arms around him from the back and wanted to unbuckle his belt. "Let's start all over again from the beginning," she said. "No other men, I promise. I don't know why I did it. I thought they could give me something you didn't. Or they would take something I was offering that you wouldn't. We can start with sex. Right now. Right here."

These are private matters, you would say, I would say. Best kept that way. To hurt no one.

When Igor asked him how things had gone in Springfield, Jim said: "You really want to see this final scene? We were the only ones there, Lou and I. How would you know if I were telling the truth?"

Igor had to listen. It was his job. But I didn't. Even now, years later, I told him I'd rather not. No one wanted to know. Certainly not her children. No friend. Not Maria. Nor Francine. When it's over between a man and a woman, it's over. Worse than that, each wants the other dead: so there can be no witnesses. And there are things you don't talk about. It wasn't so much the events, the self-abasement of a troubled woman, but that he chose to retail it—simply because it was a part of his life. With all its dramatic highlights: the details that stick: the glossy lipstick, lacking only the rouged tits. He had fallen for the modern confessional mode, about which Milo said, "Yes, yes, but with Jim they're the confessions of others. Our friend is a walking, smoking Freedom of Information Act. You note he always comes off best."

Of course he retouched the scene. Louise had been subtly written out. Only what she did remained, not what she thought or wanted or feared. Jim hadn't bothered to ask. In the way you don't question a nightmare, you just struggle out of it. "I had a terrible dream last night," people say (I have), and then they force it on you. Terrible stuff. I resisted, but I couldn't help seeing.

"So the truth isn't important?" Jim asked me. "Down to the last detail?"

"Have your truth," I said. It wasn't our truth, and it wasn't the whole truth, but he was the one who had to live with it. Just don't tell me. I said, "Lou hasn't retailed it. Why do you feel you have to? I don't want to know." I didn't want to know if it was hot or cold that night in Springfield, if Lou had been shivering naked or sweat poured down her in rivulets, if he were drunk past the *mens rea*, nor what was in that suitcase he kept talking about?

"The salesman's bag," Jim said. "Don't you get it?"

No, I didn't. What salesman's bag? He never said anything about a bag.

"Well, it came as a prop, didn't it? She brought it with her. It was in the room, by the window. My knees knocked against it while she held me. It contained her costume, that dress, her mother's, her intentions. How about the adjacent rooms she'd booked? Her intention. It was a trap."

But the one who was trapped was Louise. A kind of rage was rising within me. Her intention? I said I didn't want to know. Why was he rattling on?

What on earth had she been thinking of? He argued, oblivious: "She waited in the next room with her suitcase, she brought it in with her, she dressed in my room. It was what she wanted. It had nothing to do with me."

No? Wasn't Louise like Feli: rising up from the dead and asking to be loved?

"It was planned," he said. "The old me would have succumbed. Every time I went back to her. No matter how she had humiliated me."

When you're drowning, I thought, it's not your intention to yell "Help!" I said, she was the one who was losing. Not you. You've always been the Big Winner, haven't you?

Loss—at least so he thought back then, before Maria walked out on him, before Francine was about to do as much—was not some big deal. What's lost: things, people, minds, God, purpose, innocence, limbs, children are lost; you can't accommodate to that you're going to have a hard time.

Could he even imagine what Louise was thinking in the room next door, waiting for him while he was off drinking with a bunch of Italian lowlifes, his pair of Sals and Marios? Anyone can answer that one. She was hesitating on the brink. Maybe she'd just about made her mind up when the door had slammed in the adjacent room and Jim had walked out looking for dinner.

A curious thing happened that had never happened to me with Jim before. I was standing there in the hotel room with him, but also I was myself, miles away, sitting in my room watching them while he talked. It was like a Ghost Dance being enacted: that is both real and moving, and imaginary, like Fate. It started kind of slowly. That is, I thought about this woman who had been his wife, and whom I didn't know except through him. Like all the Mothers she must have been—at times, not always—deeply unhappy. And how she had lost her balance in this world she and Jim (Babes in the Woods!) had created and populated. In the immediate, she was responsible for part of what was happening. She had been dishonorable.

Then I asked myself, as I asked about Francine, did Louise ever really love Jim, or was he simply a refuge from a Mother who stole her food and discarded her so gleefully? Had she looked to Jim for salvation? A mistake! But she was doing so again, and he had discarded her as her Mother had, as Jacob had discarded Feli.

Now she was trapped. She'd gone—in that tawdry hotel room—as far as she could and farther than she ever thought she could, and once again it hadn't worked. Jim had been unreachable, cold and bitter. Or just too drunk for anything to register.

I think Jim was still talking. But one doesn't talk during such a ceremony. To visit the past is sacred.

All I heard was something like, "…like our first night together…legs locked about me…"

Louise was two or three years older than Jim, it occurred to me. So that when they married, he was still the boy-child I'd known, the one who was not old enough or mature enough to be told what I'd done. As I still couldn't tell him, it had to be that he still wasn't wise enough. And just as when I was sixteen, I hated it that I couldn't tell him. Because I wanted to share everything with him. Including that worst of sins.

I was angry all over again. If only he would stop telling me about Springfield and Louise. Just as I was about to get up (while still standing in that hotel room in Springfield) and hit him, something even more curious now happened, for I now found myself standing and taking him in my arms. Even at our age we have feelings. Yes, of that sort. It was more than desire. It was an urge towards him, completely instinctive: as one might, if called, rise from the circle and join the ghost-dancers. The impulsion was to this wounded man, who would go on wounding others unless a woman could love him: love him for himself and not for what he played himself, with such skill, at being. And in real time, in a real world, as someone as real as him, as when we were kids and in a garden. I felt as Louise must have felt when she was Miss Louise Inskip and wore a top hat and boots and was wildly over the top.

It was I who kissed him gently and started to lead him back to my bedroom, and undress, and whisper endearments.

He was, however, like a man possessed. He couldn't stop talking, he wouldn't.

There is a gesture my Grandma could use with Grandpa Knoblauch when he was too merry or too drunk or started speaking about things which he only knew about because of her and which it was wrong to share because they belonged only to her people. When that happened her face became as implacable as basalt or sandstone, that only time and weather can erode. She would stand very straight and face him. Her right arm would rise very slowly and step level with her jaw. Then suddenly, with thumb and forefinger joined, her hand would reach right past her mouth and lips and back again. Like yanking a curtain shut. Abruptly. It was her people's gesture for no more and Grandpa Knoblauch would fall silent, terrified.

She had made that gesture to me, just once. When I came back home and began to tell her I was pregnant.

Now I made it to Jim and acquired some of her strength.

Part three
Maria

'Let my beloved come into his garden'.
The Torah teaches gentle manners: the bridegroom
should not enter the marriage-chamber
until the bride gives him leave.

Except in winter, I would see Francine a lot: at a distance. She would drive by, sharp in shades, by now in a second-hand BMW she bought off the Net, be walking with Jake, always distracted, still wobbly on his bike, taking him to Mrs. Vojtyla's. Mannish, I thought: her height, her firmly exercised butt, her gait, the way she fixed things (including that car). Mannish and obviously admirable: for elegance, cleanliness, fortitude. For being so clearly herself. Yet I asked myself why she had scoffed at the piano-teacher's bunnies fleeing in the storm? Because fears like that were woman stuff? I mean, I understood. The wind had taken the bunnies. Things fled all the time. The stars weren't animate, nonetheless they rushed through the sky and fled every morning. For Mrs. Vojtyla that must have been petrifying. She'd built her life on what was fixed: as her music remained locked in her head: the way her Chopin had been, whom the Kid's fingers now harmed.

How did his *maman* feel about that? How did she feel about anything? She told Jim she had no heart. Okay. I looked at her anyway.

As the eyes of women turning forty often were, her eyes were hooded and sad.

My Grandpa Knoblauch had loved hunting, and on the parlor wall when I was a kid, we had a sort of oleo (anyone now remember what an oleo is?) which showed a cornered vixen. The vixen had the same sort of coloring Francine dressed in, the middle colors of fall, which is why it suddenly popped into my head. The vixen was looking back at where she'd just come from, and so doing she caught your eye wherever you were in the room. She'd obviously just gone to ground. In the foreground were the dogs, baying, and the huntsman high up on his horse.

I asked Grandpa, "There must have been a moment when the vixen thought she had escaped?"

And because he hated for me to be unhappy, he replied, "Maybe she will, honey. How do you know she won't?"

"But that precious moment when she might have got free, that was just before what the artist painted. Wasn't it?" Somehow I knew that just at that critical moment the lady fox had stopped somewhere just a few seconds too long, looking this way and that for some way to escape. And now she's lost the moment to bolt. All she sees now is the huntsman, and she knows he's tenacious. And the dogs. She knows they want to tear her to pieces.

I said to Grandpa that in all pictures there's always the way things should have been. How the vixen lived, what she was.

He said back that I should be careful thinking along those lines. "Supposing when you died you had to go through the whole thing again, backwards, with the mind you had and the memory you had, but like it or not, each year you grew younger? Would you go through it again?"

Now when I see Francine, I think: she thinks she's bolted for good. Only her huntsman's quite heedless of that. He's tenacious enough to climb down off his horse this fall, call off his dogs, look her in the eye, and say—in the accents of affection, because he really does love her—"you're safe, I won't hunt or hurt you any more."

And the hound shall roll over on his belly and wag his tail? Ha!

"This marriage," Francine said, "is dead and gone to heaven."

There were good moments, he insisted, moments when Francine suddenly became habitable, when she smiled, was kind, hugged. "They should lead somewhere, don't you think?" But hadn't, not for some time now.

"You're asking me?"

What was it then? He wanted to know. Was she just offering solace, was it just part of her generalized kindness? Just this last Sunday (we're talking about late March now) she was looking out the window, noting their forsythia had a touch of bright green. There were tears in her eyes. Jim said, if she was really gone, why hang about drinking coffee?

He'd read her their horoscopes in the morning paper. His signs were good; hers suggested romance. That did make her laugh: "Me? Romance? *C'est pas mon genre.*" It wasn't her thing. Everything he had to say had the same message: you can't run. He told her: "You've got to understand I still have the hots for you. I'm sorry. Yes, for your body as well as your mind."

When he said that sort of thing she looked down and away: he should have been saying something else.

He was trying to block her bolt hole and making light of her predicament. "I know I'm old and getting uglier, ha ha—bad teeth, unruly temper, but." He said it as though that were a joke. But that wasn't it, she thought; she'd lived with those teeth and that temper for fifteen years, and not all of them bad. Her flight wasn't something optional, dependent on the mood of the hour or whether his coat fit; it was in her nature. "Look, it's quite simple really," she said. "It's like losing your faith." "Come on let's all go for a walk," he'd say, and she'd revert to being a woman with obligations, still a wife. The Kid, her cub, wobbly-cycled on Hemperle Road. Mrs. Vojtyla waved from her window, seeing only a family out for a walk. He waved back, shaking his head. He said to Francine, "Look at us.

Who'd believe it? You've fallen out of love, this family's supposed to lie down and die? Why?"

He wanted some hope. Hope's a natural resource: but it gets depleted, then it dries up.

Maybe that was one of the days I saw her. She looked down at her far-away feet and said something like, it didn't have to happen now; she could bide her time.

"It might be less falling out of love than realizing I may never have been 'in love,' with you or with anyone else," she answered. "That's what I mean by someone losing his faith. I'm just not made for the marriage lark. And when I'm gone, you may think it's not made for you either. Face it, it was a leap of faith to marry me. Imaginative, but not real, Jim. I didn't really believe it and you didn't either. You made yourself love me; you're still at it. The original transcendental man: you make things real that aren't."

What a force the Mothers were, he thought. At once undefined, elemental forces, glorious atoms, force-fields, full of gravity, and, like all natural forces, unstable, fretful, full of shifts, of weather as of tectonic plates. Underneath, hidden, everything moves.

In his heart it was with his future as with the late March sky overhead. The weather of daily life, of living together, was sullen, the wind chilled. It seemed a very political sky: a bunch of Mothers (low clouds) were gathering in banks, looking solid as a landfall, making statements and speeches, giving with their home truths as they saw them: men are this and men are that; you are, you aren't—selfish, really interested, etcetera, etcetera. They couldn't take off without giving a reason. Yet they knew they controlled male weather: high or depressed; cyclone and anti-cyclone; El Niño and la Niña. They fostered spring and stripped the leaves off their trees; they did the snowing and they did the burning.

No question here of ideology: theirs was always the beguiling politics of the everyday, of bedroom and kitchen cabinet; they plotted and decided as they filed and paid bills (spiritual and temporal). He wasn't good at this.

"You may be right," he answered Francine. "But this is a family. And it's a real family."

"And? You don't do things because you're a family. You do things because you have to. You and I should know that. Families exist to be survived, they're a kind of advanced survival test for growing up. You think I don't know I'm hurting you and hurting Jake? I can only hope he'll love me later because I'm who I am, not because I'm his Mother. Families are like that. I'm sorry. I know you think otherwise—you're a romantic."

The Kid pedaled up alongside, using his mother's shoulder both to steady himself and to assert what pals they were. But it was his father he asked whether birds heard thunder or just felt it.

She wondered how much birds heard. Maybe not much. But she didn't let Jim answer, for who knew what he might say? "Why do you want to know?" she asked her beloved and singular son.

"Because I've been watching birds. They all look upset by something and I thought I heard thunder."

They both looked at the sky. Quite right. A nasty bank of cumulus was tilting towards them like an upturned table. "We'd better get home," Francine said. "It's lunch time anyway."

"You go on ahead," he said. "I kind of like storms."

"We know that," Francine answered, dry as morning toast.

As mother and son raced ahead, Francine's long coat flapped; her head was up, her legs kicked like a trotter's, her feet far away. The Kid, knees out, steered erratically ahead of her. So queerly awkward, both of them.

The storm overtook them just short of the house. The rain fell on them with absurd solidity, like fat sponges; they ran, and Jake cycled, with hilarity.

Last in through the door he glanced in the front hall mirror. He saw his mother, only now she wore his beard.

"Give, give, give is what women do," Francine said. "Then they crack."

Jim said: "Let me tell you about my mother."

Feli didn't crack. She wept lots, but she perdured. Nothing could have prevented her from loving her man for life and right into the after-life. She thought non-stop about her Jacob, whom she never stopped seeing as a tall, handsome, upright man. There wasn't a drop of relinquishment in her. Was her son so different? In her head, even twenty years afterward, Feli could detail every room in the Philadelphia house. Jacob's suits hung in the closet of her mind. He never really went away. She observed his rituals, kissed his pillow, and told her boys what a fine fellow he was. He doubted that Francine would create such a shrine. She wanted to protect her son, who was all she had.

"It was only when Jacob died, he who'd made what she called 'this terrible mistake,' that she felt better. Death puts an end to the past. It's a lot better than divorce, which is nasty. Once he was dead she could rue her loss with equanimity. No one else was going to enjoy him. So wait till I'm dead."

She didn't think he would die. Not for a long time. Jim was a dodger of bullets: of heavy smoking, abscessed teeth, drunken driving, carelessness, missed doctors' appointments. He'd be cavalier to the end, a man who'd place his last dollar on the turn of a card and win. But when he went, as he would, she'd be alone anyway. So why not be alone now?

In some dreams Jim danced with her, whirled her about, and admired her gallantry, her courage,—the terrific good face, all that care, all those sit-ups—that she put on the disasters that lurked in her body, waiting to pounce from her infected past. The outside was fine, but Francine knew all about the threats that lurked within. And there lay her accommodation too, in accepting death as relief.

When it came to daily life, however, no *parfum* clung to the walls of that old house any more. It had all happened to him before, with Maria, and he was far too afraid of death to leap off a cliff.

"Why is love so unequal?" Feli might well have asked. That is, if she'd ever communicated the commotion in her soul. "Why do we have to lose what we love best?" Might as well ask why the Kid's sister died during the brief year he and Francine had spent in Italy, whose coffin he carried on his shoulder on a hot day, sweating, up the steep hill to the cemetery.

The good moments—or so he explained to himself—accentuate the sheerly awful. In this photo-opportunity called life, divorce was the negative taken into the darkroom. There, spectral figures navigated on the film: that's me and that's her; this was a wedding, that a birthday, this a Christmas, that a drunken lunch with the bright light reflected off his glasses. On undeveloped film her teeth were brilliant but her mouth was a blank; dark was light, light was dark; in the background deep green hedges flared, the bright sky was black. Develop it and it became the marriage that had been.

The Mothers were at their deadly forties; to their astonishment, it had gone by so quickly, life. To think they'd wasted it on him, as Feli had wasted hers on Jacob! It was now or never! They buttoned up their collars and wrapped scarves about their slender necks; bravely they sallied forth to shop for solitude, or someone kinder, gentler, better.

The times were not favorable to men. The genders were skittish, manliness out of fashion. It wasn't a pretty picture. But he didn't think that was the root of the matter. 'One's company, two's a crowd,' was what he came up with. When you listened to the horror stories the ex-wives told—the time he smashed the kids' toys at Christmas because they were being too greedy, the way he blew smoke at Francine's mother even though he knew there was asthma in the family—you wondered if women had ever been happy?

"Do women remember anything but the bad times?" he asked Francine.

She said they'd remember the good ones if there were enough of them and they weren't just times the men thought were good.

He pointed out to her that she'd caught the American contagion. Look round you, he said. Try on the Art Institute, the better firms, check *chez* your Health Provider and among the envious academics we both know—everywhere, men who had been performing the same repetitive actions all their working lives, flirting with wealth, sticking gloved and lubricated fingers up rectums to check a prostate, running enterprises great and small, clutching the next step up the ladder, were looking over their shoulders. The company, the firm, the practice, the department, will downsize. Apply this to marriage, he said, and you'll see, so will the wife. What's the past to Americans today? It's something's done for, get rid of it. As no one repairs, no one re-builds, it's the same with marriage: you may start your dying at birth, you also start divorcing on your Wedding Day.

Vixi, ergo sum, I lived, therefore I am, Francine thought. Wasn't she entitled to a life?

If you wanted an example, there was Grandma Tilly on the wall, Jacob's Mother, one of those powerful, autonomous ladies. When Jim's father and his sister Ros were growing up, no-nonsense and Science were held over their heads: to each his own way to make. Tilly had cool blue eyes shading into grey, masses of hair wound up, a strong chin, a powerful soul. Conviction was what carried you through life. A pure American of the Age of Success, she wasn't having any. Her husband Charley wasn't there. He tinkered, he dreamt. In the family he was disappeared.

He told Francine about her: "Powerful women, Tilly and Ros, *ma belle.* Cool as you are. Undeceived."

"Just listen to you," she replied. "You don't like them, do you? These undeceived women? You'd rather they all suffered silently from their men. Well, I won't any more. You're furious. You might ask yourself, why the rage? Or ask Igor—he seems to have some sort of handle on you. He's not surprised that I want out. Ask yourself what have these women done to you? What has any woman done to you?"

"Left."

He said: "In France, where the road crosses a track, they have this sign that says: 'Beware, one train can hide another.' It's the same with divorce."

I wasn't around for Jim's bad fallings-out. As usual he was trying to account for something he called his "bad luck" with women. A bend in the road and a few shots too many of bourbon spared me my Greek. Because I wouldn't have divorced. Not ever.

Milo was the example in Jim's circle of friends. He had had ample experience of the picturesque chambers obscenely called "Family Court", where Lou spent whole days picking Jim apart: custody, fees, alimony, child support, visitation restrictions, school fees, holiday arrangements (Christmas by Madam Justice ran from two days after to two days before the New Year), travel for the children at his expense, life insurance her favor, household furnishings—books and music included, "for the benefit of the children"—to the petitioner. "Plucked," as Jim said. Or, as Judge Irving Mandelbaum put it, "This court sees no reason why the Wife should suffer any diminution in the standard of life which she and her children have heretofore possessed."

This year I gave Jim his birthday dinner since Francine was off visiting M. Pasquier, her sick father. I spent at least two days cleaning up my cottage, and the first ten hours of the day itself worrying myself sick about whether my dinner was up to Jim's standards—or would I once again fall flat on my face. I invited his old pals: Igor because Jim was always steadier when he was around; Otto and Heda, who'd known us both since time began; and Milo (Prudence was at home with the baby) because he cheered Jim up.

In one deep way, his birthday is a sad day for Jim. It's the day Maria walked out. Every year he sends her a red rose in a manila envelope. Now this rose doesn't outlive the u.s. Postal Service. So what Maria gets is one dead red rose.

As I was among all these people who loved Jim, who had a stake in Jim, who wanted to save Jim from himself, I tried to explain this to my guests. To Heda in the kitchen before Jim came, who was perennially late. Heda said, "Maria opens the envelope or she doesn't?"

Standing around, seeing what was cooking, wearing his baseball cap, Milo looks too old, too battered by life to take anything except survival seriously. His eyes are hooded like a lizard's and you wait for his tongue to dart, except that he talks slowly like he writes, and each and every part of a sentence has to find its right place. "I say he's a nutter. Divorce is the price you pay for being dumb and marriage is just one of a lot of potholes. A smart man reads the street-signs that say 'Perdition, ten miles.'"

"You did it," said Otto.

"I'm bad at traffic. My car seems to know the way to Perdition. Anyway, I've wised up."

"That doesn't answer Heda's question," I said. "What does Maria feel? She opens the envelope or doesn't?"

Said Milo: "Jim never closes one of these deals. The women try; you just can't shake the man. But I'd advise him against sending Francine any dead roses. She's got a sense of humor. Don't ask me. What do I know about women? I write them out of my life. They want to send me roses, they can get in touch with my lawyers. Roses! The thought never crosses their minds."

Heda was bumbling about my tiny kitchen as if it were a drawing room. She felt compelled to pass round the pirashki she made. She's not a good cook, she knows that, but she does her duty. She ruminates. In the middle of the night she'll digest what she was thinking about or what someone said and she'll turn on the light and talk. For her, you understand, divorce was a dirty word. It's not something you say if you're a decent person. Mrs. Frank (the McIlvennys couldn't come), when she wriggles her big feet out of her shoes, feels exactly the same way. They're both Catholics.

Time went by. I fretted over my roast. Jim was now a half-hour late.

Otto leaned toward Milo's good ear. "I happen to know she does open the envelope. She told me so. She says she feels sad on that day. She sticks the rose in water and sometimes it comes back to life."

"He adored her," I said. "It was a cold current took her away".

Milo said: "You know, I thought Francine was it. Ultima Thule."

Heda said Francine was looking for an apartment of her own. "She's moving out."

Then we talked about Jim's kids, whom he often called "the heart of the matter." In fact all of us present who were Catholics, and the two who were Jews, Igor and Milo, had been pressed into service as godparents, plus of course Frank and Mrs. Frank. We all had special feelings for these children, seen over decades and through every kind of tribulation. A tribe into which an apparent alien, the teen-age Jake, born years after the last of Jim's previous families, had been unwittingly thrust. At first, on holidays or during occasional visits, they appeared a mere gaggle, six heads luxuriously furnished with Louise-hair, auburn curls like wood shavings. They had begun to differentiate—into rival alliances and shifting hatreds—when Maria came along. The next three were made of Maria stuff. They were *Liebeskinder*, as Jim called them: love-children, because in them he loved their mother. And then there was the ill-starred Aurora and the perfectly-balanced Jake.

I was not to talk or write about them, but because Jim was late, I said, "For a long time the kids were scared. After Maria left, I mean. They didn't know which Jim they would find when they saw him again."

Of course the kids genuinely loved their Dad and would have liked to love him more—had he allowed it; but Jim took everything personally. That was what had worn his wives down, and what his kids saw of him was often a cold, or furious and disapproving eye. You simply couldn't live in Jim's world. Lots tried. The kids had tried. After the Mothers.

"They shouldn't have been scared," kind-hearted Heda said. "There was always a way through to Jim. It's called love. Watch how Jake melts his heart."

On that we agreed. I'd seen Jake burst into tears when rebuked and say, "I love you Papa." Then Jim's universe would come back into coherence. That's what his kids could have done. And of course that was what Jim should have offered.

By then it may have been too late. Maria—that self-contained, decisive beauty in whom he had invested his whole fund of love and trust, body and soul without reserve of any kind—had given him a short, sharp lesson: Don't get carried away! Don't count your chickens! And walked out: when he was carried away and did count his chickens. As he'd rightly said at the time, "I'll never love that way again. I couldn't afford it." And he hadn't. Not with Natasha Gilpin, nor with Francine. He loved them both, but it wasn't the same. They knew that.

And now Jim was going through the whole thing again. Worse now, Jim's children—the girls were Mothers, the boys were married to Mothers—sided with her: not against their father, but for Francine's right to be. To leave him was the rational thing to do. Expectable, foreseeable, inevitable. "And f*** you too," he wrote his oldest daughter. "Don't come mewling to me when it happens to you or you decide to do it to your husband."

Then Jim arrived and we stopped talking.

As the first cutting Canadian high steadied over the Great Lakes, chilling the air and silvering the lawns, we all remembered how bad his summer had been. It didn't take much effort to remember—all the lousy things that had happened were written all over him. Up and down the neighborhood we'd hauled in the deck chairs and lit fires. Jim didn't do a damn thing, as though he wanted to hang on to his misery.

Look, he kept up a good front; he talked, he laughed, he drank, he ate. But his hand shook, he smoked and only poked at his food, and he went through most of the three bottles he brought. I thought he'd cry over the cake. I wanted to cry myself.

Basically, the way animals do when they sniff imminent death in another of their kind, we stayed away from the Mounts. Otto and Heda and I saw the three of them most Sundays at church, but as Otto said, the family that prayed together didn't always stay together, did it?

"How can a good Catholic divorce?" Heda asked. "I wouldn't go to church if I were Francine."

What did Heda really mean, since she wasn't Francine and couldn't have been, since she could not conceive of divorce? I had to step in. I said that for Francine it wasn't a matter of divorcing—I was sure she still admired him in all sorts of ways, maybe even loved him much of the time—but at heart, I didn't think Francine ever thought of herself as married. And, I added for good measure, maybe Jim hadn't thought of himself as married to Francine. It was something quite different he felt. Like religion, it seemed to me. I didn't think Jim had a real faith, the simple, accepting faith of Otto and Heda. But he had an almost desperate desire for faith, a craving for authority, and a deep-rooted fear and loathing for evil, I thought, in the same way that he craved to be married to Francine. Forever.

Still, I thought of the gift it was, going to church, bringing the three of them together for an hour or so. But nothing good lasts, does it?

Back from church, the Kid fled to Mrs. Vojtyla's and from thence to the neighborhood kids. Apart from "settling details" (who got the house, which car, what did Jake cost, what if later he wanted to go to school far from both of them?) which took place in their kitchen, there was only decomposition and ire.

So that finally his marriage and its diminution reflected badly on all of us. We all loved and admired Francine, and yet when Jim involved us in his dramas, we were of little or no use. He'd become a high-tension wire and we fluttered about him like kites or swallows, reeling, aware of the electricity he gave off and its danger. Instinct said, don't get too close.

3

Frank felt the same risk and called Jim into his office. "You cracking up on me?" he asked. It was a serious question, though Jim shrugged it off as "just a bad patch" he was going through. Frank said, "Dean

Jaeger called me from Law School to say several students have complained about sexist remarks you've made, you've blown two recent
cases, several people have heard you say you're thinking of quitting.
What's more, you're drinking far too much. Francine calls my wife
and says she's scared of you; the Kid can't make you out. You call
that a 'bad patch', Jim? Or a skid?"

Frank went so far as to consult Igor about his partner. "In
a hematoma," Igor said in his usual gnomic manner, "the blood is
suffused throughout the area of injury and continues to suffuse after
the injury has stabilized. You think there aren't mental and spiritual
hematomas? Some bruises you don't get over. Jim is currently set on
loss. But he's resilient."

I think there were awful things in Jim's life, especially in his
censored young manhood, spent between myself and Lou, a time he
never talked about. Maybe that was the worst thing about the years
after he vanished from my life: that he couldn't talk about them.
He'd talked about his missing father, his desolated Mother—those
were still-recent wounds. But other bruises followed, and there were
many of them.

Blood suffused, yes. Starting with his military service: In
Poland, in Silesia, and in those extraterritorial (the word was his)
places, the camps. Even later, blood flowed about him. There was
the Indian with the cleft skull on the road in Guatemala and bathroom floor in Puerto Rico, inch-deep in Lou's post-partum hemor-
rhage—He "handled" them, he saw them, but he didn't let them
shake him. "And don't forget," Igor once said, "the blood of his
profession, the scene-of-crime pictures, the visits to the morgue, the
blood on the hands of the people he defends."

No, I don't think he forgot them. Especially not the bloody
nature of innards, women's blood.

When I try to recapture that summer of rage, I think of Jim
pacing up and down in my kitchen—thickened, knotted, hands
clenched at his side in a way that would make anyone think he
knew that if they weren't held in they'd leap to murder—saying,

"What's wrong with hate? If we allowed love, indeed exacted it of our society—that we should love all its oddballs, the shiftless and unabled—why should we mistrust our deepest instinct of all, the one which tells us that this man is our friend and that our enemy?"

One weekend in there, Jim's oldest son Henry came up for a weekend to see his Dad. He picked a particularly bad one.

When Henry reached Hemperle Road in his rented car, there were three youths of indeterminate sex loitering on the front lawn in pump-up sneakers, earrings, and muscle-enhancing tank-tops.

"They're fetching and carrying for Madame," said his father at the door. "They're from the Art Institute."

"She's not here?" Henry asked.

"Here and not here," his father answered enigmatically. "Come on in. I'm about to throw this lot out. Francine wants her clothes and odds-and-ends. The boys look like they'd just die to try the former on."

"Where's Jake?"

"Around. And about."

Don't ask me how his father was. Since crack of dawn I'd been over at the big old house myself, hobbling about like a crone, trying to make some order, at least in Jake's room, a teen-age emporium of baseball cards, unused toys, broken basketball hoops on closet doors and several weeks' tee-shirts and shorts on the floor. Big houses have many cupboards. These, too, were full of pitiful remains: rollers from when Francine had worn her hair long, jogging outfits that remained long after the jogging stopped, a careful accumulation of one-of-a-kind panty-hose. Like many of the things that I also can't bear to throw away.

The few times Jim came up to tell me what he wouldn't let out of the house (anything that wasn't strictly Francine's) I could see he was heavy-lidded and not quite sober. At nine-thirty in the morning, and more as the morning wore on. Jim stayed downstairs in the kitchen, not wanting to see what was going on. He was shamed by Francine's going. It reflected on him. A trail of red wine—balance wasn't Jim's thing—led from the front door to the kitchen, the glass in his hand was nearly empty and his sweater, with burn-holes, was on back to front.

I think poor Henry was shocked. And though Henry was deeply loyal to his Papa (but didn't say so) his father somehow blamed him and the rest of his kids for giving aid and comfort to the enemy.

Like any *ci-devant*, a shade of himself, wandering through the back streets of alien cities pursued (in his mind) by the police of the new age, there was no accommodation in Jim: he had a clear idea who the enemy was. The enemy was the change in his life, his habits, and the flow of his feelings. He had adored Francine, he'd told everyone what a *fortunatus* he was, and he thought that was that: his friends would always be his friends, his enemies the enemy. A king was a king, this superior to that. That was why he couldn't accept that yet another woman was giving up on him.

Henry didn't want food; he wanted to talk.

"Look at what I made you," his Papa said, brandishing the lid of a pot bubbling with a brisket and onions. "It's Sunday lunch, I'm not going to change my habits because Madame has decided to move out. This is what we do on Sundays."

Henry didn't want to drink; he wanted to talk.

"Don't be silly," Jim said, pouring him a glass. "We always drink. What's the matter? Have you gone effete down in Baltimore?"

"No, I came here to see you, to talk. It's hardly a time for celebration."

"Drink up. It's Sunday, it's lunch-time."

"Can I help?"

"*Abbandonate ogni speranza*! She's not going to change her mind."

That was when I was standing lop-sided in the kitchen door and heard Jake, preceded by his bouncing ball, come in the back door.

Should he say things like that with rage in his heart when the

Kid was around, who wandered innocently into the kitchen, who was ever ready to pick up and run at his father's fury, who literally quivered as Henry took him up for a kiss? Henry would have walked out himself if he hadn't thought it would hurt his Papa even more. And, being Henry, a proud father, if he hadn't thought he ought to make sure Jake was O.K., who had simply had the sense to disappear to his beloved TV.

Later Henry walked me home (probably wondering who I was, but he had a comforting arm) and said he wondered, should he meet his father in a roomful of people, would he like him? "I mean we're all genuinely sorry about Francine. We all wish it hadn't happened. But we also know none of his wives found him an easy man. We certainly didn't."

Well of course they didn't. By then Henry had been around for forty years and survived four Mothers in their complex comings and goings, he'd seen Jim up and down and rarely twice the same, in appearance, attitude, flow of feeling or just plain ordinary life. There was something touching and innocent in asking me (of all people!), "What do you do with a man who refuses to be happy with what he has? Who won't accept life's ups and downs? In a matter of months there'll be a fifth Mrs. Mount, whether he marries her or not. He's so goddam indestructible. But he really doesn't like women. They all get to figure that one out."

Just like his Pa, Henry was more than a little intimidating with his certainties. But I didn't say I thought Henry was barking up the wrong tree. No Sirree. Little old Aissa's job in life is listening.

Henry said that was why his sisters ("They're loyal as hell, but they're women") felt more for Francine than for Jim. After all, Francine too had invested her all in their father, and they knew from her explanations—Francine wrote remarkable letters, funny and deadly—that she considered this break-up her Biggest Failure.

It was a Bible thing with Jim, Henry argued. "His mother threw him out of Paradise."

Well, hardly, I thought. Feli had wanted him happy. All the women in Jim's life, myself included at fifteen-sixteen, would have died to make him happy. They sacrificed themselves for that: and when they couldn't, they left. Even Maria. So why wasn't he happy and grateful to them? The Mothers had a good share of the Happy Life: what happened? Maria was the real Eve in a real garden of Eden. But was that really what Eve wanted, that teen-ager with her knee flexed back against the famous tree, an apple in her hand? She just wanted Adam happy?

No. I have a letter from Jim telling me his Eve had walked out. Maybe in the first year or two that was what she wanted, he wrote. "When she wasn't a Mother, when she didn't even know what it was yet, or how to go about being one. That was when she took a bite from the apple and handed it to me."

The simplest answer, I told Henry, might be that Jim wore them all out. A terrible flame burned within him and consumed them one by one. Wasn't it possible to think (though I didn't say this to Henry) that they'd also been frightened on behalf of their children?

"It's all rather sad," Henry said.

Amen. Like the dead red rose Jim sent Maria every year.

Sad because while I was taking all this in, I could remember Francine as she was when Jim brought her back from gay Paree. Otto, who'd met them at O'Hare, was the first to tell us about her. What was she like? "Smart, tart, savvy, employed, straight out of rehab. She doesn't know what she's getting into."

Recently, Francine told Heda that when she married Jim she hadn't been looking for anything special. "I wasn't anything special. I was doing fine on my own. Day by day." She had been twenty-eight and just fine thank you very much. Then she met "this older man who had no beard back then but long hair, bracelets, a rich assortment of teeth. Smart and full of himself. Very sure."

He'd been so obviously at loose ends. Between women. Used to a body in his bed and children in the house. As for herself, she had been bored with her job; he had money—at least as much as his wives had left him.

"I thought I could make it work. And why not?"

Why not? Fifteen or sixteen years later there was Francine—still dutiful, not wanting to hurt, wearing Mitsouko, an elegant starched blouse and long, loose trousers hitched high up on her waist—but no Jim glowing by her side. There was no proximate cause to her disaffection, to this death she felt in her heart: just apprehension. You couldn't tell what the weather was with Jim, she said. "He thinks it's just part of the Zeitgeist," Francine said. "It isn't. I'm not one to jump ship before it's too late. I could have done a lot worse back then, I've learned a lot, I think highly of him, but I'm just not made for this marriage lark."

4

Small wonder that in the death-throes of his great autumnal love affair with Francine, he wanted to talk about Maria, the spring-time of his life. Back there lay ten years of his bliss. Something like that gets stored up, like heat in a bed. Hanging on Henry's arm as I walked back to my own house, I felt I was holding Jim's from fifty years back. It felt good, as it must have when Jim and Maria started out. There is a lovely clarity to the arm-in-arm, one steeped in trust.

The women strewn about Jim's life, including me, including observers like Heda or Mothers like Lou and Feli, stared at holiday snapshots of Maria and said, some of them dismissively, "young girls are beautiful." But Jim's women were all beautiful, and all young when he took up with them. Even I was beautiful once. We should say, instead, that Maria was so very young—eighteen—and young in a very special way, that a woman has only once, before she knows a man. In that sort of youth, nothing has obtruded. There's been no sackage. No reshaping, no sag. It's all *élan*. You know, that confident thrust into the future, toes out, careless legs. It's unformed and expectant.

Is experience, knowledge, the opposite of innocence? Is that what Eve felt when thanks to the snake she found out what Adam would do to her?

I got occasional letters about her. Along with love, with the perky, the enthusiastic, the I-could-dance-all-night, with a surplus of barely-checked sexual energy, some struck a deeper note, like one I found recently: "You see something there; not everyone sees it. You see promise and you see danger. For instance that nothing will last." Love and risk.

I don't know how he worked taking Maria to the Sonny Liston-Cassius Clay fight in Maine. Maria must have told Frank she needed to go home to see her folks in Pawtucket, Rhode Island. Frank was a softie and he would have said yes. I know that some of the money behind Liston was client money (would such people ever have been clients in a staider age?) that Jim had brought in, and that's how he got his ringside seats. It's also how the "runaway pair" (as the headline said) got spotted by the Chicago sports writers Jim, a rock-hard sports freak, frequented.

If he had meant to hide his flight of fancy with a girl half his age, being on nationwide TV under the bright lights at ringside was a crazy way to go about it. They sat on the hard edge of the penumbra all around the ring. Their faces were lit, illuminated by the lights that reflected off canvas and rope, and off the two fighters' glistening, sweaty black bodies.

Frankly, I think Jim was, temporarily (if the ten years to the day he spent with Maria can be called temporary), in his element. Celebrity, which old-fashioned lawyers like Frank avoided like the plague, had become fashionable, and the Jim of those days had a natural feel for aura, and he was star-struck besides: by this new public life, by Maria, by the way people looked at her. She turned heads; hers was turned.

What Jim wanted to tell me went beyond that, and telling me about it, even thirty years after, he was still as excited as Jake might have been, running into the house with a stream of wild talk about a dead bird he'd found or the game-winning single he'd hit.

Somehow Jim had got into an unedited video of the fight, and of Cassius' dressing room after. He and Maria can only be seen clearly once. You have to stop the frame at that, as they were being dragged along among cameras and cables. But you don't need more than that one scene to imagine the rest: to see Maria ringside with the money and the tarts, the money being flashed around, the blacks with gold chains about their necks, Clay's body with its girlish waist, the dark, brutish quality of Liston; to hear the slop of the water-buckets, the plop of sponges, the pop of rubber mouth-guards, the thud of gloves.

It's frighteningly clear just how much the pair of them were turned on.

Frightening because little Maria was a good girl. She'd never seen that sort of violence. But good little girls can be turned on and lose their heads. Heat and excitement feed their appetite.

You look back on them, as I do, and you see the fight was only a prelude to the main event, which is when they drove back to the motel, top-down, just before dawn. She holds her hair out of her eyes alongside him. The headlights veer in spruce and scrub (girls in open cars!) She is still shaking when they arrived at the Pinewood Lodge, but she made the reservation back in Chicago. She knows they have but one room and one double bed.

Thinking she's got a late customer, the manageress is out there on the tarmac in her quilt dressing-gown. She stares opaquely at Maria and watches the teen-ager follow her man in. The place she's standing in front of—a picture postcard cluster of would-be hunting lodges backed up against the woods—has stuck in Jim's mind. And the way she slammed the Office door shut with disapproval. Also the pine-paneling, the baseboard heater that hardly took the chill off the air, the TV suspended on its bracket opposite the bed, the tiny shower-and-toilet they would have to share, the poplin bedspread, the two-coiled cooker with its jar of instant coffee on a shelf above.

"Of course she was scared," Jim said. "I was scared. I was responsible for her, for everything she handed over to my care." Because she'd said "yes," he explained. And walked in after him, knock-knee'd, waiting, biting her lower lip and trying to look calm while he fried the steaks they'd bought earlier, and opened the bottle of wine with the Swiss Army knife he always carried. What else could he say, since it had all happened: with her splendid consent, her fearfulness, his tender regard, and had been like nothing else in his life, as far from Lou as you could get? Even to her tears afterward.

Even when he reached Frank the next morning at ten Chicago time, eleven in Maine, and learned how their pictures had been digested with Chicago's hefty breakfasts, Maria still slept: with a child's smile and, on her dark, downy upper lip, little beads of sweat.

The most even-tempered of men, Frank blew up. "And how do you think her parents feel about seeing their daughter out with a still-married lawyer with six kids who's twice her age? You know she's some sort of niece of mine, her folks called me up. They wanted to know if their Maria was on another case in Maine."

"What did you tell them?"

"You want me to lie to my own family? I told them I didn't think she'd make out in the office. Wonderful girl, make anyone happy just looking at her, but probably too inexperienced for a small firm like ours. I said I'd find her another job and I'm going to. Either she goes or you go, Jim."

"Make it both of us if you're going to go all moral on me, Frank. I don't just love this girl, I'm stark, raving mad about her."

As Jim said, how could you describe to Frank, or anyone, that she then woke up with such gratitude that tears filled her eyes? Or how they left Maine eastward to Vermont in that same open car, driving through the night and arriving at White River Junction frozen? What it was like to sit in the early morning diner among the sawmill workers staring at her, until the stores opened and he could buy each of them a rough, red woolen cardigan with a thick, bright zip, one which on her, a head shorter, reached her knees? To watch her trot, legs splayed like a filly, up Main Street at the end of which, quite dazed, she'd left her bag in the car, wide-open?

Crazy about her? Absolutely true. She's the one naked on Jim's wall. That tells you. He took that picture in the Pinewood Lodge on that trip. The double bed she's sitting up on, three-quarter profile and naked, is the bed they shared, those are their sheets. Is that an eighteen-year-old's body? (No, it's a woman's body.)

Hindsight is a killer. Today I look beyond the flesh and full-ness and I see something remote and detached. She isn't looking at him or at the camera; she isn't contemplating herself: it's as though body and mind have been sent to distant foreign posts well apart. And that was something Jim didn't see, the still, determined waters running deep: until it was far too late.

The way he talked to me when they came back from Lewiston, from something very like wild first love, was disturbing. It lacked all restraint: "The irresistible sweetness of fucking someone as pliable and responsive as a loaf of bread rising." He said things like that. He couldn't get over his admiration, his Luck! Yet did I want to know the details? She was a kid half his age, was there a whole lot to say about that?

Other pictures—she lies curled in a hammock, shirt on, lean-ing over the edge—show the same drift into the somnolence of sex. While the mind is again busy elsewhere! Has a spell been cast on her? That's what Eleanor, her mother—it is she whose sister is mar-ried to a McIlvenny—said to her: "You were always a sensible girl, sometimes I don't recognize you any more."

Sensible? Jim would laugh at that now. He laughed at it then. Maria sensible? Read your Judge Coke, Aissa. "Carnal copulation, slaughter, seizing what's not your own, those are things of the senses, they're sensible. Crimes, like justice, are in the head. Damn me at law if you want (he was in high good humor), but I was being sen-sible. I loved the girl! What would you have me do?"

The day-dreamy bit, as if she's just risen from bed, her lips swollen, was the Eve side. Then head triumphed over heart (as was probably the case eventually with Jim), she pulled herself together and was the efficient girl who made McIlvenny *&* Mount tick. Her brief, happy Pawtucket life followed the same pattern. After a long, drowsy adolescence, two summers in a shoe-shop—facing one ankle after another, this one swollen, that one weak, after the indecisions over insteps and heels, the pinches of protruding at-right-angle toes of ladies fat and thin and teen-age boys mentally barefoot, not to speak of a bottom-pinching boss who made her reach for the top-shelf boxes for a better view—would have made any girl think surely she could do better, that there had to be something beyond the huge comfort of family and home, more satisfying than Roger Cormiere, her putative beau, who was like spindledrift and played the clarinet in her high school marching-band.

There was something better. Roger was swopped for a freshly-landed Italian waiter with whom she was resolutely chaste, and shoes turned into records. It was done with her usual decisiveness—as indeed she left Pawtucket for fame and fortune in Chicago. The new job involved a daily commute and learning all she could: about the Beatles; then about built-up shoes for her gay outward-bound legs; then about short skirts and the town's first ever hot pants ordered up from New York. A winter of that and the new high-school graduate felt ready for the big city. She consulted her aunt-by-marriage, who wrote Frank McIlvenny, who…

From the very first time I saw her, I thought Maria knew what she was doing. Her insides had been training her up. They reacted violently to touch and sound and impressions, hence the ready blush. If her mind, as we were all to find out, was judgmental, dispassionate, even cold—oh, not at all unlike Francine's—in body she was a sanguine, healthy girl. She'd been prepared, she was ready. She had the husky voice, the beguiling, innocent smile, the full lips, the dainty ears, the baby-smooth skin, the tennis racket in the closet, and an I'm-dancing-with-myself way of walking.

I can't say that what she came to Chicago for was what she found in Jim, an older man, a success, someone who knew and could teach her, but her mind was pre-disposed by an unsatisfactory Cormiere, a repressed Italian waiter. Any girl as sensible as Maria could tot up her assets: her body, her liquidity, a fount of emotional arousal. Plus smarts.

The truth is, there was no one like Jim where she came from. Who bought her a car—just like that!—so they could ride top down round the Maine lakes and dark woods with the wind blowing right through them. She loved him all right, no doubt about that: he was everything she'd only heard about. I'll tell you something else: when Adam and Eve slunk (is there such a word?) out of the Garden, they really did want someone to see their shame; they'd been up to stuff the rest of us have been doing ever since and they wanted us to know it was fun. He loved her picture in the papers; she loved the Pump Room with Milo; she loved being seen for what she was, a gorgeous, ripe kid in love.

And on Jim's side, whatever Frank's tirade, who as the senior partner was something akin to God, Jim wanted everyone to know he could see no wrong in appropriating perfect breasts or that fresh smile or those languid, chocolate eyes; frankly, as he'd freely admit, he couldn't keep hand or eye off her.

The odd one out was Miss Louise Inskip, aka Mrs. James Mount. Now lodged in her parent's house in Baltimore (while it was up for sale), she was pursuing her suit, expected to win it and enforce it. That, too, made the papers, and via the papers, me. What an old-fashioned thing to do! When one and all were coupling without a by-your-leave, with flowers in their hair, and having offspring called Sweet-Pea, Dylan and Sunday! "She wants the kids back," Jim said. "Frank's defending. I feel sorry for Lou, but she's nuts."

And Frank said, sensibly (as Igor had), by way of warning him that he was flying higher than most kites: "You know she'll get them in the end, don't you? You don't stand a chance."

At least Frank didn't carry out his threat to fire Maria. "I keep looking at her, expecting some sort of change in her," Frank said. "But she's just as she's been from Day One, sweet, willing, modest, self-contained. Everyone loves her. I can't bring myself to talk to her about Jim. You just know there's nothing she can say about that part of her life. You and I are well out of the loop, the whole universe is. He eats her up."

5

When I think back to those days, I see a country stuck somewhere between utopia and discontent. If I'd put bells and bracelets on my ankles, which I didn't (I opted out on behalf of all the kids I'd gone to school with who were in Viet Nam), Heda and Otto would have been profoundly shocked. There were lots of people like me. Neither Milo nor Igor could join in: Milo was lofty, and for Igor, the shrink, life meant he couldn't join anything. But also plenty of perfectly normal people didn't join the orgy. Jim did. In fact he seemed made for this new world of naked, feely freedom; he went in at the deep end.

It changed the way he looked—hard as that was at his age. He sprouted hair and flowered shirts that reflected a confessional thrust to his mind. No need to conceal anything any more. In that previous—unhappy, unsuccessful, very youthful—life of his, what had really been going on, Lou's rats and pregnancies and other shameful physical details, had not been retailed to his friends. Philadelphia manners prevailed and Mamma was watching.

This new Jim was alarmingly public. The second Mother, Maria, was different. Conventional breeding marriages, calling cards that read "Mr. and Mrs. James Mount", were out. Just about everyone I knew rejoiced in Jim's new-found happiness. The papers still kept after them, but hey, as Jim protested, he and Maria weren't making choices: life was like that today. If the motto of the day was to let it all hang out, then everyone became a flasher. Though not I. I watched, wary as ever.

This new America and Maria hit him at the same time, which was causing him a commotion in his soul, making him feel twenty again or less. Maria was echt, straight American. Before Maria, he might have felt a vague nostalgia for the places and simpler pleasures he had learned in Philadelphia or New York and Chicago during the war. When they got together he knew how little he had fitted and belonged. This Jim wouldn't have married Louise Inskip, who had weird folks, who was an artiste, who bred without measure, ("pregnant at touch," he uneasily joked), and in whom lurked unappeasable and un-American desires, lovers, other women, sun, huge fruit, neurotics. Nor would he have spent all those years looking over his shoulder for his mother's do's and don'ts, at possible failure, at mistakes which could range from not holding a fork right to divorce. Where real Americans were optimists like his father Jacob; his Mother had brought him up on her own disappointed love.

Good dreams, Grandma used to say, are rich with the past; bad dreams tell you the future. Until Maria came along he had those bad dreams. He'd go Feli's way.

When he called Feli to tell her he'd found the girl of his dreams, she said, with that poisonous sweetness with which she controlled Tony in her New York apartment, and with the accent that was growing on her after she busted her hip and could no longer get out easily, "I don't understand, who ees this Maria?" She understood well enough, only she was a Lou-backer, grateful for those many grandchildren—at least some of whom were bound to be nicer than Jim.

"Who is she? She's the girl I'm going to marry."

"How will you afford eet? You are going to make more children?"

Money was certainly in the equation. My very first conversation with Maria, she confessed she didn't understand why Jim was always broke. With all the money he made, why did he poormouth? She said, "I make a buck-seventy-five an hour and I feel rich!"

A matter of expectations, I said.

She said her father had been shocked that Jim gave her a car, and shocked she'd taken it. A useless car that wouldn't take kids or a lawn mower. "He means well," she said of her Dad. "He just wishes he could have given me a car. But his is a '49 Dodge! His pride and joy."

You see, apart from me and Father Pzyrnik, whom Jim and I occasionally visited in the Virgin of Sorrows Home for retired clerics, what did he know about un-rich America? He knew plenty of low-life, jungle-bunnies, bail-skippers, bent judges and lawyers—that was the distortion of the law. But upright, solid, hard-working people? So he was a Democrat. But what he understood was Authority. That was in his Italian blood. "Sir Walter Raleigh," he said. "Like me he had an English face but an Italian heart." And if I looked inside it, that Italian heart would chill me to the core. Italians were deadly and insidious, spies, plotters, poisoners. Italians were a much better reflection of the real world, where the tough beat the weak.

But that was after Maria was gone. A period when he said he could no longer sleep, and when he did, would dream in whole sentences and admirable paragraphs. "The author of all that prose is an intimate enemy. He knows all about me. He probably is me. He reviews all my decisions, ridicules my pretensions, passes judgment on my life. I never dreamed while Maria shared my bed."

Did he dream about her? "I often dream about women," he said. "Mostly you and Maria. I get to do the desiring. You say, 'I love you Jim,' and I know it's true, you do. But you're like Natasha: you can't trust yourself to me the way Maria did. We each wanted the same thing. We knew when. We knew where. Whenever, wherever."

No mention was made of Maria's family until a couple of years later when they went to Rhode Island to celebrate her twenty-first birthday.

6

From a motel in Leemore, California, Jim called me to tell me he just remembered his father's favorite song. *The Tumbling Tumbleweed.* It just goes tumbling along. He was drunk, or very near.

"You in the bar?" I ask.

"I'm in my effing room. I've got six channels of porn, honey. One for every taste. In the Previews the girls look like they're in pain. Anyway, I'm not watching them, I'm reading the Bible. Genesis. Or What Makes Women Tick. According to the Jews of old. You still there, Aissa?"

"Sure I am. Are you drifting along yourself, you dear old lonesome cowboy? You tell me what makes women tick." I wasn't entirely sober myself, what with writing about the girl who represented (I mean in the negative sense, say Maria had never come along) my last half-assed chance to get together with Jim. "You there, Jim?"

No. He'd got clumsy, he'd pushed the wrong button, the phone had fallen in the bath. I knew exactly what was going on. He was brooding about Francine. Before he went on this chasing-Sunny-rainbow-trip out West, he spent all his time, as far as I could see, writing her letters. He posted them on her pillow, the nights she came back at all, propped them on the kitchen table, sticky-taped them to the wheel of her car. They were all about the past, pleas for what was left of his life, not that much (she said, "Don't be so dramatic"), and she answered them diligently from the Institute. Diligently and reasonably. Not wanting to hurt. Or not more than she had. She said she just couldn't put the clock back, even if she wanted to. But, he protested, she'd been the air he was used to breathing, hers was the skin he regularly touched, to which she said: "You should have thought of all this loving back when I was around."

He found the telephone and called me again. So he could tell me that when he thinks of her he gets aroused. No, because he wanted to talk.

Had he ever told me about their honeymoon in Spain when

he found her slouched unconscious on the tiled floor of a bathroom in a remote *posada* at which they'd arrived too late to eat—even by Spanish standards? "There was a lizard staring at her upside down on the wall, high up. Good reason to stare, the lizard had. Francine had passed out. From what? I carried her back to bed. It was boiling hot, she was shivering. I couldn't figure it out. I had no idea she was sick. Nor did she. We didn't have just good times, the early days would have got mixed reviews, but I was a happy man then. I knew she was my late-in-life, last-chance miracle. And don't ask me what happened. Don't tell me I'm always happy with beginnings and miserable with endings."

"I haven't said anything. But I do wish you were happier, then you'd get more rest."

"I called her," he said. "I just wanted to talk to Jake. He was asleep."

"Honey, it's way past midnight back here."

"You know what the bitch said?"

"If you'll forgive me, I must say I do. She's been saying the same thing for months, and she's not a bitch and you know that. She's been a fine wife to you. But what she wants now is for you to let up on the nostalgia trip and the grief and the whole idea you're losing something that you never really had."

"Oh."

"Then maybe you'll be happy."

Motels were a habitat for Jim. The anonymity suited: fill out a card and call yourself Nabokov, Einstein, Paderewski, who cares? I could have signed Rita Hayworth on the way to Mexico—who'd have noticed? What's in a motel to remind you who and what you are? A sponge-bag, your smoke, your breath. They are all between places, "handy" (to the airport), or "near" (the beach, exits and entrances off the Interstate). You wind up in Quality, Comfort, Holiday, Great Western… your junk, your past and present, your accumulations are somewhere else called "home". If you have one. Perfect places with everything the undischarged bankrupt, the traveling rep, the tossed-out husband, the shiftless waitress or the out-of-work manicurist could want. Outfitted with fantasies, king-sized beds that have been slept in by thousands, three out of four of whom are alone. Beds so vast Elvis might be coming to stay, or black basketballers, who lie across them diagonally, the smell of whose pump-ups impregnates the carpets. Who checks up on you? Who even sees the bottle in your brown paper bag? There's the deadly TV: if you really care about the girls' high school basketball championship. There is so much nothing around you, you can think of anything, you can be anyone.

Jim gets drunk there when he's unhappy.

7

I suppose on the face of it Maria looked easy. Pretty girl walks into office, boss (who's twice her age and has a marriage problem) falls in love, and love is a democracy, right? All marriages start from scratch. But, like me, Maria was at least half a working-class girl. Shades of Dreiser—a Terre Haute slum boy who wound up in Chicago—and his *American Tragedy.* Jim didn't drown her as Monty Clift did Shelley Winters, of course, but he lost her in the end, and that was a costly loss. Inversely, it was only she he desired. And she dropped him.

Maria was really that kind of girl, and though she melted readily into Jim and his life, it caused her problems, problems of frugality and waste, of assumptions about what could and couldn't be done. The magic frayed in daily life, as it was to do with Francine.

Her Mom, Eleanor, who was a Hare of the big Catholic-Charities-giving Hares, had quit high school in her junior year and married Joe Fonseca, a school janitor and part-time odd-job man. She wasn't pregnant, she didn't have to marry him, she just did. At which point she was written out of the family and its money (Ford dealerships), and moved in with Joe and his family. It was five years before they could afford a home of their own.

In America we talk about being liquid. Money runs like water, and water always finds its own level. The man who could write a check for a car, even if he had to ask Frank to advance him the money from the partners' fund, was not like Joe and Eleanor Fonseca who'd just finished paying for their first washing machine on the installment plan. What Joe Fonseca earned went not to divorce and not to cars. It went to help Isabel, Noémia and Teresa to march up the altar, glowing—all in the same dress, their mother's, which she'd sewn herself. It was laid aside for the kids they were having, for Pedro and João to go to community college. How could they begin to understand a man who was divorcing the mother of his six children? What sort of man did that? Maybe, if Maria married, they might forgive her for what Jim and she were doing. Yet Maria had never talked about marriage, neither to Jim nor to her folks.

Knowing that, you can understand why Maria didn't want to show off her sporty new MG (and status) on her twenty-first birthday and why they left the little red roadster behind, in downtown Pawtucket, which in early March wasn't a pretty place. Not when they had to walk a grungy half-mile on a nasty cold day. Not with dirty snow piled up on sidewalks and packed hard. Not where busted plastic kitchen chairs marked the turf of those who'd shoveled.

To us in Chicago, Pawtucket was invisible, the Fonsecas were invisible. You saw people like them in the corner shop and you saw houses like theirs from the train window. But you didn't really see them. Jim didn't really see them, he didn't fully grasp how much of Maria's heart belonged to Dad and Home.

They loved Maria, but she puzzled them. A close-mouthed girl, they said amongst themselves, not into truth-telling or taking advice, independent about boy-friends. Then she took a job far away. Now there was this matter of a divorce and how long it was taking. She could have explained that Louise was technically the "wronged woman", that she kept asking for more child-support, more alimony, and that she'd gone straight to her lawyer when Jim bought Maria her car, that she wrangled about the children being plunked down with a girl young enough to be Jim's daughter. It happened in what was now her world, but not in theirs. Divorce didn't make Maria bitter; I don't think it much interested her.

If I got along well with Maria it's because we understood one another. I understood hard scrapple and beans as they understood daily *caldo verde*, the soup of greens which Jim loved; and because I think she knew that if it had ever worked out with Jim and me the result would have been the same.

It was to me that Maria said, during her first winter in Chicago, "You think it's easy for me?"

The kinds of people Jim knew and hobnobbed with had always been invisible in another way: Maria knew they were there, but she didn't see them either. She was the pretty girl who had fitted their shoes, sold them their LPs, biked past their houses and delivered to their doors, and what she had seen was no more than their ankles and their front doors. She wasn't invited in. It wouldn't be right. In Chicago, we all loved her; I don't think that made the gang—Milo and Igor and even her Uncle Frank—any more really visible to her.

Now she said: "I know I've changed a lot since I met Jim. I hope the folks don't expect me to be what I was before I left home." I told her that her family wouldn't change because she changed. They don't. Feli didn't, the Inskips didn't, the Pasquiers don't. And probably Jim won't.

At her home nothing had changed. First, Jim peered into the kitchen where the Fonseca grandchildren were being fed at another table by their short, harried Mothers: baby-food, crisps, taco shells, fruit loops, mash. They formed a web of dark hair, Maria's among them, of heads that bobbed between babies as they talked and made encouraging yummy sounds about the ice-cream to follow. Then he retreated back to the entrance hall and stared through the parlor door at Maria's twenty-first birthday presents, heaped high in the dining-room under sheets.

The table was huge. Jim was still standing there, wondering where to go next, when Joe Fonseca came up from the cellar behind him, carrying two bottles of the red wine he made. "It's a billiard-table really," he said. "Belonged to my Uncle Alberto. Had a parlor in Providence. Billiard Parlor. Beautiful green light shades. You ever see one?"

From the hall, Jim could see in every direction. Back in the kitchen, Eleanor was staring short-sightedly into the open door of a fiery oven. A turkey glistened and Pedro (a brother) was summoned to get it out for basting. In the dining room, Joe was patting the table like an old friend. "I got it free. All the billiard players died off. Uncle Albert too. You play billiards?"

In Puerto Rico he had. It gave you diarrhea. He didn't think that was the sort of thing that got said in the Fonseca house. "Don't get hooked," Pedro yelled to him from the kitchen, tilting the roasting pan and basting. "The cushions are as dead as Uncle Albert and you can only use two-foot cues. Add to that, the old man cheats."

"Because of the wall," Joe specified. "It weigh three thousand pound. Five men and me it took."

"Hey João," one brother yelled to another in the hall with an armful of folding chairs. "We got the balls any more?" Pedro had a low, furrowed, brow and patent-leather black hair. He must have been out getting the chairs somewhere because he was wet and his thick forearms glistened with hair like raven wings.

"It's got the boards on, Pete."

"What?"

"The table. For dinner."

"We'll play after," Maria said in her sensible voice. "Dad can beat anyone. And he doesn't cheat."

The turkey was back in the oven but Eleanor was still staring at it through the open door, which was safer than talking to her daughter or her daughter's man, who flustered her, being more or less her own age. The heat from the oven flowed through the room irregularly, as if whoever was fanning it got tired and stopped and then started up again. The turkey was not this boyfriend of Maria's, so it got her full concentration. A turkey she could understand. Jim went and stood by her. There was a big earthenware casserole on top of the fire.

"You like black beans?" Joe Fonseca asked. That, Jim learned, was typical of Joe. He was sensitive to Eleanor's every feeling. He knew his wife didn't know how to handle this. He asked Jim if he would open the wine.

Jim said, "I love black beans." He took the bottle from Joe's hand.

"With rice," Joe said. "Here we eat Portuguese." He gave a contemptuous glance at the next generation wolfing down its packaged gunk. "In their home they do what they want." He gave Jim the corkscrew. A straight up-and-down corkscrew.

When the bottle was open, Joe poured a glass for Jim and then one for himself. The Mothers and Maria and the children had all disappeared. "Elly, you want a glass?"

"With dinner," she said, looking up and smiling at him, brushing loose hair from her eyes.

"Can I help?" Jim asked.

"They're already too many hands round here," she said, looking back down, but not before, briefly, meeting Jim's eyes. She had Maria's dark eyes, though not so lustrous, and they had stayed on Jim a few seconds. The hair she'd brushed back was lighter than Maria's and had a single streak of white. It was a disturbing look, both puzzled and afraid, meek and avid. It was Jim who backed down when her eyes took him on, not knowing what to do with his hands, saying to himself she's Lou's age, she's my age.

Eleanor was neat, short, spare and pale, any fat worked off. Jim would have said etiolated, like a plant that's been re-potted at the wrong time of year. The effect of their actually looking at one another was curiously sexual. The young girl she'd been peered out from over her apron, and in Jim's eyes she suddenly became a six-teen-year-old playing house. Nothing overt of course—what you got up front was what she intended you to see, one version of her life: penny-pinching piety, time served on her knees, maybe not scrubbing the rectory corridors but praying her heart out. Underneath was another matter, and Jim saw the teen-ager Maria so often talked about, the one who went down to the furnace-room at school—it was, memorably, the eve of Pearl Harbor—because she wanted Joe, and offered a simple custodian herself and her carefully bouffant hair.

According to Maria, Joe had chased her out that first time: like a priest casting out demons. Yet by January, though no Hare came to the wedding, she'd been married to him, and Joe had accepted what he thought of as his destiny.

Now that, like Feli, Eleanor has succumbed to dementia, Jim calls that look of hers "cupidity." Which wasn't lust. Jim said, "She wanted me."

For love, or sex, or rebellion, Eleanor had traded in her life of ease for a pair of washed-out eyes, hard-rubbed knuckles, and multiple pregnancies (those "too many hands"). Now her daughter was falling for the cushy life, and going to get it. The resentment was so strong it was almost lewdly out in the open. Perhaps she didn't just imagine her Maria and Jim making out in Maine, maybe she was really there in Maria's place. "Or don't you think," Jim asked, "that Mothers can be envious of their daughters?"

At first I thought that was a crazy thing to say, then I thought: Jim's sexually charged, he gives off heat, and many women, even knowing the risk they were taking, can't help themselves.

Huddled with the rest of the Fonsecas, Jim stood in the hall. Darkness had fallen outside and Joe switched on the chandelier, a smattering of bright glass stars, over the dining-room table. The only other light came from the parlor opposite, a black-and-white TV screen snowing silently by itself. Joe and Pedro, the oldest son, stood by the pool-table, dining-room table, each holding one end of the sheet for the unveiling of Maria's present. Maria watched from the hall door, children about her feet like scattered slippers. Jim counted twenty-eight Fonsecas singing "Happy Birthday."

Joe said, kissing Maria, "from all of us," then the sheet was whisked off to reveal a gleaming black-and-gold, second hand sewing machine in superb condition. Sisters crowded around to show Maria the many attachments, for zig-zags, cross-stitches, buttons, their brothers had tooled up for her. They fingered its tensions, stroked its feed, the dog and needle clamp, its variety of bobbins, its spool pin, pushed the power-button and, startled when it set in busy motion, Maria clapped her hands to her cheeks, laughing with pleasure at a machine that promised socks, repaired collars, curtains, summer frocks and baby clothes with embroidery. A statement of her duties. She said, "I can't get over it!"

Jim said the machine was to retain its mystical potency throughout their time together; and remained for two years after Maria had gone. Its current and its hum tied her to her family. It was like her, like them. It was like Maria's house, utilitarian, modest, and possessive. Its wood and shingles, the ribbons of concrete down one side, the garbage cans aligned, its solitary and scrubby tree by the street-light, the tangle of wires that headed recklessly away, were an ineradicable part of her. People, objects, and now an invitation to sew.

8

Early Maria is very clear in my mind. Often it's a Sunday. Jim would be away or buried in his office downtown catching up, always catching up. If his kids were with Lou, Maria was on her own. After mass, she'd come up to us, to Heda and me, full of youthful piety and carrying, high-colored herself, an ivory-colored missal. I don't think I'm reading her backwards (that is, from what she became) when I say that Heda and I found her both full of enthusiasms and appetites, enchantingly so, but also often still and self-contained. Perhaps only the way young girls can be after Holy Communion. Not self-contained as Francine is now and Maria would become later: like big cats that lie in wait. It was Heda (well read in the lives of the saints) who first pointed out to me that having Jesus inside her—after head down, tongue out at the altar rail—did something physical for a girl often painfully literal. Jesus as Lover is not as far-fetched as it sounds when you read the lives of cloistered nuns. In church or in the apartment he had then, on Dorchester, what Heda called "the eucharist effect" was always totally visible. She took in God, she took in a man. The old-fashioned Pawtucket way, between hill and mill: the way the town was, she was. And Jim confirms Sunday afternoon as their favorite time.

It didn't take long to grasp that, with Jim or without Jim, Maria had no intention of giving up anything of her past, not really. She clung to the new fashions in an innocent way, she found them (the music, the glad rags, her delicious shoes) fun; at the same time she was prudently tied to things she'd done and been all her young life. She could dance herself silly in the new way of dancing, weaving about, not touching, but also she could be found, with the Mount kids in tow, dreaming on the sidelines of a high-school football game: as though still watching her brothers play, she in white sweater and short skirt leading the cheers.

When she'd had the sleep which she badly needed—I saw her as still a growing girl—she'd call up wanting to know if there wasn't something she could do, and before she got pregnant the first time she often spent whole days on some archdiocesan charity I'd found her. She cheered old ladies, delivered meals and wound up visiting prisons (Joliet frightened her). I don't know why for the charitable stuff, which was also the away-from-Jim stuff—perhaps because these outings she was reminded of her mother's insistent humility—she wore conventional skirts, hand-me-down jackets and even a scarf around her hair which was growing out, thick and dark. The places she went, she was as if back home, with no need to be fancy for Jim's sake. Here, too there were Mom-and-Pop stores, car-crowded streets and wooden stoops, the criss-cross of fences, chain-link and picket. She could imagine this was where she'd skipped and hopscotched; and over there was her bus stop or the way to the shoe-shop she'd worked at or the house of the man who'd managed the record-shop where she'd first heard the Beatles.

Those nice, earthy links made her feel safe, and therefore Jim too felt safe with her, which didn't mean that he felt safe generally. Safety is a feeling and you can no more buy it than you can buy love. When he looked up from his own life and concerns, the Singer sewing-machine which hovered nearby, a benevolent black-and-gold angel, represented Maria. That was her life, this was his. She never complained, but for two years and many after she had to suppress her cravings: for her Dad and scrubbed floors, for the oil-cloth on the table which Jim wouldn't allow, for the yard in back where Joe grew his giant tomatoes. What one is, after all, is the safest thing there is in the world, and Maria had to find safety in herself. For safety was not something Jim could offer her. Love, children, money (more or less); fun, yes. The certainties that come with safety—no.

Anybody could have told her that Jim was dangerous. Ask me. I think safety—surely this applies to the relations between two people—is an illusion. No one is really safe. Ever. Not even dead. Which, briefly, is when we stop performing and our successors start reviewing us.

Safety means being at peace, at least with oneself, and Jim wasn't. Hence his volatility, hence the danger. There's no doubt that's what those years with Maria—right to the very end, to 7.45 on the morning of his birthday—were safe for Jim. But they were safe at her expense. He was safe in his feelings for her, in his own love. Wasn't that enough?

No. The very old are selfish the way Jim was. They don't mean to be selfish: their present little fragment of life is all they have left. Bit by bit they get separated from their selves, from their memories, from what makes them human; and without memory, what anything really means is gone. It happened to my Mother and to Jim's Mother. All my Mother had left was sensation: cold hands, remembered slights, sticky candy she once had, patches of sun, and the conviction that the hands she saw on her lap were not her own;

as Jim's Mother had Jake's hand in hers which she took to mean, come on out and play.

I never knew if my Mother was with me; I suspect none of the Mothers knew if Jim was with them. Did he recognize them? Was the "you" that lay with him the same "you" from years ago, or from earlier on in the same evening when he was talking so clear and brilliant—exactly as clear and brilliant as his startling blue eyes—that you could not, I could not, help but love him.

Jim didn't lack memory. Often he just didn't connect. Or he connected only when he wanted to. Old people have outlived the things we think give life significance, so they're naturally egotistical and needy for the basics: food, warmth, light. He adored Maria; she was all those things and more—food, warmth, light and reassurance. Did he really know who she was?

For many people, even me, adoration is sufficient. Apparently for Maria it was not. She couldn't understand how he was one thing one minute and another the next.

It was money, of course. Take their trip to Mexico, not to be compared with mine.

It went wrong over money. She wasn't responsible for his wallet being stolen. She wasn't responsible for the money Lou sucked out of him. She'd offered to go back to work, Frank said that was fine. That wasn't the point. Jim had grown used to being the kind of man who had money, the kind of money that made it possible for him to buy her a car or take her with him on trips, to pull her by the hand through the London boutiques and pick out her clothes. However, once the divorce from Lou became final, he no longer had that kind of money. He made a lot, he spent freely, Lou took what she could: school fees, moving expenses, trips to see his children or for them to see him. Mexico showed this all up. His wallet had been stolen and all they had with them was the few grubby pesos she had in her purse and the twenty dollar bill she always shoved in her shoe.

They were on the ferry by the time he found out his wallet

was missing. Standing by the rear rail she watched him frantically search his sweat-stained jacket. His wallet wasn't there. "Look," she said on the ferry—twenty minutes too long a ride—"Bad things happen. There are alternatives." She said it calmly. She was always calm. They needn't stand squinting at the bright green shore of the river and Alvarado that they were drawing away from. They didn't need the bright blue sky and the crazy sun that beat down on their heads, or to hold dirty bowls of worn little clams in a hot sauce, a very hot sauce, in their hands. Nor try to eat them with their fingers, which the pepper burned: though she'd wanted to try everything at least once. She missed her baby, left with her mother, Eleanor. She wasn't responsible for his mood and there was no need for it. They had alternatives, like going home. She liked to be clean, and wasn't, often feeling polluted as his babies leaked down her thighs. She had a headache, she felt car-sick, she might be pregnant again. Pregnant in a short little red silk dress he'd bought her on the way down—in the market place in Orizaba just before the high central plateau fell down towards the sea at Vera Cruz.

He spent all his time in Orizaba lecturing her about Porfirio Diaz—Dictators seemed to come to mind when he was in one of his moods. He looked as he often did, his mind crowded with thieves and pimps, pulque and Mexican vomit, cops who'd put the bite, the *mordida*, on him: as though he'd gladly smite his enemies, all of them; watch the little flower of blood form smack in the middle of their copper foreheads, over their flat noses, under those ebullient curls, over those lax, cynical, not-very-bright eyes. Oh, the details of Jim's angers! And he didn't even know yet his wallet was gone! Yet, after a litany of Mexican caciques he'd gone on to tell her about our trip and that miserable *indio* with his brains leaked out on the highway. Out of malevolence, was what she was made to understand. He couldn't get himself killed somewhere else?

Alternatives, eh? he said now that the wallet was found to be gone. "That's just dandy. My wallet, my cards, my driving license." Was it in Orizaba or later, in Vera Cruz?

She said, "It must have been in that awful *café* in Vera Cruz.

You didn't have to show them how much money you had in your wallet. You were asking for trouble."

"Sure. I ask for trouble. I want to get robbed."

Well, yes he did. Like a man diving into a whirlpool. Bad had to get worse.

He wanted to know why had they gone into the café in the first place, and she thought about that. They'd arrived in Vera Cruz hot and stopped in the first hotel they found and gone straight to bed. The heat was a hot hand that felt you up, that got to know your skin. Their room gave on the main plaza. They'd been close then. She thought she'd eased him out of his political kick. Afterwards, half asleep, dreamy, she remembered being mesmerized by the pains-taking wheeling of the fan in the ceiling. Then there had been a silly quarrel—she should have known better than to ask just then—when he wouldn't let her call home in Pawtucket to see how their little son was. They were on holiday, damnit. And she'd said, things had to be attended to. They only got worse if you didn't.

"It was hot," she said. "You wanted to eat." She could tell Jim was edgy. He took her hand impatiently before she'd even brushed out her hair: straight from a lukewarm shower. He kept pulling her behind him: this restaurant looked lousy, that bar had no life.

"Let's go back to the hotel," she said. "I'm really not hungry."

"Why do you want to go back? I promised I'd take you to Palenque."

She could have said, as I did, that she didn't belong here.

"In here," he said, tugging her into a small cantina behind the hotel. Why there? It was late, towards midnight, and it looked like a rough crowd inside. He sat her down at a little round table near the door. Dark Mexican eyes looked her over, butchered Mexican hair gleamed under the sparse bulbs along the walls. He went over to the bar and muttered something to the barman, came back with two beers and a shot-glass of tequila. He drank seriously. The barman brought over some hard, tasteless cheese, the heel of a loaf of bread, a few olives on a saucer and hot peppers.

When he had got himself drunk enough, the locals stared

at the bearded gringo trying to dance by himself among the scatter-rugs of mangy dogs, the high, dusty boots of the locals, gliding by the old men clacking dominoes at their table and the *maricones* at the bar (definitely not the tourist season), spitting out long sentences about his *mujer*, the first one, and what a rip-off marriage was, emptying out his wallet on the plastic-topped table: "All this, *todo eso*, and more, every month! *Coño!*"

She tried to get him out of there: if that was his idea of a good time it wasn't hers. But he would pull her up from the table and take a few steps on the floor with her. In these moods he was hard to refuse: how would he react? She tried to make a joke of it: it wasn't her kind of dancing, please. The music sounded remote, the mariachis were out on the plaza with the stunted shrubs their room looked down on. He didn't stop. He was showing her off around the floor, she could look up into his hard-set face or up from his arms into gold teeth and bandit moustaches. They'd had enough of the gringo. Now they'd like a little fun of their own. "Please. Let's go home."

"We're going to Palenque."

The Mexicans pressed him out. They danced him out was how Maria remembered it. All men, and the *maricones* who had been at the bar, pretending to grab for her while Jim backed to the door, reaching over Jim's shoulder, grabbing the red dress, while a piebald dog had its hem in its teeth. He didn't remember. That was where he left his wallet. She heard their laughter out in the street, punctuated by the click-clack of dominos.

He was still angry the next morning, digging into his trouser pocket and peeling off hundred-peso notes, slapping them on the counter, then climbing into their rental car and hurtling south with the sea on their left.

Now the ferry drifted in towards the far shore. He had his engine running hard. He said the car had a sticky accelerator; all these rental companies were shit. He banged into the car in front, bumpers tangling, noise like scaffolding collapsing. There was an argument instead of an earthquake. Cars emptied out. Her window was up on faces that peered in and might crash through the glass and spread all over her. Some were laughing, teeth brilliant; some jeered through puffy lips; some pounded on the windscreen. It was last night all over again. The clams stirred uneasily in her belly. Six, ten or twelve men jumped up on the bumper of the car in front of them and, released, Jim gunned the engine and swerved by at the foot of the ramp.

For two hundred k's he didn't say a word.

Surreptitiously, she double-checked in her bag. The passports they still had—she'd taken care of them. But the wallet was gone. What would he do when they ran out of gas? He must have been calculating, thinking up something, maybe (if they could get there) holing up in a good hotel in Merida or before, calling American Express. Whatever he was thinking he couldn't say it. Couldn't admit he'd been a fool. Couldn't consider her.

She looked across at him. His face was still white hot, then red hot. She said, "We can call up Frank, he'll help us out."

He jammed on the brakes. Two cars sped by them. Then he reached across her, opened the door and pushed her out. Mad, mad, as her brothers kept telling her. He was going to show her Palenque and the ruins of the Maya come hell or high water. "I promised you," he said, the flat of his hand on her shoulder.

The macadam was hot, she stumbled, scratched her knee (it bled) and the wind sent stinging dirt flying into the wound. The worst part was knowing how much he loved her. It meant there was nothing she could do about whatever was wrong with him. She was a bandage that wound round his wounds. And of course what had happened could be, would be, forgiven when five minutes later, crestfallen, deflated, Jim turned back and rescued her, took her in his coppery, beautiful, muscled arms. Forgiven with rue, sweet kisses and many promises.

Then in clouds of evening mosquitoes, the sky afloat with dog-fights, the pyramids would be climbed at Palenque, a night spent among archaeologists on camp beds, coffee at the first plaza they came to. A test in the *farmacía* ("Is not entirely reliable," the girl said, but Maria knew) across the street had her pregnant again, and he did fly her back to Chicago after a luxurious weekend in Merida ("Can we afford this?") in which they played tennis and swam and got their new credit card hand-delivered.

He loved her. His damned joy, she said, the way he looked at her. It made the air sing, rippled in waves. She knew what it was, he told her often enough: you could lie in her arms and never feel a thing, that was their healing power. Those arms had a little dark fur, like that at the roots on a rabbit or a cat. That was why for years he felt less whole after she'd gone. The anger would rise. Natasha couldn't solve it, it was sending Francine on her way.

Kneeling at night by the bedside, her prayer-book bound in ivory-colored plastic, she said, silent, "Lord, joy is deeply disturbing. I'm bound to him by his joy. How can I deprive him of that?"

She felt he was making a vast mistake about her. She was just an "ordinary girl" from an ordinary family; she didn't want to be celebrated, feasted, adored. She didn't even want to be loved that much.

Which wasn't quite true. She had wanted that much, the night of the Sonny Liston fight; she could tell she'd given him something he'd never had. A clever man and a well-hidden one, he couldn't conceal that. But oh, sometimes, the tedium of that, of his encroaching hands and wily talk, of new clothes (a cute tennis dress with lace) and a new racket, new balls at every set they played in the dusk. There were times when she longed, and plotted, to get away from it. For simplicity. Not to have aroused so many expectations.

What stayed with her when she was back in Chicago, was the violence. Her dead Indian. She wanted to know how I'd seen the incident, what it meant to me, because she didn't think Jim had the slightest idea how close he had been to getting them both killed by those awful people.

I said something like, "In the movies or in photographs dead people look surprised. Mexicans don't look surprised at all; they look like they expect to be dead."

Had I really looked at the dead man? I got blood on my shoe?

She had a brother who was a cop and she'd told him about my trip. He said that what Jim did, fleeing the scene, was normal, anybody would have.

"Down there it was scary," Maria said. "Jim acted like a Mexican."

9

Around the time my Mother died, at the end of the 'Sixties, I used the money she left—she was a lifelong scrounger and saver—and bought my house out here. That put Jim and Maria geographically far away. I didn't see much of them. I know their third baby was unanticipated, and like everyone else who knew them, I heard talk that Jim was planning a surprise wedding on her thirtieth birthday, when he and Maria would have been together a whole ten years. But on the few occasions I went into town to see Father Pzyrnik and saw Maria after church, I found her ever more bemused, more speculative, more inward-turning, puzzling out the pieces of her life by concentrating on her babies' lives: herself all milk; he daily more zealous, as one is with desperate cases.

I also heard that she'd begun to have little niggling "accidents" (or so she called them): tripping, falling, dropping things. Nothing that she took seriously—she who was always so healthy! Nonetheless, at Igor's urging, she underwent a battery of tests—with inconclusive results. Jim now says it may have been an arrhythmia. They didn't really know. Perhaps it was just exhaustion. The exhaustion of keeping up appearances.

It wasn't just the money, though that was something she talked about a lot. Lou had set herself up in a remote part of Extramadura in Spain, and the tax on his marriage to Lou constantly multiplied. No doubt Jim's carelessness contributed. The only time we met downtown for lunch (I still got about in those days, and we met in a Chinese restaurant by the University, a place she was sure Jim would not think of eating), I thought she was really looking for advice. Or maybe reassurance.

She wasn't sure that what he was doing to her was really "normal."

"What do you mean?"

Awkwardly, she talked about his intrusiveness. The way he was "taking her over." It had always been a bit that way, she said, but it was getting worse. "I wondered—I'm sorry to talk to you about this sort of thing, but I don't know who else to ask. I mean is it normal that a man thinks you belong to him?"

It seemed that whether naked or dressed in his gifts (how could she refuse them?), he watched. She felt watched in her shower and when she wanted to go to sleep. Before breakfast and after. In or out of an apron while she labored on a *crème brulé:* "As though I'm to be available at all times."

Even with her legs raised in stirrups in the delivery room, he'd watched. Later she lay exhausted and asleep, new daughter by her side. Every time she woke up he was still watching. When they brought in breakfast the morning after, he took her picture when she asked him to take the baby's.

In a way she was ashamed to say these things to me. I asked her if she'd told him to stop. She said she'd recently said, "What would you do if I left you?" and he'd answered, "You never would."

"Would you?"

"I'm not sure. I wish I knew."

I try not to talk about those times with Jim—I know they hurt him deeply. But when I insisted, he said: "You women are all bloody marvelous liars. I asked Maria all the time if she loved me, was she happy? I was going to marry her for Christ's sake! She never said she wasn't. I asked the same thing of Francine. I told her how much I loved her, and she said, 'I love you too, Jim.' Well, are you all liars?"

I said: "Only when we have to be."

There was also this business of Jim bursting into tears. All the Mothers bring it up. Must be from his Mother, they say: a sign of his instability, his failure to accommodate to ordinary life. Lou once told Milo that Jim regularly got the weeps in the fall, at the smell of burning leaves, at earth turned over; Maria said that music did it to him, or the movies; sometimes sex, said Natasha. Judicious, cool Francine said tears came when he finally realized he wasn't going to get what he wanted. Francine doesn't believe in histrionics. Life was about problem-solving: she'd solved two—Jim and Marriage—and she'd be o.k., thank you very much. After four hundred sit-ups her muscle-tone was just fine. You get on with life.

"Francine's not cold," said Heda, fond of her. "She's crisp, like clean air. She could take Jim to the cleaners; she doesn't."

"All right. Not cold. Rational. Wary of feeling. But men don't cry. At least not in my family. Can you imagine Milo crying? At a funeral even, he'd be button-holing the grave-diggers."

Heda and I had a good laugh over that. But it was no joke. Jim knew the tears were in him. Like a faulty valve in his heart. Recently he said they were just another sign he was growing into his Mother: who also had love and no place to put it.

More than anything, Maria was bewildered. Was she supposed to pay up by filling all the voids in Jim's life?

He wept and got up in the middle of the night. When the baby woke up, Maria found him with his head on his arms asleep at the kitchen table, dregs of wine beside him dry in the glass. Which was her table; it was where she paid what bills she could. "I can't go on like this," she said.

Jim remembers the walls of their apartment were hung with lone riders on horses, windmills, and brief white houses drawn or painted by the kids. "I got to thinking of them as 'Lou's kids' as opposed to 'Maria's'." Or poems in Spanish. The place stank of wax crayons and absence. o.k., so the hall was littered with fresh toddlers on trikes, and he loved his kids, but it went through his mind all the time, he said—how long would they be around? They might be blown away by the lightest breeze. It had happened with the first six: like Mrs. Voyjtila's cats they'd been spirited away. Mothers owned the rights to supraterrestrial flight: as though every day were All Hallow's Eve and the Mothers could swoop down and seize the living. Like his mother in her cigar box, beckoning him down for a kiss: Just a little kiss, my darling.

If the children he now had with Maria were out of sight it meant something had happened to them.

Meanwhile, she broke a leg skating, and I only heard about it six months later. Then she misjudged how hot the water was in the baby's bath.

In the playground, while Maria was holding the year-old baby under her chubby thighs for a quick pee, their firstborn was bitten by a dog. Whose dog? Jim wanted to know. What had she been doing?

A dog, she said, it was nothing serious. Fanny was peeing. Then she heard growling.

Who was the dog with?

Some Mother.

What did she look like?

Stuck-up, Maria said. She wore a fur coat and her little boy was in a sailor blouse.

The next day, carrying the pistol Frank kept in his desk in his parka pocket next to his house key—reassuringly normal—Jim shot the dog dead, close up. Right there, on the asphalt, under the empty trees. No one else was there. He didn't tell her anything about it for weeks. He shot a dog. How did he know it was the right dog? He wanted to kill a dog.

With Frank one day in court she sat and tore all the depositions in a case into tiny pieces.

Frank sent her home to Pawtucket for a month with her kids.

As she had from the Dominican Republic, Lou now wrote

regularly from Spain. She always ended with "regards" to Maria. "I hear she's not well," Lou wrote. "I hope it's not serious."

Jim called Pawtucket to tell Maria that. Any excuse would have done to talk to her. "Why does she do that?" Maria asked. "She must hate me."

"Mothers stick together and details kill," he replied. "How is everyone?"

"Everyone's fine."

"I guess I don't mean much to those kids any more. I've missed the last baby tooth and the first crush."

Maria said to tell Lou she was all right.

"When are you coming back?"

"Soon."

He cried ahead of time. Before bad things happened. His clock was set to autumn: when the last leaves would be shed.

Except that she left in the spring: just when hope rises.

10

Francine's current depression, Jim says, has to do with its being eight years since Rory died. Thanksgiving was upon us, but what was there to be thankful for? Since she hated Thanksgiving anyway—regularly serving up things like her rabbit *moutarde* instead of turkey—this year Francine was away in Italy with the Kid. Who wanted to see his sister. When I see him out on the street playing ball and talking to himself, it's his dead playmate Rory (the one he never got to play with) he's talking to. Occasionally I see him with an odd little dark girl I don't know (someone on the road's summer grandchild?); they hold hands and whisper. A year or two more and they could be Jim and I.

From Belfort (where Francine stopped to see her parents) they drove to Pisa and then up to their village which Jake only just remembered: that was the wall he used to walk along to the caffé that was where the dog drowned in the flood, caught in the mill-race.

The mill-house was overgrown but smoke rose from its chimney and, in what had been the garden Francine had created, four cars were penned like cattle. The gate down to the house was padlocked. No one stirred. Jake chattered to cheer his *Maman*, and when they got to the cemetery found the grave, brought the ladder, placed the flowers. But the wooden angel Jake had brought on their last trip had been stolen from Aurora's grave. Jake spent the rest of their holiday collecting, on different beaches, bits of sea-glass, all of special colors, for Rory to play with. As though he'd be back soon.

This is the kind of loss I can understand. And early knowledge of death is a good thing. Death taketh away. Because it's a fact and you have to live with it, you can.

But Maria's imperturbable leaving? It happened thirty years ago now, and you can't offer angels or sea-glass to the still living. That's why losing someone you love is worse than their dying. There's no All Souls' Day for the split.

A few days before his birthday, Maria said, "You remember what I asked you? What would you do if I left? You wouldn't even consider the question."

"When was that?"

"It doesn't matter when. Do you remember?"

"Sure. What was I supposed to answer, my love? That there'd be dancing in the streets?"

"What you thought."

"And what did I say?"

"You said I'd never leave."

As usual, Jim hadn't been paying attention. He reckoned what Maria had said was just a passing remark. But as Milo said, "When a woman makes a remark like that, there's always a purpose." He should have added that men like Jim don't listen because they don't want to hear.

Pretty recently, in the first early spring after the third baby and when Maria came back from Pawtucket, they had moved to a farmhouse about an hour inland from Chicago. Maria seemed more or less as she'd always been, but Igor had told her to rest as much as she could. Above all, she ought to stop brooding about how her mother was losing track of herself and Joe had been forced to send her away. That's not what you're suffering from, Igor said. You need to stop running to keep up with Jim. And to Jim he said, Maria needs peace and quiet. So Jim had scraped together enough to put money down on a farmhouse in which they would live happily ever after.

The house stood on a plot of level land and had trees on three sides of it, mainly pine. Old snow was melting, the ground was spongy, and rain blew into his face when he went to the mailbox for the paper. Long before the sun was due up he'd risen and, while listening to hear whether any of the children were stirring (their furtive morning sounds), stood in the door to look back at Maria. She still slept like a child, one hand tucked under her cheek, the other draped over the edge of the bed where the night-light burned. Her lips were parted; the sheets sprawled about her hardly moved. That deep, steady breath—like the gleam of the sewing machine that stood on its own table by the window—was all constancy. It contained the memory of the night before. His *Fortuna*.

Downstairs, he laid out the children's cereal and then read the paper. The smell of coffee filled the kitchen. It was Jim's neutral hour, the one that belonged to himself. He needs this time; when the world wakes up, he's long awake. Anywhere in the world. Even when the two of us were in Mexico, when I'd come down from our room, deathly afraid someone would talk to me on the way in Spanish, worried that he might disapprove of the way I looked or what I wore, he would see me with surprise: as though he'd forgotten I was there.

Now it was Maria who came down, and it was his birthday. On the table, next to the morning paper, was Tyler v. Federated Plastics, a complex worker's comp case which Jim lost. He'd just taken up his pencil to mark passages of the judge's directions—when he heard her on the stairs. ("Negligence is a vast subject," he told me. "I should know.") She wore a terry-cloth robe and she said, "I'm leaving."

At first he didn't understand, and the telephone on the wall rang. The kids in Spain wanted to say "Happy Birthday." Lou had given them a minute each. What had he got for his birthday, what did Maria give him, how were they going to celebrate, had he got their parcels? All this time Maria was sipping the coffee he'd made. Expressionless. But not in the way she usually was before her coffee. In the way you might be if you didn't want to notice someone else was in the room.

"Love you, Papa," the last one said.

He put down the telephone and looked at Maria. From upstairs he heard Fanny, the youngest, babbling unintelligible words to her brothers. She thought she was having a conversation, but though she had intention, she had no language. What he saw in Maria was her implacability.

I wish I'd had her guts with my Greek. But I didn't have to. He resolved the matter in his own way. Once he'd gone, I fled. I'd started drinking to give him substance, then I drank to escape myself, and the memory of that year. Maria didn't need to flee: she'd already gone.

Jim looked around, bewildered. What happened now? Fanny needed her diapers changed. There was a whole early morning ahead.

Maria said, perfunctorily, "Thanks for the coffee. I'm going upstairs to get dressed. I'm being picked up at nine. I've made all the arrangements." Picked up? Going where? What arrangements? "You'd better see to the little one."

It was quick. Like the *estocada* they give bulls in the ring. I'm all for the coup de grâce myself, but thirty years later Jim's still bleeding. It was her seeming pliancy, I tell him. She wasn't what he thought. Not the child-bride snatched up into felicity on the wings of the 'Sixties, but the severe judge of her own weakness, which was that pliancy. "If she gives you a chance to argue, to plead in court, she's lost."

She had thought out how and when she would undo what she had so freely and pleasurably done.

Maybe Jim had thoughts of pleading his love, the children. That too she foresaw. Going back up the stairs she turned around and said, "There's somebody else. I'm in love with him and he wants to marry me."

That did it. Happy Birthday.

Later, Fanny was on his hip, chortling. The boys had been quieted with ice-cream on their cereal: with a promise of cartoons if they were good. He warmed Fanny's bottle, who kept saying "Ma-ma-ma-ma." The boys didn't ask. Not yet. This was a weekend morning, so she must be sleeping. It was when he went back upstairs to change Fanny that he glanced out the window and saw Maria walking up to the mailbox as he had a couple of hours ago. She carried a single, small suitcase, and it struck him that it was her suitcase. Probably the first suitcase she'd ever had. It was the one he'd strapped to the back of his car in Maine. It reminded him of Lou's suitcase that she'd had in Springfield, on that last night.

He thought: she's not taking much with her. Not her children, not her glad rags.

He held Fanny's tiny hand and had it wave at her mother, but Maria didn't look back. When he put Fanny down on their bed (he could still feel a trace of warmth in it from Maria's body) he opened up the cupboards (painted a horrid, shiny green, must do something about that, he said to himself) where Maria kept the diapers. The diapers were there, but nothing else. Nothing at all. Same story in the bathroom. Even in the laundry basket. Such premeditation.

He ran to the bathroom window just in time to see a dirty gray car (Was it a Dodge? Had he seen it before?) pull away. He could make out Maria in the front seat, who did not turn her head to look back, but he could not see the driver. Who was presumably the man she said she loved.

A note on the refrigerator door reminded him to pick up his birthday cake at Marion's Bake Shop.

Already Maria wasn't very clear in his memory. Only how she had been at first. Yet it seemed she hadn't really changed in the ten years they'd been together. Her body had grown imperceptibly with the children, but not in any way that changed her appearance. He'd left no mark on her.

He called the Fonseca's once or twice, to find out if they knew where she was. They said they didn't. This didn't surprise him either. She'd taken up with him without their knowing; she'd brought him into their house almost defiantly; and now she could go off without so much as a word.

Jim is simply a fact in my life. I heard from Otto that Maria was gone, that the farmhouse was sold, and I expected to hear from him. I suppose that's my role in life. But I can't pick up his pieces. I can listen to him, I can't do anything else for him.

I didn't at all like how he took Maria's departure. Least of all the gloss he put on it. That what women give, they take away. And (from the first letter I got, in mid-summer after her going) that nowadays they gave less and took more: "They can take away your breath or take away your life." He just wanted an explanation, and from experience I knew it wasn't from an earnest desire to learn from his mistakes.

Thirty years have gone by and he's still arguing with her. As with his mother, with Lou, and now with Francine. Considering, that is, that Natasha Gilpin was the only one who didn't (in the ultimate sense), fall for him.

Recently, he said, comparing Maria to Francine: "I had Maria in my arms the night before. By morning I had just words. Few words. The first thing a guy does is ask, what did I do to deserve this? And now Francine wants to know, what have I done to deserve her?" For as Jim said, Francine might have considered her marriage her own failure, but to him and everyone else, he'd forgotten his good fortune and he was the one who'd failed her.

Nothing Maria ever did was modern. New clothes, new music yes. But an old-fashioned girl, very upright. He wouldn't have loved her if she had been modern in the way Francine was. For Francine is a modern woman. He'd tried the other kind, then he tried Francine.

I don't see how you can blame all these mistakes on bad luck. I also guess how lucky I am not to have been one of those mistakes. Supposing I'd had more dress sense, wanted to travel, and had been able to welcome him into my bed? And hadn't got rid of our child?

II

Ritchie Urquhart ("ER-cart" is how you say it) was as soon as possible Maria's husband, and Jim had seen the Dodge before. The man had been to an outdoor Sunday lunch the first summer they had the farm-house and while the "Lou" kids were there. Maria had said he was someone she'd met in Chicago, and now he was taking his vacation "in the neighborhood."

Jim thought he was a nice enough guy. Before he drove off (the Dodge) that Sunday, Urquhart said, "You're a lucky man." It was a very conventional thing to say, like "You have a lovely wife, three lovely children, a handsome, a good, a safe house, a normal life."

Who wouldn't want that? Jim said, "Don't I know it."

Anything else?

Sure. " 'Ritch' said how he spelled his name got him laughed at when he was in school in Wheeling, West Virginia. The whole family were miners, but 'Ritch' wasn't. He was short, soft like sponge-cake, and gentle. Turned out he was some sort of preacher fellow."

Just what Maria saw in him Jim couldn't say. "When I look back, all I see is her. The way she ran about pleasing everyone, the kids especially, her legs kicking sideways the way they always had."

Oh yes, there was also the fact that Urquhart was married and had two children of his own. It seemed to Jim that he had talked about them quite freely.

The main thing was that the little ones shouldn't miss their mother. He wondered if he could still find Lou's Hondurans, the ones his mother had dismissed for going about in bare feet. With Fanny in a kind of basket, while Otto and Heda, who hadn't any children, looked after the boys for the afternoon, he went by Holy Child.

Father Pzyrnik was long dead, and the new priest said he'd pray for him and ask around if there were any woman to look after three young kids. The innocent way Father Soares talked led Jim to think the priest thought Maria was dead. Maybe he hadn't understood, because no woman was found. He moved back into town, and did the job himself.

A whole summer went by before Maria called and said she'd like to see the children. Then she came alone every Sunday and took them out for a walk. She was very subdued on those occasions, as if recovering from an illness. Maybe she was. She had cut her hair short and wore a chain-store skirt and top. She was sorting things out, she said, living alone, making a little money working in a drug store. "His wife's having a baby." She meant Urquhart's wife.

Ritchie was leaving his wife when she was bearing his child? Maria didn't say anything, but Jim could tell she was discomfited. "When's she having this baby?"

"This week sometime. Any day now. She's at the Baptist Hospital."

It was a crazy thing to go there. It wasn't Jim's business, then or ever. All Jim ever said was, she ought to know.

"Are you the father?" the volunteer asked at reception.

"A, not the." She looked at him as if to say he shouldn't be joking. "I'm a relative," he said.

She ran her finger down a list. "It's a baby girl."

He went up five flights then down two long corridors. He thought: at least she'd had the baby and everything was all right. That would make it easier to tell her.

Once by her bedside he had second thoughts. She was such a skinny thing, Belle. You could have lost her in the pillows piled up. All ribs, bone and spine, then the soft part in the middle, which was wrapped up in a huge diaper. Her skin was sallow and unhealthy, her hair long, dark, uncurled and sweaty, her lips bloodless and swollen. She must have been biting on them throughout the delivery.

"Who the hell are you?" she asked. Actually too exhausted to listen to an answer if he'd given one. Nor did she say anything more for several minutes. Then it was to ask for water. She pulled herself up on her elbows.

"Find my glasses," she said. "I can't make you out. You a doctor?"

He handed them to her and she put them on and stared at him briefly, without any great interest.

"I need a cigarette," she said. "You got one?"

Now that he looked at her more carefully, he noticed bruises all over her: on her arms, on the one thigh that escaped the sheets and dangled over the side of her cot. She said, "Yeah, I know, you're not allowed to smoke in here."

He handed her a cigarette and lit it for her. A nurse who came in looked as if she wanted to slap the cigarette right out of her mouth. And Belle seemed to be expecting the nurse to do just that.

The words went round and round in his head: how he regretted to be the one to tell her, but he thought she ought to know, her husband and his wife, and when he got to that point he stopped.

The bruises on her were in various stages of yellow, purple and messy brown. He thought, perhaps she likes it, being beaten. Urquhart wouldn't do that, Maria wouldn't know about it. Illogically, that made him even angrier. The words just came out, in the right order, the way he'd thought them. Belle stared at him wild-eyed: he must be crazy to say such a thing to her.

Then another nurse came in, bearing a bundle wrapped in a soft pink blanket which she laid on Belle's thin chest, on her really tiny tits. The face that peeped out of the blanket was black.

Belle took another drag on her cigarette and said: "I don't know what your problem is, but I've got to be getting on with this, don't you think?"

Part four
Natasha

Desire is physical, as is sex,
and I've never understood people elevating the latter
to some cosmic and deeply emotional experience.

Sheer fantasy, had to be, Jim said. Fantasy which everyone has but nobody shares. Except people who mistake it for what's real. Off the top of his head, girls' knickers for boys, worn warm and hidden. Vegetable sex in girls, intrusions everywhere, rotting excitement, and an ice-box full of gourds, cukes and outlandish carrots. Unsexy fantasies. Men get off dreaming they run the world: it's Red Square every day, they're on the balcony and everyone's cheering. Millions buy into lotteries and spend what they haven't won on what they think is "the good life." Killers dream of knives, mystics go for God. Shut the door, darken the room, drop the blinds. If you don't, fantasy runs up against reality. Very destructive.

The fat man was back, he said. Sunny Farber's fantasy was that he'd slept with Jim's wife, the high, haughty, ultra-chaste Francine.

Where? When? How? He wanted to know. Long ago, last week, last night? In what undress or clothing? In that hotel above the restaurant where Francine brokers her future with the one-armed lady in red, her boss Myra Cox?

True, there had been a thickish new gold chain about her slender neck, the sort of thing vulgar men give their temps after they've left town. It could mean anything. It probably meant nothing.

Sunny's way of introducing the subject had been to say, airily, that he was thinking of renting an apartment in Chicago ("I have plenty of business here"). He'd asked for Jim's advice, discussed prices, looked around the old house sniffily—it wasn't his sort of place. Then he said, no wonder Francine feels stir-crazy this far away.

Sunny who didn't stop there, was already on tricky ground. He said, "You should have stuck with your mother. You need a Mother." He emphasized the word. "Someone who looks after you."

What did that have to do with the apartment he was looking for?

Jim kept staring at Sunny. The fat man's head bobbed busily as he talked, and his puffy chest expanded and contracted. It made Jim think of pigeon-grease. Pigeon-grease shining through thin hair, light refracting in selected spots, like lusters on a neglected chandelier.

Jim called up Milo and invited himself over for dinner (there was no one to cook for at the big, old house). Prudence squatted gracefully on the floor with the new baby. He couldn't wait to tell them this malarkey about Sunny and Francine. Unfortunately, Milo wasn't much help, artists being absorbed in their own distresses. Milo was in a jokey, not-really-listening mood. He told his old pal Jim abut meeting an old geezer in a Miami drug-store where they both took breakfast. The old geezer said—He was "a pouchy old bachelor with Madras silk around his straw hat, wide as a cummerbund"—that the only sex he'd ever had in his life was with the wives of his friends. "So I thought to myself (said Milo) why is this old geezer telling me this?"

"No you didn't," Jim said. "The first thought was, has he had my wife?"

"It's simpler than that. He said, 'You're a big-time writer, I could share my experiences with you.'"

194

"For a consideration?"

"Certainly not. He was too lazy to write it up for himself."

"I can't stop imagining Francine crushed under all that fat."

"…He was from Skokie," said Milo, continuing the trail of his own thought.

"How do you think I feel?"

Now Milo turned his attention to Jim: "So…What does Francine say?"

Shocked, Jim said: "Surely you don't think I'm going to ask her."

If Milo did think so, he didn't say so. In times of complaint, how useful are even the oldest friends? Any more than today's doctors? You offer doctors a problem full of intriguing possibilities and they say, "Sorry, we don't know very much about this condition of yours…" This while they sit in white coats at their desks—their unshined shoes creep out below—poke at your pain, consult the computer, offer dazzling tests. Friends, too, listen, which is another form of auscultation. But they too don't want to take sides; they prefer to straddle life and death.

Anyway, we could all see it. Milo was growing old around the edges. His hearing-aid was hidden in a drawer under socks. The death in Jim's heart had to yield to the death-around-the-corner in Milo's. Chasms lay between Milo's thoughts. "I was saying something, what was it?" The Old Pal was blurring, or was it other people (like himself) who were blurring, who no longer mattered that much, who sat there in Milo's Grand Rapids-furnished study, as stationary as the old black-and-white TV in the corner, snowing?

Each time he saw Milo now, his old pal was casting off. Not his body, which was astonishingly resilient—to a diet of pills and things-that-couldn't-be-eaten, to casual infections, to troubles in the esophagus and heart—but from the oldest port-side of all, the troubled Self. Memory came up clogged with seaweed and barnacle; the anchor-chain clanked.

Milo said: "I've had enough of myself. I've said what I have to say, I'm just adrift."

Sunny sat in the kitchen of the big old house as if he owned it. As if Jim no longer had a right to be there. Pointing out that the Kid's ball-bouncing was no longer to be heard. In between, he cast occasional sidelong glances at the walls, so encumbered (some might think) with the accumulated wreckage of Jim's life—"Your brother looks more like your father, more forthright…"

One insult after another. The rage Jim felt was the same rage that Francine so feared: "And the Kid's scared of you too," she'd taken to saying. "He never knows what you're going to do or say next, how you're going to react."

"Of course the forthright stuff, you know, the tough American," Sunny was saying about Jim's father, Jacob, "is the way he thought of himself. It was all for show. Hetty had him by the balls, he'd never had sex like that. She took him to the cleaners, flushed his system. That's what new wives do for you. You look at your old man up there on your wall with a slouch hat and what do you see? A man who didn't know what he wanted."

Sunny's patter was outrageous, but Jim couldn't respond. Not if Francine…

The very idea was even more outrageous. It was momentarily blocked by a brief vision of his father at Marion in the lawn championships, his racket gleaming. What was Sunny on about?

He wasn't on about anything. He was simply insidious. He was a large presence too, but of a different kind from Jacob's. Jacob was angular, all sharp edges. If Sunny had been a loaf of bread, he would have been a tribute to the power of yeast, whose asexual warmth and dividing, budding, filament-making, produced such a dangerous opulence. Where would it stop?

Then Jim remembered, also from his Philadelphia days, a breathless girl, pale and pigtailed, her eyes hidden behind great, round spectacles, who told him how her aunt's house (somewhere in Virginia) had been lifted off its foundation by yeast she'd left rising in her cellar. Maybe Sunny would just keep expanding and lift this house off its foundations.

Then Sunny was getting up, refusing another coffee from the

espresso machine, and taking a picture of Francine proprietarily off the wall. "She looks real cute here," he said. "Though even then I don't think she'd rate highly in the sack."

"What would you know about it?" It was when she'd grown bangs to hide the scar from the accident, when all around her skin was luminous and set off her eyes. "Put it back," Jim said.

"It's just a photograph. Not the lady herself."

"I know that."

"As for what I know about her, why don't you ask her?"

"Put it back." Because if he didn't, Jim would knead him back into his original shape and he'd have to start expanding all over again. "Put it back and get the hell out of here."

"You never asked her about me?"

He'd heard Francine say, a year ago now, "a Mr. Farber called." Nothing more than that. No special intonation in her voice. "Just what are you trying to say?" Jim asked the fat man.

"I'm pointing out you don't even think it's possible. Francine and me. Francine and anyone. You don't think she has a life. Just like your father, I guess: so goddam self-absorbed you don't even see what's going on, the way he didn't see Hetty was having it off, what Robbie was doing with company money. I offer you a deal, you don't even see it."

Sunny said things like that without anger, the California way. In small talk. The way he just "dropped in" as though he smelled the BBQ going in the back yard and wanted to say hello, walking up to the house with those well-oiled balls of his feet making it seem he glided up the front path, up the stairs by the front door. Not necessarily thinking Jim wanted to see him. No, as though he couldn't turn him away. No one turns away money, which was what he appeared to be offering.

Fate walks up on you like that. That's why Jim hated going to the hospital to have his EKG. You go there with some silly little organic spasm and come out of the tests with cancer. What did you get when Sunny walked in through the door?

I suppose his point of view was completely antiseptic. You

looked through a microscope and what you saw was what you saw. The tumor wasn't in you. Most likely Sunny thought, where was common sense and rationality in this man? Women were all on a game of some sort; they gambled with their assets. You could have any of them if you had money or power and a modicum of persistence. So what made this old-fashioned Catholic would-be macho think Francine was any different? He'd come here to help. Several times. At his own expense. Jim's brother was dead, now Jim was the goddam heir. Without Jim the whole business would never get sorted out. Hell, there was enough there for everybody! You couldn't shake the man's belief in profit.

"Who's Robbie?" Jim asked.

2

Mrs. Vojtyla (now I know her name is Iris) was around Francine's age, maybe even a few years younger. Which was something Jim hadn't noticed until he opened the door to her. Those curled-up talons on her, the fright life had given her, had always made her seem older. Today, however—having no idea why she'd been invited to Jake's father's house—she was wearing a long skirt of midnight blue and a lavender silk blouse with long sleeves closed at the neck with an ivory brooch, as if she didn't want much of herself seen. It didn't keep Jim from seeing she was, fear apart, a good-looking woman: long black hair, often brushed and very straight and fine. Handsome eyebrows, delicate ears, a good long neck.

It was a full-blown autumnal afternoon, a time of sexual energy in someone his age. Through the kitchen window she could see the vast, tumescent garden Francine had rescued from the wild:

big, sodden leaves, roses, rambling, trying to breathe and unfold one last time. On her way she'd noted the Bechstein ("I'm sorry about Jake." "Sorry?" "Sorry he's given up on the piano"), and, ushered into the kitchen and poured a glass of wine while Jim worked at the stove, she found herself being stared at by the photographs on the wall. All the Mothers in their delectable youths looked down on her, one of them naked.

"I'm sorry," Jim said. "Perhaps you didn't expect to be alone."

"Your wife, Francine…It was always she who brought Jake over."

"She's not here."

As Jim made no attempt to explain himself, or his invitation, she felt she ought to account for her own nerves. Why she had ceased to think of herself as a woman. She said: "I guess since Harry… since Harry died, I don't get out that much. All our friends were Harry's friends."

As Jim remembered, Harry had killed himself, thrown himself under a subway train. He'd been accused of fondling a student and Mrs. Vojtyla had locked him out of the house. Something like that. They had had no children. The idea that these bare bones were all he knew about Mrs. Vojtyla moved him towards her. He found his stubby hand lying on hers (she didn't withdraw it), and her hair, bunched up with a couple of pins, unwound. Perhaps she caught his glance. She licked her lips, which were full, until they shone.

There was an urgency in the way she ate the risotto and the salad which followed, a blur in her eyes, as though she wore contact lenses which hurt and caused watering.

He said something banal, like there's no dessert, and she fell into a fit of giggling. He offered a brandy; she asked if he had something sweet. He did.

Later she stumbled on a loose carpet following him up the steep back stairs and he said nothing got fixed any more, Francine had been the house engineer.

Then he was staring at her moon breasts, her blouse pulled up, her hair sprawling on the pillow, on her side of the bed, her hands, coiled and trying to uncoil, clutching the sheets (not perfectly clean) from underneath.

Perhaps she heard snatches of music, incomplete phrases. They, like Jim, made her tense, afraid and unable to speak—of all the things she'd kept in since Harry died: her concert pictures and diplomas smashed on the floor; the bored kids (not hers) who didn't want to play Bach or anything; that she knew her plastic bunnies hadn't fled in a storm but been stolen by kids from up the road who rode by on their bikes and taunted her. She couldn't mention Harry, or ask Jim some simple question about why Francine had gone and where and how was Jake. So she kept silent, her hands fell still, the music stopped and she waited.

Of course Jim felt he had to tell me. He said: "You don't make love out of pity. The truth is, how could you talk about how it was, after."

3

He had met Natasha Gilpin twice. The first time was in England. Though Natasha was not English and was lovely, it was about English girls Jim wrote—as always care of Otto and Heda, because for nearly most of the 'seventies I did not want him to know where I was. They have gentle voices, he said, and a queer shyness we know nothing about in Chicago. In their short, high-summer dresses—sprawled on deck chairs in parks, striding confidently along with shopping bags, or sitting out front of pubs, their shaven legs crossed—they were all highly desirable to a man living in what Jim called "Interim", the queer, unnatural state between wives. (Wasn't it marriage especially, and family in general, that was unnatural? Francine would ask.)

Life went on—his children saw to that—but Jim himself was
Nowhere. A furnished apartment without takers. I got the long-dis-
tance resonances. Of the ladies who loped through.

Mostly, each time it was our story all over again. He and the
ladies explained to one another what had gone wrong; why their guy
was gone or why they'd left their guy. How they were marked by
failure. They had put their Best Foot Forward and still they'd failed;
they so much wanted to Do Better This Time Round, yet each had a
sense of being used goods. Even as sperm sought egg and egg, sperm,
each was jealous of those who had gone before, who had trodden
what flesh, received those practiced kisses.

He could be quite funny about it: as though, unmarried, he
suddenly had clearer sight. He bore none of the prospective wives
a grudge: one for bidding seven spades to open the first time they
played bridge; another for trepidating on the edge about her exiled,
dismissed or lost Bill or Oscar—How will he manage without me?
For not making out, for backing off, for asking more than he could
give. There was the Chinese lady for wrapped herself round a tree
on her way to him. This one who wrapped the wrong kind of skin;
that one tried to become an instant Mom to his many kids. (The last
thing they wanted was another Mother.)

The first time, in England, with the Maria kids in tow, over
for a Bar meeting, he'd gone to a garden party. At these parties the
English mill about, drape themselves on sofas, desultorily watch
cricket on the TV. It's a garden party because the garden was where
the drinks are, the tasty, thin sandwiches (soon gone or wilting), and
the assorted, well brought-up children are of unidentified parents.

This particular garden, which belonged to a publisher of aero-
nautical books, consisted of a long narrow lawn dotted with deck-
chairs, glasses left on the grass, one fruit tree (maybe a pear tree) and
two linear, herbaceous borders. The sun was low, the shadows long.
Overhead, airplanes, like noisy lawn-mowers, cut the sky.

Natasha Gilpin was squatting at the back of the garden, taking a cutting from a plant. What he saw was a pleasant, soft butt
stretching a dress of blue rayon and a lot of curly black hair.

I'm sure Jim's senses were attuned. He'd probably chatted up a few of the girls there, it was getting late, and he'd promised his baby-sitter he'd be back by eight-thirty. That aside, what happened was that he had barely got to introduce himself, and she to tell him that she was half Russian, before she stood up, cutting in hand, and said, "Why don't you take me home and let's go to bed?"

Which he did, even if "home" was a rented flat and he had to leave Natasha in his car while he went up and handed the baby-sitter a wadge of notes, telling her to take the kids out for dinner wherever they wanted, asleep or awake, as long as they weren't back before eleven.

At five to eleven on the dot, matter-of-fact, Natasha leapt out of bed, showered, and slipped back into her blue dress, under which she wore nothing more than a schoolgirl's cotton panties. With a parting kiss, she said, "That was nice. I had a really, really nice time."

She, too, was in Europe just for a visit, though she often came here for "work" and had a million friends here. Did he like England? He said he loved it.

"Well," Natasha said, "You can't have everything in life. I should know."

She, too, was leaving soon. In Evanston there was a husband and two children. Later, Jim found a scrawled piece of paper under his pillow with her telephone number. Back home.

Natasha was the Mother I came to adore. She was so straightforward: as uncomplicated as she was uneducated. She was also funny, tireless and undiscriminating. She bore no grudges, and the only thing I ever knew her to worry about was whether she was putting on weight. She knew Jim by instinct and talked a lot to me (as she did to everybody) because she loved gossip and was constantly surprised ("Really? I never dreamed he was queer!" "You won't believe this, but I just found out my mother was Jewish. Isn't that wonderful?") In daily life as, presumably, in bed she was matter-of-fact. Why make a fuss? Fish were fish and got fried; you got sick, you went to bed; you had children, someone must want them.

She had survived an unhappy childhood and was settled comfortably in an unhappy marriage. Her father, some time dead, was a bald and severe Minnesota historian (of the Dutch Republic) and her mother (whose origins she had just been told about) a mop-haired refugee brought out of Russia at the age of three and schooled to find a husband, preferably a rich one. Mr. Gilpin had been rich, but left his all to Natasha's younger brother, who would not, he thought, squander his money on toby jugs, biscuit tins, and other kitsch. Natasha would say candidly, and believe it, that she was the disappointment her younger brother had been created to make up for.

She married at sixteen, as she said, to make up for being disinherited. The old man was dying and Natasha knew marrying would piss him off. Her choice fell on Hubie Conklin, though she seldom referred to him as anything but "the husband." Hubie was slow-spoken and moneyed. He was all right, she said, in small doses. But not much interested in sex, or her, his job, or his children—apparently generated in two fits of distraction. Maybe because he already had a child from a previous marriage. Of this child, Natasha said only, "He's mental." She meant the poor boy, now twenty-something, wasn't normal. She worried that her own children, exactly the same age as the Maria Mounts, would inherit this faulty gene. That was why she daily organized their lives, down to the last detail. She said she probably would like them: when they grew up and she could be sure. They were, she admitted, "catastrophically beautiful," and modeling suited them: Emma because she was vain and Cosmo because he was bone lazy.

For Natasha the consolation prize was Hubie's money and his house. She was deeply attached to both money and house. Her mother had taught her the rules she'd come to America with: what you have you hang on to, whatever else you can get, grab.

They met the second time at one of Milo Frankl's weekend parties by the shore, where she was going around taking photographs commissioned by one of the fashion magazines whose covers she had, when younger, when thinner, often graced. The "estate" was rented. (To the end, Milo never bought anything—houses, cars, wives—that he could rent.) At the moment he was very flush: a big advance, a movie deal in the works, and the last wife, a Slovak biologist, for once defeated on the score of major alimony.

She spotted Jim on the pier by his baggy pants and hands thrust deep in their pockets, and marched a waiter up to him with a bottle and two glasses. "Know any summer jobs going round?" she asked.

Why did she want a summer job? Jim asked. "It can't be for the money."

"Just to get out," she said. "I need something new in my life. Or maybe someone. That's the deal we have, Hubie and I."

"He doesn't object?"

"Why should he? I do his shirts, I put dinner on the table, I look after the kids."

On one of the Frankels' enormous fingers of lawn—some stretched down to the water, the boathouse, the pier, the float a hundred yards out, the gunmetal water beyond; others led to the tennis court, to Milo's studio, to Penelope's vegetable garden with its array of stiff pepper-basil plants and opulent tomatoes—she told Jim her childhood hadn't prepared her for anything in particular. Enough manners (and the occasional accomplishment, like photography) to enable her to "marry well," as well as her mother. Hence Hubie. Hence photography. "You know, other peoples' weddings are more interesting. I did Milo's."

"Which of the many?"

"Ha-ha. This one." She squatted and snapped dead rose-heads. "If something needs doing I can't help myself," she said. "Do you think Prudence would be furious? She hires gardeners for this sort of thing. Prudence is an old chum. We were at school together."

I love the thought of her looking up at that moment, the perfect mid-thirties *jolie laide*—too wide a mouth, breasts too triangular, eyes of a too-bright blue, her dress taut on her body, always so true to herself—and saying plainly, "Still on the rebound, are we? Still mourning the loss of our Great Love?"

He didn't get over things that easily, Jim explained.

"Then why get into them in the first place?"

Just right for Jim, I thought. A little brass. Snap him out of mid-life mourning. I think she'd figured him out in five minutes in a London garden. Not all of him, but the part she'd have to take in hand. He needed a woman in his bed; she offered herself without attachments or afterthought. She had her own mind, her own money, her kids, and the fiercest determination. If he'd let her, she'd make him happy.

That second meeting they played a set of energetic tennis on the Frankel court (grass). Natahsa played with perfect good sense, never even trying for a shot she couldn't reach. They then wandered back to the house arm-in-arm, put away one of the anglophilic Prudence's vast teas, and had their choice of bedrooms upstairs. She said, and she meant it: "I've missed you."

Dinner was very good (Prudence was also a fine cook) and they had powerful appetites. They went back upstairs unnoticed and much refreshed. At a little before midnight she said, "I've got to go now."

Jim said unless her kids were with them he never saw her past midnight or much before eight. That was no problem.

But Jim was, and Natasha talked to lots of people, including me, about Jim. "I can make damn sure he doesn't have any children by me," she said, "but he's got this marriage mania. Hubie and I have a deal, and I'm not going to go back on it."

I suspect she got all sorts of different advice about Jim. No two people saw him the same way. That was because he didn't like having to choose among the many people he liked to think he was. Every day was a re-invention of himself: of his appearance, what he wore, what he wanted, who he was with, of what was coming next. It wouldn't surprise me, tomorrow or ten years down the line, were Jim to walk in through the door to tell me he'd become a horse-trader in the pampas, or was now a woman and ran a bordello in Vancouver. Each would be perfectly true in his eyes. And convincing.

Me, I liked the child; or at least the teen-ager I remembered best. Natasha liked the excitement. She was the ultimate realist: well beyond Francine in acting out of pure acceptance of the world as it was. It was what she called a "jolly" way of looking at things. That much of Jim was fantasy didn't deter her; she might not even notice.

She did get a job out of that second meeting: unpaid organizer of a Mount family summer. Official lady for August and probably beyond, the beyond ultimately lasting a whole ten years. It was no minor task. And involved (literally) thousands of miles in a series of clapped-out cars running between two households. She was shocked by the state of Jim's finances, then by the accumulated dirt and disorder of his apartment. For the latter she kept rubber gloves in her handbag. The former was not so easily resolved.

In August, the Mothers released their children, known to each other as the LouMounts and the MarMounts (the FranMounts came later.) That meant nine of his and two of Natasha's. A lot of air-fares. The three MarMounts were relatively cheap. They came up from Biloxi, Mississippi, where Urquhart had something to do with Civil Rights. He was paying off Belle, so there was no spare change there. The house they rented that summer cost six grand. Natasha cheated on her household money for her half and said her husband would never notice. Besides which, Jim refused to sell his Bechstein.

4

There was a fire on August fifteenth. A chunk of woods a few hundred yards behind their house went up, bright yellow and black, into the sky. Natasha watched, mesmerized. She had no idea of danger. The telephone wires went and they were lucky the wind was blowing from the Ocean and a torrential rain doused the fire. Was it Jim's barbecue and noted carelessness, or the way he had of flicking his cigarettes and knocking out his pipes wherever he liked?

Another afternoon, he and Natasha stand at the top of the cliff while the kids straggle back up the path from the rocky beach up to the house. The path winds awkwardly through windswept pines. Jim's so busy counting kids filing past, towels on their shoulders, balls and impedimenta in their hands, it takes him a while to notice Natasha has gone back down to the beach. Then, down below, he catches sight of her dark hair glinting, and why she's gone back down. She has her little Emma by the hand, who alternately stumbles on loose rocks and is lifted over driftwood. Natasha's voice carries: Emma has left behind her plastic bucket and Natasha is fierce about possessions.

He sees Emma down there, bawling, and no bucket—that's what the sea does, it taketh away. Natasha is struggling with a raffia basket heavy with wet towels and swim-suits. Now she shouts at her little girl to stop crying. Emma, who is three, sits down on the sand on her plump little bottom, a perfect miniature replica of her mother's. The scene is painful to watch. Who gives a good damn about a plastic bucket?

The material Natasha does, the way she cares about her knick-nacks and dressers. Natasha's back is to the sea and he can hear her distinctly: "You are a wicked little girl, wicked." He sees her bend over and pick her kid up in her left arm and start towards him. Emma is still bawling, but Natasha is shouting even louder: "Will you stop crying? Will you stop crying?" It goes on in a mechanical crescendo: "Will you stop crying? Stop, will you stop, stop crying?"

Then Natasha reappears trudging up the path below him. She has a rock in one hand, and every accent is a blow on Emily's head. Will you stop crying, thump! Will you stop crying, thump!

Disobedience. Exactly what she'd been like as a child, this awry part of herself is being repeated in her daughter: who must be punished as she was.

Jim thinks he is very calm when he says, "If you ever do that again, Natasha, I warn you: I shall kill you."

She drops the rock and bursts into tears. She has not even known what she has been doing; the rock in her hand is a complete surprise, as is the blood streaming down Emma's temple.

5

Back in Chicago that Fall—there were no negotiations, not even talk—Natasha really took charge of Jim and his messy life. Once the kids were back with the Mothers the apartment could be scrubbed, scoured and mercilessly emptied of its junk. With her brief, turned-up nose, and big, buttery, bright red mouth, rubber gloves of bright yellow, a red bandanna around her hair, galvanized buckets, scrub-brushes, she spent weekends and snow days looking like a formidable Polish char. Underneath her pale skin there was steel and fire and generations of keeping up appearances.

"You don't want this, do you?" she said, holding up a sweater out at the elbows. In a week she'd filled plastic bins with Jim's many pasts. Clothes she ran up to the parish house, papers she burned, bugs she exterminated. In my house, only the windows defeated her (the cottage settled and the frames were askew). In winter she just threw the doors open instead: she was one of those women who don't sweat. One week she turned out two big plastic bags with thousands of dollars' worth of clothes on my bed.

"I don't wear any of this stuff any more," she said. A perfect solution for me, as I'd never learned what to wear and was happy to have what had already been chosen. It was charity and she'd been doing it forever. Always loudly and stopping only for cups of instant whatever ("If I can't tell the difference, why should I buy 'real' coffee?"). Then she'd pack me into Hubie's Lincoln and take me to lunch or to the man who did her hair.

Jim said, all freshly shaven himself (the beard didn't come until he was in his sixties), that you couldn't allow Natasha into your life, it would never be the same again, and also you couldn't keep her out, she was a force of nature, more insistent than weather.

Whatever she wanted to know she just asked: if Jim and I had done it when we were teen-agers, and if I hadn't ("I certainly did!" she said) what was I scared of? How very little Hubie liked sex. Was Maria really worth the torch Jim carried—he talks about her as if she's a goddess?

She was inside you in a trice, and not fickle. But over children a certain noticeable rubbing took place, times when logistics or importunities delayed meetings, upset plans. Tiny, explosive wars broke out off-stage once or twice a year. Natasha staked out allies among the Mothers, who were—at a distance, on occasion—all too ready to agree Jim was a "self-absorbed shit." "You do wear us down, love," she said.

Once, she thought she was pregnant in spite of all her precautions. "It was thirty-seven days of pure hell. I could put up with him, but not with being a bloody Mother again. And when at last it turned out I wasn't, I almost left, just in case it happened again."

Which girls got the better dresses, his or hers, which girls got the lessons. Those were vexing matters. Cosmo stole money, Emma was a lousy fiddler. Such things should never be said, but Jim never understood that words could hurt.

When Jim gave her dinner on her fortieth birthday, she broke down at the table, her eyes filling with tears. She said that was the end. No more birthdays thank you very much. "When Emma's twenty-one I'm going to kill myself."

A woman of such energy kill herself? Who whizzed about town from tennis-lesson to a friend in trouble, to the antique dealer and the crooked mechanic who sold her the cars she cracked up? Jim sent her to see Igor, but she only went once, made deeply uneasy by self-examination.

And yet Jim and I both came to see in Natasha what Jim called: "the skull beneath the flesh." The death's head when her hair wasn't teased out and her skin looked pale as moons, the inertness of her eyes when for no reason at all she would doggedly go to sleep wherever she was, in tears of humiliation that an old friend hadn't invited her to a wedding.

In this very house she would bring, as though it explained her life, her "book," the photographed faces and bodies, hands, lips, feet and eyes, models carried round in transparent plastic folders to sell themselves. Tatty, disordered (so unlike her), the pictures stuck in any which way, the pictures were meant to show me what she had once been. If I said how beautiful she was, she could say, "Look at me now. You see? I was thin once!" That allowed her to flip the pages to an anorexic Natasha—big hair, no tits, as fashion demanded. I said she was more supple, more beautiful, more vivid now, and she said, "You don't really think so." On another day she would open the book towards the end: to when she married Hubie (wedding dresses) and pregnant (maternity dresses) with Cosmo. By the end of the book she'd dwindled to chainstore catalogues. Then she'd look up with anguish—how had her body grown and her soul shrunk?—and then anyone could see the skull beneath the skin..

Jim and I should both have paid more attention. The signs were all there, and plenty of false alarms. She had a pet, hip doctor who fed her amphetamines; she went weeks barely eating, living on Nescaf. She'd be expected at Milo's for dinner and be seen instead with the sort of fringe-people her husband, Hubie, frequented, many of them queer. I once found her passed out face-down on my bed with her head under a pillow. Twice she went to a private hospital for what she said were "female complaints" and emerged weeks later, listless, complaining of being terribly tired. The second time, she said she couldn't decide how to die.

She never failed, however, to return home to Evanston.

In terms of the sheer survival of uterine families Natasha—her Mother before, acquiring the rich Mr. Gilpin who disinherited the daughter, and the daughter after, doing the same with Hubie—came from stock fitter than any bug at Armageddon. As beetles were immune to radiation or flood or asteroid, so their inherited carapaces and simple mechanisms were proof against Jim, against the world. The Mother wrote suicide notes to herself, the daughter got beaten with a rock: they flourished.

When finally Jim proposed they should marry—Why not? They were a "couple" all around Chicago—Natasha refused curtly. She said: "I can't bear to part with anything."

She meant property, not people. Or made people into property. Hubie sat among her biscuit tins and Victorian china on a mythical mantelpiece; her children were bundled hither and yon, pushed into different ultra-clean clothes that changed with the seasons, trained in sabre and modern dance, told the niceties of betting at the races, their pony ribbons flaunted. What counted was acquisition.

6

Natasha did not die as she expected or wanted. When Jim invited her to go to Paris with him (a complicated case of infringement of copyright by a Wisconsin perfume company had come up), she was more or less the age Francine is now: the tense forties, that strenuous age for women, who go from grub to butterfly and spread their gorgeous wings with ease, only to age and find no place and few new men to fly to.

Could she get away? Day after day her alarm went off in the early morning, she showered, pulled on her jeans, ran a brush through her wet hair, and pecked him on his cheek on the way out. Why could they never share a coffee in the morning at home? Jim said: "What's so specially exciting or seemly about creeping out at six a.m. to go back and do your husband's shirts? You could get up at nine, you know. Can't Hubie take your kids to school sometimes?"

Her eyes were large with the movements of the day: breakfasts, the school run, car to the garage, then Emma to her fencing lesson, Cosmo (behind at school) to his tutor. "How can I?" she said, tears welling in her eyes. Paris would have been lovely, she loved him, but at half past six, struck by a witch's wand, she was a Mother.

"I have a present for you," he said on her birthday, another on which her reiterated deadline for dying would pass. "I hear the husband's away. Can I drop it off?"

She said, "I know you're furious because I can't go with you."

"I'm on my way over to show you just how furious I am."

The trip seemed immensely long and complicated. How had she managed to make it almost every day for ten years?

It had its mysterious side, this house where Natasha spent her other hours. Where Jim expected his things to be, her husband's were: on the backs of chairs, hanging on hooks. And where he expected his own children, he found Emma and Cosmo, like seasoned interlopers. He felt like a voyeur in the Hubie-and-Natasha kitchen, dazzling with equipment.

Then he noticed she had puffy eyes as she ripped the paper off his gift, a prized cookie jar from Appalachia; worse yet, the jar did not make her face light up. On the contrary, she had started sniffling. "Is something wrong?" he asked.

"No. Nothing at all." She searched for a handkerchief and used a paper towel straight from the roll instead. "It's just so stupid. And hurtful. I've just found out Hubie's sired a bouncing baby boy on a tall, Germanic lady who works in the college library. It makes me sick."

"I only just found out. There's this massive bill from the flower shop. Some things," she said, walking about furiously, smoke rising from her pretty lips and pert nose, "are just 'not done.' It's very irritating." Was some of Hubie's money going to get diverted away from Cosmo and Emma?

"It's so unfair. I mean, I don't go round getting myself pregnant."

These fortuitous events, unlike the fixed ellipses of the planets, can have big effects on our gravitational fields. Hubie's new child meant Natasha felt more strongly than ever that she had to defend her home, this very kitchen where they stood, its serried rows of cups hooked onto shelves, its knick-knacks, knotty pine dressers and Toby jugs. A tea-cup out of line hurt her. And why not? All of us search for immutables. Her snub Russian nose deep in a Nescafé, she said, "Now you see why I can't go to Paris."

"I thought you'd just found out."

"I always knew something like this would happen."

The "something like this" meant Hubie, but could as well have applied to Jim. She wouldn't marry. Jim would. Their parting was not without regret and tears. It wasn't that they didn't love one another after their fashion. All of us make up our childhood losses in different ways. The waif in Natasha had been made up for with things, the things that her Mummy and Daddy denied her and she now stored up for her kids. They were her hedge against deprivation.

It was only when he came back from Paris with Francine that he found out Natasha was in hospital, and then only because I told him. "You mean she had another shot at it? At killing herself."

"No, I think it's worse than that. She was operated on for a malignancy two days ago."

"Jesus!"

"A brain tumor. Igor's been to see her. She's been incredibly brave about it."

I'd seen her go in with her nightie, a toothbrush and a book in a brown paper bag. "It's no big deal," Natasha had said. "They make a hole in your head and take it out." Life as a fact, that was her strength.

"How long's she known about it?"

"It was a birthday present."

"Does Igor think she'll make it?"

"If she fights it. Maybe."

"Yes, but will she?"

"Fight it? You bet. I've been told to go out and get her some sample wigs."

I've watched obsessions with death, with what Francine calls "Bolivia" (for oblivion.) My Grandma dreamed and lamented the death of seventy warriors shot off their horses as though this had happened in her own life rather than two generations before her time. To her, death came without the dimension of time. It was always present as one was alive, as life was ever-present when one was dead. My parents fussed about it, making substantial and complicated arrangements about "after" which didn't stand up when the long-postponed day came round. I knew all about Jim's deep fear of it—he didn't want that Indian on the road or any other omens. I could understand that, given the way his father had played with death, teased it out, flying, courting danger, skiing down that mountain in the middle of the night, walking back up, who was still dying, if Sunny Farber was to be believed, somewhere reaching out from the next world to proffer a posthumous fortune to his surviving son. Tony knew he was killing himself by degrees, it was a self-admiring act for him, as though dying were some special skill he had. Which brought those girls to him at the end, as to one of the gunmen of the old West.

And here was Natasha, for whom death was like a roll of the dice, who both liked it and feared it, but whose body (independent of her mind) refused it. Luckily for Jim, she didn't share her secret life (or death) with anyone. She just asked me if I could ride with her and take the car someplace because the parking fees at the hospital were outrageous.

Part five

Francine

Love is a growing or full constant light
And his first minute, after noon, is night.

W hen she found herself married to Jim, Francine couldn't imagine how it had happened. Not for a second. The actual hitching, the mayor in his tri-colored sash, was absurd, the reception in the family house in Belfort equally ridiculous. It had been a *coup de tête*, a rush.

Given the shape she was in and what she'd been through in the past few years, she couldn't say for sure what got into her. These whims, her Mother said, she'd always had them, the way a bad cook reaches out and throws this or that, sun-dried tomatoes, onion grass, into his dish. "So you just fancy stepping out at ten o'clock when you're supposed to be in bed?" Whack!

No matter how often she screened the scene in her mind she couldn't come up with an explanation. The words were out of her mouth before she even thought what they meant. It was her usual awkwardness. It was that she couldn't take people seriously. It was that she liked to be funny (it was a relief in the Pasquier house), and liked to make smart-alecky remarks. It had to have been a feeble attempt at a joke. Some joke!

217

The first time she allowed herself to be dead cold sober again she knew it had been a mistake. But she'd allowed for that. There'd be a margin of error. Maybe she'd just go to bed with him. What she couldn't understand was him. Why on earth, heading for the airport to marry the Chinese pianist in Taiwan, had he said yes when she said she thought he ought to marry her and not the pianist he was having fantasies about?

When Francine first saw him walk through the office she thought he was a rich fag: bracelets on his wrists, long hair, big eyes the size of remote-sensing disks, and fine talk. Interesting. Fun. After that she didn't actually think again because for all sorts of reasons, mainly rain and it being Friday night, his taxi to the airport never came and he said, "How about a drink?"

Technically, she didn't properly see him again until she found herself on their honeymoon up in the Spanish mountains staring out at a big, cold moon through their bedroom window. Because she got drunk, as she regularly did. The hills outside that *hostal* were dotted with dark scrub that moved. They turned out to be stealthy sheep pretending to be Birnam Wood and browsing towards whatever this place her husband had chosen was. A castle? A convent? A series of prolonged hangovers made it so she didn't care what it was as long as it had a bed she could fall onto. And preferably not wake up.

When he undressed up in their icy room, she saw him as hard-fit, preening and too damned sure of himself: a muscular torso, no hips to speak of, no sign of baldness or hair in the wrong places; good legs which she admired. Just missing teeth which made him hesitate to laugh out loud.

"A car crash," he said. "I'll get them fixed if you want."

"They don't bother me," she said; and he didn't.

She fell asleep and he wasn't bad about that. At least he didn't wake her up. But in the morning, he was there. She thought, who is this guy?

One thing Francine—the Francine I got to know—didn't lack was self-irony. In some part of her mind that wasn't frozen in the unexpectedness of being married to a man she knew nothing about, she acknowledged having thought for a good part of that summer "abroad" and away from her "treatment" that she ought to get married.

It was an idea no more consequential than a hundred other oughts: she ought to go to see film X because her French cousins kept on talking about it and she ought to straighten herself out, she ought to stop doing harmful things to herself. Maybe she ought to kill her Mother and get it over with. Or maybe stop being proper, as it had been beaten into her that this was what life was all about. The sense that turning thirty wasn't far off, that her sisters had done it (marriage). The boredom of turning up daily at the parfumier as if she were a well-brought-up, well-turned-out girl doing P R because she loved it and loved Madame's effing perfumes, when in fact until two months ago (after a nasty police bust which led them to pack her off to Paris) she'd been her parents' child from hell: but her own boss. Master of her own self-destruction.

There was no order or priority in these thoughts. They were all equal. And all pointless. Because they didn't amount to anything until she opened her fool mouth while he was still talking and said, "I think you ought to marry me."

Ought?

It would be her parfumier whose suit Jim was settling and it had to be raining buckets outside. Very doubtful circumstances, she would always say. Fate. Shit waiting to happen.

Jim's view of their meeting was different. Just because he was in Paris he really hadn't felt like singing in that much rain, though the song went through his head. No, he was on his last night in Paris and stuck in a plush ante-chamber to Madame's office, impatient and needing Madame's signature on a deposition. Meanwhile he was being a sodden, bearded Chicago lawyer shedding water from a coat with an astrakhan collar and holding an umbrella with two collapsed ribs. Not until Francine spoke was he even aware she was in the room. There was a shape in the corner of the room, and the shape was bent over a table writing something pugnaciously with a big black Mont Blanc pen. The shape held the pen in some peculiar way he'd never seen before.

He did his business, got his signature, and came out again. Only then did he get a proper look at Francine, who uncoiled from her chair (to her full height) when Madame asked her to find a taxi for Monsieur Mount. (Who was due at Roissy at nine because he was getting married.)

In Jim's version what came across was mainly how impeccable she was. Impeccable the way lots of French girls are, without effort or deliberation. She was boy-tall, very thin, very *soignée*—clean, sweet-smelling, well turned-out. She wore her hair, which was straight and slight but touched with henna, longish, and kept in place with two combs over her ears and a fringe down her brow. Those ears were delicate as bats', silky, long. What she wore was all simple but expensive: a pair of fawn trousers that went a long way up, a cream shirt, a jacket of knitted wool and leather. How old was she? Late twenties?

She said a taxi would be impossible to get on a Friday night. With this rain. She would take Monsieur back to the Bristol.

And he would buy her a drink.

Well yes, they had a quick drink, or maybe two, before setting out to find where she'd parked her car, and he noticed a thing or two more about her: such as, that she didn't so much walk as lope; that she looked down all the time, and not where she was going; that she wouldn't share even his busted umbrella, so her wet head looked like sealskin; and that he didn't usually lose his car as she seemed to have.

He said maybe they should look more systematically for the car. They talked that over in another café where they also managed some Beaujolais and a ham sandwich heavily stuffed with butter. He says that was probably where he talked about the mythical eighteen-year-old Chinese pianist and the fact that Natasha, with whom he'd been more or less living for the last decade, wouldn't marry him anyway.

And she said, "Look, there's my car, I knew I left it somewhere around here."

He thought they were going to the Bristol. Instead she drove recklessly fast in the general direction of the Eiffel Tower. He didn't want to ask her if she knew what she was doing, and noticed (between lurches) that the glove compartment in front of him was stuffed with traffic tickets.

They stopped in a rush in front of a bar beyond the Ecole Militaire. She said she had no idea where they were and she never came this way. They went in anyway. Algerians played cards, a television cowboy was talking in French over their heads. Francine ate nuts, showing clean, strong white teeth. He recalls the champagne not being very good.

"There was a certain perturbation in her eyes," he said. "They didn't always look at me." Besides, the way Jim told it, no sooner had they knocked back most of the inferior champagne, than she had begun talking a lot: in a weird jumpy way, the way a liar will do when his defenses have been breached. That was when she said it was selfish of him even to think of marrying a foreign pianist who wouldn't fit in at all in Chicago, especially—she was emphatic about that—a Chinese pianist, and a Chinese pianist who was younger than some of his children, if he had all the children he said he had. How would they feel about her?

"Have you given any thought at all, *avez vous réflechi à elle?*"

About Emily Wong? Not at all. He'd been with Igor to a concert she'd given—the performance crystalline, the girl immensely lovely. The next day he'd sent flowers to her hotel, the day after he'd taken her out to dinner, the third day they'd played four-hand Schubert together at his house, and she'd stayed. A week later she was gone to visit her parents who lived in Taipei, and he'd said he'd come out there straight from Paris where he had to go. What should he do, then? Nothing else had worked out. The Chinese were traditional, maybe she'd stick around.

Francine's eyes had turned disconcertingly clear. She said, "I think you should marry me."

I know what he said. On a slow count of ten he said, "You're on kid. How about next weekend?"

Francine didn't just go to bed with him, she didn't go to bed with him at all. Not yet. Because he refused. He drove to her apartment, an almost entirely bare attic room on the Rue de Lille, and demanded coffee, which meant she had to re-connect the stove and hope there was some coffee in the house. And did he mean American coffee?

Well, obviously he was rich, because he was shocked (she could tell, even with her back to him, untangling wires) by the way the wires, loose, dangling, naked, by-passed the meter by the front door:

"You mean you get your electricity for free?"

This was a problem? Something told her this wasn't the time to explain that the room belonged to her cousin Odile, and Odile was...

Not knowing a damned thing about Jim, and somehow committed to marrying him (she checked her watch to know what day it was) in a week's time, she wasn't sure how he'd react to the fact that Odile had been harboring an Italian terrorist in the room, and therefore you couldn't very well have the electricity people checking the meter.

There was a lot to explain, but as all this—meaning marriage and this man in her room—was really happening to somebody else, she supposed that it didn't matter that much.

He said cheerfully: "Shouldn't we be calling your folks?"

That was biting into the reality apple. "*Il est quelle heure?*" What time was it in Hartford (and though they were French, that was where they lived and where she'd grown up) Connecticut? *Merde.* Seven. Reality set her scrambling for co-ordinates. Where and when had he said they'd do this mad thing, get married? Had he really said it? And she hadn't said she was only joking?

The next thing she knew, he'd asked for the number and he

was dialing it for her. She could hear the rings and then someone picked up at the other end and he handed her the instrument. "*Maman?*"

The phone seemed not to be transmitting sound, but images. The wretched, perfectly ordered, suburban living room she'd fled, the flower pattern of the sofa, the TV, the piano on which *Maman*, counting carefully, the four girls clustered behind her (Papa was generally watching Forest Hills), had picked out their French musical heritage, *Sur le Pont d'Avignon* and *Malbrough s'en va-t-en guerre*. Stuff like that. A smell of offal hung over the kitchen while next door the Ryan kids, a dozen or more, had cook-outs and burgers, which was what she'd longed for.

She nearly hung up while Mme. Pasquier, breathing heavily, shouted "*Allo, oui. Allo, j'écoute!*" Her own voice, making her sound about twelve and still dressed in a pinafore, echoing distantly, said things like, yes he's fifty-something, he's got a dozen children, you know, more or less, and of course he speaks French, didn't everyone?

Meanwhile, her mind was telling her the following: Ha! Bet the first thing you thought (that Francine, full of secret hatreds, was also talking to her Mother) when I said, "*Bon soir, Maman, c'est Francine*", was that I was calling from jail or the local loony bin. Never thought I'd get married, did you? Never were sure I was really a girl, were you? Can't dance, doesn't know where her feet are (far away, as remote as the rabbit ears on the TV that I'll bet Papa is watching right now), a girl who'd rather fix cars than sew, someone so thoroughly undesirable, hanging out with the lowlifes in Hartford, *devenue trés américaine*, you bet, completely sold on American life—not like her unfailingly *comme il faut* sisters who wanted to grow up just as they were told they should—anything rather than this phony French shit, including the goddam stupid table manners and kissing everyone when you walked into a room…

"*Allo! Ça va, ma chérie?*" Papa's turn. She saw him looming behind the small, leathery figure of her mother. He was in his flannel bathrobe and he had an ear-piece to his ear (an authentic French touch) and he was trying to get a word in while *Maman* did her *son-et-lumière* number, lit up from inside and blathering.

So that when she handed the phone over to Jim and she was no longer watching and hearing a video of a self that wasn't her at all, she thought how much explaining she had to do to this man she was supposed to marry. How come she was so fucked up in the part of her no one got to see, in which fucking-up *Maman* and Papa had their roles, hers active, his passive.

Now she would say that there had been a delicious moment, while Jim charmed the plaid skirt off Celestine and told Papa how keen he was on tennis himself, his father having played against Borotra and the other *Mousquetaires*, in which she saw a window of opportunity. If she told Jim what she was really like there was no way he would marry her, the truth was the way to get off the hook.

In Spain it occurred to her again that this alien presence, now her husband, was entitled to know what he'd taken on. But then he'd already had to sit through her melt-downs at the wedding and Papa's ramblings on the dance-floor, he'd seen what her family was like and she'd let slip some of what it had been like to grow up with them—the size and thickness of the belt Celestine used on her, whack! Why Papa didn't feel he could move out of his chair while that was going on before his very eyes: and it hadn't bothered him at all. If indeed he even heard her. Or if she ever gave *Maman* the satisfaction of crying or shouting.

Still now, knowing where Francine's private sorrows lie, I find it hard to take. Deliberate, repetitive, scheduled, cold-hearted harm. Francine must have truly stuck in her Mother's craw. Because Francine just would not be loved. Love isn't something you can push on another. But such must have been Celestine's despair that the belt, Papa's shaving strop and, once, the leaf-rake, seemed the only way out. I reckon Papa was stuck to his chair not out of indifference but because he could neither bear it nor do anything about it.

For a week then, on their travels—a lot of *caldo verde* in northern Portugal, a briefcase left behind at the frontier in which he'd fished around vainly for his passport (locked up in the Bristol's safe), the inquiries from the Guardia Civil at the frontier who wanted to know why his *Señora* was wearing a veil (she'd scarred her cheek from eye to ear mounting the curb in Paris two days before the wedding, doing everything she could in the hope the marriage wouldn't go through), a day tramping through Seville, unaccountably missing all the things the guidebook said they ought to see—she left him notes under his pillow.

The notes, in her odd, angular hand, referred to the real her who'd gone bad early because she thought it was hypocritical that someone should be making love to her who knew nothing of what she was really like. They were deliberately coarse: what the cops tried to do to her in Hartford the first time she was busted, what Dollar Bill gave her for certain transactions, the time she burned down the trucker's log cabin way above Denver because she passed out smoking in bed, the probable condition of her innards after so much abuse. Or for the notes she substituted a marbled school notebook open at the page where she listed Jerry, Frank, Connall—a number of cousins who'd had her in the house they'd just been wed at, and each and every single other man (one-night-stand or other, who'd had her.)

Though she still hoped these messages-in-a-bottle would convince him that she was less than worthless, perhaps even dangerous, like a virus or a condition, he continued to behave as though he neither saw nor heard. He may have thought that was the past. While he believed in the future.

Also, though she often doubted it had happened, she had been married to this man, hadn't she?

For Jim, marriage was a safe condition: it kept all his bits and pieces together. To his euphoric eye, nothing could have been more perfect than this chance and, as he saw it, final marriage, one performed—the only one performed—as marriage should be, with awesome words, relatives in tears or good cheer, a mayor in a sash, and a vast family house with fifty new people to meet and charm, and some of his own (flown in in haste and at random) to show what he was capable of, genetically. His alpha and omega, wasn't it!

Start with Lou and VD checks, with the Inskips on booze and Feli whining; end in Belfort in high style.

It's not clear to me how much he actually saw the Belfort house or the Belfort Mairie for what they were: a characteristically French way of making sure that everything looked right.

I know he arrived at the station before Francine was due, that he took his hired car out to the house, looked up the driveway and then turned back. It was vast, gabled, pink-stoned and set in a park. It brought to mind, he said, the troubling question of Hartford, Connecticut, and a number of other questions. He could barely remember what the lovely Francine had said that night. Papa was something to do with twine? *Maman*'s family—had Francine really said so?—had been in trouble after the war for collaboration?

In a way I'm better off than Jim is. He displays the color snaps of his wedding to Francine and what I see is a bunch of people whose bones are soft so that they seem to be settling down onto the nearest ledge, heads in shoulders, torsos in the pelvic basin, but all dressed to the nines. With hats! Down a generation, those famous male cousins of Francine's, those whom she suggests "initiated" her serially and severally, the Jeans and the Raynaults and Benjamins, look equally lop-sided, from drink, hallucogens or over-anxiety, while the females (whom he had expected tall and proud like Francine) seem compressed into their dresses as though their hats weighed too much.

Or looking at the house, I note that wisteria and creepers of all sorts have set its eyes all aslant, that there's subsiding on the right, that what looks (the remains of a fence still show) like it must have been a tennis court is home to hollyhock and thistle, that the cats and dogs in the foreground of the picture are uniformly wall-eyed or overweight, that the ground is marshy, the grass mowed in haste to coarse stubble.

"You're quite right." Jim says. "There were only three bathrooms in the whole house. I don't know what the girls did who had to sit on bare porcelain. I didn't care. I wasn't going to live there, was I? I mean, the set-up wasn't perfect. Nothing is. I got snobbed by a lot of frogs who didn't know any better: Oh, for an American I spoke French so well, *presque sans accent*, there it was—the '*presque*'—the 'almost', after all the fuss my Mother had made about it! They thought all Americans ate on the trot and burgers only. I can deal with that sort of French shit."

No, he was a happy man. A new life lay ahead of him, uncharted, a bit bizarre. No doubt reassuring to have Igor over as best man. He'd had the stitches taken out of her face and brought Francine with him to Belfort, since the police had zapped her driving license.

I got a full account from Igor, who said: "Our friend sounds quite in love."

"It's a condition," I said. "You know that. Jim can fall deeply in love in a week or a day. He's like radar, spotting objects in the sky he can fall in love with."

"At least his Mother's not going to be there. I talked to brother Tony. He said it was really too bad, because Feli dearly loved weddings. As long as they were one per person. Of course she no longer knows who Jim is."

"And Tony? Tony's not coming over?"

"I think Jim offered him a ticket."

"But?"

"I don't think he'd make it. Not with his lungs and everything else. But what he said was, he couldn't leave his Mother."

"She's in a home."

"I know that."

I think of Francine's poor *Maman* too. ("I've met the *Maman*," Igor had said. "Never marry a girl until you meet the Mother. But in this case, I don't think Francine will take after her.") Like Mothers since Eve she was fixed in her ways, and just passing on the bad times she had from her own *Maman*.

It was Papa who liked having four pretty girls. "A sort of fantasy," Jim would say. "He wore long white flannel trousers to play tennis in, but I would describe him as flirtatious."

Celestine was made of sterner stuff. Her daughters existed to be dutiful, Papa's job, since he'd long retired, was to be an extra hand. And when she thought about Francine at all, who went her own way and laughed in her face, she had early on concluded that Francine was some divine mistake, a François gone wrong.

A lot fell on her with this marriage: doing and explaining. What sort of man had the intractable Francine thrown herself away on? No doubt some hippy type. Even as she dealt with *traiteurs* and champagne merchants, as she and remote in-laws and cousins dusted, cleaned and sought to warm the old family fief (from which she and her husband had exiled themselves by selling their share), it fell to her to set out, in a dozen ways, the charms of a future son-in-law she had not yet met. Especially his French, which gave her hope; and not his age, which she thought disproportionate. She didn't much like her other sons-in-law, but at least they did what they were told; from what she'd been able to find out about Jim, he seemed unlikely to comply.

At the same time, she had to elide the fact that her daughter, still in her twenties, was about to become an instant step-grand-mother. And somehow gloss over all those children. It was common enough in her day, but now such generative power was out of fashion. On the other hand, whenever she thought of Francine as a bride, it seemed to her implausible that someone as lean and ambiguous would easily be bred on. Not that she dared mention the subject to her daughter. The one time she tried, Francine said she'd been into casual sex since she was fifteen and she'd never got pregnant, why on earth would she now?

That flat statement was the sort of "realist" argument Francine often used, and Jim had come to complain about: for its coldness, its sense that what is, is, and cannot be changed. However, when Jim's oldest daughter (one of Lou's) suggested at the wedding it was about time he stopped breeding, he said, "Francine is a modern young woman. These days they practice economic contraception: so they can hold down jobs, work out in the gym, keep their bodies, party. It doesn't seem likely."

The dear daughter said, in her mind knowing the answer (yes, yes and yes) said: "What do you think women should do? Fold diapers, wash your shirts?"

His many kids got called, yanked from dinner—unavoidably he heard the mess of their own children, his very own phylum, in the background, seeing smocks on the girls and wadded diapers on the babes—or hauled out of bed themselves, by the telephone summons: "I'm getting married, get yourself on a plane. Yes. Saturday, that's right. I know it's the day after tomorrow. Strasbourg is the nearest airport, unless you want to come by way of Switzerland."

As for the lucky girl, he said they'd have to wait to find out who she was: French seemed to define her. Cool and smart.

What should he have said to his lovely daughter? What could he have said? No child will ever understand its parent's sexuality, much less try to visualize these awkwardly old people at it. And if one did, that would be bad. Very bad.

Feminism, he thought, had probably done more harm to civilization—and civility—than both wars and the Holocaust. Those may have been dread events in history, but lives lost to war or horror could be replenished; buildings could be rebuilt. But not so easily a careful structure, a vast web of human relations.

He did not answer his daughter. He saw no reason to do so if she thought diapers and doing the wash was all womanliness and motherhood was about.

But she didn't. What she thought was that her father was that sort of a man. And he wasn't. Thank God Francine had told him, practically at the start, that she was no feminist.

Maybe half his children came. Jim didn't count them. But those present thought their father looked very happy, information which they did not pass on to their own Mothers.

"We'd agreed we wouldn't see one another until the wedding—I got just one call about the accident, she'd given the police my name as her fiancé," Jim said. "On my mind was whether she'd actually show up. And would I recognize her?"

As he drove to the station to pick up Igor and Francine, the huge lion (which was meant to remind the Belfortains that this controverted territory was forever French) lay couchant by its castle, half hidden by wisps of mist. The air was impregnated with smoke after the early autumn swailing, as from a summer's worth of unused fireplaces; it smelled of chestnut and hams hung in chimneys. The constant rain of Paris had yielded to late patches of sun between clouds that looked bruised and swollen; the light on the station platform was lazy and horizontal. Fat weather.

Only Francine stepped down from the train. There was no Igor. It took Jim some time to pick her out: by her height. She wore a pink pill-box hat with a white dotted veil. The effect was reminiscent of Feli and her Italian family, very 'thirties and 'forties and curiously handsome. It went, he thought, with silk stockings (she wore those, too). She carried a suitcase so light it might as well have been empty. At first she walked the wrong way, and when she turned about, all but walked right past him.

"I fancy the veil," he said.

"It tickles," she replied, raising the veil to plant a fugitive kiss on his cheek. Which was when he noticed the sixteen stitches between her left eye and ear. "I had a little accident."

"The police called. I vouched for you. I said you were an honest woman, or about to become one anyway. Are you all right?"

"Let's not make a fuss about it. A girl only gets married once. Some friends threw a party and I got mixed up on the way home. I thought there was a street there and there wasn't. Anyway, I didn't think I could face it without," she said. "You have no idea the hangover I have."

"It" being marriage. Which she presumably meant she couldn't face without drink or crash.

"Is marriage that awful?" he asked.

"I wouldn't know."

The stitches, she thought, might be hidden with enough

make-up. Though perhaps cosmetics would be no help to the *trac* she felt. "Pure stage-fright. I've never bought a hat before, and I never will again. It's not me. And I won't be able to drive for a year. That's official. I guess I'm in your hands, or should that be 'on'?"

Did that mean she'd never marry again, which would require a hat? A week later in Spain she said once was enough.

He delivered Francine, weaving slightly, to her many cousins and sisters, met Papa (he looked like an Arab, sported a white moustache and legs up to his chest) and *Maman* briefly and inconsequentially, then went off to meet Igor, who'd called to say he'd taken the next train. Osteoporosis, Jim thought. To have one's head fall into one's chest leads to depression. Not enough milk in the war. That's why all these people look like discarded hairpins.

Despite Igor's flowery apologies when they got back to the house, Celestine let them both know she was put out. It was an awkward hour to arrive, she said. People were so thoughtless. She took best man and groom through an enormous kitchen—mousedroppings in the corner, and cats wondering why these people were there when it was not summer—to show them the crew of girls still cleaning up. She hoped he wasn't hungry, she said, though if he were actually starving something could no doubt be found. All this in French, to Igor, whose French was paltry.

Igor said, lighting up as he always did when rattled, that all he wanted was to rest.

"So you see," Francine was to tell me, "the proprieties were all observed. That is the specialty of hypocrites."

"Very good then," said Celestine. "You are in the *salle de billard* upstairs, someone will show you the way."

No one did. But Jim made several inquiries from elderly relatives seeking their bridge partners—"*Non, non, c'est le docteur Klima, il est mon best-man*" "*Ah! Vous ne jouez pas au bridge?*"—and found their way, Igor puffing, blowing smoke, to the attic floor: to what had once been a playroom. It did indeed contain a billiard-table, though its green felt had been ripped in many places by many previous generations. Likewise a grand piano minus many of its keys, a portrait of some notarial Pasquier ancestor whose eyes had been eaten by worms, and a lumpy Napoleonic sledge-bed the heat did not quite reach.

"Well, this is an adventure," Igor said when they'd puffed up three flights of stairs. "You didn't tell me about the Mother. I thought it was one of your rules—post-Lou—never to marry a girl without meeting her Mother."

"Marriages may be, but families aren't made in heaven. I'm marrying Francine, not the Pasquiers. Rest well, Igor."

"Eternal rest is what I want."

Shortly afterwards, the fly on Jim's wall I have become sees Jim padding along the threadbare hall carpeting on the floor below. There, too, the light-bulbs are dim. He is barefoot with a thin undersized towel about his waist and looking for a bath, a shower, or something besides the ewer of water and bowl in his room. The walls are hung any which way with lithos and bills of sale, gimcrack bookshelves, locked doors, all of which he can barely make out. An icy draft blows from the open window of the toilet at the end of the hall.

He is half way down when Celestine arises from the stairs and freezes Jim still. He sees first her hair, which is dark and "practical," then the rest of her which is flushed, her lips sanguine, little carmine dots on her cheeks. Her gait is short and scuttling like a scarab. She, roughly his age, is out of breath and puts a hand to her bosom, which is well-organized.

Now she sees that Jim's feet are bare and he is hardly covered. Disregarding his bare legs, towel and broad, hairy chest, she says: "Would you mind putting on some shoes? Feet perspire and leave a smell in the carpets."

There is no reason for Jim to be amused, but he is, enormously. "*Oui Maman*," he says, scuttling back to his room, suddenly a little boy again. It is that which leaves him panting, hilarious and naked on his bed.

The comic moment is the first thing he shares with Francine when, late that night, after dinner, he runs across her in a back room, alone. She is going to laugh, too, but not whole-heartedly, and breaks off from his kiss first: "*À demain*, then," she says.

"See you tomorrow."

Right then, however, as he lies down on his narrow bed, two children (not his, presumably the offspring of one of Fracine's innumerable cousins) burst from a corner cupboard and flee across the room chased by several others who stop in mid-chase and pretend they are terrorized by the big, naked body lying on the bed. The last two are little girls in pinafores and bright sweaters with the French double bows in their hair. They stop a moment in their *cache-cache* to whisper solemnly, "*C'est le mari de Francine.*"

Then they flee with a great clatter of little shoes before he can say anything.

He thinks how mysterious, and how pleasant, it is to join another family.

2

When he talked about his marriage now, as it was falling apart, he felt the same nostalgia he had felt that evening in Belfort. It was made far worse for him because it took place during one of these blessed American summers, summers which are both disciplined and unruly. The sun beat down steadily. Jim knew the lake, a few miles away was glinting and oily, but here Francine's garden, freshly watered, grew in a hubbub of leaves and petals. It caused him a pang of acute pain. Francine had ruled that none of this ever happened: they were never really married, never happy, did not make Jake whom they both loved, not even lost their daughter whom they had buried together.

In Malaga, and later at the beach-house he rented for the last few days of their honeymoon, he twice found her sitting propped against the tiled walls of the bathroom, a vacant expression on her face, and furious—when he reached out to her—that he should touch her. "Can't you see?" she said. "You can't possibly want to be married to me."

The second time he found she had taken all the pain-killers he carried with him for his necrotic teeth, and not remembering how many had been in the bottle, he drove her back to Malaga and hospital. Where the bearded Spanish doctor said that was a close thing, *Señor*, and Francine, behind a pleated, white screen said, "I'd rather be dead." There were cigarette burns on Francine's long arms. When he saw them in the hospital room in Malaga, she said she'd done them to herself, she wanted to know if she could feel.

The stick-its Francine had been dotting about had only just begun to refer to "Bolivia." Bolivia was her word for oblivion. Later, she mentioned needles: "The needle says I'm not me."

Jim could understand that much. In French they call an orgasm *la petite mort*, the little death. And didn't the executioner Pierrepoint refer to the "release" when his victims dropped? Being dead was just an advanced form of not being yourself. You get sick of yourself; you can die. Being someone else, anyone else, is better. "No doubt she thought being dead would be better. That's what Natasha thought before she walked up to the door: then she thought better of it, a lot better."

When they got back to Chicago, they'd opened up Natasha's cranium and removed a tumor, which looked like a large rat-dropping, with hair attached. Piece of cake, she said. Didn't feel a thing. Bundled up in a robe, her shaven head bandaged, a lop-sided bobble hat on top of that, she walked outside in the cold cadging (as Hubie wouldn't let her have any) cigarettes off Jim.

"They make me sick," she said. "They're *verboten*! Igor would have a fit if he saw me."

He asked about the biopsy. "Oh, malign, I think," she replied cheerfully. "They worry about it, you know, moving around, going places. You always said I had a peasant constitution, so I guess I'll be all right."

To me Jim said, "She didn't even ask! Oncologists come round in white coats, their hands behind their backs, and tell her things. I'm not sure she listens. Igor says it could come back anytime. She has chemo ahead, months of radiation. She'll take it as it comes. Some people, when they do crazy things like swallowing pills or trying to kill themselves, you don't ask, 'Should you?'"

In his view, women were more reckless than men, but about most things (pregnancy, adultery, sex and more) Natasha wasn't so much reckless as heedless. She seemed to understood neither implications nor consequences: just survival. He said. "I'm sure she wouldn't have minded dying. When she woke up after the op, she said she guessed she wasn't meant to die."

She accepted what the dog brought home for dinner. One day it was Jim; another, it might be death—or indeed, life. Francine said at the time: "Go figure which is the luckier for her."

As his beloved *Maman* packed her things in the big old house, saw lawyers and looked for somewhere to stay (I was one of the neighborhood women she asked), the Kid was having whole days like that: as if death, or no longer being who he was, was what he wanted. He banged upstairs, kicking the rubbed treads on the stairs, slammed the door to his room behind him, put himself face down on his bed and buried himself in his duvet, which was ironically bright and cheerful, a view of the sea. He didn't even want to be held. Or comforted.

Jake brought back to Jim his own childhood, and he had to go back to Igor to control himself. "Not a crutch, not a luxury," he said to Francine. "A good man like Igor is a form of exorcism. You've got some things to exorcize. A Mother. You've got a Mother and I had a Mother."

It was probably back then, a few years before I met him, that Jim was attracted to being someone else: so that in his own child-like way he could feel what Feli had felt when she poured her own tears into his eyes. Jake's bouncing ball, his sudden refusal to be with them when they were together in the house was like young Jim, kid to his father, bolting out of the house, swimming his resentments across the inlet, a half-mile, throwing a ball against a wall for hours. Always he had to come back, for kids live where their parents live. None of it worked. It didn't get rid of the rage; it didn't help him sleep. Instead Jim would lie down in his room to die for his mother, and she would lie in her room and blow her nose ever so softly so as not to wake him up. Now he remembered himself as being ravished by the thing itself, the act of dying. Once dead—he made dying last—sleep would take over. The last thing, each time, was a smell of moist lilies, a breath of cool air, his fingers playing with the velvety pads and buttons of the coffin in which he lay, a gentle subsidence of earth that trickled into the corners of his mouth.

It is quite common to think one deserves to be punished. Sometimes there are so many things to be punished for that one doesn't know for which of them one is being punished. In the same way, I'm sure Francine, who is nothing if not calculating, each time had a foretaste of being beaten. And did what would bring the belt, her Papa's, down from its hook in their closet.

This morning, too. I saw Francine drive slowly by our houses, Mrs. Vojtyla's and then mine, as though she might perhaps stop, and slowly enough for me to see she was clear-eyed: like a painter standing back and viewing how far he'd come from his early works. Like Igor, I was struck by the sadness of her eyes.

In contrast, Jim grinned, bared his odd teeth, worked his beard, and looked like a man just starting out in life. He proposed to survive this shipwreck as he had the others.

"Women and children first," he'd joke. "I've got my water-wings." He took to bringing over good bottles from his cellar. His lips looked liquid, his eyebrows went astray. We drank far too much. Francine behaved as though nothing had really changed; all she'd done was come to her senses. She insistently wrote his children, visited his friends, cultivated new ones, worked on her body, gave up smoking, gave up drinking. A thief of feelings. He thought she told

Milo and Frank and Igor things about him which made it awkward for him to see them.

Francine was his most recurring subject. He, too, had a bit of the painter in him: the obsessive way painters return to the same subject—always as though they missed something last time they traced that neck, those eyes. Then he'd stop, blink, and look at me.

"With Francine I thought I'd landed," he said.

3

The mill-house, to which his mother and brother were to come at the very worst possible time, and which Jim, having reached the age when he could take extensive time off, bought one summer when they'd been married for a few years, was really the scene of successive unravelings in their life together.

Jim either cleared the ground or built up walls against the torrent that flooded every winter, or spent whole days with his books in his study.

Such a wonderful ironic subject he was working on, Francine wrote me wearily: Omission. What duties of care one has. Can one be guilty for failing to do something? Are we expected to be heroes when we see a man fall into the drink? If we can't swim? What is the whole truth if we leave something out of a story? "It's a nice theoretical problem. It doesn't engage him with the real world, in which he's often at sea. I play catch-up with American Express; I keep finding new debts, envelopes he's never opened. He doesn't pick up phone messages. Think of all the friends he has on the wall—Does he ever get in touch with them? Who remembers his kids' birthdays? I do. He talks a lot about his father, but in a way I can't ever seem to get him down pat. Just what did the Mounts live on when Jim was growing up? You know who he is when he's there, amiable enough. But there's a kind of vagueness about off-stage. I'm sure you know what I mean."

In the next letter she wrote about going to a doctor who came to their remote village in the hills behind Pisa on Saturday mornings. "It's a half-hour climb," she said, "and I kept wondering what could go wrong back at the house, if Jim wouldn't set it on fire, if some creditor wouldn't rip out the telephone or cut off the electricity. If Jake would be all right. Then when you get there you go into a waiting room, which on weekdays is where the post office is, with the doctor's 'office' behind, in what must be where they sort the mail. The doctor is young and wears a hat, his patients are mostly old women who've lost their husbands and suffer from loneliness like I do. You sit there for maybe an hour—There's nothing better to do—and at the end of that time you know all about their ovaries and the rest of their plumbing, how their husbands approached them (like sacks of grain), all stories they must already know from other Saturdays. Their inquisitiveness is fierce. They stare at me angrily: Where are my children? I have only one. Why? Is it because my husband doesn't approach me? He's not impotent is he? I had to fight them off about Jim. And still they knew more about him than you could believe: where his letters came from (he must know important people, only important people get letters), that he watched football in Romano's caffé down by the trout farm below the mill, what time he got up, why was he cutting down trees at the wrong time of the year?"

She didn't say why she'd gone to see the doctor, but now she was willing to tell me: she'd been having serious, consistent pains in her liver. "I thought it was because of the local wine, or maybe my past was catching up with me, as I always expected it would. The doctor asked me about my periods, and I didn't know the right word for it. He kept saying '*mestre*' or something like that and making graphic gestures until he lost patience with this stupid foreign woman. '*Sangue*,' he then explained. Blood."

I could hear her laugh at herself. Hers is a lovely laugh. It lies somewhere deep inside herself, and it's as though she were always surprised by it. "I told him I had no idea when the last one was." She never thought about them, she hardly had any. When he said that as far as he could see she was pregnant and should go down to Pisa to take the test, she didn't believe him.

"Well, I was wrong. And that presented problems. I had something in me that belonged to Jim (which turned out to be the delicious Jake.) That was the way Jim looked at it. You have to understand, I'd never been pregnant and never expected to be, I had no one to talk to, I didn't know the language, I was in a mill-house in the middle of nowhere that was cold and damp even in summer, and I wasn't at all sure I wanted to be a mother or would be a good one. I wasn't even sure I wanted to go on being married and carted around from place to place with a man who was so restless and so unpredictable."

The following year they returned to the mill-house in the fall and stayed through January with little Jake. It was the first year Feli and Tony turned up, with Tony coming down with pneumonia and mixing whiskey in with the oxygen in his tank, while Feli was furious to have to drink tea from a cracked cup.

"She said she was too old to be left alone with Jake, so all that meant is that I was more stuck than ever, because Jim certainly wasn't going to emerge to talk to his Mother. He couldn't without the two of them trying to settle old scores. I remember it as a time when I put to good use the learning how to lie I'd practiced with my Mother. I'd been taught the least I could do, asked if I loved her, was to say '*Oui, Maman.*' I had become a very good liar, but it wasn't something I liked having to do. Fortunately I had Jake, and you don't have to lie to kids when they're six months old."

Two years later Francine was pregnant again. "The last thing I ever expected to happen," she said. "I'm simply not a Mother in that sense. Of course you don't need to be told how Jim reacted to being a father again, at sixty-something. How then could I not be happy? It's true I adored Jake, who was then two. Did that mean I wanted another one?"

Then Jim had the mad idea that since his brother had re-married his second wife and gone West with her, leaving Feli alone in New York (under threat of being put in a home if she couldn't cope on her own), Feli should come and live with them. In the mill-house.

"We'd tried that once," pursued Francine. "It had been a disaster. Even in summer it would have been madness because of the way the two of them, Jim and his Mother, clashed. To do it again in winter, and with me pregnant, was quite unthinkable."

By then, Feli had shrunk. What kept this nearly-ninety-year-old shade of herself earthbound were her swollen legs, her feet that fitted only into large felt slippers. Two heavy bathrobes clutched about her, she limped heavily and reverberated, her cane stamping on the mill-house's stone floors. Her hands trembled, very little hair held her skull together, and her eyes were washed out, as if they didn't care to see what was around her.

"I hated the house by then," Francine continued. "Rory wasn't really visible, and Feli refused to take pregnancy into account. 'Another mouth to feed,' she said disapprovingly. 'Poor Jim already has so many, I can't keep up with them.'

Apart from the local graveyard, which Feli took in carefully, making inquiries about cost—"It takes influence to get a slot," Jim explained. "Who wants to be among aliens in the next world?"—she hated everything, the weather, the situation of the house, that there wasn't someone around to clean, that this was such a large house whereas she and Tony had been used to two rooms in Manhattan, and her daughter-in-law, Francine, was surly, while Jake was underfoot, noisy and disorderly.

"Where was grandmotherly love?" Jim asked. "Once a week, if the river was falling, we went down to town," Jim says. "Just to get out of there. Mamma's spirit was thwarted, she was like a ghost fighting to get back to life. When she didn't talk about whether she ought to have a by-pass operation or just die and be done with it, she complained: this might be Italy but it wasn't her part of Italy; Tony was sick out West, 'that woman' wasn't looking after him, his 'horrible children' never went to see him; the money she'd saved ("Despite you two boys") was mysteriously diminishing—she refused to see Tony's hand in this.

By the time Francine was halfway through her pregnancy—they knew it was to be a girl and called Aurora—Feli had begun to forget what she'd said the day or the minute before, so everything had to be repeated, like "We're going out tonight."

"Who's that?" she would ask.

"Francine and I."

"Didn't you say she was having a baby?"

"Yes, she's having a girl, Mamma, Aurora."

"Such a peculiar name. I don't think I know any Auroras."

"Francine's left some soup on the stove."

"Who?"

"Would you rather come down to Pisa with us?"

"Oh no, a little soup is all I need."

 Did she want to come?

"What if your brother called and she wasn't here? You know she's going to outlive him," said Francine, slipping into a loose dress left over from her first pregnancy. "Come on, or we'll never get out of here."

In the car, always reasonable, Francine said calmly, "It depends what kind of life she'll have after the op. But that's not the answer your mother wants. She wants you to say, don't die, I can't live without you. That's what your brother tells her. And for him it's true. He's her burden, she's his. It's like the president and the senate: she doesn't want your advice, she wants your consent."

They left elaborate instructions for Feli about how to use the telephone, and what a party line was. Jake was sound asleep upstairs and Francine showed Feli where Jake's juice-bottle was if he woke up. Briefly lucid, Feli smiled her crooked smile, and said reproachfully: "You'd think I'd never had any children of my own," and Jim didn't say it had been sixty years ago, though he thought it. Instead, as they left, he stopped by Romano's caffé, which was hard by the main road, to ask his wife, Pia, if she could just call the house, say around nine, to make sure everything was all right.

That night was one of several about which Jim was confused. What happened on which occasion—though each one was at least metaphorically connected to the others, all bound to birth and its terrible burdens—he could not say for sure.

This one was later known as the "False Alarm." It began with Francine being taken ill after dinner. The cramps were so severe that Francine had to get out of the car as they were on the ring road and going home. She stood doubled over for some while in front of a shop (which Jim thought was a flower shop) with its corrugated metal shutters up. He recalled a number scrawled on the shutter: in case of an emergency.

It was an emergency, but he couldn't do anything for Francine who was obviously suffering, all the while saying that, really, there was nothing wrong.

Pregnancy and its ups and downs is a mystery to most men. Not to Jim. He'd brought procreation down to its common denominator, as expressed by the Mothers and their various deliveries. On the one hand, this was reassuring to the Mothers; on the other it was unreal. He wasn't having the baby, they were.

With me he would say cruelly that since birth had been common to all the Mothers he'd lived with, it did mark them off from those who, like myself, have not gone through the same ordeal (or the happiness that follows), as also from those who cannot participate, such as men. The most striking aspect of such occasions, as Jim recalled them, was the helplessness of the Mothers, the way doctors and nurses deprived them of their Selves, and the helplessness of those around them: because they could not give birth for them.

"You can die for someone else," Jim said, "but you cannot give life for them."

The night of the False Alarm he turned back and rushed her to the *pronto soccorso* attached to the hospital in Pisa. Francine was really out of it and lying in the back seat groaning. He didn't tell her where she was going, because she, who knew all about pain, would have protested that she was perfectly all right, it was probably something she ate.

He found a phone, slipped in his *gettone*, and called his Mother to say he would be delayed, as Francine seemed to be in labor. His mind seemed to have slowed down, he said, and he let the phone ring at least five minutes before seeing that another man (presumably another haggard father) was waiting patiently for him to finish. Or start. There was, however, no answer at the mill-house. Feli could have been asleep, but it was as likely that she had forgotten where the phone was, far away from her own room.

He found Francine on a gurney on the third floor, still fully dressed. A row of women lay on other gurneys lined up against the wall. All of them wore gowns and puffy slippers. Two of them were smoking, one was eating slices of salami which her mother put one by one into her mouth.

"Apparently there are no beds available yet," Francine said. She looked dazed.

A nurse came by with a watch. "How long since the last contraction?" she asked. Francine shook her head. A while later the nurse came back and asked the same question. Francine shook her head again. "*Fa male?*" the nurse asked. It hurts? "Where is her Mother?"

"In America." Jim told her.

Francine wanted something to drink. "The wine we had at dinner must be making me thirsty."

The nurse asked when the baby was due. Jim told her: in about twelve weeks.

"*Dio mio!*" she said. And to Jim: "Come with me." "Everyone has a Mother. Your wife does not speak Italian? Is she prepared?" Then she said to Francine, as she turned the gurney into a tiny cubicle, "*Svestirsi*. Take your clothes off. Ask her if she would rather shave herself," she said to Jim. She hurried off to call a doctor.

To the nurse they were curious people. Jim said. In what sort of a country did they make women this tall, so thin, with hips so like a boy's? In America they go to hospitals without a nightdress or a mother?

Why was this image (a shaven or unshaven wife) so persistent in Jim's account? And what kind of a question was that, to ask, is she "prepared"? Did they mean "prepared" in the pre-op sense? Or ready?

No one is prepared. Jim knew that, Francine much less so. The degree of pain is always unexpected, and for Jake she had insisted on being under anesthetic. No one tells you, except grandmothers-to-be. That is what they are for, even if age made it impossible for Feli to understand what was going on.

By the time the doctor showed up, her pain had eased, and he sent her home with dire warnings. A false labor was not uncommon, but it often meant that the child might be born prematurely. She should always be ready, he said.

By Rory, Francine had been through one delivery, but that did not make her better "prepared" when, a few weeks later, again all of a sudden, Jim had to rush her down to the *pronto soccorro* a second time.

"Do I have to shave myself?" Francine asked. "I don't think I want to go through with this."

What could you say? From the last time, she remembered the woman feeding her daughter salami and the distraught way in which the Mother put away the salami and broke into suppressed tears as her daughter was wheeled away, a hand waving feebly from a tangle of sweaty sheets.

This time Francine was on one of three gurneys in the corridor outside the delivery room. At every cry, she winced. Sweat broke out on her forehead and on her upper lip. "Am I next?" she asked. Jim shook his head.

Again, they wanted to know if Francine was prepared. And the obstetrician nodded at the nurse and said, "The delivery room is not a place of mind over matter."

What I suspect is that for a woman so accustomed to being in charge of herself, pretty much invulnerable in mind but not in body, the idea that this (birth) was happening to her; that she couldn't do anything about it, was terrifying,.

"You have to treat it," she said later, "as though it's happening to someone else."

Someone else is being wheeled along long corridors which, now that sun's up, are thronged with relatives and shifts going off work. There's a man with a long canister serving coffee in paper cups, people are reading the morning papers, the sunlight is bright. "Even in Chicago, where I spoke the language, no one will tell you anything. What did Jim say with Jake? He said everything would be all right, it would soon be over. Well, it wasn't. But at least I didn't know anything about it until I woke up."

I don't think it was anxiety that got to her (here again, with Rory, she wanted to be put out and not feel a thing, but they said that with a premature baby they would need her help) as much as the disgust of someone normally more fastidious that a cat. You could keep the outer world at bay by cleanliness, but what could you do with what's inside the body and must out: snot, feces, sperm, blood, puke? The insides of a body, she once said, are vast and complex, and if we wore them outside (and our smooth skin, washed hair, eye-lined eyes, rosy lips inside) people would flee. She has a whole other body within, a perfectly round, small, beach-ball-shape that stretches her skin and makes it impossible to see what the doctor between her legs is peering at. She sees no more than a patch on his head where his hair is thinning. And this body inside her has to come out. Like it or not. And she didn't like it at all.

All her life until Jake was born she had been whole. She had done things to herself—burning, puncturing, piercing—but that was different. And the men who had "done it" to her when she was young didn't count; they were just an easy way out, "trips" during which she imagined a hundred things that weren't what was actually happening. Whereas now, the doctor says she's going to have to concentrate on this, on bringing Rory into the world. However she can't concentrate on "this", whatever this is, because no sooner does she catch her breath after one bout of pain than another builds up. She feels deeply stupid blowing out her lungs in little pants, like a dog in summer. She says, can't he give her something for the pain that comes with the contractions? He looks up from under the sheet (which is like a canopy over his head) as though she'd asked some unusually stupid question. Of course not. Actual delivery hasn't begun yet.

Oh. It's early days yet, is that the idea? All the time she pants and squeezes Jim's hand—never reassuring, since he's the cause of what she's going through—she has the feeling that she's done something wrong. The child shouldn't be born now; she wasn't ready. Who was doing this to her and why? The torsions and contortions in her belly were a sure sign of disaster.

But now she suddenly finds herself in a brightly lit room, and everything is suddenly speeding up and enlarged, or multiplied. There now seem to be two, no three, four nurses with whiny rubber gloves; the obstetrician has not one bald batch, but two, or there are two doctors with bald patches. The only thing anyone says to her is: "relax" or "push now." There go the globular lights, which have dark centers and rims of harsh white light. They swivel or busy themselves overhead: now they're over her, now behind. The lights, ever more of them, glint on the chrome of the stirrups which hold her legs high over the level of her head. There is a clatter of instruments. What are they doing? What are they going to do? Jim now has both of her hands, which he holds behind her. She notices he is sweating; she notes she is wet. The pain no longer seems to stop at all. If it stops in one place, the small of her back, it intensifies in another; her thighs feel molten. The words all those people say around her turn liquid; she can read the words that drip down the white walls and mingle with sunlight. Every once in a while a nurse darts around the metal, squeezes past trays and mops her face. Francine's eyes are rolled so far back she can't really make the nurse out. A man she hasn't seen before runs into the room with a tank on some sort of a trolley and the nurse who's been wiping her face now puts a rubber mask over her nose and she is forced to breathe in ice, sweet ice, then for a few seconds (it seems like) her brain seems to sing and her forehead goes numb.

In a sudden moment of lucidity (she remembers herself shouting, "Can't you stop this?"), the pain becomes infinitely particular, the way ice can seem to burn. She is breaking into several fragments, huge cliffs of ice, which are severing themselves from her and falling, in a series of smaller fragments, each of them twisting, into dark waters, and these, in turn, are rising above her knees.

Jim is pouring water, much too slowly, down her throat.

Two, three, four doctors are shouting at her to push. To push now. One last time. She hears a howl, which must be her own. The fragments of herself are only two now, but they are being pulled apart, and only in the part of her which is still one (it must be her mouth), is this animal (it must be herself) howling. Come on, push, it's nearly there.

She thinks of herself as back in the mill-house. The butcher who comes round once a week in his white van is standing by the open back doors and holding a rabbit up by its hind legs for her to see, bones showing, blood seeping. But it is Rory. Not a rabbit.

Then she was—when Jim came back the following morning with his Mother in tow—in a ward with six beds. There were cots and grandmothers by each bed. On the bedside tables were used dishes, flowers. Babies slept or bawled; breasts engorged behind lace bed-jackets; newspapers spilled from sheets.

Francine's bed had a cot at its foot, only it was empty. Jim had brought the only nightgown she owned that buttoned down the middle: with a bright slip of a scarf around her neck, Francine looked chic. A passing nurse felt Francine's small breasts for firmness and said, tomorrow.

Tomorrow what? "What happens now?" Francine asks. "They don't tell you anything here. I want my baby."

"Perhaps tomorrow," Jim says.

"I haven't held my baby yet. I haven't even seen her."

Jim had. She was dark and cross-looking; very small. The doctor had told him one never knew with premature babies.

And there was a grandmother by Francine's bed. This of course was a miracle. Somewhere Feli had gathered together her scattered wits (it was to be just about the last time) and emerged with them all in one place. At the mill-house, as Jim had been preparing to drive back down to Pisa, she was insistent and peremptory. "I'm over twenty-one, you know," she said. "I'm perfectly well, and you can't keep me from seeing my daughter-in-law. I have paid for a girl to stay with Jake…Here she is now."

For some time that morning she sat like any Mother on a rickety wooden chair, her hair wispy and her glasses smudged. Some minutes were occupied with carefully peeling a pear for Francine, all by the feel of her shaky hands. Later, from her black little-old-lady's shopping basket, she produced a bottle of Spumante, which she said Tony had asked her to buy for them. When she'd finished her glass, she walked around the other beds offering the Mothers a glass and peering down at the babies in their cots. Then, still carrying the bottle, she vanished for a quarter-hour and Jim finally found her staring through the glass walls of the nursery, presumably looking for her grandchild, and lost.

The third time at the *pronto soccorro*, two summers later, was obviously the worst.

4

It rained in March and April; the river rose. If it stopped raining, an icy mountain cold settled in: with a sun that warmed only the skin and a wind that cut. The sheep on the slopes above the mill-house steamed. To the joy of Rory and Jake, the shepherd, whose name was Achille, brought the thick-wooled beasts, many of the ewes pregnant, down in a jangling of bells for a coffee with grappa at the mill-house. In those days, while Francine had more or less recovered her health, and as a girl, the youngest sister of Romano, the local bar-owner's wife, had been hired to help out, Francine was often withdrawn and engaged in endless private tasks (writing letters, laying fires, sewing, reading, mending, swabbing the distant floors of rooms they never used—but also smoking too much, leaving half-finished glasses of wine by various fireplaces that needed constant tending) like someone who knows she has failed to do something but doesn't quite know what it is.

But from her window at the far end of the house, over the mill itself, Feli shouted furiously at Achille and his flock below. The animals were frightening enough—a cloud of smelly, steaming wool that trampled down the little bit of order the family had made by the river: borders with stones, sometime-soon-flowering plants, and flagstone paths to walk on when the ground was sponge or mud—Achille frightened her even more. He was an alien, more beast than man, she had said on other occasions. He had a huge moustache, his hair came halfway down his back, his trouser buttons were never fastened, he was drunk all day long, and obscene, and why did her son live in such a place and among such people? *Con questa gente*, she said, as though a new breed had risen from caves deep in the valley.

Down below, Jake—not yet "the Kid" because there were, unexpectedly, two of his kind—looked up at his grandmother with a puzzled expression; his sister sat on a stone getting her leggings dirty, and cried at the sudden noise among the bells.

With babies and the very old, Jim would say, the most you can do is appease them. If they're angry or befuddled, you calm them, hug them, distract them. He tried, but neither Feli (distraction) nor Rory (hugs) would calm down, so he sent the shepherd and his flock back on the road; then and only then was Feli appeased, but Rory, deprived of her bells, cried even harder, and even Jake (who had magical powers with her) was unable to stem her tears.

"All right," he said. "We'll all go for a walk."

One of Feli's stockings was down about her ankles; neither boot was laced up. While he hooked his Mother into her heavy fur coat, one that went back to Jim's own childhood in Philadelphia, she insisted on knowing (refusing to let him put her clothes together until he did) when he was going to talk to her—seriously—about the operation. "I've been thinking," she said vaguely; but when he said they could talk about it while they were walking, she held on to his arm fearfully and said, "God is telling me I cannot go while your brother still needs me. If I don't do it, it's just a question of time."

"The children are waiting. We ought to get going. There should still be some sun further up the hill."

"Your wife should be looking after the children."

"She's getting better. She'll come if she wants to."

"She's not coming because of me," Feli said, refusing to budge. "The first one was good to me." "Lou? Nonsense. We've been through all the arguments, Mamma."

"You don't love your brother."

He did, but Tony was an open book to Jim. Tony wanted to liquidate his past. The past affected his breathing even more than his emphysema. He wanted his Mother in the home so that he could breathe.

He put her arm through his and guided her down the stone steps, then past the mill and its noisy sluices and through several rooms that had once stored the ground grain, and finally out through the kitchen where he hoped (he told me) to run into Francine. "That dreadful month of March," he said, "was the only time I'd ever seen Francine weaken, lose her direction. She was a fine, and a funny, Mother. Normally, she would have run to her when Rory cried. She doted on both of them, but I could tell she was living with fear, and I thought maybe that was why she wasn't coming down from wherever she was to look after Rory.

"The children had become in some inexplicable way something less than substantial for her, like morning mushrooms. It was as if she couldn't trust them to continue. I know it sounds peculiar, but I honestly believe she lived those days that turned into months with the taste of death in her mouth. The death could be her own, or it could have been the children's. Despite the fact that until then even Rory had been unutterably healthy. Whatever the cause, this fear was utterly real to her.

Later, of course, I found out that she'd gone—an ordinary part of her daily routine—to the caffé down by the main road to have her coffee and pick up the newspaper. I don't know why this didn't occur to me at the time."

I think I do know why. Talk of death, his Mother's, his own, anyone's, always clouded Jim's mind. He turned away from thinking about it the way, while asleep, one struggles to get out of a nightmare by waking up. His Mother wasn't frightened by death as he was; she was simply obsessed with Tony, who was all she had left. He was. Scared. Not with its silence, not with his eventual absence (happens often enough anyway, he said), not with the farewells, but with the actual moment—the encroaching cold.

Even stepping outside into the cold and strapping Rory into her rickety pram, Feli would not give up. "Please," she said. "Just tell me what you would do if you were me?"

To say, leave it in God's hands, would have been hypocritical; he didn't have her faith. He said, "I couldn't answer her. It was cold. Our cold up in that mill-house was that deathly sort of cold, and I didn't want that for anyone."

The four—Jake flinging stones into the hedges, Rory still furious in her bumping pram, Feli thumping her thick stick, himself deeply uneasy—made their way up the driveway and onto an old farm road that led up to where Achille waved a bottle at them from the hill-top. He said to his mother and Jake, "You two take the pram and I'll try and cope with Rory. Jake, take your *Nonna*'s hand."

"I'll take the baby," Feli said stubbornly, already bending over the pram in picking her up. "She's very hot," Feli said. She held Rory reluctantly, as though she were only doing so out of duty.

"She gets that way when she yells."

Of course he should not have let Feli have her way. The hill was steep, her walk faltering, the child struggling in her arms. Only Jake, liberated, took off up the hill with the pram a fast car in his hands.

A few hundred yards away, Achille must have imagined this mad family (the villagers couldn't imagine anyone rich, which all foreigners were, living on such poor land, good for little but pasturage) was in more trouble than it was and came running down the slope towards them. He stopped just short of Feli and rang the sheep-bell he had dangling from his little finger at Rory, who first beamed—like a shaft of sunlight, Jim said—and then screamed.

"*Sior!*" Achille shouted over Rory's cries. "*El la strega che gli fa piangere!*" (Feli was a witch making the child cry, which to Achille was simply an obvious truth) and with a gesture like a magician's finding a card in a total stranger's breast pocket, he had Rory, no bigger than a lamb, tucked under his arm. Where she immediately calmed down, with another huge smile on her face as she reached for the bell on his finger.

At least that was what Jim thought he heard: it's the witch making the child cry. He didn't immediately see, he said, that his Mother had toppled backward; or didn't react quickly enough when Achille bent down and held out his free hand out to help Feli up, and when she shrank away from him, muttering bizarrely, he simply grasped her arm—as if she were a sick animal—and pulled her to her feet.

Of course the shepherd had little contact with human beings at all, much less with women. Or with witches who shouted at him whenever he appeared with his sheep and the kind *signore* gave him a cup of coffee laced with a little *grappa*. But it was clear to him that she needed his help, particularly as he could see she had lost one of her boots in her fall. Jake, up above them, had turned around, delighted, and Achille had handed Rory on to Jim, so that he could fetch the boot and help the old woman put the boot back on.

No one could have foreseen that as he bent over, Feli would grasp her heavy stick as he leaned down to recover her boot and bring it down on his head. Nor, when he fell, senseless, that she would approach Achille and pat him comfortingly on the head—as though she hadn't meant to hurt him. Or that when she stood up again, her hand was covered in his blood.

How could Francine trust him? Who had no idea where Jim and his mother and her babies had gone, who'd come back and found the house empty and was about to go looking for them when the ancient police car come down the driveway, making her think right away, that's it, they're all dead, and hastily planned her own. Who then saw Feli come out of the back with blood on her hands, on her stick, and, now, as she drew closer, suddenly alert, with Francine looking closer, blood on her fur coat.

Before Francine could say anything, Feli was repeating incoherently: "That horrible man, Jim left me with him, I can't stay, you tell him he has to take me downtown (downtown?), I have to get away, yes, find Tony, get away."

In the background, she saw the local policeman saluting. Behind him, Jim, holding Jake by one hand, eager to tell his *Maman* all, and Rory in the other, fast asleep. How could she?

5

That was the beginning. From there on it went from bad to worse, Jim said. All that long eventually-hot spring, which was always a hopeful time, when the sun finally moved round the shoulder of the hill behind them, the waters receded, the leaves burst out, and into the beginnings of hot Tuscan summer, with its rancorous thunder, the burning plush of the local buses, unknown to any of them, Rory was noisily dying.

Though it didn't look like that. It looked like colic, then like bad temper, then like fury. Some days her temperature would skyrocket; others were not peaceful. Rory was never at peace), but left the child exhausted. The local once-a-week doctor and the others they consulted weren't much help. Up there in the high hills the locals were stoical from long experience. Not all children survived. The doctors said fevers were endemic in the area, always had been. So it got to be that Jim and Francine accepted that the fever should mount, break, recur. Whenever they decided to leave, to go back to Chicago, Rory pulled herself back from whatever brink she'd been on and became merely a tempestuous child. She yelled, she screamed, and then she would be perfect again. He said: "It's easy enough to say what we could have done, should have done. But her frailty, her swings, her crises were more like giant tantrums than an illness."

I think neither he nor Francine were entirely sure what was wrong with their child. Besides which, Rory had her miraculous moments that would make them forget everything in their attempt to get to the heart of her.

Jim's memory of her, and Francine's too, is that of a child you could beguile with sheep and bells, but whom you could also engage with things she couldn't possibly have understood—at which she'd fall quiet, eyes wide open, taking everything in. Wise. And if they suddenly stopped, or got distracted, she was furious, as if saying: you think I don't understand, but I do.

"What could I do?" Jim said. "I just looked at her and admired her insistent attachment to being. It turned out they were screams of pain. Some of the time, when I held her, I could feel her burn through whatever I wore. But I thought it was a sort of brain fever, the body being overwhelmed by feelings that were too strong for it. It didn't occur to me that she could die. What can you know ahead of time? No child of mine had ever died." He shrugged. "No one in the house, nor the village doctor, recognized or admitted it. At least not until the summer, when it became obvious. And then, in the hospital in Pisa, they advised against moving her, and the specialist said that operating—if it was her intestine that was infected—was dangerous. And I finally understood, as I think Francine did, that we were powerless. Matters were in God's hands. It is the worst feeling you can ever have or imagine, a hundred times worse than dying yourself. Though it was not something Francine and I ever said to one another. If she were going to die—and in many ways we would ourselves die with her—then it should be where she was and always had been, where for whole stretches she could still be quite magnificently alive."

I suppose it's traditional that part of his anger should be directed at God, but what sickened him most—because he so dearly wanted his tiny daughter to live—was ever the thought of those Mothers who thoughtlessly rid themselves of such beings. That was something he came back to time and again. He believed that however small or frail or defective, what curettage or a pill expels is human. He and Francine were bound in a struggle for their own survival, and smart Aurora's, while others frivolously scraped and flushed.

This was and is so deep in Jim, so utterly physical, that I've never been able to face it. I don't think anyone has been able to. It is one of those emotions that are far past reason, as it was for his brother's crazy daughter Tessa, the one who could hear all the unborn children of the world as they shrieked in the night, who told him he had but to listen and he would hear them himself. And perhaps, too, though he hadn't yet met Mrs. Vojtyla, or her deaf cat, this was when Jake first learned, watching his *Maman* and his Popeye fight the obvious day in and day out, that silence is often better, and safer.

For the mill-house to concentrate exclusively on this battle, which began in earnest with the summer, as they were readying themselves to fly back to Chicago, perhaps in the fall, before the cold, first Jim's brother had to turn up again—slightly larger than life and frayed at the edges—and whizz Feli off. At least that was the intent. It would be his last outing, and hers, and I assume Feli paid for it.

"See Naples and die," said Tony. It was a joke that fell flat, but then taste was never one of Tony's strong points. After the holiday, which would end in the Agrigento of her childhood, Feli said she would be operated on; and, as if that were news, that a place was now available for her in the Spellman Home, where Jake was to visit her two years later and she was to die in her mind while Tony died on his hilltop in a car, a smile on his face.

But when the time came for Tony and Feli to go, he did and she wouldn't. She stayed and prayed. Often downstairs, alongside her son.

Those must have been dark days. In moments of silence, when Jim talked to her, Rory would look up at him with dark eyes and say, "save me." Francine couldn't bear it. Jim couldn't bear it.

"To live through some things," Jim said, "requires what we call 'heroic virtue'. I don't have it. I told Rory to hang in there, she didn't want to go someplace where winter goes on forever. For your mother, I said. For me. But she couldn't wait. The fever, whatever it was, had come back and wouldn't go away."

My Mother said we should never have come to a place that was so far away. But she took the brunt of Rory's outrage at what was happening to her.

"By then we knew we had no choice."

This time, they left the empty house, packed Jake and Rory in the car and drove straight to the *pronto soccorso* in Pisa. The evening was harsh, the silver slivers of the olive leaves took on a sinister glow as the sun started setting, the cypresses along the road, and the way Jim raced, turned into a black tornado. When they reached the ring-road—by then it was dark and a shower had fallen—they passed police cars that were super-washed and bright-colored.

In the emergency room, the attendants either spoke very loudly or walked silently by on sponge soles as though the three of them didn't exist. Again, color figured. The staff were Ethiopian black, the walls ochre half-way up and then white. Francine was now—now that the crisis was upon them—excessively composed: considering that the baby was burning up in her arms, a sick doll in a parenting class. With huge artificial tears that shone.

They sat down on metal chairs, one apart, Francine holding Rory, Jake on Jim's lap, asleep. He thought his mother was sitting reproachfully between them. She had plenty to say but didn't dare open her mouth.

Trolleys were wheeled by, clattering with emptied plates. He said, "I can't see what we're doing here."

Francine was pale: she either couldn't or wouldn't talk. They were another painting, called "Waiting". In the foreground a mother and a father; behind them hurrying figures and cypresses. He mumbled: "They won't be able to mend her."

His Mother, who in his mind at least insisted on being present, nodded. She wore a dress he remembered from the 'forties: of blue rayon, with a lace collar.

A black doctor walked over toward them—he had a white cap on his head like a short-order cook; from the cap extruded patches of tight, wiry hair—and indicated a corner with a white curtain, which he then drew aside to reveal a cot, presumably for Rory. The gesture seemed theatrical.

The cot, however, was filled with cleaning materials: buckets, a mop, detergents, rolls of paper towels. He spoke to them in signs as though neither of them knew Italian. He reached for the baby, in fact touched her head, but Francine refused to part with Rory. Jim thought she was being unreasonable, so he stood up to urge her to let the doctor have the baby.

He must have done so too abruptly because the doctor looked scared and took a step back. "*Poverina*," he murmured. "If she lasts the night we will see with the surgeon in the morning. There is nothing you can do here."

They sat down again, as before. A while later Jim heard long, noisy sobbing—he also heard the doctor's steps retreating through the double doors and along a long corridor. At first he thought it was his Mother making a scene. But his mother was at the mill-house. And it couldn't be Francine, Francine never cried. But as soon as he sat down the crying stopped. So it might have been himself crying.

An hour might have gone by—it could have been much more,

or no time at all—before a nurse came hurrying by, obviously going to some other part of the hospital. She had very bright spectacles, a bright blue cardigan over her white uniform, and a bright red smear on her mouth as if she'd just been eating pasta. When she saw them, she suddenly stopped and stood there in silence, her arms akimbo. Then decisively she walked to the reception desk where the attendants were playing a very loud game with tarot cards in between patients who came and went, to whom they gave certificates, reading them out loud: "Mastrogiovanni, construction worker, born 1937, unfit for work." That sort of thing, quickly done. The nurse pulled her blue cardigan around her and rapped on the desk. The game suddenly stopped.

The nurse said: "Find this woman a bed immediately. The baby should at least be allowed to die in her mother's arms." Her voice was loud and commanding. She came back over, looking around to see if anyone objected, and then took Francine by the arm and led her away. And why should she have whispered, if it was obvious the baby would die? Francine certainly accepted it as a simple fact and went off with the nurse and her daughter. All Francine said, looking down at Rory, was: "She looks just like your Mother."

Later the nurse returned and took him gently by the hand. "They are resting," she said. "If you want to stay with your son, there is a bar open all night."

Jim said yes, he knew.

"You go through there (she pointed at the double doors) and go right at the end. You'll find it easily." When he seemed to hesitate, she said: "I'll know you're there, and if there's any news I'll send for you."

Brandishing her stick, his Mother wanted to know why they hadn't brought anything with them, a night-dress for Francine, a tooth-brush. He was to remember distinctly her saying 'Pepsodent' and suddenly showing him a very bright smile like the ads in his childhood, or like one of her smiles from his earliest memories of her.

In the bar he lay the sleeping Jake down on a bench against

the wall, covered him with his jacket and sat down at the bar. Looking at a clock in the corner he was surprised to find that it was well past midnight—not that time mattered, or existed in that place, where yesterday's news was strewn on the floor. There was a desultory card-game going on at one table. The room would fill and empty in some undiscernable but comforting rhythm: sleepless patients in striped robes, fathers exiled from delivery rooms or reluctant to intrude on the world of Mothers, porters, ambulance drivers, interns going off duty, or coming on, nurses of all sexes, two cops, a weary surgeon in green, obscure men who were obviously "regulars". The TV was affixed to the wall and in those dead hours was tuned to the private channels—housewives stripteasing, sports call-in shows, cooking displays.

The bar-man was a fat, fascist sort of man with fleshy lips and a few strands of hair. Like a priest, his job was to listen to all the world's stories, and like many a fat man he was deft and quick on his feet. Jim's first *grappa* appeared right away, quickly enough the second, and those after. Then the barman went back to the other end of his counter and continued doing crossword puzzles in a fat book, waiting for someone who wanted to talk.

"I couldn't talk to him," Jim said. "I couldn't talk to anyone. I knew I couldn't get through to Francine, and even if I could have, what was there to say? I know she grieved as much as I did, but she couldn't bring it out into the open. Never could. Not grief, not love. I couldn't even pray, I felt there was no one to listen to me."

He stayed there until the very small hours, when the streets outside hushed and no one was coming in or out. The card game was over, the players going to work or finally home.

Then, true to her word, the nurse walked in briskly (where did she get her energy?). She said the surgeon was on his way.

Surgeon?

Yes, he must operate. There was an obstruction in the little girl's intestine "I will come again when it's over."

Over?

Yes, the operation. *Speriamo*, she said. Let's hope. *Poverina.*

Avra sofferto molto. She said it always seemed unjust, didn't it? That a child should suffer at all.

And my wife?

She was sleeping. She was sleeping. The nurse looked at him and said he should get some sleep too. Then she gently ruffled Jake's hair and left.

He was glad to see her, but also angry. Why should she bother him about an operation when it was obvious what she expected? And would come again to tell him when it was over? Over? He thought, it must be no bigger than vermicelli, Rory's intestine.

6

Later—it must have been much later, perhaps he'd briefly fallen asleep, his head on his arms—the Signora came in and sat at a little round table at the opposite end of the bar, where the shadows on her face shifted with the images on the TV high up behind the bar. The nurse had long gone, and Jim was preparing himself for the inconceivable, convinced that despite the operation, which was now going on, or would soon begin, their child was dying.

Jim saw her first in the mirror. She was not old, but dressed pretty much in black. She had long, thin arms over which she constantly pulled the sleeves of her dress. Like Jim's mother, she had a fetching little gap between her top front teeth, one of which was slightly askew. Something in her look reminded him of Francine, early that evening, which seemed days or weeks ago, coming into his studio. He heard her say, as she might have said "the kitchen sink is blocked again"—"Aurora is having a fit, I think." In his eyes, she was tall and lovely, but also distressed. Or bewildered. He had the same feeling about the Signora, who also reminded him strongly of his Mother. Not as she was now, but as she had once been.

He then turned round to see to Jake, but Jake had gone. The barman put his hand on Jim's sleeve and said, "The nurse came and took him off. She found a bed for him. This is not a good place for children, *Signore.*"

A flame sprouted on the mirror. The Signora was lighting a cigarette. The light of the match made her look even more like his mother: dark hair, oval, olive face, Feli's resigned eyes. Only his mother had been, when she still smoked, forever awkward and uncertain with a cigarette in her lips. A cigarette grew damp in her mouth, and carried her lipstick. But her hair had fallen the same way as the Signora's. Though Feli did not cross her legs. The Signora did, high on the thigh. On the other hand, the longer he looked, the more she was like his Mother at about the same age, around forty, and he thought, briefly, that the Signora looked as Aurora might look, were she to live, at that age. If Aurora, too, had been struck by some disappointment.

"I cannot explain it," Jim said. "I just felt drawn to her. Perhaps she had been through something like I was going through?"

Meanwhile, without being asked (the Signora was obviously well known there) the bar-man brought her tea in a glass. Jim heard him say, "Another bad night, Sante?"

When Jim joined her at the table, she said, in English: "American?"

There were vigorous hairs above her knees, he noticed. He couldn't remember whether Feli had, but he doubted it. He said yes, he was...

There was also something in her way of speaking that was Feli's. As when she was telling her boys that they would be happy in California. Whereas what the Signora had said was that she would be happy if she could go to America, especially California.

"You were unhappy there," he said. "You cried all the time."

She said, only briefly puzzled, "You won't be unhappy with

me. I can be whoever a man wants, or anyone." After a short pause, she said: "You mustn't get the wrong impression. It's just that some-times I can't get to sleep, and then I get lonely. I live very near. I often come here, just for company. This place is always open."

"Signora…"

"Oh, I'm not the Signora. I'm Sante. The Signora lives in the same building as I do. Was it the Signora you hoped to see? She hasn't been here in a while. I suppose you know that she lost her baby, and her husband left her. I've known her for years. In fact, I know her so well, I often think we were made for each other. You must have noticed that we both always wear the same clothes."

"I love the way your hair falls across your face as you light up."

"You love me, then?"

"If you tell me why you invent this other woman, this Signora."

"This used to be her table. Only now she has a weak heart, blood does not reach her extremities. Feel my hand. You can feel my heart is good." He reached across the table, but she took her hand away. The marble of the table was very cold. "She comes here to see the cardiologist. He is always telling her she needs an operation. Naturally she's not sure about that. If you were in her place, would you have an operation?"

"You want to live? Then yes, you should have the operation."

"She lost her baby here. In this hospital. It's not surprising she hesitates, don't you think?"

"Everything all right, Sante?" the bar-man asked.

Jim thought, at least he could be sure a baby had died. Perhaps not the imaginary Signora's. Possibly Sante's. Or it could be that the Signora had read something in his mind; or it was the easiest way to explain her state of mind. It could be a form of explanation for her life. Feli, too, would tell the same story when she met someone for the first time. How Jacob had left her alone with two growing boys. Her story was always monotonously told in that same order: Jacob's departure, her unhappiness, the boys. As to the Signora's dubious heart condition, that too was her intuition. It was what she was afraid might happen, as he was afraid of what was happening to Rory somewhere in this very building, but remote from him.

He was glad Sante didn't ask many questions—in fact preferred to talk about herself, or this Signora. He was glad she just sat there smoking and drinking tea, but wished he hadn't seen the hair on her legs. From time to time she would light another cigarette and smile at him. Each time the Signora, or Sante, or his Mother, lit up, he looked over his shoulder, expecting to see the friendly, competent nurse standing there with the news that it was all over. But the more often this happened, the more he was aware that the cigarette didn't look right in her hand; she held it wrong; she worried it with her lips and it grew red at the tip from lipstick. Unaccountably, he had a memory that this cigarette in his Mother's hand had always excited him. It was doing so now and he started to tell the Signora how he had tried to love his mother, whom she was so alike, but he hadn't been able to tell her that she ought to die, because living when you're not really alive was even worse than dying.

The Signora looked distressed by this turn in the conversation. If it was love he wanted, she offered a car outside. "*Per la morte, me ne frego,*" she added. Screw death. The Signora could be anyone a man wanted, she said. She boasted about it. And she was every bit as good as the Signora. Death didn't bother her. Life did.

"You've already said that," said Jim dully.

"I know. She repeats herself endlessly. It's as though on any Monday she is repeating the previous Monday. This Monday she'll save for next Monday."

"It's Saturday."

"Just a manner of speaking," she said.

Her car was parked so close against the long wall outside the hospital grounds (and why there if she lived right across the street?) that they had to climb over each other in the back seat before she hoisted up her dress and clutched him, shivering. Despite the sun slowly rising, hitting the ochre top of the hospital.

Not really his mother, surely. Yes she was, he said. As well as

Sante and the Signora. At least then. During. "Give the Signora this money," he said, handing her the last dollars in his wallet. "What will she be doing now, do you think?"

She readjusted herself in the front seat, puckered her lips, applied lipstick. Smoothed down her hair, lit a cigarette. "The same as every morning," she said. "I told you she could be whoever you wanted. You miss your mother, I think?"

"What happens to girls when they become Mothers?" he asked back.

"How would I know? The Signora lost her baby. Now she thinks she's going to die."

"You think she will?"

"I think if life is all repetition, that's a new experience, death. They say that when you're really dying, you don't notice it."

Jim returned upstairs feeling far calmer. As if something had died in him and no longer was causing him trouble. He told me that what he'd done with Sante was not really different from his meeting Lou at the station all dolled up as Lou; neither was it different from what Tony's other daughter, Mandy thought she was doing when, divested of her sheaths of nylon and frilly blouse, she had offered herself to her beloved Dad—"by way of consolation for their two rotten lives."

There was a whole new set of people manning the counter at Reception. The nurse who seemed to be in charge, not the one who'd been so helpful the night before, told him there was no news. He should come back during visiting hours.

He was about to leave, to leave, wondering if he should look in on Jake when a doctor came down the hall Jim had just walked from the bar and, taking him by the arm, led him into a cubicle with a real door, not a curtain. Jim supposed it was where they give out the truly bad news.

The doctor sat down on a chair on one side of a narrow table and motioned to Jim that he should sit down on the other. They'd done everything they could, he said. The child had been weakened by her long struggle, by the pain, and in fact poisoned (*avvelenata*) by her own digestive system. As he stood up and put his hand on the doorknob, he said: "Try to get your wife to cry. It will help her." He then accompanied Jim back to the counter where, Jim was made to understand, there was paper work to be completed.

The new nurse said it would be better if Francine and Jake stayed for a day or two, but she would understand if she felt better at home. "She can go after the formalities have been completed."

Jim inquired about these "formalities." After listing the various reports and certificates that would have to be filled out—"it has been a busy night"—the nurse added that Rory seemed to have come without a bonnet.

"You will need a bonnet to bury her in," she said.

When the shops were open he went shopping for a bonnet. The women in the shops he went to looked so happy that he had a new baby (was it a boy or a girl?) that he didn't want to tell them why he wanted a bonnet. He just said it was for a girl, a very little girl.

Later he took Francine and Jake home to the mill-house. Jim said to me that after that night you could hear Jake anywhere in the house and he'd be talking, apparently to himself. At least he never admitted that really he was playing with his sister, or telling her what was going on.

7

The graveyard was on a high hill, well above even their village, their church and post office with the doctor's Saturday office at the back, to which several times a week Jim or Francine climbed. Nearer to heaven, Jim thought now, and Jake, who with his mother or father climbed up there as he had when he was too young to remember, to put the polished glass of the sea on his sister's grave. Opposed to the way bodies like his mother's, which he would be visiting again years later, on Hallowe'en, turned to ash in a box, sank deep into their soil. There, raised in tiers, the tombs rose higher than many ladders, half way up cypresses, and bore oval frames with enlarged snaps that recalled, in amateurish fashion, widows and fathers and bike-kill boys—"They ride their motorbikes and scooters straight into trees or oncoming cars," Jim said. "We could hear them down below: the roar of an exhaust pipe; the sheering sound of a skid, like paper being torn; the noise silence makes after an accident; then the remote sound of a police car or two growing nearer. Is it a good thing to die young? I never heard a sound when Rory died."

The whole village was there, in the church and after. Mourning brought them all out, and almost all the women brought flowers, or at least one, while the men, among them Achille and his twin brother, Ettore, showed their respect by wearing their Sunday suits and, despite the heat, the dark, broad-brimmed hats they wore only for christenings, marriages and deaths.

Greeting them at the dark door of the church, with all the villagers in the piazza before it waiting for the poor *stranieri* who had lost their daughter and were leaving her with them, amongst their very own, the young priest said, "*È in paradiso.*" And then added, in English, "In haven," by which he meant heaven, but as Jim said, the former would do.

That whole week leading up to the interment, he told me, had been taken up with "arrangements." He and Francine had been kept busy making all the "arrangements".

There was an abnormal calm in the house. Jake did not touch his football; Francine packed up their things in silence and planted a peach tree which she hoped would continue to grow long after they were gone; and he spent many hours in the village office concerned with the price of vacancies in the communal cemetery, the payment of taxes, permission to leave the country and the like; and then several more with the young priest over the cost of the ceremony and its style ("the simplest possible"), the music to be played, whether he and Francine were "*praticanti*", practicing Catholics, would they take communion, and where had the little girl been baptized ("in the hospital," Jim seemed to remember)? The calm, he said, was the most difficult thing. Far more difficult to live with than screaming, which was what he wanted to do.

Carrying Rory up the hill had been painful. How could something so terribly small and angry weigh so heavily? He wept and Francine was all in white.

He said I was right to think of Rory's death as the beginning of the end, for every August afterwards Francine withdrew still further. Until she finally left altogether, leaving scattered belongings in closets and recesses under stairs in the big old house: here a pair of womens' boots, there a tennis racket, a plastic bag of panty hose (Extra Tall). Only the Kid's room remained intact, though he wasn't there.

Part six
Aissa

If Jesus died and came back to life,
how come he never let anyone
know what it was like?
(the Kid)

One thing I notice as I bring this to an end is that I seem to have started writing quite apart from Jim. Ever less have I needed his witnessing, his words, his authenticity. I have changed myself. Simply the labor of getting up from my rocking chair and my sherry—usually very early in the morning, hours before the papers arrive—has brought me back, in ways both silly and strange, to the young girl I once was, the one who admired and loved the man I've been writing about.

Is it the case that, as we grow older, our sentences (the written ones, not the judgments made on us) grow longer, more unhurried, and more interrupted by doubt and speculation? And how can we be so sure, when we listen to someone recount what "happened", that it happened the way they say it did? Much less likely is it that they perceived what "happened" as we would perceive it. Much as we might like to be—the great saints were—transparent (that is, something obvious, visible to all) we are not. Our opacity is at the heart of what we relish about ourselves, and what is a human being without secrets?

As my Grandma said when I was a girl, the best way for her people to kill, who in the early days (those of her grandfather) had only bow and arrow, was through the heart or in the eye. To make sure of the first, you had to be strong, to split the breast bone or drive a splintered rib into the heart; but for the second, you had to be able to aim, you had to have an eye yourself. You might kill if you attacked the heart, but also your arrow might bounce off or stick in the flesh and be wrested out or broken off; if you hit the eye, you hit what your enemy saw with and you struck at what makes a human being, his mind.

I find Jim serene these days, carefully locked away in himself. Again, my Grandma comes to my assistance. In his old age, she said, her grandfather, a noted warrior whose name translates as Human-Being-Who-Dirties-His-Hands, had nothing left to do. No wars, no decisions (the settlers on the northern plains took them for him), and only descendants who sometimes came to see him. He continued to live in the old ways, but not actively. He could not see well enough to hunt or shoot. Food was brought to him, and the wood necessary for his fire, the blanket in which he wrapped himself up. His only public function was to tell stories, or to be asked puzzling questions. These questions were puzzling because the circumstances in which they could be answered had so radically changed. If one of the few young men left in the reservation asked, for instance, what is courage? he could not answer the way he would have answered a generation or two back, because the courage required was of an entirely different order. You did not stand in the way of a locomotive, yet the fire-box was more destructive than the most traditional of your enemies. At heart, Grandma said, he was alone with himself, which is what any one of us is at the end.

Thus all those elements in Jim's life which seem to me mysterious (or not fully explained, because he cannot account for them himself) are as mysterious to him as they are to me, and hence, perhaps, to anyone reading this.

I think in particular of the conversation with Lou in the depths of their garden in Puerto Rico when she sought to dispose of a child within her which Jim clearly thought was also his child, was their child, and therefore inviolate; or his reiteration of his niece Tessa's dire visions of a universe populated by the souls of the unborn. I find it fascinating that he could be calculating (or cynical) about other forms of violence, such as the dead Indian on a Guatemalan road, but that deeply distressed by anything that was a part of himself.

Is this irrational obsession—and perhaps also his many children and their many Mothers—in any way due to my own pathetic sixteen-year-old's flight from motherhood? My destruction of what would have been his first child? Did he know, and never said? For I am quite sure he would never have "understood," or countenanced it. Nor tolerated my fears, which he always railed about as though he had none of his own. Had my Grandma not died even as I found out I was pregnant—from that one shot in the dark!—things might have been different. Or had I not known how supportive my own parents would have been, and dear Otto, the putative child could have been cared for (had things not worked out with Jim) within the ample skirts of the Archdiocese. Yet, I could not go that way. It would have deprived me of my very self, all that I had. Very young and very passionate about one another, different in every way, we knew about Sin, for which one was Punished. As we were.

Or again, his repeated (and half-suppressed) desire to be the women in his life: was that because they, too, were a part of himself? What was the source of his imprecise fear of our female biology, the part of ourselves that is hidden to others but so potent to us?

I can offer no more answers than Jim can. They are distresses of an inexplicable kind, and no less real for that. Precisely what does he blame his Mother for? For giving birth to him? For loving him? For crying in his presence? For taking his brother Tony to husband (of a sort)?

When I ask Jim to explain why he accords such an importance to Sante (just who is the Signora? Does she exist? Is she a figment of Sante's imagination or of Jim's?) and why she is intimately involved with the death of his daughter, and in far more terrible ways with his Mother—There, I've said it! Was he making love to his Mother, as his niece did to her father?—he said that he had last faced such moral indifference, something so affectless, in Poland when the war ended, a period in his life about which he had heretofore said almost nothing.

I think it was in 1945 (Jim is ever imprecise about dates, as though he were not quite sure himself how his life fits time) that he enlisted in the army. I think at the time he probably wanted to prove something to himself, to deny a childhood morbidly absorbed into his Mother's defeats (I am just guessing); if so, it did not work—in the sense that the war, a manly affair, soon ended, and there began that long process in which conquerors and conquered alike return to a "normal" life. I mean "normal" in the sense that it has to be lived, got through, while judgments are being made on actions of all kinds.

As luck (or ill fate) would have it, his legal training (just beginning) and his languages qualified him as an interrogator. Late in the game, when all the big fish had been caught, and what was left was the dreadful underside, the defeated common guards, the corporals and sergeants and other *Unteroffiziere* who had worked in the extermination camps, many of which were now filled with other victims of the war, the utterly displaced, those who no longer had a country, a home, a family, or any possessions other than the clothes on their backs.

I gather he was, for several weeks at least, assigned to one such camp in Poland, though by then Poland had been more or less incorporated into the Soviet Union. I believe him to have been the youngest of a group (which included a French officer and several Russians) which acted as a sort of liaison in the nascent study of war crimes and crimes against humanity. It would be in winter (the winter of 1945–1946, or the very hard winter of the year after) and Jim had a room in a requisitioned house in a small town, the camp itself being two or three miles away.

One day, after several difficult interrogations, all of which centered on denial ("I never did anything"), on the law of hierarchy

("I was just an ordinary soldier, I did what I was told"), or on a much more vital challenge ("You weren't here, you can have no idea what it was like"), he had missed his last transport back to town and decided to walk, even though it had begun to snow.

After he had walked a mile or so along a road which he described as utterly flat, featureless (all the trees that had once lined it had been cut down for fuel) and straight, with nothing but vast, empty fields on ether side, he saw a lone figure walking ahead of him. Impossible to say anything more about it, whether it was man, woman, boy, girl, or old or young. All you saw of most people, Jim said, was an overcoat. Perhaps an old overcoat. Perhaps a greatcoat taken from a dead soldier. Perhaps one made of blankets, sewn together if you were lucky and had needle or thread, or held together with safety pins (if you had any), or simply tied together with string or webbing or bandages.

Whoever this was, was walking far more slowly than Jim, who had somewhere to go: a meal at the Soviet canteen and a bed in a room heated for two hours between eight and ten. The result was that he soon caught up with the mysterious figure. Had it noticed that someone else was now walking alongside it? That this someone else (Jim) had lit a cigarette and held it out? Whoever or whatever it was, it had its head down and plodded onward as though Jim did not exist.

No doubt you notice that, as Jim did, I use the word "it": because when you'd seen what Jim had seen, "it", or sometimes "they", were the words that best described the world he worked in: on tables of statistics, body counts, production levels, personnel records—that was how people seemed in those days. If they had once been people, these desperate, ghostly figures, prisoners or guards, inhabited a world of generalizations, not specifics, That is, if they were husbands they no longer had wives or fulfilled the normal functions of a husband; if they were children they had long ago abandoned the world of childhood, of play and imagination.

In fact he was surprised, he said, to have noted a few details. It had a hat of some sort on its head: either a cap, a wool hat, or a bundle of cloth, and something around its neck—perhaps what had once been a shirt. The figure also had shoes, though these were wound about with the same sort of bandaging it wore about its neck.

Jim slowed his pace to adapt, and posed a few gentle, very simple questions (Where are you going? Who are you?), trying several of the languages the figure might speak, German, Polish, Russian. The questions weren't answered. It was as though this figure, barely human, but a person nonetheless, didn't even acknowledge his existence.

How could he not believe in ghosts, in the dead seeking to talk to the living? he asked. If he stood before the figure to stop it in its relentless walk, he felt sure that it would pass right through his body like cold, or perhaps volatilize and join the smoke and snow that figured in all the photographs he'd studied, picking out faces among both the dead and the living and, in the case of the latter, facing them across a desk and saying, "Is that you?"

I could imagine his surprise, he said, when a corner of a rag lifted and he saw a part of a face—when that was the last thing he expected. He said he could see right away that this mysterious, solitary walker was indeed quite real. And still young, though it was hard to tell the age of anyone who had been in any of the camps, or might have walked, as far as he knew, at the same obsessive pace, thousands of kilometers from where it once had a life. The face was so difficult to identify with the person that might once have borne it, that Jim was quite unable to tell me if it were a man or a woman, a boy or a girl. If it had been a girl, he said, it was likely that she'd been pretty, in the way young girls are; and if a boy, vestigially awkward and unprepared, as most boys are.

It was just a moment, he said, then a wrapped-about hand pushed the bit of rag up like a visor, the eyes behind it glanced at him momentarily—as if asking, what strange creature is this that walks the same way I do?—and it continued on its way.

That meeting, Jim said, was exactly what he meant when he'd told me what Sante had said that night while his daughter lay dying upstairs, that if life is all repetition, one step after another until you come to the end, then death is something new. "That's who—if in fact she had been a girl—she must have thought I was: Death come to greet her."

Of course, staying behind, he watched the figure. Her, as he by now had decided to think of it. An hour later, she had passed right through the little town, right past his room, without once lifting her head or looking side to side. There was nothing strange about it, Jim said: in those days thousands, if not hundreds of thousands, were on the roads from one place to another.

But still you could ask him until you were blue in the face, and Jim would not be able to tell you why this particular encounter left its mark on him. The circumstances in which that one fleeting meeting took place? The place? She resembled his Mother at some particular junction in his life—perhaps one in which his Mother, having briefly met his eye, moved on? Yet I recalled his saying that he collected images of unconsolable women (in fact he cites one of them), and I am certain they must all have resembled that one. In just the same way that I am certain that Jim did not mention the composer Chabrier and his miscarried siblings in their bottles by accident. They refer, obliquely, to what is aborted; and to what his niece said: that few people can be silent enough to hear the unborn.

So we accept that there are mysteries forever present even in those we know best. I can ask myself, why did I fail? Why was I so terribly afraid of him? And why was he so consistently interested in me and, in his own way, so devoted to me, that for years he was the source of the few rich experiences that came my way?

I say to myself: Mrs. Vojtyla and I are alike. We are the "stranded" women Jim referred to when he was first exploring Hemperle Road. And now I think that was possibly the attraction Jim felt to that ultimate not-the-girl-next-door, Francine, with her hooded eyes and private griefs, her inner belief that everyone would be better off without her.

Here, as in all stories, there are lacunae. There are a thousand things I do not know. Jim's children, though familiar to me from his talk and devotion, were not my familiars. He did not want them included. Too much the heart of his matter, I suspect. I don't know his friends as he knows them. And he, who would be furious if I told him a story and brought it to an abrupt end, who would turn to me and say, "Yes, and then? What happened to them after that?" wouldn't like the way I scant the subsequent lives and consorts, partners, whatever, of the Mothers. I treat them, however, as he did: as not part of his life. Yes, Jim's concerns were that exclusive. There was Himself, and what he folded into himself, and then there was the rest of the world.

The hardest thing for me to accept has always been the terrible thesis he proposes, that Mothers are destructive. If the process of compliance and acceptance, of impregnation, gestation and parturition, is as inherently wicked and Jim sometimes seems to say it is, then we would all join the unborn. Yet one of the gifts of setting so many of his contradictions down is that I think I see in myself what Jim only barely understands in himself, that is: the way we try to keep ourselves whole. Surely it is that which was at the origin of my fears when I was madly in love with Jim—that I knew he would destroy my wholeness, as he did with many of the Mothers—and that is why I survived. And Maria survived who snuck away to the car waiting for her. And Natasha survived, who wouldn't give up her possessions.

Of course Jim's life is not finished, any more than mine is, or Milo's, or Igor's—I notice, alas! how he crowds them off the page!— but in its essentials, at our age, the lines of our solitude, and theirs, are well-established. Jim, I said, seems serene, even alone in the big, old house; the Kid grows up; Francine still loves Jim in her way, she wishes it had been possible to make him happy, if he'd allowed her to breathe. They get along well and live close by each other. The only time I have felt him bristle is when Francine, playing her role as a free woman somewhat too strongly for someone so frail, announces—to someone she and Jim might meet at a dinner, the movies or the like, that she's divorced. Then Jim says, not always gently, but always politely, "Madame, here, is divorced. But I'm not."

As our lives are not over, there are loose ends. For instance, the awful Sunny Farber. Or Jim's mysterious father. He assures me he has them in mind, and that he's putting down the elements of that story.

And then there are those who think Jim will re-marry. No, he said: "Henceforth I shall be as the mayfly, that lives but twenty-seven days, and considers that adequate for its needs."

About the author

Keith Botsford

After a notable early career as a novelist and editor, Keith Botsford describes himself as having been "sidetracked" into journalism (*The Sunday Times, The Independent, La Stampa*), working variously as sportswriter, food columnist and US correspondent. He lives in Boston where he is a professor of journalism, history and international relations, and edits, with Saul Bellow, *The Republic of Letters.*

The fonts used in this book are from the Garamond and
Friz Quadrata families

Other works by Keith Botsford are published by The Toby Press

Out of Nowhere

Editors (with Saul Bellow)

As I. I. Magdalen
Lennie & Vance & Benji